"I find myself at

"I know you're up to something," Aidan continued, "but since my family has taken you to their bosom, I can hardly toss you out on your ear."

"I live here now," Emma said, her gaze daring him to disagree.

"And why is that?"

"You didn't want any explanations," she reminded him.

"Perhaps I was too hasty."

"The information window is closed." Her ironic smile made his temper spark, but he was determined to keep the upper hand.

"What if we agree to an exchange? One piece of info for another?"

"I don't need to know anything about you. I don't care."

"Look at me." He strode to where she sat, pulled her to her feet. "Actually, there's only one thing I really need to know."

"What's that?"

"I'll show you," he said, capturing her mouth beneath his.

* * *

Christmas in the Billionaire's Bed
is part of The Kavanaghs of Silver Glen series: In the mountains of North Carolina, one family discovers that wealth means nothing without love.

CHRISTMAS IN THE BILLIONAIRE'S BED

BY
JANICE MAYNARD

MILLS & BOON

Published in Great Britain 2014
by Mills & Boon, an imprint of Harlequin (UK) Limited,
Eton House, 18-24 Paradise Road, Richmond, Surrey, TW9 1SR

© 2014 Janice Maynard

ISBN: 978-0-263-91487-0

51-1214

Harlequin (UK) Limited's policy is to use papers that are natural, renewable and recyclable products and made from wood grown in sustainable forests. The logging and manufacturing processes conform to the legal environmental regulations of the country of origin.

Printed and bound in Spain
by CPI, Barcelona

Janice Maynard is a *USA TODAY* bestselling author who lives in beautiful east Tennessee with her husband. She holds a BA from Emory and Henry College and an MA from East Tennessee State University. In 2002 Janice left a fifteen-year career as an elementary school teacher to pursue writing full-time. Now her first love is creating sexy, character-driven, contemporary romance stories.

Janice loves to travel and enjoys using those experiences as settings for books. Hearing from readers is one of the best perks of the job! Visit her website, www.janicemaynard.com, and follow her on Facebook and Twitter.

For all the wonderful authors who paved the way at Mills & Boon. I read your stories growing up, took trips around the world, and dreamed of writing my own romantic heroes one day…

One

Aidan Kavanagh stared at the cream vellum card edged with tiny holly leaves and berries and shook his head in reluctant admiration.

Game. Set. Match.

His mother had won the war without firing a single shot. The last thing Aidan wanted to do was visit Silver Glen, North Carolina, during the holidays, but Maeve knew he wouldn't miss his own brother's wedding.

The first of his siblings, Liam, had tied the knot recently as well. That event had been a huge, splashy society affair at Zoe's home in Connecticut—a hop, skip and a jump from New York City. This time Aidan wouldn't be so lucky.

It wasn't that he didn't love Silver Glen. He did. But

going home for Christmas brought back too many ugly memories. So, he chose to visit his large, close-knit family at other times of the year: Easter, Mother's Day, the Fourth of July…and October, when the fall foliage in the mountains was at its peak.

But December? No. In the last decade, he had managed it only once and only then because one of his brothers had been in the hospital. Aidan would have felt like a total jerk if he had let his family down.

That visit had been both uncomfortable and unpleasant. His mother and brothers had walked on eggshells around him, everyone far too aware that Aidan carried the weight of past tragedy. He'd done his damnedest to prove to them he was fine…that he had moved on.

Unfortunately, no one had been convinced by his deliberate facade of Christmas cheer. Least of all Aidan himself. Because the truth was, December sucked. He was fine. His life was good. He was content. But not even his family knew the worst of what had happened so long ago.

He stood and stretched, tossing the offending invitation on his desk. The view from his office window stretched from the Statue of Liberty all the way to the George Washington Bridge. Aidan loved New York City. The constant pulse of life. The fact that he could stop for lox and bagels at three in the morning and no one batted an eye.

Most of all, he loved the anonymity. No one here cared about his past or even his future. The emotional breathing room had become as essential to him as food or water.

Growing up in Silver Glen provided an idyllic childhood—at least until his father's death when Aidan was a young teen. The little alpine-like town would always be home. But living in a fishbowl where everyone knew his business became unbearable when he was twenty-one and his entire world crumbled around him.

Moving to New York had been his salvation. With a hefty nest egg of Kavanagh money—long since repaid—he'd started a high-end real estate company. The lessons he'd learned as a youth working in his family's swank hotel stood him in good stead. Although the Kavanaghs were very wealthy, the crème de la crème here in the city took that definition to a far greater level. Aidan enjoyed the challenge of matching socialites and business magnates with their perfect homes on the rooftops of Manhattan.

His phone pinged, reminding him of an upcoming appointment. Once more he sat down, then picked up his favorite pen and rolled the heavy gold cylinder between his fingers. He had inked his first real estate deal with this pen. Beyond the leather blotter, the wedding invitation lay innocently. He read it a second time, finding its elegant cursive font no less stomach tightening than he had before.

December 20th. That meant Aidan would need to be in Silver Glen no later than the weekend before. Knowing his mother, she would undoubtedly have planned a series of social events to fill the days leading up to the wedding. And then he would be expected to hang around until the family celebrated Christmas together on the 25th. Almost two weeks. Might as well be a lifetime.

He glanced at the paper calendar his assistant kept updated on the corner of his desk. She was as tech savvy as the next person, but she had discovered that Aidan liked to keep tabs on his schedule in more than one medium. The month of December was notably blank.

No one, with very few exceptions, shopped for high-dollar real estate during December. His clients were too busy hosting parties, overspending on their spoiled children and taking trips to exotic locations. Which meant, unfortunately, that Aidan was free to do as he pleased.

Or in this instance as he did *not* please.

For a moment, he flashed back, his vision blinded to the present but very aware of the past. Two young women. Both beautiful. Both charming. Both full of life and fun. And he had lost each of them.

The familiar burning sensation in his gut was more than a mix of guilt and regret. It was a longing for what he would never have. Absolution. A woman and a family to call his own.

Spending Christmas at Silver Glen would undoubtedly resurrect a host of old memories that he'd rather not face. But if he were honest, the memories lived with him everywhere. The painful part of going home was having other people *share* the memories. The empathy and concern on the faces of his siblings and his mother would be his downfall.

He didn't want their love to heal him. He didn't deserve that. And he didn't want to *feel* anything. Family knew his weak spots. Family refused to let him cling to the cloak of indifference that made it possible to live from day to day.

Aidan Kavanagh was a charming shell of a man, interested only in closing a deal or cashing a check. Ask anyone. The persona was one he had crafted carefully to keep people away. After loving and losing three times in his life, he was through with emotion…with caring.

In Silver Glen, especially at the holidays, he would have to be himself—the young man who had enjoyed life and reached for happiness with the careless naïveté of the innocent. He would be forced to open himself up to the warmth of family celebrations that would make him terribly vulnerable.

Could he do that and still survive?

Doggedly, he reached for the peace he had created here in the city. Emotional anonymity. A pleasant shield that kept other people from inflicting hurt.

He didn't hurt. He *wouldn't* hurt. Loving his family was a given. But beyond that, he had nothing to offer. Loving and losing meant vicious, unrelenting pain. Only a fool would walk that path again.

Emma Braithwaite leaned into the bay window, perched precariously on a stepladder that had seen better days. Creating the shop's storefront display was usually the highlight of her workweek. Today's theme, not exactly original, was teapots. Twitching the edge of a lace drape into place, she tried to visualize what her handiwork looked like from the street.

On the other side of the glass, a woman stopped and waved madly. Emma smiled. Even through the reverse gold lettering that spelled out Silver Memories, she recognized her visitor. Maeve Kavanagh, matriarch of the Kavanagh family—mother to seven sexy, über-masculine, wildly attractive grown men, and heir to the Kavanagh fortune.

Maeve's husband's ancestors had literally created the town after discovering a rich vein of silver deep in the mountain. The family story took a tragic turn when Maeve's feckless husband, Reggie, became obsessed with finding the remnants of the mine. One day he climbed into the hills and never returned.

But that bit of local color was from long ago. Maeve was now a vibrant woman in her early sixties who managed to keep tabs on her brood and run a thriving business up at the Silver Beeches Lodge. A little bell tinkled over the door as Maeve entered. Her dark auburn hair—with only slight traces of silver—was done up in a stylish bun.

Emma climbed down from the ladder and straightened her skirt.

Maeve waved an envelope at her. "I know etiquette dictates I mail this to you, but I couldn't wait. Here. Take it."

Emma accepted the cream-colored envelope with a grin. The missive was thick, the paper expensive. When she opened it and examined the contents, she understood the older woman's enthusiasm. "Another wedding?"

Maeve's smug smile said everything. "Indeed. And this time right here in Silver Glen. I know it seems hurried, but Dylan's adoption of Cora will be final on the day after Christmas. He and Mia want to be married and have their family complete."

Emma tucked everything back in the envelope. "I'm honored to be invited."

Emma and Mia had met several months ago at a coffee shop around the corner from Silver Memories. Since then they had become friends. Emma knew Maeve had been extremely kind in including Mia's parents as hosts for the wedding. The Larins had given birth to Mia late in life and now lived in Florida on a fixed income.

Maeve waved a hand. "Don't be silly. You're practically part of my family now. Mia raves about you, and I've enjoyed getting to know you these last few months."

Not long after Emma opened her store, Maeve had dropped by to shop for a set of occasional tables to use in a lounge at the Silver Beeches. It was thanks to Maeve that word had spread and the small shop had become a success so quickly.

"May I ask you something personal, Maeve?"

"Of course."

"Is the baby's father in the picture? Mia never speaks of him, and I didn't want to upset her by asking."

Maeve shook her head. "Dear Mia chose to have a baby via a sperm donor. When she and Dylan got together, he fell in love with little Cora. They make a beautiful family, don't you think?"

Emma smiled wistfully. "They certainly do." She had often seen Dylan and Mia and the baby out walking on afternoons when the weather was still warm.

Silver Glen was a small, cozy town, even though it boasted a strong tourist economy. Movie stars shooting on location often took up residence, as well as wealthy travelers who loved the peace of the mountains. The town's alpine flavor reminded Emma of a Swiss village.

"There's one more thing," Maeve said, her expression cajoling. "Mia told me you're not going home to England for Christmas, is that right?"

"Yes. I spent two weeks in September with my mother for her birthday. She's handling the loss of my father better than I expected. And she has plans to tour the Greek Isles during the latter part of December with a group of her friends."

"Then I want you to spend the holidays with us. Mia's parents are coming only for the wedding itself. So I know Mia would enjoy having you around. We're gathering for several occasions at Dylan and Mia's home. My older son and his wife are still building their new house. And of course, we'll have some special events up at the lodge, too. What do you think?"

Emma didn't know what to say. She wasn't afraid to be alone. In fact, her childhood had been solitary more times than not. She enjoyed the peace and tranquility of her own thoughts. And she was not a Kavanagh. Surely her presence would be awkward.

Maeve spotted a silver rattle and a matching small cup from the 1950s. "I knew I remembered seeing these," she said triumphantly. "One of my college sorority sisters just became a grandma for the first time. This will be the perfect gift."

As Emma rang up the purchase and took Maeve's credit card, she wondered how large a wedding the Kavanaghs were planning. And then another thought struck. One that made her heart race.

"Will all of your family be able to attend on such short notice?" Emma had never actually confessed to Maeve that she knew one of her sons very well.

For the first time, Maeve lost a bit of her excitement. "I hope so. My third son, Aidan, lives in New York. We don't see him all that often. And besides…"

She trailed off, her expression indicating that she had traveled somewhere unpleasant in her mind.

Emma wanted to know badly. "Besides what?"

Maeve's lips twisted, her eyes shadowed. "Aidan had a very bad experience some years ago. It happened at Christmas. He comes home to visit, but not at the holidays."

"And this wedding?"

"We hope he'll make the effort, but who knows…"

What would Aidan think if he saw Emma ensconced in the bosom of his family? She hadn't set eyes on him in a decade. Her original intent in coming to Silver Glen during the late summer had been to speak with him and bring some closure to what had been a painful time in their lives. She had hurt him badly, and she wanted to explain and make amends. But she discovered he no longer lived in the town of his birth.

Her recent birthday had brought home the fact that life passed quickly. Regret was an emotion fraught with negativity. After healing a decade-long rift with her father back in the spring, she had realized she wanted to move forward and to make better decisions than she had in her early twenties.

It was entirely possible that Aidan had not clung to the memories the way Emma had. She might be nothing more than a footnote in his past life. According to Maeve, he sounded like an entirely different person than the boy Emma had known.

The fact that Emma had chosen to settle in Silver Glen permanently had more to do with the town's charm than it did with Aidan. But her initial motive remained. Even if her apology meant nothing to him, it would clear her own soul of lingering regret.

She couldn't control his response. In fact, he might not even show up. But if he did, she was determined to do the mature, responsible thing and own up to her mistakes.

Emma wanted to grill her visitor, but she had already overstepped the bounds of polite curiosity. "I'm sure he realizes how important it is."

Maeve gathered herself visibly. "You haven't given me an answer. And I warn you in advance that I'll only accept a yes."

"Then I will say yes with pleasure." And a healthy dose of trepidation.

"That's wonderful, Emma dear. My invitation is selfish actually. Everything you say in that delightful British accent makes me want to listen to you for hours, but I have to fly."

"I'd say *you're* the one who has the accent," Emma teased. "You, and the rest of Silver Glen. I've practiced my drawl, but it never seems to come out right."

Heading out the door, Maeve shook her head, laughing. "Let's face it, Emma. You're the quintessential blue-blooded Englishwoman. Fit to marry a prince if Kate hadn't snatched him up first. If you had a slow-as-molasses speech pattern, no one would ever believe you were an aristocrat."

In the sudden silence created by the departure of her vivacious guest, Emma felt her stomach curl. She had known this day would come eventually. It was a major reason she had chosen to roost in Silver Glen. That, and the fact that the town reminded her of the cheery Cotswolds village where she had grown up.

Sooner or later, Aidan would appear. If not at Christmas, then in the spring. The thought of seeing him face-to-face both elated and terrified her. She knew they were far beyond second chances. Too much time had passed. His life experiences had no doubt changed him, especially the tragedy to which Maeve alluded. Too many turns in the road. But Emma wanted to speak her piece. And she would make him listen.

He deserved to know that she had loved him beyond reason and sanity. That his leaving had nearly destroyed her.

Perhaps she was kidding herself. Aidan might not even remember her. Maybe she had magnified the importance of their university romance. Aidan had come to Oxford the fall semester of his senior year for a term-abroad experience. He had literally bumped into Emma on the street in front of a pub frequented by students.

They had both laughed and picked up their books and papers. Aidan offered to buy her dinner, and that was that.

Her heart actually clenched in her chest, the pain of

the memories still fresh after all this time. Would he look the same? Would he think she had changed?

And what was she going to say to Aidan Kavanagh when she saw him again?

Two

Aidan braked carefully and rolled to a stop in front of the courthouse that reigned over the town square. Darkness had fallen swiftly, proof that they were nearing the shortest day of the year. All around him, buildings were decorated in lights…some twinkling white, some a rainbow of colors.

New York City loved to deck itself out for Christmas. But nothing about Christmas in the city was as disturbing as this. As if it were yesterday, he remembered Danielle's delight when he first brought her home to spend the holidays with his family. She had loved the decorations, the town itself and the fresh snow that had fallen.

At least this year the roads were dry. Even so, the image of a long-ago snowball fight brought a small smile to his lips. Danielle had approached everything about her life with the enthusiasm of a puppy.

He was surprised and grateful to find that at least a few memories of their last days together were good ones.

Glancing at his watch, he knew he had lingered long enough. Though Dylan and Mia had invited him to stay with them, Aidan preferred the privacy of a hotel room up at the lodge. Then, it was nobody's business if he couldn't sleep.

His mother had a nice condo in town, though his oldest sibling, Liam, still had a suite with his wife, Zoe, at the Silver Beeches Lodge. They were in the process of designing and building their dream home, but it wouldn't be finished until the following summer.

Liam would be sleeping with one eye open, waiting to make sure that Aidan showed up safely, even if it *was* almost 3:00 a.m. *Why can't you fly down here like a normal person?* he had complained.

Aidan wondered that himself. The grueling hours on the road were supposed to have prepared him for his upcoming ordeal. Well, hell, that was a little too melodramatic. It wasn't as if he hadn't been back to Silver Glen time and again after Danielle was gone. But only once at Christmas. And then only to see his brother in the hospital and make sure he was okay. A little fruitcake, a few packages and as quickly as he could manage, he had returned to his home in New York.

This trip, however, there would be no reprieve. Maeve had already warned him that she expected his presence at an assortment of events and activities. Her third son had strayed beyond her reach, and since she had wrangled his presence via the unexpected wedding invitation, she planned to make the most of it.

Aidan put the car in gear again and cruised around town slowly, expecting at any moment for a cop to pull him over and demand an explanation for his nocturnal prowl. Things looked much the same as they had during his last visit. Except that his brother Dylan's pride and joy, the Silver Dollar Saloon, was once again open for business.

When Aidan had come home for the long 4th of July weekend, the Silver Dollar was still being repaired and renovated after a fire in June. Fortunately, no one had been injured, but he'd heard more than one person bemoaning the fact that the town's most popular watering hole was closed indefinitely.

He looped back toward the square, passing Silver Screen, the community's one and only movie theater. Way back in the forties and fifties, someone had decided all the stores in Silver Glen should be named with the theme of silver. As a marketing ploy, it was brilliant.

The town had grown and prospered, drawing visitors and business from all over the country. Despite his unease, Aidan found himself feeling distinctly nostalgic for this charming valley that had been his home for twenty-plus years.

As he turned the car one last time and headed for the narrow road that would take him up the mountain to the lodge, his headlights flashed across a darkened storefront that didn't look familiar. Silver Memories. From what he could see of the window display, the merchandise appeared to be antiques.

He frowned, almost positive that the last time he'd visited, this particular spot had been a leather shop. Operated by an ornery old guy who made saddles and guitar straps to order.

Odd. But then again, at Thanksgiving, he'd been in town barely twenty-four hours.

When he made it up the mountain, he pulled onto the flagstone apron in front of the Silver Beeches Lodge. After grabbing his bag and handing off his keys to a sleepy parking attendant, he sent a text to his brother. I'm here. Go to bed, old man. See you tomorrow.

A neatly uniformed employee checked him in. After that, it was a matter of minutes to make it onto the elevator, up to the top floor, down the hall and into his quiet, dark, pleasantly scented room.

He kicked off his shoes, plugged in his phone and

fell facedown across the bed, prepared to sleep until someone forced him to get up.

Emma kept one eye on her customer and the other on her laptop. The elderly woman came in a couple of times a month, mostly to window-shop. She actually sold Emma a few items from time to time, clearly in need of cash to supplement her social security check.

Since the white-haired lady seemed content to browse, Emma refocused her attention on the website she'd been perusing. Catriona's Closet was a designer boutique in London that had been Emma's go-to spot for special occasion clothes when she still lived in England. Fortunately for Emma, the shop now boasted a strong online retail presence.

Trying to decide between a cream lace duster over a burgundy long-sleeved jersey dress, or a more traditional green velvet cocktail number with a low, scooped neck, was impossible. With a few quick clicks, she bought them both, with express shipping. If she were going to see Aidan face-to-face, she needed armor. Lots of it. From the cradle, she had been taught the finer points of social etiquette. Mingling socially with the well-regarded and diverse Kavanagh family would pose no threat to her confidence.

But seeing Aidan again? That was another matter.

Finally, the customer left without buying so much as an embroidered hankie. Emma sighed. Her father, if he had lived, would have been horrified at his only daughter stooping to something as bourgeois as *trade*.

The Braithwaites were solicitors and clergymen and physicians, at least the menfolk. The females generally presided over tea, rode to hounds and threw dinner parties, leaving their offspring to be raised by nannies.

Emma had been eight years old before she understood that her dear Baba was not a member of the family.

Shaking off the bittersweet memories, she prepared to close the shop. This time of year, business fell off in the afternoons despite the holidays, so she rarely stayed open past four o'clock.

Outside, people hurried about their errands, braced against the stiff wind and the swirling flurries of snow. Emma would have much preferred to go upstairs to her cozy apartment and snuggle under an afghan, but she was completely out of milk, and she couldn't abide her tea without it.

Bundling into her heavy, raspberry-pink wool coat, she wrapped a black-and-pink scarf around her head, tucked her billfold and keys into her pocket and walked quickly down the street.

At the next block she shivered, impatient for the light to turn green so she could cross the street. So intent was she on making it to the other side that she didn't notice the silver Accord running the light until it was too late.

Her heart beat sluggishly, everything easing into slow motion as she hopped back. But not before the reckless driver clipped her hip, sending her tumbling airborne for several long seconds and then crashing into unforgiving pavement.

Though she was aware of people crowding around her, she lost herself somewhere internally as she catalogued all the places that hurt madly. Teeth chattering, she forced herself to sit up. Nothing appeared to be broken. A man crouched beside her, his scent a mix of warm male, cold air and an oddly familiar cologne.

"Don't move," he said, his honey-toned voice sharp with command.

She was glad to accept his support behind her shoulders. The world swam dizzily. Vaguely, she heard the wail of sirens.

Shortly after that, brisk strangers loaded her onto a gurney and lifted her into an ambulance. Though she protested as much as she was able, no one seemed prepared to listen to her. Her scarf had slid halfway over one eye. She was fairly certain her leg was bleeding.

The EMTs wasted no time. The vehicle moved swiftly, cutting in and out of traffic. Closing her eyes, Emma winced as a pothole caused fresh discomfort. Fortunately, the hospital was not far away. Before she knew it, she had been whisked inside and tucked into an emergency room cubicle. The dizziness was getting worse. She had enough presence of mind remaining to wonder if she was in any kind of serious danger.

A nurse came in to get vitals. Suddenly, the same deep voice with the bark of command sounded nearby. "How is she?"

"She's conscious. We'll have to get her up to X ray."

"I'm fine," Emma stated, her determination diluted somewhat by the high, wavering condition of her voice.

The nurse left. Though Emma's eyes were closed, she sensed the man standing nearby. His presence had a narcotic effect. She felt safe…as if he were keeping an eye on things.

"Don't go to sleep," he snapped. "Let's get this damned scarf out of your face."

She felt him untie it and draw it free. And then he cursed. "What the hell? Emma?"

She struggled up on one elbow and stared at her white knight. Instantly, shock flooded her already compromised nervous system. *Oh, God.* "Aidan. I didn't realize it was you. Thanks for helping me. I'm sure everything is okay.

You can leave now." The words tripped over each other as her limbs began to shake.

He'd gone white, his eyes wide with what appeared to be a combination of disbelief and horror. "What are you doing here?"

A smile was beyond her. Tears threatened to fall, but she blinked them back. This was not how she'd imagined seeing him again. Not like this. Not without warning. She swallowed hard. "I live here," she whispered.

"The hell you say. Is this some kind of a joke?"

The outrage in his voice and on his face might have been tinged with a hint of panic.

His fury was one blow too many. With a whimper of surrender, she fell back onto the exam table as the world went black…

Aidan strode out of the hospital at a pace little less than full-blown retreat. His heart slugged in his chest and his hands were ice-cold. Of course, that might have been the weather. He'd left his gloves in the car.

Emma was here. And Danielle was not. *Emma*. He repeated her name in his head, still seeing the look of dazed comprehension that filled her wide-set gentian-blue eyes. He was very familiar with those beautiful eyes. Not to mention the porcelain skin, the perfectly curved pink lips, the patrician features, and the silky, fine blond hair that fell past her shoulders. Emma…Good Lord.

The buzzing in his ears was probably a factor of the wind. But then again, his blood pressure might be in the danger zone. His emotions were all over the map. And how ironic was that? He'd made a science of becoming the superficial guy with *no* real emotions.

The lie had been practiced so deeply and so well, he'd begun to believe it himself. But a chance encounter on the street had cut to the heart of his charade. He was injured, bleeding deep in his gut, raw with pain.

Yet Emma was the one in the hospital.

He had no obligation to go back inside. He'd done his part. She was in the hands of professionals.

Standing beside his car, he slammed a fist on the hood…hard enough to bruise his fingers. He'd known that coming home at Christmas would be a test of how well he had healed from the past. But never in a million years had he imagined a confrontation with Emma Braithwaite. She was supposed to be in England, happily married to Viscount Supercilious. Raising upper-crust rug rats with Harry Potter accents and carelessly chic clothes.

Damn, damn, damn…

What would happen if he merely walked away? If he didn't ask for explanations? Could he pretend that the last two hours were a dream? Or a nightmare?

Another ambulance zipped into the admitting area. The flashing lights and ear-piercing siren shocked him back to sanity. He'd left Emma passed out on the exam table. True, he'd notified a nurse immediately, but after that he had fled. What would his brothers think if they could see him now?

They already teased him about his city polish and his propensity for take-out every night of the week. Even Liam, who dressed as befitted his position as co-owner of the prestigious Silver Beeches Lodge, was most at home clambering about in the mountains. He'd already taken Zoe camping and made a new convert.

The Kavanagh brothers, out of necessity, were physically and mentally tough. You didn't grow up with six same-sex siblings and not learn how to handle yourself in a fight. But as much as Aidan loved his brothers, he had always felt a bit out of step with them. He'd wanted to travel the world. He'd been strangled by the small-town lifestyle.

Regardless of the differences in personality and temperament, though, Maeve Kavanagh had taught her sons about responsibility and honor. Perhaps because their father had been lacking in that area, the lessons had stuck. Only the worst kind of cad would leave a woman alone in a hospital with no one to look after her.

Cursing beneath his breath, Aidan gulped in a lungful of icy air. This couldn't be happening. What terrible sins had he committed in the past that karma was so very ready now to kick his ass?

Minutes passed. All around him, people came and went. Hospital staff heading home for the night. Visitors walking toward the doors with worried faces. Aidan barely noted their presence.

Though it shamed him to admit it, he was actually terrified to go back inside. What if Emma were badly hurt? What if even now she was slipping into a coma?

As if it were yesterday he remembered pacing the halls of this very same hospital while Danielle struggled to live. It was a lifetime ago, but the agony was fresh and real. As if it were happening all over again.

He wouldn't allow that. Not on his watch. He had no clue why Emma was in Silver Glen. It didn't matter. He would make sure she was okay, and then he would walk away.

Just like he'd been forced to do ten years ago…

Three

Emma moved her shoulders and moaned. "My head hurts," she whispered. When she tried to focus her eyes, rectangular ceiling tiles above her bed marched from one side of the room to the other. For some reason, that drunken motion made her think of the intricately plastered frieze in her childhood bedroom. She remembered trying to count the individual roses on days when she was ill in bed and stuck at home.

Sadly, this generic space was not nearly as beautiful.

At some point, an unknown set of hands had replaced her clothing with a standard issue hospital gown. The warm blanket tucked up around her shoulders should have felt comforting, but instead, she found it claustrophobic.

Despite her discomfort, she shifted until both arms were free.

An older nurse with kind eyes patted her hand. "You have a concussion. Try not to upset yourself. The pain meds will be kicking in any moment now."

"How long was I out?" She could swear she had only closed her eyes for a moment.

"Not terribly long. But enough for us to get a couple of X rays. They were concerned about your leg, but nothing is broken. You'll have to have a few stitches on your cheek and shin, but that's not too bad considering what might have happened."

"Oh…good…" Someone must have pumped wonderful drugs into her IV, because even with the pain, she was floating on a cloud of worry-free lassitude. Something important nagged at the corners of her mind, but she didn't have the clarity to summon it.

Time passed. Perhaps minutes or hours. She had no clue. She was aware of drifting in and out. Surely it must be dinnertime by now, but she had no appetite.

At one point she was startled by a loud crash in the hallway. Turning her head toward the window, she noted that it was dark. How odd. She remembered heading toward the supermarket for milk. And though the details were fuzzy, she recalled the accident.

But after that things blurred.

When she awoke the next time, her body rebelled. Turning her head, she gagged and reached for the button to summon help. The woman came instantly, offered a basin and spoke soothingly as Emma emptied the contents of her stomach.

The nurse's scrubs were covered in Christmas trees and snowmen. "It's normal, I'm afraid," she said. "The medicine helps the pain, but some people don't tolerate it very well. Try to sleep."

She lowered the lights again and the door swished shut. Feeling dreadfully alone and miserable, Emma was no longer able to stem the flow of tears. She sobbed quietly.

A warm hand stroked her hair. "Hush, Emma. Don't cry. Go back to sleep."

Her eyelids felt weighted down. But she forced them open for long enough to make out the shape of a man seated in a chair beside her bed. "Aidan? I thought I dreamed you."

His laugh sounded rusty, as if he hadn't used it in a while. "I'm afraid not."

"Why are you here?" The syllables slurred together. She was so very tired.

Still he stroked her hair. "It doesn't matter. You're going to be okay. Go to sleep."

When she awoke toward morning, her brain was clearer, but her body felt as if she had gone three rounds with a professional boxer. Maybe the medicine was worth it after all.

In one surreptitious glance, she ascertained that the room was empty. The taste of disappointment filled her mouth. Perhaps Aidan had been a dream after all.

An aide came in with breakfast. Emma's stomach flopped sickeningly at the scent of scrambled eggs, but the tea bag on the tray caught her attention. When the woman arranged the rolling table across Emma's lap and raised the head of the bed, Emma thought she might be sick again.

Breathing deeply, she closed her eyes and remained perfectly still until the feeling passed. At last, she summoned the energy to brew a life-saving cup of Earl Grey. With a dash of sugar, a squirt of lemon and a dollop of artificial creamer, the result was not entirely acceptable, but it was better than nothing.

She was poking at a lumpy biscuit when a female physician entered the room. "Ms. Braithwaite. How are you feeling?"

Emma shrugged. "Like I was hit by something big and hard?"

The doctor grinned. "Aptly put. We've patched you up,

and all your stats are good. Don't get me wrong. You're going to be in bad shape for a few days. But you were very lucky. It could have been a lot worse. I'm thinking of releasing you later today once I see how you do with your meals. Is there anyone at home who can look after you? So you don't have to be on your feet too much?"

Emma opened her mouth to speak, but before she could answer, a man stepped from the hallway into the room. "I'll get her settled and make sure she has help."

Aidan. She couldn't have been any more surprised if the Loch Ness Monster had paraded down the hall. Apparently the sexy phantom in her dreams was entirely real.

"That won't be necessary," she said firmly. Even as she spoke, she scrambled mentally for other alternatives.

Mia would be willing to lend a hand, but she had a baby to care for and a wedding to plan. And Emma definitely was not going to ask Aidan's mother for help. Which left Mrs. Correll, the retired lady who worked part-time at the antique store. But the older woman battled arthritis and couldn't climb stairs.

Emma hadn't lived in Silver Glen all that long. Certainly not long enough to have an extensive list of friends on hand to provide casseroles and sympathy soup.

Aidan ignored Emma's protest. He gave the white-coated physician a high-wattage smile that made her blink twice. "I'll make sure she follows your orders exactly, Doctor. You can count on me."

The doctor departed. Emma stared at the man who once upon a time had been her knight in shining armor. "I can explain," she said, eager to clear the air.

Aidan held up a hand, his gaze wintry. "I don't want to hear anything about the past or why you're here. I'm not interested, Emma. I'm going to take you home and sleep on your couch overnight. But that's it. I have no desire to hear anything you have to say. Are we clear?"

Her heart sank. She had hoped his animosity might have dwindled after all this time. But, no. She was an unwelcome obligation to him. Nothing more. Not even worth the effort of polite conversation.

Her throat tight, she nodded. Though it pained her to admit it, she didn't have the luxury of arguing with him. If Aidan's assurances of aid were enough to get her dismissed from the hospital, then she would swallow the words that wanted to tumble forth in a plea for understanding.

She watched him focus his gaze on the muted television as he feigned great interest in an infomercial for egg separators. His profile was dear and familiar, but the boy she had once known was gone, replaced by a man with even broader shoulders and a physique that was honed and strong.

His dark brown hair with a hint of red was expertly cut, his clothing masculine and expensive. The young university student she remembered had flaunted shaggy locks and a succession of rock-and-roll T-shirts that showcased his flat abdomen. Close-fitting denims had outlined long legs and a tight butt. His grin and American accent won over every girl in a ten-mile radius. But at the end of the day, he went home to Emma's off-campus apartment.

Shaking off the poignant memories, she stared at him. He'd said *no explanations*, so what else was there to talk about?

Abruptly, he turned to face her. "I'll ask the nurses' station to call me when they're ready to dismiss you. In the meantime, I have errands to run."

And with that, he was gone.

* * *

Emma ate and drank and did everything that was asked of her. For one panicked hour she contemplated faking a relapse to avoid being alone with the painfully distant man who looked so much like the Aidan Kavanagh she had once known. But as much as she dreaded being beholden to the glacial-eyed Aidan, she also wanted to get out of this noisy hospital and back into her own bed.

After a long afternoon of additional tests and X rays and blood work, a physician's assistant showed up and announced that Emma was free to go. Aidan appeared just as she tried standing beside the bed to dress in her sadly damaged street clothes.

He cursed quietly. "For God's sake. You're going to fall over." Her tights were badly torn. Aidan took one look at them and tossed them in the trash. "You'll have to go bare-legged on the way home," he said, "but I assume you live close?"

She nodded, humiliated by the way he tucked and pulled and fastened her bits and pieces as if she were a helpless child. Tension radiated from his large frame. Her head pounded, but she was damned if she would show weakness in front of this brusque stranger.

When her few belongings were gathered and in her lap, an orderly eased her into a wheelchair and gave Aidan a nod. "If you'll bring your car around to the front entrance, sir, I'll meet you there with Ms. Braithwaite."

Aidan nodded and vanished.

Emma wouldn't have minded a tour of the hospital, or a quick peek at the maternity ward with all the brand-new babies. Anything to postpone the moment of truth.

If she hadn't been in so much pain, physical and mental, the pun might have made her smile. Aidan didn't *want* to hear the truth. He'd already judged her and found her guilty. He believed that she had betrayed his trust. In his defense, the evidence had been pretty damning.

Outside, the wind was no less biting than it had been the day before. Only now it was dark as well. By the time she sank into the passenger seat of Aidan's fancy sports car with the heated leather seats, she was shivering. He grabbed a jacket from the backseat and handed it to her.

"Wrap that around your legs." He paused, staring out the windshield. His granite jaw flexed. "I need your address."

She sensed that having to ask for that one small piece of information pissed him off. Muttering the street and number, she leaned back and closed her eyes. The car smelled like him. Maybe he would let her sleep here. The prospect of making it all the way to her bed was daunting to say the least.

He parked at the curb in front of her business, his hands clenched on the wheel. "Here?" he asked, incredulity in his voice.

"I have an apartment upstairs. You don't need to stay. Really."

Ignoring her statement completely, he half turned in his seat and fixed her with a steady gaze that left her feeling naked…and not in a good way. The hazel eyes that had once twinkled with good humor were flat. It was difficult to believe that *anything* about this older, tougher Aidan twinkled.

His jaw worked. "Correct me if I'm wrong, but I was under the impression that Lady Emma Braithwaite was an heiress. To the tune of several million pounds. I can't fathom why she would be here in the mountains of North Carolina running an antiques shop when she grew up in a damned castle." He was practically shouting at the end.

"It wasn't a castle." His sarcasm cut deep, but it also made her angry. "You said you didn't want any explanations," she reminded him. "If you don't mind, I'm very tired and I need to take some medicine. If you'll help me up the stairs, you can go." She managed an even-toned, reasonable response until her voice broke on the last word. Biting down hard on her bottom lip, she swallowed and inhaled the moment of weakness.

After several long, pregnant seconds, Aidan muttered something inaudible and got out, slamming his door hard enough to rattle the window beside her. Before she could brace herself for what came next, he opened her side of the car and leaned in to scoop her into his arms.

She shrank back instinctively, unwilling to get any closer. He stumbled when her quick movement threw him off balance. "Put your arm around my neck, Emma. Before I drop you." Irritation accented every syllable.

"Are you always so grumpy?" she asked. If anyone had cause to be out of sorts, it was she.

He locked the car with the key fob and settled her more firmly into his embrace. "Don't push it."

To the left of her storefront, a single narrow door gave entrance to a steep flight of steps. The building dated back to the early days of Silver Glen. When Aidan took the key from her and let himself in, she wondered if his big frame would make it up the stairwell, especially carrying her.

But he was a natural athlete. She never even felt a jostle or a bump as he ascended to the second floor and her quaint apartment. His chest and his arms were hard, though he carried her carefully. If it were possible, she thought she might get drunk on the scent of his skin and the faint starchy smell of his crisp cotton shirt.

A second door at the top required a key as well. By

now, Aidan should have been breathing heavily. Emma was five-eight and not a slip of a woman. But he managed the final hurdle and kicked open the door, reaching with one hand to turn on the light.

She knew the exact moment he spotted her sofa. The red, velvet-covered Victorian settee was designed more for looks than for comfort. It was definitely not meant for sleeping. Fortunately, she owned a more traditional chair and ottoman that were tucked up close to her gas-log fireplace. If Aidan were determined to spend the night, he would be under no illusions as to his accommodations.

The apartment was fairly warm. When she'd left the day before, she had only been nipping out to grab the milk, intending to return in little more than a half hour. That was a blessing. If the rooms had been ice-cold as they sometimes were, her misery would have been complete.

He set her on her feet in the bedroom, not even glancing at her large brass bed with its intensely feminine white lace sheets and comforter. "Can you get ready for the night on your own?" His hands remained on her shoulders, though it was clear he was lending physical support, nothing more.

"Of course." Her right leg felt as if someone had delved into it with an ax, and her head was a heartbeat away from a painful explosion, but she'd die before she would admit it. She had been brought up not to make a fuss. Her father hadn't liked female *histrionics*, as he called them.

Aidan stared down at her. For the first time, she saw something in his eyes that told her the past might be gone, but it was not forgotten. For the space of one brief, heart-stopping breath, she was sure she witnessed tenderness. But it vanished in an instant...perhaps never there to begin with. He unbuttoned her bedraggled coat and eased it from her shoulders.

"Where are your pajamas?" he asked.

She wrapped her arms around her waist. "I'll get them. Go fix yourself a cup of coffee."

One eyebrow lifted. "You have coffee?"

In England, she had done her best to wean him from the uncivilized beverage. "For guests," she said stiffly.

He nodded once and walked away. Sinking down onto the bed, she told herself she could manage to wash up and change clothes. It was a matter of pride and self-preservation. Having Aidan help was unthinkable. She was far too aware of him as it was. His physical presence dwarfed her cozy apartment.

In the bathroom she dared to glance in the mirror and groaned. Why had no one seen fit to give her a hairbrush? Moving as carefully as an old lady, she removed her rumpled and stained blouse and skirt and stripped off her undies and bra. Bruises already marked her skin in a dozen places. She had been given strict instructions not to get her stitches wet, so a shower was out. With a soft washcloth and a bar of her favorite lavender soap, she managed a quick cleanup.

When she was done, she realized that she had forgotten to get a nightgown from the bureau. Wrapping a towel around herself sarong-style, she opened the bathroom door and walked into the bedroom.

As she did so, she caught Aidan leaning down to put a cup of steaming hot tea on her bedside table.

Four

Aidan froze. If Emma's eyes grew any bigger, they would eclipse her face. Though it hurt to look at her, he forced himself to meet her gaze with dispassion. "Drink your tea while it's hot," he said. "I'll see what I can whip up for our dinner."

In her tiny kitchen, he put his hands on the table, palms flat, and bowed his head. So many feelings, so many memories...

Emma laughed up at him, her skin dappled by shadows from the willow tree that served as shelter for their impromptu picnic. "Why the serious look?" she asked.

She lay on her back, arms outstretched above her head, eyes ripe with happiness. They had borrowed an old quilt from her neighbor. The faded colors only made her more beautiful in comparison.

"I have to go home soon," he said, unable to comprehend the upcoming rift. "What will I do without you?" He sat upright, his back propped against the tree trunk, trying not to think about how much he wanted to make love to her at this moment. But the perfectly manicured English park was filled with adults and children eager to enjoy the warmth of a late fall afternoon.

Emma linked her fingers with his, pulling his hand to her lips. "Don't spoil it," she whispered, for a moment seeming as desperately dejected as he was. But immediately, her optimism returned, even if manufactured. "Remember—you'll graduate in the spring, and then we'll have all sorts of choices."

There was no acceptable choice if it didn't include her. He managed a grimace that was supposed to placate her. But from the expression on her face, he knew she saw through him. She had since the first day they met.

He lay down at her side, not caring if anyone raised an eyebrow. Propped on an elbow, he brushed the back of his hand down her cheek. "I can't leave you, Emma. I can't..."

But in the end, he had...

Inhaling sharply, he slammed the door on recollections that served no purpose. That day was so far in the past, it might as well be written up in the history books. Perhaps in a chapter labeled "youthful indiscretions."

Turning his attention to practical matters, he examined the contents of Emma's fridge. The woman lived on yogurt and granola and fancy cheese. His stomach rumbled in protest. But he'd have to make do with a gourmet grilled cheese sandwich.

He found a skillet and spooned a dollop of butter into it, listening to the sizzle as he strained to hear movement in Emma's room. Even now, the image of her half-naked body remained imprinted on his brain. All that creamy English skin. Long legs. Hair the color of spring sunshine.

He dropped a chunk of cheese on the burner and had to fish it out before he set off the smoke alarm. His final efforts were not visually pleasing, but the sandwiches would keep them both from starving.

Leaving his meal in the kitchen, he took Emma's plate to her door and knocked quietly. She would be dressed by now, but he didn't want any additional surprises. He knocked a second time and then opened the door a crack. "Emma?"

The lights were on, but Emma was in bed, fast asleep. Curled on her side, she slept like a child with a hand under her cheek. A neat row of stitches near her ear reminded him anew of how close she had come to disaster.

He glanced at his watch. He hated to wake her, but if she awoke later in pain, it would be worse. He put the plate on the dresser and crouched beside the bed. The instinct to touch her was one he had to ignore.

"Emma," he said quietly, not wanting to startle her.

She moved restlessly but didn't open her eyes.

"Emma."

This time her eyelids fluttered. A small smile curved her lips before she realized where she was and with whom. Immediately, a mask slipped over her features. "Aidan. I told you to go. I'll sleep 'til morning."

Fishing the bottle of pills out of his pocket, he shook a couple of tablets into his palm. "The doctor gave you enough pain meds to last until we can get your prescription filled tomorrow. You're an hour past due, so you'd better take them. And at least eat a few bites of food."

She took his offering with visible reluctance and washed it down with two sips of tea. When he brought the grilled cheese, she stared at it. "You cooked for me?"

He felt his face redden. His lack of expertise in the kitchen was well documented. "It's a sandwich," he said gruffly. "Don't get too excited. I'll be back in a minute with a glass of milk. That might help you sleep."

When he returned, she had managed to finish half of the meal. He held out the tumbler of milk and waited until she drained most of it. Already, the simple exertion of eating had taxed her strength. She was as pale as her bedding, and he saw her hands shake before she tucked them beneath the sheets and settled back into her original position.

"Do you want the lights off?" he asked.

"I suppose. Please leave, Aidan."

He flipped off all except the bathroom light. Leaving that door cracked an inch or so, he took one last look at the patient. "Go to sleep. Everything will be better in the morning."

The chair and ottoman were more comfortable than they appeared. With the gas logs flickering and a couple of woolen throws in lieu of blankets, he managed to fall asleep. His dreams were a mishmash of good and bad, past and present.

Somewhere in the middle of the night a crash jerked him out of his restless slumber. Leaping to his feet, he headed for Emma's room, almost sure the noise had emanated from that direction.

He found her in the bathroom surrounded by the broken remains of a small water glass she kept on the counter. "Don't move," he barked. Her feet were bare. Scooping her up, he avoided the worst of the mess and carried her back to bed. "Why didn't you call me?" he grumbled.

"I didn't need a witness for *that*," she snapped. Even drugged and injured, she had spunk.

Smothering a smile he knew she wouldn't appreciate, he tucked her in and straightened the covers. It was still another forty-five minutes before she could have anything for pain. "How do you feel?"

She shrugged, her expression mulish. "How do you think?"

Evidently, the ladylike manners were eroding in direct proportion to her unhappiness. "Sorry I asked," he said drolly, hoping to coax a smile.

But Emma turned her back on him. "Don't be here when I wake up," she ordered, the words pointed.

He shook his head though she couldn't see him. "Do you want me to bring in the medicine when it's time?"

"No." She burrowed her face into her arm. "I can take care of myself."

Emma had cause to regret her hasty words only a few hours later. When pale winter sunshine peeked into her room, she stirred and groaned. Today was worse than yesterday, and that was saying something. Of course, part of the problem was her stubborn pride. It was long past time for a pain pill, and she was paying the price.

She eased onto her back and listened. The apartment was silent and still. For a moment, she panicked about the shop, and then she remembered it was Sunday. Well, she wasn't going to get any relief until she took something, so she had to get out of this bed.

Cursing softly when pain shot up her thigh, she grabbed hold of the foot rail and found her balance. Her slippers were tucked beneath the edge of the bed, but if she bent to retrieve them, she was fairly certain her headache would ratchet upward about a million notches.

Tiptoeing on icy feet, she went in search of the elusive pill bottle. What she found was Aidan, sleeping soundly beside the hearth. Her shock was equal parts relief and dismay. His longs legs sprawled across her ottoman, his shoes in a jumble nearby. Though his neck was bent at an awkward angle, he snored softly, irrefutable evidence that he was actually slumbering.

She counted the breaths as his broad chest rose and fell. Though she couldn't see his eyes, she knew their color by heart. Hazel, beautiful irises that changed with his mood. Lately all she had seen was the dark glare of disapproval.

His thick hair was mussed. The top three buttons of his shirt were undone, revealing a dusting of hair below his collarbone. The intimacy of the scene curled her stomach with regret and sharp envy. No doubt there was a woman in New York who had laid claim to this beautiful man. But Emma had known him before...before he had acquired the spit and polish of a successful entrepreneur.

As he slumbered, she finally caught a glimpse of the boy she had known. After all, even at twenty-one she and Aidan had been little more than teenagers. They'd had no clue what forces could tear them apart, no way to understand that life seldom produced fairy-tale endings.

The old Emma would have curled into his embrace, not waiting for an invitation, confident of her welcome. Wistfully, she allowed herself a full minute to watch him sleep. But no more.

Easing past him, she spied the bottle on the end table, scooped it up and retreated before the lion awoke and caught her gawking at him. Her bravery extended only so far.

Though she would sell her soul for a cup of hot tea, that luxury would have to wait. The simple task was more than she could handle at the moment, and she had leaned on Aidan far too much already.

Thankfully, he never stirred as she retraced her steps. The partial glass of milk from the night before still sat beside her bed. It wouldn't have spoiled in this amount of time, and she needed something to coat her stomach. Wrinkling her nose at the taste, she swallowed the medicine with one big gulp of liquid.

Though she had heard Aidan clean up the mess in

the bathroom, she knew it was foolhardy to go in there again with bare feet. So she forced herself to slowly and carefully retrieve her footwear from its hiding place beneath the bed. When she straightened, she saw black spots dancing in front of her eyes and her forehead was clammy.

Even so, her immediate need was pressing. After a quick visit to the facilities, she washed her face, brushed her teeth and shuffled back to bed. She didn't even bother glancing at the clock. What did it matter? She had no place to go.

Aidan breathed a sigh of relief when he heard Emma's door shut. He'd heard her the moment she climbed out of bed. Feigning sleep had seemed the wisest course of action. But he hadn't anticipated how strongly her silent perusal would affect him.

What was she thinking as she stood there and stared at him? How did she reconcile the way they had left things between them years ago with her current choice to live in Silver Glen? She had to possess an agenda. There was no way she could call such a thing coincidence. She was far too intelligent to try that tactic.

The only explanation was that she had come here intentionally. But why?

He told himself it didn't matter. And he almost believed it.

Scraping his hands through his hair, he sat up and put on his shoes. As he rolled his neck trying to undo the kinks, he wondered how long it had been since he'd spent a platonic night on a woman's sofa.

Emma would probably sleep for a few hours now that she had taken her medicine. Which meant he had time to drop off her prescription, grab some breakfast and dash up to the hotel for clean clothes and a shower.

The first two items on his list were accomplished without incident. But when he tried to access the back stairs at the Silver Beeches to avoid any awkward questions, he ran in to Liam coming down as he was going up.

His older brother, dressed to the nines as always, lifted an eyebrow. "Look what the cat dragged in."

"Don't rag on me, Liam. I haven't slept worth a damn."

"At least not in your own bed. I thought all your lady friends were in New York."

Aidan counted to ten and then to twenty. Liam was not giving him any more grief than usual, but Aidan wasn't in the mood to be teased. Not today. His jaw clenched, he offered a simple explanation, knowing that Liam wouldn't let him pass without at least that. "I ran in to a friend who was having a bit of trouble. I helped out. That's all. Now if you don't mind, I'd like to go to my room and get cleaned up."

Liam leaned against the wall, his arms crossed over his chest. "This wouldn't have anything to do with the young woman who was hit by a car day before yesterday…downtown?"

Aidan stared at him. "Damn it. That's exactly why I don't live here anymore. Nobody has anything better to do than gossip."

"People were concerned. Silver Glen is a tight-knit place."

"Yeah. I got that."

Liam's face changed, all trace of amusement gone. "I know it's hard for you to be here this time of year. But I want you to know how glad we all are to have you home for the holidays."

The knot in Aidan's chest prevented him from answering—that and the sting of emotion that tightened his throat.

His sibling knew him too well to be fooled. "I'll let you go," Liam said, his eyes expressing the depth of their relationship. "If I can help with anything, let me know."

Five

By the time Aidan picked up the prescription and made it back to Emma's place, almost two hours had passed. He had taken her key with him, so he let himself in quietly and placed his packages on the table. Peeking into the bedroom, he saw that she still slept.

The extra rest was good for her. And besides, the sooner she was stable, the sooner he could leave.

He shoved the carryout bags he had picked up into the fridge. The greasy burgers and fries came from a mom-and-pop joint down the street. The Silver Shake Shack had been there since he was a kid. While Emma had converted Aidan to drinking proper English tea, he had been the one to teach her the joys of comfort food.

His immediate mission accomplished, he sprawled in the chair again and scrolled through his email. No big surprises there. Except for the one from his mother that said: Dinner at eight. S.B. dining room. Don't make me hunt you down.

He laughed softly, knowing that had been her intention. Everyone wanted Aidan to be in a good mood. To be happy. He understood their concern, but he was fine. He was here, wasn't he? They couldn't expect more than that.

Evidently the smell of his lunch offering permeated the apartment. Emma wandered out of her room wearing stretchy black knit pants and a hip-length cashmere sweater. She had done her hair up in a ponytail, and wore bunny slippers on her feet.

She gave him a diffident smile. "Hey."

"Hey, yourself. Doing any better?"

"Actually, yes. Was that food I smelled?"

"Some of the best. I put it in the fridge, but it hasn't been there long. We can zap it in the microwave. Are you hungry now?"

She nodded, heading for her small dining table. Her gait was halting, so he knew her leg was bothering her.

While Emma sat and rested her head in her hands, he managed to rustle up paper plates and condiments. "I ordered you one with mustard, mayo and tomato. I hope that's still the way you like it."

Her expression guarded, she nodded. "Sounds lovely."

The silent meal was half-awkward, half-familiar. Emma had changed very little over the years, though he did see a few fine lines at the corners of her eyes. She had always been more serious than he was, conscientious to a fault. The one thing he couldn't help noticing was that her breasts had filled out. The soft sweater emphasized them and her narrow waist.

When the food was gone, down to the last crumb, he cleared the table. "Do you feel like sitting up for a little while? I'll give you the seat by the fire."

"That would be nice."

So polite. Like a little girl minding her manners. Swallowing his irritation at her meekness, he hovered as she made her way across the room. He wouldn't touch her unless she showed signs of being lightheaded. When she was settled, he stood in the center of the room, hands in his pockets. "If you have an extra key," he said, "I can check on you later and you won't have to get up to answer the door. I have dinner plans, but I'll bring you something hot to eat before I go."

Staring into the fire, she nodded. Her profile, silhouetted against the flames, had the purity of an angel's. He felt something in his chest wrench and pull. The shaft of pain took his breath away. That wouldn't do. Not at all. He was way past dancing to Emma Braithwaite's tune.

He made a show of glancing at his watch. "Will you be okay for the afternoon on your own?"

"Of course." Her chin lifted with all the haughtiness of a duchess.

For all he knew, she might actually *be* a duchess. He hadn't kept up with the details of her life. Anything was possible.

She pointed. "The spare key is in the top drawer of that desk by the window. I think it's tied to a bit of green ribbon."

He rummaged as directed and found what he was looking for. As he pushed everything back into place, his gaze landed on a familiar-looking piece of paper. When he recognized what it was, he felt a mule-kick to the chest. "Emma?"

"Yes?"

He held up the offending card. "Would you care to explain why you have an invitation to my brother's wedding?"

Emma groaned inwardly. Could things get any worse? Aidan's original animosity had faded as he cared for her. Now his suspicions were back in full force. His expression was glacial, his demeanor that of judge and jury combined.

"Your mother gave it to me," she said, the words flat. Let him think what he wanted.

"My mother..."

Emma nodded. "I'm sure Mia asked her to. Mia and I became friends when I moved here a few months ago."

"How convenient."

As bad as she felt, her anger escalated. "I don't know what you're implying, and I don't care. I don't have to explain myself to you. Leave the key and go. I can manage by myself."

His face darkened with some strong emotion as he crushed the beautiful invitation in his fist. "You have no food in the house. I said I would bring your dinner. Now if you'll excuse me, I have things to do."

The way he slammed the door as he walked out was entirely unnecessary. She already knew he was furious. And that was just too damn bad. Emma had as much right to be in Silver Glen as he had. If he cared to listen, she would be happy to explain. But she had a sneaking suspicion that Aidan Kavanagh was too darned stubborn to hear her out.

Aidan wondered if he were losing his mind. Had the trauma of coming to Silver Glen at Christmas finally made him snap? When he left Emma's apartment, he sat downstairs in his car for several long minutes, trying to decide what to do. Finally, he drove out to Dylan's place for a visit. If he should happen to pump Mia for information in the meantime, that was *his* business.

Dylan answered the door, his face lighting up as he grabbed Aidan in a bear hug. "Thanks for coming home, baby brother. It means the world to Mia and me. I couldn't have a wedding without you."

Aidan shrugged, uncomfortable that everyone was making such a big deal of his visit. "Of course I'm here. Why wouldn't I be?"

The empathy in Dylan's steady gaze made Aidan feel raw and vulnerable, neither of which was the least bit appealing to a grown man.

Mia broke the awkward silence. "I'm glad you're here, too. And so is Cora."

Aidan took the child automatically as Mia handed her over. Cora gave him a sweet smile that exposed two tiny front teeth. He kissed her forehead. "Hey, darlin'. You want to go joyriding with Uncle Aidan? I'll show you where all the toddler boys live."

Mia rolled her eyes. "Why is it that no one in the Kavanagh family knows how to talk to girls?"

Dylan looked at her with mock outrage. "I might point out that *you* fell for some of my best lines."

Mia kissed her soon-to-be-husband on the cheek. "Whatever helps you sleep at night…"

Aidan grinned. He'd expected to be a little jealous of Dylan's storybook ending…and Liam's. And perhaps on some level, he was. But even so, he was happy for his older brothers. It was about time the Kavanaghs found something to celebrate.

Reggie Kavanagh had died when his boys were young. Liam, at sixteen, had been the only one close to adulthood. Truthfully, it wasn't exactly accurate to say that Reggie died. One day he simply went off into the mountains and never returned. Looking for the silver mine that had put his ancestors and the town of Silver Glen on the map.

Aidan tried to shake off the memory. He could still see his mother's face at the memorial service. She had been devastated, but resigned. Apparently, Reggie had never been the husband she deserved. But then again, life wasn't about getting what you were owed. It was more about dealing with what you were given.

In Aidan's case, that meant surviving loss. First his father. Then Emma. And finally, poor Danielle.

Cora's pudgy little body was warm and solid in his arms. A baby was such beautiful proof of life's goodness. Aidan needed that reminder now and again. He glanced at his brother, who apparently couldn't resist nibbling his wife's neck since Aidan was running interference with Cora.

Aidan complained. "In case it's escaped your notice, your innocent daughter is right here in front of you. How about a little decorum?"

"Decorum sucks." Dylan grabbed Mia for a quick smacking kiss on the lips. While Mia giggled and turned pink, Aidan put a hand over Cora's face. "Don't look," he whispered. "The adults are being inappropriate."

Laughing, but starry-eyed, Mia rescued her daughter and cuddled her close. "She'd better get used to it. Dylan wants at least two more."

Aidan lifted an eyebrow. "Seriously?" His brother had changed a lot in the last year. He was happier. More grounded. Less defensive about his place in the world.

"I like having kids around." Dylan's crooked grin said he recognized Aidan's astonishment and understood it. There had been a time when Dylan was the ultimate party animal. Now, however, he had embraced the role of family man with enthusiasm.

It didn't hurt that beautiful, quiet, smart-as-Einstein Mia shared his bed every night. They were an unlikely couple in many ways, but somehow the two of them together made it work.

Mia glanced at her watch. "Are you both going up to the lodge to eat with your mom and the rest of the clan?"

"You're not?" Aidan was surprised. His mother's command performances demanded proper deference.

Mia shook her head. "I've been given a dispensation. I want to get Cora to bed on her usual schedule, because we're going to Asheville tomorrow to find her a dress for the wedding."

"Cutting it a little close, aren't you?"

Mia shook her head. "Blame it on your brother. He's the one who decided we had to get married ASAP."

"Because?"

Dylan spoke up, his face a study in love and devotion as he eyed the two women in his house. "I'm adopting Cora," he said. "The papers are going to be finalized the day after Christmas. I want us to be a family before the New Year."

Conversation wandered in less serious directions after that. Dylan offered Aidan a beer while Mia sprawled on the floor to play with Cora. Aidan decided in that quiet half hour that he couldn't go back to Emma's. Not today. He had things to figure out, and he needed space and time to understand what her motives were.

When he and Dylan joined the two females on the floor, Aidan addressed Mia. "I need a favor, since you and Cora aren't going up the mountain for dinner."

She untangled Cora's fingers from her hair. "Name it. I need to build up all the family points I can get."

He chuckled. "It's nothing bad, I swear. But did you hear about the accident in town on Friday afternoon?"

Mia nodded, pausing to blow a raspberry on Cora's tummy. "Someone ran a red light and hit a pedestrian."

"Yes. I happened to be there at the time and followed the ambulance to the hospital. The woman's name is Emma Braithwaite. She says she's friends with you."

He felt a lick of shame at manipulating his sister-in-law. But he needed to know if Emma had disclosed the relationship she shared with Aidan.

Mia's gaze was anxious. "Is she okay?"

He nodded. "Home resting now. A concussion and some stitches. She didn't want to bother you because of the baby and the wedding. But it seems that she's fairly new in town… right? And doesn't know many people? I was hoping you and Cora could run over there and take her some dinner."

Dylan's eyes narrowed as though he sensed something was going on but wasn't sure what. "Who died and made you Clara Barton?"

"I watched the accident happen. All I had in mind was heading to the hospital and making sure she was okay. But when I found out she didn't have anyone to help out, I offered to get her home and settled when she was discharged."

"How convenient."

Hearing Dylan voice the same sarcastic response Aidan had used with Emma made him wince inwardly. "I don't know what you're talking about."

"Give me a break, Aidan. I've seen Emma. She's tall, blond and gorgeous…with a voice like an angel. You were smitten and decided to go all Galahad on her poor, helpless self."

Mia looked up with a frown. "I'm sitting *right* here," she said.

Dylan gave her a smoochy face. "Don't worry, my love. You know I'm into short, dark and cuddly."

"Oh, dear Lord," Aidan groused. "You two are embarrassing little Cora."

Cora, oblivious to the repartee, played with her toes.

Aidan weighed the facts. Clearly, Emma had made no mention to Mia of the fact that Emma and Aidan went way back. So if she wasn't using her past relationship with Aidan to ingratiate herself into the Kavanagh family, what was her deal?

* * *

He wrestled with his suspicions all evening, in the midst of a loud, argumentative, completely normal dinner with his siblings and his mother. To be honest, he'd forgotten how much fun it could be when they were all together. Usually when he came home to visit, at least one or two of the crew were missing...spread out here, there and yonder. It was increasingly difficult to corral all the Kavanaghs in the same place at the same time.

Maeve hadn't forgotten, though. It was at her insistence that they were all gathered under one roof tonight. And this was only the first of a series of holiday moments scripted by the matriarch of the family.

Liam's wife, Zoe—still with a new bride's glow—fit right in. Unlike the introverted Mia, Zoe loved a social gathering. She laughed and flirted and played the role of naive newcomer with verve, all under the indulgent eye of her besotted husband.

Aidan tipped a metaphorical hat to his mom. With Dylan's wedding, the whole Christmas season and a brand-new, soon-to-be-adopted Kavanagh kiddo, Maeve had scored a trifecta.

He left the Silver Beeches Lodge with a smile on his face. Though his room was upstairs, he was too wired to sleep. Instead, he climbed into his car and drove toward town. The closer he came to Emma's place of business, the less he smiled.

Parking at the curb below her windows, he stared up at the light. Why had she come to Silver Glen? He told himself he didn't care, but that was a lie. The Emma he had known in college was neither devious nor vengeful. Though, that was a very long time ago. Had she somehow decided to blame him for the meltdown of their relationship?

Only the most naive of assessments could attribute anything positive to her unexpected appearance in Silver Glen. His immediate reaction to finding her was suspicion and wariness. None of this made sense.

But even knowing that she had made the acquaintance of at least of two of his family members and that she had never once mentioned to either of them her connection to Aidan, he didn't want to believe the worst.

Truthfully, now that he had spent some time with her, it was impossible to hold back the flood of memories. Feelings he thought long dead pumped adrenaline into his bloodstream. She was like a drug in his system. He had detoxed after she nearly ruined his life. But the addiction was still there. Waiting to be resurrected.

If he had an ounce of self-preservation, he would stay the hell away. He'd crafted a decent life for himself—an even-keeled existence with no surprises, no regrets. No highs, no lows. It was safe…and financially remunerative. Even without his share of the family business, he had plenty of disposable income. And many friends of both sexes to help him fritter it away.

Emma's unexpected incursion into his life shouldn't even be a blip on his radar. Yet he had spent the night at her place. The same old Aidan, looking out for a woman who didn't want or need his protection.

He knew better.

But did he have the guts to turn his back on the one person who had taught him both the incredible rush of desire entwined with new love and also the soul-crushing agony of betrayal?

Six

December in the mountains of North Carolina was a capricious season. It could either be snowy and cold, balmy and sunny, or—as was the case this year—wet and gloomy.

Emma leaned against the windowsill, hands tucked in the pockets of her chenille robe, and watched water droplets track down the glass. Her view of the street below was distorted…like an image in a dream.

For four days she had expected Aidan to return, and for four days she had been disappointed. Now, there was no denying the truth. He was not coming back.

Having Mia show up on her doorstep Sunday evening had been the first sign. Though Emma was delighted to see her friend and little Cora, the fact that Aidan had promised to bring her dinner and then delegated that responsibility suggested he had been caring for Emma only out of a sense of duty.

She was the one who had wishfully attributed his emotions to feelings of affection. Which was ludicrous, really…she fully admitted that. Aidan had good reason to despise her. Only the honor and integrity instilled by Maeve Kavanagh into each and every one of her sons had compelled Aidan to come to Emma's aid.

Twitching the lace sheers back into place, she contemplated the outfit that lay draped across the red velvet settee. Tonight was the first of Maeve's holiday events—a fete for Dylan and Mia. Since the wedding plans had been thrown together so quickly, there hadn't been time for a more traditional bridal shower.

Because Dylan's home was fully outfitted, particularly with the addition of Mia's things, tonight's invitation had requested gifts to one of three charities in lieu of toasters and stemware. Emma had already written a large check and tucked it in her shimmery silver clutch. As a small thank-you gift to Mia and Dylan for their friendship, she had wrapped up a memento—an antique silver picture frame engraved on the lower edge with the words, *'til the end of time...*

In her imagination, she saw a young war bride tucking it into her soldier's pocket as he headed off to the other side of the world. Emma was a romantic. And a proud one. At one time, she had believed that every woman could find her soul mate. Now, older and wiser, she wasn't entirely sure. But she still hadn't given up on romance, even if it was mostly for other people.

Quite honestly, she didn't want to go tonight. Her leg still hurt, though it was much improved, and her head ached if she tried to do too much. But the doctor had cleared her to go back to work.

If she planned to open the shop tomorrow after a several-day absence, she could hardly expect Maeve to understand if Emma cried off tonight's festivities for health reasons. She was trapped by her affection for Mia and Maeve and the many kindnesses they had shown her as a newcomer to Silver Glen.

On the upside, if Aidan were avoiding her, it would make tonight more tolerable. Maybe they could sit on opposite sides of the room. She didn't have a problem with that, at all.

She sat down and stroked the fabric of her formal dress. Strapless and Grecian in design, the column of platinum silk was actually quite comfortable. A Christmas gift from her mother, the dress made the most of her height and her pale skin. Instead of washing her out, the color was surprisingly flattering.

Regrettably, because of her painful leg, she would have to forgo her favorite, sparkly three-inch heels. Silver ballet flats would have to do. In the meantime, she would practice not tripping since the skirt was bound to brush the floor.

Mia had insisted on sending a car to pick up Emma at her apartment. Though Emma thought it a wasteful luxury, she had to admit that *not* having to drive was a relief.

The hours of the afternoon crept by. The cleaning lady came and went, leaving the small rooms spotless. Afterward, Emma took a bath in the old-fashioned clawfooted tub, leaning her head back and closing her eyes as she escaped to a sweeter, less volatile time in her life…

Aidan met her at the library, his hushed greeting drawing disapproving stares. Perhaps because he dragged her against him and gave her an enthusiastic kiss. He was always doing that. The uninhibited American and the repressed Englishwoman.

"Did you get your paper turned in?" she asked, loving the way his eyes ate her up. Aidan made her feel like the world's sexiest woman. It was heady stuff for a girl who had spent much of her youth as a wallflower. Crooked teeth, a slight stammer and paralyzing shyness had made boarding school a nightmare. At home, things were not much better. The few village children who were her age were either intimidated by her title or openly

sullen, resenting the money that made her life easy in their estimation.

Aidan stroked her hair, his eyes lit with humor and lust. "My paper on the wives of Henry the Eighth? Yes. Barely. All I could think about was getting you naked again."

They had been lovers for a week. Seven glorious days that had changed her life. "Aidan," she said urgently. "Hush. I don't want to get tossed out of here."

"Won't dear old Daddy take care of any demerits?"

"Don't joke about that," she said, shivering as if a ghost had walked over her grave. "He would kill me if he knew that I—"

"Let your virginal self be ravaged?"

Her grin was reluctant. "You are such a scoundrel."

He slapped a hand over his heart. "Me? You must have me confused with someone else. I'm the man who loves you, body and soul..."

From the living room, she heard the chiming of the hour on her mantel clock. It was five-thirty already. Her pumpkin coach would be arriving in little more than an hour.

Climbing out of the tub, she dried herself with a thick Turkish towel and sat in front of the mirror to twist her hair into a complicated style befitting the dress. When that was done, she applied makeup with a light hand. A bit of blush, a hint of glittery powder at her cleavage. Mascara to darken her too-pale lashes, and finally, a spritz of her favorite perfume and a quick slick of lip gloss.

Hobbling into the bedroom at a much slower pace than usual, she dragged open her lingerie drawer and selected a matching set of silk undies in pale celery green. Since it was too cold and damp to go bare legged, she added a lacy garter belt and cobweb-thin stockings with a naughty seam up the back.

She might be dateless tonight, but that was no reason to let her spirits drag. It was Christmas, damn it. And she intended to squeeze every last bit of ho-ho-ho cheer out of the occasion. Aidan and his judgmental attitude could take a hike to the North Pole and stay there for all she cared.

It was becoming increasingly clear that her move to Silver Glen might have been ill-advised, at least when it came to Aidan. He didn't want to hear anything she had to say. But fortunately, he would be gone soon—back to the big city where he could wine and dine every woman in Manhattan if he wanted to.

Emma had finally found a place where she felt at home. After so many years in Boston, she was out of step with her English roots. And city living in Massachusetts really hadn't suited her, despite enjoying her job. She was really a small-town girl when all was said and done.

Here, in Silver Glen, she had a future. Her business was off to a good start. She had the opportunity to meet new people. Even if Aidan never gave her a chance to make things right between them, his charming hometown offered a cozy place to create her nest.

At twenty 'til seven, she realized that since her accident she had never actually tried negotiating the steps to the street. Slipping into her winter dress coat and adding a filmy scarf that would serve as a shawl later, she grabbed her purse, locked the apartment door and slowly made her way downstairs.

Apparently, she had taken her pre-accident fitness for granted, bounding up and down the steep staircase several times a day. Tonight, by the time she made it to street level, her leg throbbed and she trembled. Fortunately, the uniformed driver was early and immediately opened the car door when he saw her appear.

Emma sank into the comfortable backseat and folded her hands in her lap, her heart racing. Like Cinderella being escorted to the ball, she wondered what lay ahead. No Prince Charming, that's for sure. More likely a grumpy beast. Aidan had made his feelings clear.

Pulling onto the large flagstone apron that led to sweeping steps accessing the doors of the Silver Beeches Lodge, the driver halted the car and jumped out to come around and open Emma's door. The scene that awaited her was magnificent. Two huge Fraser firs, adorned with white lights and silvery stars, flanked the hotel's entrance. On the porch, a dozen more trees, each decked out as one of the twelve days of Christmas, cast a glow against the night sky.

Though the rain had stopped, the air was misty and cold, much too chilly to linger outside. Stepping into the lobby was equally impressive. Here, a Victorian holiday theme had overtaken the large public area. On a huge round table that normally supported a lavish flower arrangement in an ornate urn, poinsettias had been stacked in tiers to form the shape of a crimson-and-green tree.

Much of the traditional décor reminded Emma of her childhood during the month of December. All she needed was a mince pie and some plum pudding and she would feel right at home.

A formal doorman took her coat and greeted her, directing her toward the ballroom at the rear of the main floor. Emma hesitated in the doorway, feeling abashed at the swirl of light and color and conversation. Gold and green festoons draped the room along the ceiling. Bunches of real mistletoe hung from curling red ropes.

Twined in the quartet of chandeliers were narrow red-and-green-plaid ribbons.

Everywhere, the air carried the scent from great boughs of evergreens that adorned the massive fireplaces on either end of the room. Before Emma could turn tail and run, Mia spotted her and hurried across the floor, her smile infectious. "I'm so glad you're here," she said. "Come let me introduce you to some of our friends."

Dylan and Mia were well liked. Emma lost count of the townspeople she met. Fortunately, there were no seats at the family tables, so Emma courted invisibility by seating herself with a couple of business owners she had met soon after she'd moved in to her storefront.

Maeve had planned the evening to the last detail. First was a sumptuous four-course dinner, beginning with cranberry salad, then butternut squash soup, and finally, the entrée consisting of squab, asparagus with Hollandaise sauce, twice-baked potatoes and yeast rolls. The china, crystal, silver and napkins were impeccable.

By the time the sweet carts rolled out, Emma was stuffed, but not so much that she couldn't enjoy a piece of pecan pie.

Her tablemates were chatty and kind, including Emma in their conversations. She found herself smiling for no particular reason except that she was happy to be there.

As the dessert course wrapped up, Dylan stood and, on behalf of Mia and himself, thanked the crowd for their gift donations. He named a total that made Emma blink. Not that she wasn't accustomed to moving in social circles where fundraising dinners were de rigueur, but many of the Kavanagh party attendees seemed like ordinary people.

After Dylan's brief speech, several people toasted the bride-and-groom-to-be, and then it was time for dancing.

A small orchestra set up shop in one corner of the room. The lights dimmed. Music filled the air. Holiday songs and romantic ballads and even a smattering of classical pieces coaxed brave couples onto the floor in the center of the room.

Emma watched wistfully. She should probably slip out. This was not the time to be without a date.

Before she could make her excuses to her tablemates and head unobtrusively to the exit, Mia appeared unexpectedly with Aidan in tow. "Emma…" Her smile was conspiratorial. "I told my future brother-in-law you were feeling much better. I know you met under odd circumstances, but we should celebrate, don't you think? You could have been badly hurt. And since neither of you has a date tonight…"

One look at Aidan's face told Emma this was not his idea. "I'm sure Aidan has lots of people he wants to chat with since he lives out of town. I'll just sit and listen to the music." She tried to back out gracefully, but though Mia was quiet by nature, she was a woman of strong opinions.

Mia tugged Emma to her feet. "Don't be silly. Aidan *wants* to dance, don't you?" She looked up at her fiancé's brother with a cajoling smile.

Aidan nodded stiffly. "Of course. If Emma's up to it."

He was giving her an out…perhaps giving *both* of them an out. Perversely, his patent reluctance made her want to irritate him. "I'd love to dance," she said, draping her scarf across the back of her chair. The room was plenty warm. With two large-scale fires blazing and the body heat from a hundred guests, she was definitely not going to get a chill.

Mia, her job done, waved a hand and went to reclaim Dylan for the next dance. Emma and Aidan stood in a small cocoon of awkward silence. He wore a tux, as did most of the men in the room. Only in Aidan's case, the formal attire fit him so comfortably and so well, he seemed in his element. A man who, no doubt, had a closet full of such clothes back in New York.

He was bigger than the boy she remembered. His shoulders—barely contained by the expensive fabric of his jacket—were broad, his belly flat. When he took her hand and pulled her into a traditional embrace, she felt a little giddy.

Was it wrong to be glad that Mia was bossy and that Aidan was too much of a gentleman to make a scene? Emma bit her lip, looking anywhere but at his face. One of his hands, fingers splayed, rested against the back of her gown just below the place where bare skin met soft fabric.

She had intended to make light conversation, but her throat dried up. A wave of nostalgia and sexual yearning swept over her with such force that she stumbled once. Aidan righted her effortlessly, his strong legs moving them with ease across the crowded dance floor.

When Aidan spoke, she actually jumped.

"Relax," he said, his tone frustrated. "I'm not going to out you to the room. No one needs to know our dirty secrets."

Her spine locked straight. "We don't have any dirty secrets," she said, enunciating carefully.

"Then why haven't you told my family who you really are?"

Finally, she allowed her gaze to meet his. If she had expected to see tumultuous emotion, she was way off base. His face was a pleasant mask, only a tic in his cheek betraying any hint of agitation. "Who am I?" she asked pointedly. "An old girlfriend? That hardly seems worth mentioning. We were little more than children playing at being grown-ups."

Finally, she stirred the sleeping dragon. Fire shot from his eyes, searing her nerves and making her tremble. "Don't you dare," he said, the words forced from between clenched teeth. "It may have been a long time ago, but I won't let you rewrite history so you can whitewash the truth."

"The truth?" She stared up at him, confused and upset. "I don't know what you mean."

"You screwed me over, Emma. Though I must admit that your prissy English manners almost made it seem like a privilege. I was a young fool. But I learned my lesson. When I told you I didn't want to talk about the past, I meant it. But apparently, it's not so easy to overlook."

"I didn't ask you to dance with me," she said, the words bitter in her mouth.

"You didn't put up much of a fight, either."

To any onlookers, it must have appeared that Aidan and Emma were conversing politely in the midst of a dance.

Suddenly, she couldn't bear to have him touching her. Not when she knew how much he despised her.

"I will *not* cause a scene and ruin Mia's party." Her tone was soft but vehement. "But I am leaving this dance floor—now."

"Not without me." The fake smile he plastered on his face was in direct counterpoint to the unrelenting grip of his fingers around her wrist as he walked casually away from the dancers, pulling Emma in his wake.

If she struggled, everyone would see.

She waited until they reached the relative privacy of the hallway until trying to jerk free. "Let go of me, damn it."

But Aidan wasn't done. He stared down at her, a slash of red on each of his cheekbones. The glitter in his eyes could have been anger—or something far more volatile.

"We're going upstairs," he said. "And we're going to hash out a few things.

"My scarf and purse are at the table."

"I'll call and ask them to hold your things at the front desk."

"Oh, good," she said, glaring at him. "At least someone will know I've gone missing."

Seven

Aidan knew the moment they stepped into the elevator that he had made a strategic mistake. The mirrored walls reflected Emma's cool, English beauty no matter where he turned his gaze. The swanlike grace of her neck. The perfect features…even the vulnerable spot at her nape that he had unfortunately fantasized about all evening.

She carried herself with the poise of a Grecian goddess who might have worn such a dress once upon a time. The only flaw he could see was the slight limp caused by the injury to her leg. She had used makeup to cover the stitches near her ear. They were barely noticeable.

From the first moment he saw her tonight with her hair intricately woven around her head, he had wanted nothing more than to remove each pin, one by one, and watch all that golden silk tumble down around her bare shoulders.

They reached his floor in a matter of seconds. Emma made no move to elude him. Perhaps she knew they had been heading for this moment all along.

When he opened the door of his suite and ushered her inside, she glanced around curiously but did not comment. The accommodations were luxurious, but for a woman of Emma's background, the antique furnishings and Oriental rugs were old hat.

"Would you like a drink?" he asked.

She perched on the edge of a chair, her hands folded in her lap. "Whiskey. Neat."

He raised an eyebrow. The girl he had known rarely drank anything stronger than wine. Perhaps she was more nervous that he realized. It was petty of him to be glad. But he was.

When he handed her the heavy crystal tumbler, she eyed him over the rim, tossed back her head and swallowed the shot in one gulp. She might be nervous, but she was defiant as hell.

Taking a sip of his own drink, he rested a hip against the arm of the sofa, too antsy to sit down.

Emma finally relaxed enough to lean back in her chair. Kicking off her small shoes, she curled her legs beneath her. For a moment he caught a glimpse of slim ankles and berry-painted toes before she twitched her skirt to cover the view.

"I find myself at a loss," he said. "I know you're up to something, but since my sister and my mother have taken you to their bosom, I can hardly toss you out on your ear."

"I live here now," she said, her gaze daring him to disagree.

"And why is that?"

"You didn't want any explanations," she reminded him, the words tart.

"Perhaps I was too hasty." He offered the conciliatory olive branch, but Emma stomped on it.

"The information window is closed." Her ironic smile and visible satisfaction at thwarting him made his temper spark, but he was determined to keep the upper hand.

"What if we agree to an exchange? One piece of info for another."

"I don't need to know anything about you. I don't care."

If the way her breasts heaved was any indication—threatening their containment—she cared far more than she was letting on.

He poured her another drink. "I forgot to ask if you were still taking pain pills."

She took the second shot and treated it like the first. Though her face turned red and her eyes watered, she never wavered. "Of course not. I'm not stupid."

"I never said you were. Everyone at Oxford was quick to point out to me that you were one of the smartest women on campus."

"Not too smart, apparently."

"What does that mean?"

"Oh, never mind." She seemed crestfallen suddenly, her lower lip trembling, her expression lost.

"I own a very lavish penthouse apartment in the heart of New York City. I deal in high-end real estate."

"Believe me, Aidan. That's not exactly news. Your mother has been singing your praises in great detail. She misses you."

"I'm here now."

"Yes, you are."

"Look at me."

He strode to where she sat, pulled her to her feet, and settled them both on the sofa. Finishing his own drink, he placed his glass on the coffee table. "Actually, there's only one thing I really need to know."

She half turned to face him, her wide-eyed gaze curious. The platinum silk molded to her body with mesmerizing results. "What's that?"

"I'll show you." Capturing her mouth beneath his, he kissed her slowly, allowing her every opportunity to resist. Nowhere did their bodies touch except for the breathless press of lips on lips.

Her scent was familiar—sweet English roses with a hint of dewy spring. He'd been down this road a hundred times…heard the same angel choirs…seen the land of milk and honey.

His heart slugged in his chest, struggling to keep up with the need for oxygen. His circulatory system was taxed to the limit, as if his blood had become thick molasses.

In his head he heard the raucous sound submarines make when diving. Something was pulling him under. Something dangerous.

Emma made no move to put her hands on him. He was the one to crack first. Helpless, desperate, he slid both hands alongside her neck and angled her chin with his thumbs.

The room was silent except for their harsh breathing. He felt as if he were floating on the ceiling, watching himself fall through the same rabbit hole. At one time, Emma's kisses had been the magic elixir that made his days in England as bright and sweet as a dream.

He was losing control. His brain knew it. His body fought the truth. Shuddering with a desire that shredded his resolve, he used one hand to tug at the bodice of her dress. The thin fabric yielded easily, as did the filmy lace of her bra. In moments his fingertips caressed the puckered tip of one breast, then the other.

Emma groaned. "Aidan…" The word was barely a whisper.

He leaned over her warm, curvy body stretched out on the sofa. Abandoning her lips with no small amount of regret, he moved lower to kiss her more intimately, using his teeth to scrape furled nipples.

So lost was he in the feast that was her body, it took several long seconds for him to recognize the moment when she rebelled. Small hands beat at his shoulders. "No more, Aidan. No more."

Groggy with shock and confusion, he sat up, moving away from her with haste. In her face he saw what they had done. In her eyes he saw the woman he had loved more than was sane.

"God help me," he muttered, unable to look away as Emma tugged her dress into place. Several strands of her hair had come loose to dangle onto her shoulders. She looked rumpled and well loved.

She sat up as well, her complexion paler than the night he'd brought her home from the hospital.

Rage and fear consumed him. He stared at her in silence, his chest roiling with emotions to which he dared not give a name. Self-preservation kicked in. He wiped his mouth with the back of his hand, removing traces of lip color. "Amazing," he said, his heart as cold as his hands. "How can you look like a princess, kiss like a siren and have the duplicitous heart of a cheat and a liar?"

Emma blinked. He saw the moment she processed his deliberate insult. Dark color flooded her face. She smacked him hard with an open palm. The sound echoed. "How dare you," she cried, as moisture brightened her eyes. "You don't even know me. Apparently you never did."

He shrugged, insolent and furious, as much at himself as at her. "I know enough. I won't be wrapped around your finger again, Lady Emma. I learned my lesson."

She lifted her chin, as though daring the teardrops to fall. "You're a miserable, hardened, shallow man. You've let your prejudices and your grudges and your righteous indignation blind you. I can't believe I ever thought I was in love with you."

"But you never really were. It was all a charade.

Though for the life of me I can't understand why you bothered. Was having a fling with an American something on your bucket list? Or did you simply want to defy your father and prove your independence?"

Emma stared at him, her lips pressed together in a thin line. If there were a prize for dignity, she would win it every time. He *knew* she was in the wrong, and she knew it as well. Yet somehow, she managed to look like the injured innocent. Making him the villain.

"I'm going home," she said, the words flat. "You've made your point. Do us both a favor and keep your distance."

She jumped to her feet abruptly, obviously intending to reach for her shoes. But she tripped on the hem of her dress and slammed into the coffee table. Her cry of pain made him wince. Blood colored the skirt of her dress, no doubt from the stitches on her leg.

"Good Lord," he said. "What have you done to yourself?"

Not waiting for permission, he scooped her up and took her to his bedroom. Flipping back the covers to protect the expensive duvet, he set her down and unceremoniously lifted her dress.

"Don't touch me." She batted his hands away. The tears she had held at bay earlier fell now. Silent wet tracks that dripped onto her bosom.

"Settle down," he muttered. "Let me see what you've done." He took her ankle in his hand and bent to get a closer look. The bones beneath her skin seemed impossibly fragile. Touching her hastened his own defeat. But he had no defense. The feel of her skin beneath rough fingertips did something terrible to his resolve not to get sucked in again. He would have to keep up his guard.

He didn't care about her. Of course he didn't. It had

been a decade. Only his libido had any interest in pursuing this inconveniently persistent attraction. Emma Braithwaite was a stunning woman. It was normal for him, or any man, to react to her sexuality. In fact, if he *weren't* affected by her allure, he would be worried.

The carefully worded but unspoken argument did little to settle the churning in his stomach.

The wound on her leg had been healing nicely, but the blow to her shin evidently had landed in exactly the wrong place. One end of the reddened seam had pulled apart maybe an eighth of an inch and was bleeding profusely. "We need to go back to the emergency room," he said.

"No. I don't want to. I have butterfly bandages at home. That will take care of it."

She tried to pull her skirt down, but he held the cloth firmly. Her bare thighs were slim and supple. *Damn it...* He cleared his throat. "You don't want a nasty scar."

"The worst scars are the ones you can't see."

Her eyes met his. Their gazes clung. Something hovered in the air. Memory. Regret.

He almost kissed her again. The urge was overpowering, his need vital and pressing. "Don't move," he said. "I have some Band-Aids in my shaving kit. That will cover it until you get home."

His miscalculation cost him. Perhaps he had misunderstood the import of their kiss, because he had been in the bathroom no longer than thirty seconds when he heard the door to his room slam shut. Rushing out to stop her, he saw the empty bed. The bed that already figured prominently in his dreams at night—only in the dreams, he was not alone...

Emma's skin glowed like pearls in the shaft of moonlight that fell through her window. The bed was narrow, the sheets unexceptional. For a student apartment, the two-room space was above average. Aidan barely noticed his surroundings. How could he with a naked Emma on her back waiting to love him?

Ripping off the last of his clothes and donning a condom, he gave her a quick grin. "Scoot over. There's no place for me."

She bent one knee, placing her foot flat against the mattress. The sight of her feminine secrets made his hands shake.

"I suppose you'll have to climb on top," she said, her smile droll and mischievous.

The sex was still new. He felt like a fumbling peasant in the presence of royalty. Not that Emma gave herself airs. But because she was so damned perfect. He was hard and ready. But still he waited.

Emma seemed to read his mind. "I won't break," she said softly. "I love it that you want me so much. It's the same for me."

It couldn't be. No one could feel what he felt in that moment...

He sat on the edge of the bed and put his head in his hands, his elbows on his knees. How ironic that he had been so worried about recollections of Danielle during the holidays, when in fact, the worst memories of all were the ones about him and Emma that had blindsided him.

The urge to jump in his car almost won. He could be back in New York by morning if he managed to stay awake. Emma would understand, once and for all, that her ploy hadn't worked...whatever it was.

But his mother would never forgive him. And he wouldn't forgive himself. It would be unbearably selfish to let his problems ruin Dylan and Mia's wedding day. Equally as bad would be abandoning his family at Christmas. They were all so wretchedly glad to see him. As if he were the prodigal son returning after a long absence.

He came home to Silver Glen all the time, damn it.

But not in December. And now he was paying the price.

Since he had no choice in the matter, he would have to take Emma's suggestion and stay as far away as possible. Otherwise, he couldn't trust himself not to beg. That was the bitterest pill of all to swallow. Despite the fact that she had humiliated and betrayed him, given half a chance, he would willingly forget the past for one more night in her bed.

It was laughable now to think he had taught himself not to feel. Of course he felt. He felt it all. Everything from the purifying blaze of well-founded anger to the crazed urge to let his lust dictate the course of the next ten days.

The choice was his. All he had to do was let Emma speak her piece. Presumably, she had some explanation for lying to him. He could pretend to believe her and they could wallow in erotic excess until it was time for him to go home to New York. The hunger that turned him inside out would be appeased.

The idea had a certain wicked appeal. But like making a deal with the devil, if he gave in to temptation, his soul would never be his own again. If he bedded her, skin-to-skin, nothing between them but the air they breathed, he might decide he could live with the past.

When whatever game she was playing ended, there was the reality that she would lie to him again. Women didn't change. He hadn't been enough for her once before and she had crushed him with her betrayal.

Could he do it for the sex? Could he draw a line in the sand and take only what he wanted? He'd sealed off his heart long ago. No woman since Emma had managed to tempt him. Except for his family, he cared about no one. He was a hollow man.

Pain came with relationships. His father had abandoned him by putting his obsessions ahead of his family. Danielle had abandoned him by dying. But in Emma's case, Aidan had been the one to leave. As soon as he learned the truth, he didn't hang around to be kicked in the teeth again. Even so, that pain had been the worst of all.

Eight

Emma cleaned blood off her leg and pondered all the ways she could murder Aidan Kavanagh in his sleep. He was infuriating and stubborn and his masculine arrogance made her want to hurl things at his head.

He still felt something for her. Even if it was only lust. But no way in heck was she going to tumble into bed with him when he thought so little of her. Perhaps she should have insisted on clearing the air immediately when he first recognized her. After all, the reason she'd come to Silver Glen, in part, was to make amends for the way she'd handled things in the past. She had hurt both Aidan *and* herself, though he bore some responsibility as well.

Maybe her stubborn pride was as bad as his, because she didn't want to make her apologies to a man who said he didn't care enough to hear what she had to say. There were a lot of things they could talk about. Important things. In her personal version of a twelve-step program, making amends was high up on the list. But it was hard to do that when the person you injured wouldn't let you do what you needed to do.

It was probably just as well. Look at what happened tonight. It was a really bad idea for the two of them to relive their college infatuation. Sex would introduce a whole extra layer of entanglement, because Aidan's family had no idea that Emma and Aidan shared a past.

Still, when she thought about his kiss, it was difficult not to imagine what would have come next. Feeling his hands on her body had kindled a fire, a yearning to experience his possession one more time. No man in the last ten years had made her feel a fraction of what Aidan could, not that many had tried.

Americans attributed her standoffishness to British reserve. But it wasn't that. Not really. She wasn't shy. She had simply learned to protect herself. Meeting Aidan at Oxford was a chance encounter. She'd been freer back then, more apt to take a chance on love.

Now, she was mostly happy on her own. Men complicated life. She had girlfriends back in Boston. And here in Silver Glen, she was already building a circle of support. She wanted to make things right with Aidan. But if that never happened, at least she had found a place to call home.

She glanced at the clock on the wall, realizing that the hour was really not that late. Even so, she was beat. Her first outing since her accident had required more energy than she realized. Suddenly, the idea of curling up in bed for an early night was impossible to resist.

After brewing a cup of herbal tea, she set it on her dresser while she changed into a comfy flannel nightgown. Then, moving the tea to the bedside table, she sat down on the mattress, plumped the pillows behind her back and picked up the novel she was in the midst of reading. She managed to finish her tea, but just barely. After her eyelids drifted shut for the third time, she gave up, climbed under the covers and turned out the light.

* * *

Sometime later, an insistent noise woke her. In the dark, she listened carefully, her heartbeat syncopated. It took only a moment to process that the sound she heard was the street-level buzzer. It rang upstairs whenever she had a visitor.

Leaning up on one elbow, she hit the button on her phone and gazed at the time blearily. Good grief.

Since the person at the other end of the buzzer didn't appear to be dissuaded by her lack of response, she got up, shoved her feet into slippers and reached for her fleecy robe. Her wound was still tender, but the Band-Aid had stopped the bleeding.

In the living room, she pushed aside the sheers and looked down at the street. There were no cars in sight except for her neighbor's familiar sedan. But even from this angle she could see the figure of a man.

As if he could feel her watching him, he stepped back, looked toward her window and made a familiar let-me-in motion.

Clearly, she should ignore him. He would go away soon.

Even as she lectured herself, her feet carried her down the steep stairs. Her hand on the doorknob, she called out, "Who is it?"

With only a couple of inches of wood separating them, she could hear the response distinctly. "You know who it is. Open the door, Emma."

Her toes curled inside her slippers. "Why?"

"Do you really want the whole town to know our business?" he muttered.

The man had a point. She jerked open the door and stared at him. He was bareheaded despite the fact that it was frigid outside. "Do you have any idea what time it is?" she asked, trying to sound irritated instead of excited. There was only one reason a man came calling at this hour. The intensity of his shadowy gaze made her pulse jump and dance.

"No. I don't. But I'm freezing out here. May I please come in?"

She stepped back to allow the door to close, and suddenly the two of them were practically mashed together in the handkerchief-sized space. "Where is your car, Aidan?"

He shrugged, his clothes smelling like the outdoors. It was a nice fragrance, a combination of cold air and evergreen. "I walked," he said bluntly. "We'd had a few drinks, if you remember."

"That's at least five miles." She gaped, unable to comprehend such a crazy thing in the middle of the night.

"Why do you think it took me so long to get here?"

"Oh, for goodness' sakes. Come on up. I'll make you a hot drink. Can you deal with coffee at this hour?"

He followed on her heels. "I'll take some of your famous herbal tea."

In the kitchen, he took off his wool overcoat and tossed it over a chair. The light was too bright. She felt exposed, though she was covered from head to toe. His sharp gaze took in her decidedly unseductive attire. Though his lips twitched, he made no comment.

He still wore his tux pants and white shirt, but he'd left his jacket behind. The shirt was unbuttoned partway down his chest. A partial night's beard shadowed his firm jaw. He looked sexy and dangerous, like a man who was about to throw caution to the wind.

What did it say about her that his rakish air stirred her? That his undiluted masculinity was both mesmerizing and exciting?

He sat down in one of her spindly wooden chairs, his weight making the joints creak. For the first time she recognized his fatigue. Was it because of the hour or because of his nighttime prowl or because he had been wrestling with himself? The third option was one she understood all too well. Why else had she opened her door?

Without speaking, she handed him a cup of tea and poured one for herself. Instead of joining him at the table, she leaned against the fridge, keeping a safe distance between them.

"Why are you here, Aidan?"

The satirical look he gave her questioned her intelligence. "Don't be coy."

She shrugged. "Does this mean you're ready to listen to my explanations?"

"I told you before. I don't want to hear anything about the past or why you're here in Silver Glen."

"What else is there?"

He stood abruptly and plucked the china cup out of her hand. "This."

Dragging her flush against his big frame, he dove in for a hard, punishing kiss, one arm tight across her back. His lips moved on hers with confidence...as if he remembered in exquisite detail exactly what she liked.

The old Aidan had never been this sure of himself. But darned if she didn't like it. Without shoes, she was at a distinct disadvantage, though. She stood on her tiptoes, straining to align her mouth with his. Everything about him was warm and wonderful. Despite his gruff refusal to let her plead for absolution, there was tenderness in his kiss.

She shivered, even though in Aidan's embrace she was perfectly warm. Too warm, maybe. She felt dizzy. As if all the air had been sucked out of the room.

"I want you, Emma," he muttered. "Tell me you want me, too."

It was a hard thing to deny when her arms were twined around his neck in a stranglehold. "Yes," she said. "I do, but—"

He put his hand over her mouth, stilling her words. "No buts," he said firmly. He paused for a moment, the look on his face impossible to decipher. "There's only one question I need answered." His Adam's apple bobbed as he swallowed. "Are you married?"

Shock immobilized her. She twisted out of his embrace, staring at him wide-eyed. "No. *No.*" She answered more forcefully the second time.

"Good." He picked up her left hand and lifted it to his lips. "Then, Lady Emma Braithwaite, will you do me the honor of taking me to your bed?" His droll smile was at odds with the intensity of his gaze. A tiny muscle ticked in his granite jaw as though her answer was far more important than he was letting on.

Emma had come to that moment in life when plans had gone awry and the road ahead was no longer clear. "Do you hate me?" she asked bluntly. "For what happened?"

Aidan was unable to hide his wince. "Does it look like I hate you? I'm practically eating out of your hand, damn it."

It wasn't really an answer to her question. "Please, Aidan. Tell me the truth."

His broad shoulders lifted and fell. Full, masculine lips twisted. "No. I don't hate you." He paced the confines of her small kitchen. "There was a time when I *wanted* to hate you, but no more. Life is short. I'll be leaving soon. I think we can chalk up tonight to what-might-have-been. It's Christmas. I'm feeling an odd, sentimental need to be somebody else tonight. Somebody that I used to know. A boy, not quite a man. An idealistic, heart-on-his-sleeve kid. Too naïve to be let loose in the wild."

For the first time, she understood that he was telling her the God's honest truth.

"I loved that boy," she whispered. "He was amazing and kind and perfect in every way."

"He was a fool." The blunt exclamation held a trace of bitterness and anger, despite his professed lack of enmity.

"I won't let you say that." Her tone was firm. Though Aidan Kavanagh was a mature, successful man, she saw in painful clarity the many ways she had damaged him. "If you don't want to rehash the past, then so be it. We'll make tonight all about the present. Come to bed with me."

He paled beneath his tan. "No regrets when the cold light of day dawns, Emma. From either of us. I need your promise. I won't be accused of taking advantage of you."

Crossing her fingers left and right over her heart, she lifted her chin and eyed him steadily, even though her chest jumped and wiggled with fizzy shards of happiness. "No regrets."

Quietly, he switched off the kitchen light and followed her to her bedroom. The sheets and comforter were tumbled where she had leapt up quickly to answer the door. Stopping beside the bed, she battled a sudden attack of shyness.

Aidan had no such problem. He removed her robe with gentle motions, and then touched the button at her collarbone, unfastening it along with three more. "Lift your arms," he commanded.

When she obeyed, he pulled the gown over her head. She wore not a stitch beneath it. He had her naked in less than five seconds.

The look on his face was gratifying. He brushed his thumb over her navel. Gooseflesh broke out all over her body.

"You're cold," he said.

She shook her head slowly. "Not cold. Just ready."

When he lifted her into his arms, she was confused. They were both at the bed already. But as she rested her cheek against his chest and looked up at him, her heart twisted. For a split second, she saw the young man who had loved her with such reckless generosity and passion.

He stared down at her for long seconds. She could almost feel his turmoil. "No one needs to know about this," he said.

Though the words hurt, she nodded. "I understand."

"Birth control?" His communication had been reduced to simple phrases, as though he barely retained the capacity to speak.

"I'm on the pill. And no health problems to worry about."

"Nor I." He shook his head as if to clear it. "I'm not sure I can wait any longer."

She cupped his cheek with her hand. "Why would you? We're both on the same page tonight, Aidan. Make love to me."

Hesitating, he stared at her with stormy eyes. "This is sex. No more, no less."

Not love. Message received.

"Whatever you want to call it is fine by me. Now if you'll excuse me, I need to freshen up."

Fleeing to the bathroom, she leaned her hands on the counter and stared into the mirror. Her cheeks were flushed, her pupils dilated. Was she making a monumental mistake? Was it wrong to share her bed with Aidan when there were so many things left unsaid?

A slight noise in the bedroom reminded her that there was no time for dithering. Either she wanted him, or she didn't. When you put it that way, there was only one clear answer.

She took two minutes to prepare. Then she opened the door, squared her bare shoulders and returned to the bedroom.

Nine

Aidan couldn't believe this was happening. How many times over the years had he imagined this very scenario? Or dreamed it, vividly erotic in his head?

As he stripped off his pants and boxers, socks and shoes, he was painfully aware that he had been hard for the better part of the evening. Dancing with Emma was a particularly wicked kind of torture. Now, naked and lovely, she stared at him, her nervousness impossible to hide. He wanted to reassure her, but in truth, he had no reassurances to give. What they were about to do was either self-destructive, or at the very least unwise. Even knowing that, he couldn't work up any enthusiasm for the idea of being sensible.

"You're beautiful," he said. It seemed a trite thing to mention. Surely the men in her life had been telling her as much since she was an innocent sweet sixteen.

Her hands twisted at her waist as though she wanted to cover herself. She was clean-shaven between her legs except for a tiny strip of blond fluff that proved her hair color was natural. Her legs were long and shapely, her waist narrow, her breasts high and firm.

If he were strictly impartial, he might note that her forehead was too high for classic beauty...and her nose a tad too sharp. But those minor flaws were balanced out by the heart-shaped face, full pink lips and eyes the color of an October sky.

He took one of her hands in his, finding it icy. Chafing it carefully, he cocked his head toward the pile of covers. "I think in December the preliminaries should probably be carried out in bed. I don't want you to catch pneumonia."

"This feels awkward," she said with blunt honesty and a crooked smile of apology.

He nodded. "It will get better."

They moved, one at a time, into the relative warmth of the bed. The sheets seemed chilled, but heated rapidly.

Emma reclined on her side facing him, head propped on a feather pillow. She watched him with fascination and reserve. "You must have lots of experience," she said, the words hinting at dissatisfaction.

He mirrored her position, though he propped his head on his hand. "I doubt we want to compare notes on our sexual histories. Do we?"

"No. I suppose not."

In her pose and in her gaze he saw the same thing that had drawn him to her when he was at university. There was no other way to describe it than *goodness*. It radiated from her. No woman he'd ever met appeared to be so unsullied, so open and warm.

Yet, he knew for a fact that it was only a facade. Emma had a capacity for deception, as indeed did most humans. Aidan made no assumptions about her. He had not listened to malicious lies. He'd gone straight to the source, had asked Emma for the truth. Even now, recalling that moment stabbed his heart with disillusionment.

Shaking off the unpleasant memory, he concentrated on the woman who was so close, her breath mingling with his. Reaching out, he stroked her hair, sifting the strands through his fingertips. "We were so young," he said. "But I thought you were the most exquisite thing I had ever seen."

"And you were brash and handsome and charmingly affable. A young Hugh Grant. Except with that adorable American accent."

Aidan chuckled. "Perhaps it's true that opposites attract. I was mortifyingly intimidated by your pedigree and your finishing school manners." He moved a fingertip lazily from her cheek to her collarbone to her cleavage. Emma's sharp intake of breath told him that the simple touch affected her as strongly as it did him.

Gently, he pressed her shoulder, urging her onto her back. As he shifted positions to lean over her on one elbow, he mapped her body with his palm. Plump, curvy breasts. Smooth rib cage. Almost concave belly. And then—the mother lode.

Keeping his gaze fixed on hers, he traced the folds of her sex with gentle persuasion. Her legs moved restlessly, her thighs widening in unspoken invitation. It would be so easy to pounce and take. But since his plan was to allow himself only a single night of delirium, he had to go slowly. Make it last. Wring every drop of pleasure from the hushed minutes when he had her to himself.

Emma's hands roved over his scalp, her fingers sweeping across his forehead, stroking his neck, playing with his ears. It was embarrassing that such chaste touches made him rigid with need. His erection was full and hard and throbbing with eagerness.

Do it. Take her. Now.

Every masculine impulse leaned toward plunder. Only the mitigating tenderness of their past reined him in.

Emma exhaled in a shuddering sigh. "When you touch me, I melt inside. It was always that way, Aidan."

Perhaps that much was the truth. He would never really know. But she couldn't fake her body's response at the moment. The warm, soft welcome at her center was slick and moist and scented with her need.

He had intended to tease them both with long minutes of foreplay. But why? He couldn't want her more. No hunger could be as gut-wrenching. He was primed and ready.

Moving over her on shaking arms, he positioned the head of his sex at her entrance and pushed with a groan that betrayed his need. Her excitement eased his passage, taking him to the hilt with oxygen-stealing speed. *Holy hell.* Either his memories were faulty or she had slipped some kind of aphrodisiac into his tea.

"Damn, Emma."

She arched her back, taking him deeper still. Her legs wrapped around his waist, her heels locking in the small of his back. "Don't stop," she begged, the words ragged.

Cursing and laughing, he moved in her with what little control he had left. "Not a problem."

To say they were good together was like saying the horizon was infinite. He'd had plenty of sex in his adult life. But whatever happened when he joined his body with Emma's defied description.

A sappy English poet might talk about roses and hearts afire and the purity of true love. Aidan took a more visceral approach. When he screwed Emma, his body went berserk. Fireworks, explosions, searing heat…incandescent pleasure.

And all that was before he climaxed.

He buried his hot face in her neck. "Once won't be enough."

She bit the side of his neck. "I never said it would."

Feeling her teeth on him was all it took. Light flashed behind his eyelids. He pistoned his hips. In some dim corner of his brain, he tried to make sure he gave her what she needed. If her wild cries were any indication, he was succeeding.

Then he went rigid as the world went black and he lost himself in the flash fire of completion.

Emma trembled uncontrollably. Most of Aidan's weight pressed her into the bed. His breathing was harsh and uneven. She had no idea if he were awake or asleep. She was hoping for the latter, because she hadn't a clue what she was supposed to say.

Wow, Aidan. That was awesome. Let's do it again.

Or…*you rocked my world. And I'm pretty sure I never stopped loving you.*

Hysteria bubbled in her chest. She was in so much trouble. How had she blinded herself to the truth? She hadn't come to Silver Glen to find Aidan and make amends for their past…or at least not only that. She wanted to win him back.

Since the chances of that happening were about as good as the possibility of the Queen dancing naked beside the Thames, Emma had a choice to make. She could slink away quietly and go home to England—forgetting she ever knew Aidan Kavanagh—*or* she could fight for him. But the emotional barriers he had built were formidable.

Confrontation was not Emma's strong suit. Aidan didn't want to hear her version of the past. Anytime she tried to bring it up, he stonewalled her. But tonight, he had given her a powerful weapon. He had shown her clearly that at least one thing hadn't changed over the years. He and Emma were still magic between the sheets.

That had to count for something, right?

She smoothed his hair with her hand, relishing the opportunity to touch him as she wished. How different her life might have been if she'd had more gumption at twenty-one…if she hadn't been under her father's thumb…if she'd had the confidence to accept that the handsome American really loved her.

But deep in her heart, she had doubted Aidan. It shamed her to admit it. And it had taken her a long time to face the truth. One reason their relationship had ended so abruptly and with such devastating finality was that she hadn't really believed a man could want her for herself.

The preteen wallflower had grown up to be a self-conscious academic. Her degree in art history was achieved with highest honors, but no one had ever expected her to use it, least of all her family. Emma's purpose in life was to marry well and continue the Braithwaite legacy.

Perhaps to someone of Aidan's background, such a notion was antiquated. But Emma had grown up circumscribed by the expectations of her rank and position in society. Her parents adhered rigidly to the tenets of their social code. As their only child, Emma's path in life had been well defined. Even so, she'd certainly had the freedom to fall in love…as long as the man of her choice passed muster in the pages of Debrett's *Peerage & Baronetage*.

Now, holding the mature, sexy Aidan Kavanagh in her arms, she couldn't fathom that she had been so foolish. His advent into her young life had seemed like such a fairy tale, she'd lived the fantasy and refused to think about the future. Which meant that when disaster struck, she hadn't been prepared. Neither had she possessed the confidence to fight back. A mistake she bitterly regretted.

Her cowardice had hurt Aidan and destroyed their fragile, beautiful relationship. Even though she had tried her best to fix things in the aftermath, the damage had been done.

Already, she wanted him again. Hesitantly, she ran her hands down the taut planes of his back, as far as she could reach. He was a beautiful man. Naked, he seemed both more powerful and more approachable.

Moving slowly and carefully so as not to wake him, she eased him onto his back. His broad, hair-dusted chest rose and fell with his steady breathing. The flat belly, muscled thighs and surprisingly sexy feet caught her eye. But it was his quiescent sex that made her sigh with appreciation. Even at rest, it shouted his masculinity.

Men were so wonderfully different from women. In her art history classes she had studied hundreds of famous nudes—painted on canvas, chiseled in marble, sculpted in bronze. But no matter how impressive the subject, there was nothing to compare to a living, breathing man.

Resting her hand on his thigh, she bent to examine a small white scar on his right hip, probably a childhood injury. He and his brothers had been wild rascals growing up, particularly after their father died. She could only imagine how Maeve Kavanagh managed to wrangle them all into becoming upright citizens of the community.

"Em, are you window-shopping or trying to get something started?"

She sat up abruptly, shocked to the core. Apparently, Aidan was a better actor than she realized. Clearing her throat, she sat back on her heels. "How long have you been awake?"

"Long enough." He linked his hands behind his head, smiling slightly, clearly enjoying her discomfiture.

She couldn't think of an excuse that would explain her intense interest in his body. So she changed the subject.

"Sorry I woke you," she said, not quite able to meet his knowing gaze. "We should both probably get some sleep. The next three days are going to be busy."

He took her hand and tugged her down beside him. "Hush, Em. Don't be embarrassed. I want to look at you, too."

But she wasn't as blasé as he was about her nude body. Dragging the sheet to her chin, she bit her lip. "I thought you might want to go back to the hotel now."

"It's the middle of the night." He chuckled. "And I don't have a car. As far as I can tell, staying right here in your bed is a damned good plan. Do you have any objections?"

Lord, no, she thought. Why did it matter if they were sleep-deprived? It was about time some of her other physical needs took center stage for a change. She could sleep when she was old.

"You called me *Em*," she said.

His smile faded. "Don't make a big deal out of that. It slipped out. That's all. Old habits."

She hoped it was more than that. *Em* was the nickname he'd sometimes used for her when they were in college. Often he would whisper it in the midst of sex. A tender, affectionate means of address that always sounded indulgent and proprietary.

She nodded, unsure what was going to happen next. While they talked, his erection had flexed to attention again. A thing like that was hard to ignore. But the expression on Aidan's face was serious.

Touching her cheek gently, he grimaced. "Tell me why you moved from England to Silver Glen."

Her heart leapt. It was a chink in the wall, though a small one. "I didn't," she said. "I've lived in Boston for the last nine years."

"Doing what?" She had startled him, no question.

"I was an art appraiser at the Sotheby's branch there."

"Why work at all?"

"You're rich. And *you* work. We all need a reason to get up in the morning."

"Why did you leave England?"

She wanted to be a smart-ass and remind him that he wasn't interested in having information or explanations. But it would be foolish to bypass this opportunity. "I had a falling out with my father. We're both stubborn people, so neither side wanted to concede. I refused to go home for eight and a half years. My mother visited me often in Boston, but until this past spring I had not seen my father for a very long time."

"And why last spring?" He seemed genuinely curious.

The reasons for her voluntary exile to the States involved Aidan, but she didn't think he was ready to hear that. Not yet. Maybe not ever. So she told him the bare bones.

"My father was an old-school autocrat. He ruled our family with an iron fist, expecting absolute obedience. When it became clear that he and I were never going to see eye-to-eye about several very important topics, I knew I had to strike out on my own."

"Must have been scary."

"It was…but exciting, too. Even so, I missed home. When my father was diagnosed with pancreatic cancer in April, the doctors told my mother he had only weeks to live. I flew back immediately, and thankfully, I was able to reconcile with him before he left us. That experience taught me it's never too late to heal old wounds."

The personal story was about as blunt as she was prepared to be. Aidan was an intelligent man. Surely he could read between the lines. It had taken until today for Emma to acknowledge to herself that her reasons for coming to Silver Glen were more convoluted that she had been willing to admit.

She wasn't committed to any man at the moment. And unless Aidan was not the man she once knew, he was not attached either, or he would not be in bed with her. If she could convince him that what tore them apart was no longer relevant—if he would accept her apologies—then surely there was no reason they couldn't make a new start.

That was a big pile of assumptions. Built mostly on fantasy and dreams. But he was in her bed, so that was a start.

Ten

Aidan tried to find his anger and his righteous indignation, but it seemed to have disappeared along with his pants. It was difficult for a man to hold a grudge while a woman's naked body was pressed against his. He stroked Emma's hip. "Enough chitchat," he said. But he smiled to let her know he wasn't making light of her revelations.

Her hair was rumpled. Dark shadows smudged beneath her eyes spoke of exhaustion. Perhaps another man would have been content to hold her. But not Aidan. Not after waiting a decade to be with her again.

Difficulties lurked outside this room. And reality. Not to mention his vivid, painful memories of the past. For the moment, however, he was content to overlook the negatives. Probably because his brain was not in control. That function had been ceded to his baser anatomy.

He kissed her softly, one hand balanced on the pillow, his fingers tangled in her hair. "I want you again," he said. His lips moved to her eyelids, her cute nose, her perfect earlobes.

When Emma squirmed, her hand brushed his erection. Accidentally, or no? He sucked in a sharp breath. "Don't stop there." The gruff command worked. Perhaps because it sounded more like a plea. When her slender fingers closed around his firm shaft, stroking up and down, he shuddered and gasped, totally unable to hide his excitement.

Emma might have seen his reaction as proof of her power over him. But instead, her gaze was one of fascination. "I don't remember what you liked," she said quietly, as if confessing a wretched secret.

"No complaints here." He forced the words between clenched teeth. She was adorable. But then she always had been. He refused to think about any other men who might have been part of her life. He didn't want to know. If he could keep his mind on the present and nothing else, everything would be okay.

"Aidan?" She abandoned her activity and put both hands on his cheeks lightly.

He turned his face and kissed one soft palm. "What?"

Big eyes searched his as if seeking answers to questions they hadn't even spoken aloud. "I've missed you."

She paused before she said those last three words, giving him the impression that she might have changed what she was going to say at the last minute.

What did she expect from him? He felt a lick of anger and shoved it away. "I'm here now. Roll over, Emma."

Suddenly, he couldn't bear to look her in the face, couldn't stand to see the gaze that made *him* feel guilty... as if he had been the one to break her heart and not the other way around.

Rubbing her firm, round bottom, he leaned over her, tucking her hair across one shoulder and kissing the nape of her neck. When they were together in the past, he had never taken her like this. She had seemed too much the lady for a naughty position.

Or so he had thought. Maybe she had seen his naïveté as comical.

"Are you okay?" he asked, cursing inwardly that he felt the need to check.

She turned her head to smile at him with a mischievous look. "I won't break, Aidan. I swear."

He took her at her word. Checking her readiness with two fingers, he found her sex slick with moisture. She squirmed at his touch. Entering her slowly, he cursed. The fit was different from this angle, but no less stimulating. Sweat broke out on his forehead as he tried to pace his thrusts. The visual wasn't helping.

Emma's pale skin was luminous. Streetlights below cast a gentle glow through the thin curtains, so the room was never truly dark. He could see the curve where her waist dipped in and her hips flared.

Reaching beneath her, he palmed one breast, then the other. The flesh was full and firm. She wriggled backward, seating him more fully inside her. He was so close to coming every inch of skin all over his body was taut with expectation.

Suddenly, he knew it had to be different. If he and Emma had been long-time lovers, nothing would have been out of line. But they were neither lovers nor longtime. They were reconnecting with a tentative passion that left too much unspoken. She deserved to know he wanted *her*, not merely a faceless hookup.

Disengaging their bodies carefully, he moved her onto her back, lifted her leg over his hip and slid home again. She cried out and stared at him with a hazy expression, her lips parted, her breath coming quickly. Pleasure was the only emotion he recognized without question. And truly, he didn't want to examine the others too closely. Pleasure was fine. Pleasure was good. He didn't need to know what was going on inside her head.

Exhaustion lay heavy on his shoulders. If he had the

energy, he would move inside her forever. Feeling the butterfly caress when her sex squeezed his. Watching the way her breasts lifted and fell as her excitement grew. Touching her intimately, stimulating her little nerve center.

But the night had waned and he and Emma were half-sated from their earlier coupling. Even still, he managed to hold off for one more minute. "You enchant me," he said.

Emma frowned slightly. His statement held a hint of accusation, even to his own ears.

"I don't need you to talk, Aidan. Take us both where we want to go."

Closing his eyes, he heaved a deep breath and did just that...

When Emma awoke the next time, morning light filtered into her small bedroom. Aidan stood beside the bed, almost fully dressed. As she watched, he finished buttoning his shirt and tucked it into his pants.

She reared up on her elbows. "Are you leaving?"

He shot her a glance, nodding. "I promised Dylan and Mia that I would help them today out at the house. The whole crew is coming over for dinner tonight."

"Mia invited me, too."

She saw him go still, witnessed the rigid set of his shoulders. His reaction hurt, but she wasn't surprised.

No one needs to know about this.

Sitting up, she clutched her knees to her chest, the sheet protecting her modesty. "If you don't want me there tonight, I'll stay home."

He shrugged, still not meeting her eyes as he fastened his cuff links. "Go. Don't go. It's up to you."

"You don't have anything to worry about, Aidan. I won't embarrass you."

He slipped into his overcoat and buttoned it. "It's not a question of embarrassment. But my mother and Zoe and Mia get a real charge out of matchmaking. I don't want to get their hopes up."

"What does that mean?"

"I never bring women to Silver Glen. If they think you and I are an item, they'll hound me without mercy."

"Surely you've introduced them to women in the past."

"No."

She waited for him to continue, but that was all she was going to get.

He sat down on the edge of the bed and touched her cheek. "Thank you for last night. It was pretty damned incredible." Finally, she was able to see past his reserve to the genuine warmth and affection in his eyes.

Her face heated. "That must have been all you. My sexual prowess ranks one notch above old-maid schoolteacher."

Curling a hand behind her neck, he pulled her close for a long, sweet kiss. "Don't underestimate your appeal, Emma."

His tongue stroked hers gently, raising gooseflesh on her arms. What would he do if she threw herself into his embrace and begged him to stay? She mimicked his caress, no longer shy about letting him see what he did to her. When she bit his lip gently, teasing him with the sharp nip of her teeth, he rested his forehead on hers.

"Don't start something," he muttered.

She winnowed her fingers through the silky hair at the back of his head. "Why not? It's still early."

"You have a store to open, and I have to get home and take a shower."

"I have a shower," she pointed out.

"I'm wearing a tux, Emma. If I have to do the walk of shame, I'd rather get it over with before there are too many witnesses out and about."

"Ah." She pondered that. "You don't have a vehicle."

"I'll call Liam to come get me at the coffee shop down the street. He'll give me hell, but at least I won't have to walk back."

"It's not the walking that's a problem, is it? You don't want people to know you spent the night in town."

He shrugged. "Small communities thrive on gossip. I'd prefer to keep my affairs private."

"Is that what this is?" she snapped. "An affair?"

"I wasn't using that context, and you know it."

"Honestly, I don't understand much about you at all. You're an enigma, Aidan. My own personal sphinx. Once upon a time I thought I knew you inside and out. But no more."

"And whose fault is that?"

They had gone from hot kisses to bickering at warp speed.

"I take it the suspension of hostilities is over?" Stubborn, stubborn man. Why wouldn't he listen? "In case you forgot, *you* were the one who came to my bed, not the other way around."

"I don't want to fight with you," he said, shoulders slumped, his tone rough with fatigue.

"Fine. Then leave. And don't worry. When we see each other tonight, I'll act as if I barely know you. After all, it's the truth."

For long, heated seconds their gazes dueled. Hers angry and defiant, his stony with indifference or bitterness or both. When the standoff seemed at a stalemate and there were no more words to be said, he turned on his heel and strode out of the bedroom. Slamming the apartment door behind him, he left her, his rapid steps loud on the staircase down to the street.

She bowed her head, raking her hands through her hair. That certainly wasn't how she'd planned to end one of the best nights of her adult life. Why did she have to provoke him? Why couldn't she be satisfied with the knowledge that he had wanted her enough to show up in the middle of the night despite his better judgment?

The pillow beside her still carried the imprint of his head. She picked it up and sniffed the crisp cotton pillowcase, inhaling his scent…warm male and expensive cologne. For a brief time, it appeared that his enmity had vanished in the mist. Reconciliation had seemed possible.

Truthfully, she was spinning dreams out of thin air. Aidan was a man. He wanted sex. She was available.

There was no more to it than that. Maybe before he went back to New York he would relent and let her clear her conscience. But based on tonight, she wouldn't bet on it.

Aidan had to endure a merciless ribbing from his older brother in exchange for a ride up the mountain. Though Liam poked and prodded and did his best to ferret out information, Aidan wouldn't be moved. It was bad enough that he had caved to temptation and ended up in Emma's bed. He wouldn't compound his mistake by letting his family know the history he shared with one of Silver Glen's newest residents.

Fortunately, by the time he cleaned up and changed clothes and headed out to Dylan's place, Dylan and Mia were more than happy to see him. Cora was not in the best of moods. The housekeeper was in the kitchen cooking all the side dishes that would accompany the meal.

Dylan was still insisting on barbecuing despite the outside temperature.

"I'll bring it all inside," he said. "When everything is done. It's no big deal."

Mia glared at him, the baby on her hip. "You're the *host* tonight, Dylan. And this party was your idea. Just because it's family doesn't mean you can hide out by the grill."

Aidan inserted himself as peacemaker, raising his eyebrows. "I thought you were the party animal among us, bro," he said. "What's with this burning desire to play chef?"

Dylan snickered. "Burning. Get it? Maybe no one trusts me with raw meat. Is that the problem?"

Mia put her foot down. "I am your *almost*-bride, Dylan. And I'd really like a bubble bath, a glass of wine and some downtime, not necessarily in that order. Instead of dragging out the grill, why can't you let Aidan handle the barbecuing later so that you can entertain Cora for a little while?"

Aidan shrugged. "She has a point. I'm here to help. Why not take advantage of my culinary skills and kick back?"

"I've seen you cook," Dylan pointed out. "You have a tendency to burn water."

Mia wasn't impressed. She hugged Aidan. "Thanks for offering. And we accept." She handed a cranky Cora over to the baby's adoptive father. "Don't disturb me unless the house is on fire."

Aidan chuckled as he followed his brother back to the sunroom. "That woman of yours is a firecracker. Plain paper wrapper on the outside, but when you get her ticked off...*boom*."

"Are you saying my wife is plain?"

"God, no," Aidan said, backpedalling. "She's amazing, of course. I only meant that she seems quiet and shy until you get to know her."

Dylan made a sound something like a harrumph. In the middle of the cozy, sun-warmed den, he reclined on the floor with the baby, letting her climb over him like a play gym.

Aidan sprawled in a recliner, telling himself he wasn't envious. He didn't want kids. Though they were cute as hell. He had almost dozed off when Dylan's voice snapped him back to attention.

"So how long are you going to grieve, Aidan? Danielle has been gone a long time. She wouldn't want you to wear sackcloth and ashes forever. You've honored her memory. It's time to move on, don't you think?"

Aidan swung a foot lazily, his leg draped over the arm of the chair. "What I *think* is that my whole damned family can't mind their own business. Do I look like I need help with my love life?"

"Who knows? Whenever any of us visits you in New York, you pretend to be living like a monk in that fancy-ass apartment of yours."

"I didn't know I needed to introduce the occasional female guest to my extended family."

Dylan tickled Cora's tummy. "Is there really no one you can see yourself settling down with?"

Aidan shook his head in amazement. "I can't believe it. You and Liam get hitched and suddenly you're handing out advice to the lovelorn. I'm okay, I swear. My life is perfect. And if it's ever not perfect, you'll be the first to know. Now, can we drop it?"

His brother eyed him suspiciously. "There's something to be said for getting laid every night."

"Hell, Dylan. You're impossible. I'll have you know

I did have sex last night." As soon as the words left his mouth, he realized what he had done. *Crap.*

Dylan perked up like a retriever spotting a quail. "Say what?"

"Nothing. Forget I mentioned it."

Dylan rolled to his feet, holding Cora like a football. "Now I get it."

"Get what?"

"You look like you've been up all night. Liam told me he had to pick you up in town this morning. And that you had given him some lame excuse about an early morning walk."

"The two of you gossip more than a couple of old biddies. Have you checked your testosterone lately? I think you may be a quart low."

"Do we get to hear about her? Is it anyone I know?"

"Nothing happened. Nothing at all."

Eleven

Fortunately for Emma, her day was full. With the sun shining, Christmas shoppers were out in force. She and Mrs. Correll barely had time to take a breath in between customers.

Mia called midafternoon. "I wanted to make sure you were still coming to my house this evening," she said. "You left the party early last night, and I was afraid you were feeling bad."

Emma blushed, even though her friend couldn't see her. "I'm fine, honestly. I've been trying to pace myself." Except for the several hours last night she spent making love to Aidan instead of sleeping. "Do you need me to bring anything?"

"We've got enough food to feed half of North Carolina, but if you wouldn't mind coming an hour early, I'd love some help with my hair and makeup. Would that rush you too much?"

"Not at all. Mrs. Correll has offered to close up the shop today, so I can be there whenever you want me."

Emma had been to Dylan and Mia's house once before when she babysat little Cora. Even during this cold winter, she had to marvel at the home Dylan had built before he met Mia. The approach was a narrow lane flanked by weeping willows that in summer would create a foliage-lined tunnel. Today, though, the trees were sparse and bare.

As the house came into view, she sighed in envy. Dylan and his architect had created a magical, fairy tale of a place. The structure, built of mountain stone, dark timbers and copper, nestled amidst the grove of hard-wood trees as if it had been there forever.

She parked in the area that had been roped off for cars and took one last look in the visor mirror. Coming face-to-face with Aidan was inevitable this evening, but even if they were going to ignore each other, she wanted to look her best.

The jersey dress she had ordered from England was comfortable and fit like a dream. The lace duster dressed it up and made the form-fitting fabric a bit more modest for a family dinner.

As she walked toward the front door, the unmistakable smell of meat cooking teased her nose, making her stomach growl. She'd grabbed a cup of yogurt for lunch, but that was a long time ago.

Mia answered the door herself. "Thank God you're here. Look what I've done to myself." She whipped the towel off her head.

Emma did her best to cover her shock, but it was bad. "Oh, dear…" She managed a smile. "We'll fix it. What did you do?"

"I was sick of having boring hair, and I didn't have time to make it to the salon, so I tried a home color—highlights actually. But all I got was this."

Emma winced inwardly. "Not to worry. But let's get started. We don't have much time."

Fortunately, the orangey red was mostly on the ends

of Mia's dark brown hair. Even so, this intervention was going to require desperate measures.

Aidan carried a tray of bison burgers into the kitchen and snagged a handful of potato chips before he went back out into the cold. Playing chef wasn't a bad gig, though. The down jacket he wore was plenty thick, and standing so close to the grill, even his hands were warm.

It wouldn't be long until his entire family came roaring down the lane. The momentary peace and quiet of a beautiful winter afternoon would get lost in the chaos. Even Cora was napping at the moment. And Dylan...who knew what Dylan was doing?

Seasoning and flipping meat didn't require much concentration. Aidan had plenty of time to think...and plenty to think about. Was Emma going to show up? Or had he been such an ass that she would decide to make an excuse to Mia and skip the whole thing?

He'd tried to speak to her before he came out to Dylan's. But when he parked in front of the antique shop, he could see through the window that her small business was packed with customers. Since he certainly didn't need an audience for a conciliatory conversation, he had put the car in gear and driven away.

After all, it wasn't as if anything he said to her last night wasn't true. But he felt bad for making her question her right to come to the party. She was Mia's friend, and Dylan and Mia could invite whomever they pleased to their dinner.

Aidan was the one with the problem, not Emma. Now, he had complicated his life even more by sleeping with the woman who had dropped back into his life so unexpectedly. Did he still wonder why she came to Silver Glen? Yes. Did he still want her? Yes.

The question was, what was he going to do about it? Already he felt himself softening toward her. Seeing her, talking to her, sleeping with her…all of that was dangerous. Clearly, Emma regretted the past. But he couldn't open himself up like that again.

Losing his father had left him to flounder in a world with too many temptations for a young boy. He'd missed his dad fiercely, but at the same time resented him for dying.

Aidan found Danielle in college and had latched on to her as if he had found his life's mate. But the magic had faded. That relationship ended in tragedy.

And then, there was Emma. Losing her had been the worst of all. He had learned his lesson. Emotional distance was key to his survival. Hats off to Liam and Dylan for committing to a future that held no guarantees. Aidan couldn't do it. Wouldn't do it. He'd had enough loss and suffering to last a lifetime.

He wanted Emma more than he wanted his next breath, but sharing her bed came with too many dangerous side effects. Emotions. Yearning. Hope. Hope for a different outcome this time.

If he had to go cold turkey to keep away from her, he'd simply have to do it. Last night had shown him a disturbing truth. He would never stop wanting Emma. And because being with her permanently was not in the cards, he had to protect himself. Even if Emma had some notion of getting back together—and that was a long shot—he was not interested.

He had to guard his impulses where she was concerned. Their interactions would take place only in public or amidst a crowd. That way he could avoid the temptation to share her bed again. He was a grown man, not a kid. Self-control was a product of maturity. Until it was time to go back to New York, celibacy was his friend.

The trouble was, everywhere he looked he could see her. In his mind's eye. Smiling at him. Flushed with pleasure. Arms outstretched to welcome him into her embrace. Her scent was in his head, the feel of her skin imprinted on his fingertips.

He poked at a half-done burger, scowling at it blindly. There was nothing special about Emma, other than her accent. If he still carried baggage from the past, it was only because he'd been an impressionable college kid, and she had made him feel like a man.

But he was smarter now. The sex last night was nothing out of the ordinary. No reason to think he was at risk for doing something stupid. He had enjoyed it, but it was over.

By the time Aidan finished his assigned task and carried the last of the main course into the kitchen, Dylan had come out of hiding and was talking to the housekeeper in between stealing bites of the appetizers. He took the heavy tray of meat from his brother. "Thanks, man. These look great."

"I guess we've got, what, twenty minutes until everyone shows up?"

"Maybe less. You know our crew. They can smell food from a mile away."

Before Aidan could respond, Emma appeared in the doorway. "I need to see you both in the living room, please."

Aidan frowned. "What's wrong?"

"Just come."

They followed her into the empty room. Emma, as always, looked effortlessly stylish. The form-fitting wine-colored dress she wore hugged her shape lovingly. If Aidan had his way, she would remove the lacy overdress thing so he could get a better look at her curves.

Dylan looked puzzled. "Where's Mia? I thought you were helping her get ready."

Emma wrinkled her nose and grimaced. "Mia had a little accident with some hair color." She fixed Dylan with a determined gaze. "You can't tease her about this, okay?"

"About what?"

"The color was dreadful, a cross between tomato-red and jack-o'-lantern-orange. We had no choice but to cut it off."

Aidan blanched. "You cut her hair?"

She shot him a look. "Not to worry. In boarding school we weren't allowed to go to the salon without our parents' permission. So anytime one of the girls wanted a new cut, I was the stylist."

Dylan firmed his jaw. "Is she crying? I want to see her."

Emma put a hand on his arm. "She's okay now. But the new 'do' is short. She wants you to see it before your guests arrive. But don't make a big deal, okay?" She turned to Aidan. "And when your family begins to show up, it would be nice if you could give them the same message."

"Of course."

Emma walked toward the bedrooms. "Hang on. I'll go get her."

Moments later a hesitant Mia appeared from around the corner. Her eyes went immediately to Dylan. "I feel like a fool." Her bottom lip trembled visibly.

Dylan put a hand over his heart. "Holy hell, woman. That is so hot." He went to her and feathered his fingers lightly over the ends of the pixie cut. "We may have to cancel the party," he said in a stage whisper, kissing the side of her neck.

Though Mia's eyes were pink-rimmed, she smiled and threw her arms around his neck. "I love you, Dylan."

He lifted her off her feet in a bear hug. "And I adore you, my sexy little fairy. Your hair is beautiful."

She pulled back, her gaze dubious. "You really think so?"

"I'll show you later," he muttered.

Aidan watched Emma, who was watching Mia and Dylan. On Emma's face was a wistful look that said she found the bridal couple's byplay romantic. Of course, that was a woman for you. Always suckers for a happy ending. Too bad those same women didn't realize life was seldom so tidy.

He glanced out the front window. "Car number one. Looks like Mom's. I'll go meet everybody if you two want a moment alone."

Mia smiled at him. "Thank you, Aidan, but I'm fine." She smoothed the skirt of her black dress, looking up at the man who would soon be placing a wedding ring on her finger. "Dylan and I are the hosts tonight. We should go greet our guests."

The two of them hurried away, arm in arm, leaving Aidan alone with Emma for the first time since he'd left her bed early that morning. "I stopped by to see you this afternoon," he said, "but the shop was really busy, so I didn't go in."

She perched on the arm of a chair. "I'm sorry I wasn't available."

"How's your head?"

"I'm still taking over-the-counter stuff for the headache, but it's not bad."

The stilted conversation was almost painful. Only hours ago they had been naked together. The mental image made his skin heat. "Last night was amazing, but it can't happen again."

"Why not?" She was pale, her expression mutinous.

"I'll be leaving soon. There's no future for us, Emma."

"Because you've decreed it?"

"Is that why you came here?" he asked. "To start over with me?"

"Not in the beginning. I was telling you the truth. I wanted to make my peace with you. To explain the past. But now that I've seen you again...now that we've made love...well, I have to wonder if there's something left between us. Something that never died."

"There isn't."

"Liar." She said it calmly, as if she could see inside the tortured recesses of his soul. "If you can kiss me and prove to me that you feel nothing at all for me, I'll leave you alone."

He held out his arms. "Do your best. It's sex, Emma. That's all. And I can get that from any woman. The young man you remember so fondly doesn't exist anymore."

"You're trying to make me angry by acting like a pig."

"Is it working?"

When she stood, the skin at his nape tingled. Emma on a mission was a formidable opponent. But he knew something she didn't. He knew that resisting temptation was not a choice. It was his only defense.

She crossed to where he stood and went nose-to-nose with him, although her nose was admittedly a few inches lower...almost at his collarbone, in fact.

He stared straight ahead, trying not to inhale her scent.

"This isn't fair," she complained. "I can't reach you. Sit down." She poked him in the chest until he took a step backward and sat down hard, hands behind him, on the edge of a beautiful oak table behind the sofa.

Now, their heights were much closer. The dress she wore had a scooped neck that revealed modest amounts of cleavage…but only if he let his gaze fall. His fingers gripped wood until pain shot up his wrists.

"Do your worst," he said, staring at her chin. His throat was so dry the words came out hoarse.

Emma leaned in. "You are a ridiculously handsome man," she murmured. "Gorgeous lips. Masculine. Sexy. Here goes…"

She pressed her mouth to his. Nothing happened except for his blood pressure shooting up about twenty points. *Focus. Focus.*

The first few seconds were barely a challenge. Her kiss was chaste, almost sweet. Nothing he couldn't handle.

Then she curled a hand behind his neck, her fingertips slipping inside the collar of his shirt to scrape deliberately across the bump at the top of his spine. *Sweet mother of God.*

Warm breath ticked his ear when she whispered. "How am I doing so far?"

He shrugged, his jaw so tight his head ached. "I've had better."

Emma's low chuckle was intensely sexual. He found himself getting hard despite his fierce concentration.

She came back to the kiss and put her all into it. When she nipped his bottom lip with sharp teeth, he gasped, giving her an opening to slide her tongue against his. Her taste went to his gut like raw liquor on an empty stomach. Hell, this was a pointless game.

He grabbed her close and angled her chin with one hand. The shock in her blue eyes gave him an enormous jolt of satisfaction. "You're an amateur," he said. "But I give you points for enthusiasm."

Then it was his turn. If he were going to admit defeat, he would drag her down with him. Pulling her fully into the V of his legs, he simply snapped. Everything he had tried to keep to himself, every needy, greedy urge to plunder, was unleashed.

Ten years of memories, of wondering, of futile anger and grief, coalesced into a white-hot need to make Lady Emma Braithwaite his. "Don't think you've won," he croaked. "This means nothing."

Her eyes brimmed with moisture, the look on her face a mixture of tenderness and wonder. "I understand," she said quietly. "Whatever you say, Aidan. Whatever you want."

Cupping her breast in his hand, he stroked the nipple through its soft covering. "I want you. Now."

Before Emma could say a word in denial or consent, a loud noise nearby shattered the mood, the one sound guaranteed to stifle a man's ardor.

Maeve's Kavanagh's cheerful greeting…"We're all here. Let the party begin."

Twelve

For Emma, the next two hours took on a surreal quality. The mood in the house was joyful and rowdy, rightly so. The Kavanaghs en masse created a special kind of magic. One of their own was tying the knot, and in true Irish fashion, they were prepared to party all night.

Despite Emma's efforts to stay in the background, Mia insisted on making sure she met everyone individually. The festive gathering at the hotel had been much larger and more formal. Tonight, however, was a time for one-on-one conversations, sibling jokes and eating.

Emma had been taken aback at the amount of food laid out buffet-style, sure they would never consume half of it. But she had underestimated the appetite of a full-grown Kavanagh male. Amidst much good-natured jostling and name-calling everyone filled his or her plate and found a seat.

Dylan's mission-style dining room table, with leaves inserted, was big enough to handle the whole crew in one sitting. Emma took a spot at the far end and across the table from Aidan. She had promised not to embarrass him, and despite what had happened moments before the party began, she was determined not to give anyone cause to think she and Aidan were a couple.

Her interactions with him were complicated enough

already without other people butting in and offering their opinions. Apparently Aidan had come to the same conclusion, because he barely acknowledged Emma's presence. It was Mia who offered her a seat, Mia who involved her in the conversations that bounced back and forth during the meal.

Cora sat in a high chair at one corner, her chubby cheeks red with excitement. It was probably too much stimulation for a little one near bedtime, but Dylan and Mia had wanted to include her.

Each of the younger Kavanagh men had brought a date. As far as Emma could tell, the females in question were casual connections at best, because all four of them had to be introduced to the group.

The only unattached members of the dinner party were Maeve and Cora, Aidan and Emma. At first, Emma was on edge. But when she realized that no one was inclined to ask awkward questions, she relaxed.

It was almost unbelievable that every single one of Aidan's siblings was tall, broad-shouldered and dangerously attractive. The deceased Mr. Kavanagh must have been a fine figure of a man. Only the youngest, James, looked more like his mother.

Emma had been reared in *polite* society. By the time she was ten, she knew how to comport herself at an afternoon tea or a grown-up dinner party. Although tonight's gathering was much less stuffy, the Kavanaghs were a sophisticated lot, well traveled, well read and comfortable with the trappings of wealth.

The discussions of books, movies, politics and the world in general were stimulating. After a while, Emma felt comfortable enough to jump in and be a part of the occasional debate. Aidan, on the other hand, remained oddly silent. He nodded and answered when asked a direct question, but he was content to nurse a beer and observe the proceedings with a small smile on his face. From where Emma sat, his little grin seemed to encompass love for his family and an enjoyment of their eccentricities.

When the housekeeper took Cora, ready to put her to bed, Liam held up a hand. "One moment please, Gertie." He stood and picked up his wineglass. "We're gathered here tonight to celebrate the upcoming marriage of my brother Dylan to the beautiful and much-too-good-for-him Mia."

A wave of laughter greeted his statement.

He carried on, looking at Mia with warmth and affection. "Mia…when my brothers and I asked Dylan what kind of bachelor party he wanted tonight, his answer was *none*."

Dylan's face turned red. He ducked his chin.

Liam shook his head, smiling. "He told us everything in the world he wanted was under this very roof. And that the two days when you and Cora become official Kavanaghs will be the happiest of his life."

Every female around the table, Emma included, gave an audible sigh…*awwww*. For the first time during the meal, Aidan looked straight at Emma and rolled his eyes with a humorous expression. She shrugged, not about to apologize for appreciating romance.

"To Mia and Dylan." Liam held his glass toward the happy couple. The toast echoed around the table.

"To Mia and Dylan."

Maeve had tears in her eyes as she gave Cora a quick kiss. When the housekeeper departed with the baby, Maeve remained standing. "This is a party," she said. "So I won't belabor the point. But I want to say that I have the most wonderful sons in the world. And adding

Zoe and Mia to our family has been a joy." She paused, moving her gaze from Aidan to Gavin, Patrick, Conor and James. "But the rest of you…"

The men all groaned, as if they knew what was coming next.

Maeve ignored their response. "I'm not getting any younger," she said, managing to look frail and needy despite the fact that she was a vibrant woman in perfect health. "You young women be careful. The Kavanagh male is a slippery species. I'd love to have half a dozen grandchildren while I'm still able to enjoy them."

Catcalls and hoots and hollers ended her pseudo-pitiful speech. Laughter erupted again as she was forced to sit down in defeat. But the broad smile on her face told Emma she was perfectly happy to sit back and watch her sons find worthy matches.

Emma wondered if she understood exactly how unlikely that was in Aidan's case.

By unanimous consent, the group moved to the large, comfortable living room. A roaring fire warmed the space and cast a circle of intimacy. Again, Emma stayed far away from Aidan.

This time the conversation turned to less personal topics. Gavin's date mentioned spending Christmas in Zurich with her family. Emma, seated beside her, sighed. "It sounds like a wonderful trip. I've heard the skiing there is awesome. Actually, now that I've moved to Silver Glen, I was hoping to learn how to ski myself."

Without warning, a dead hush fell over the group. Like Sleeping Beauty's castle under a wicked spell, everyone in the room froze. What had Emma said? She replayed her innocent statements in her head. They hardly seemed the kind of words to provoke such a response. Though the women who sat with Aidan's younger brothers appeared confused, no one could miss the uneasy silence. The expressions on Kavanagh faces ranged from dismay to outright alarm.

Maeve suddenly looked her age, and Mia's distress was palpable. *What did I do?* Emma wondered frantically. In desperation, she looked to Aidan for help. He stood up, never once looking her way, his face carved in granite. "If you'll excuse me…"

No one said a word as he left the room. Thirty seconds later, the front door of the house opened and closed quietly.

Emma swallowed. "I'm sorry," she said. "But what just happened?"

Liam heaved a sigh, his expression a combination of resignation and worry. "Come with me to the kitchen, Emma."

She followed him out of the room with her heart thumping like mad. When they were out of earshot, she leaned against the sink. "What in the heck is going on? What's wrong with Aidan?"

"It's not your fault." Liam ran both hands through his hair. "You stepped on an emotional land mine."

"I don't understand."

"Aidan never comes home at Christmas. When he was younger, he brought his fiancée to Silver Glen at the holidays to meet the family. While they were here, she and Aidan went skiing. Danielle fell and hit her head. She died forty-eight hours later without ever waking up from a coma."

"Oh, my God." Emma's stomach heaved. "I'm so sorry."

"You had no way of knowing. He's been on edge since he left New York. Coming here…in December…has been a strain. But he wouldn't miss Dylan's wedding."

"I'm going to go talk to him."

"Probably not a good idea. When a man is hurting, he wants to hide and lick his wounds."

"I've ruined the party, Liam. I should go."

Liam touched her shoulder. "Nothing is ruined, Emma. Aidan will be okay. He needs a little time to re-group, that's all."

Mia wandered into the kitchen, her face troubled. "Did Liam tell you?"

Emma nodded, her throat too tight to answer.

Mia hugged her and then stepped back. "I should have warned you, I guess. Dylan told me how bad it was back then. My heart breaks for Aidan. He's never been seri-ous about anyone since."

"I see." Emma swallowed hard, on the verge of tears. "Thank you for inviting me tonight," she whispered. "I'm going to see if I can find him and apologize."

"It might make things worse," Liam said.

He was probably right, but Emma couldn't bear the thought of Aidan wandering cold and alone on a night that was supposed to be a celebration. "Maybe," she said. "But I have to try."

Mia nodded. "I'd want to do the same."

"Please tell Dylan I'm sorry," Emma said.

"Don't be ridiculous. I'm so glad you were here. Mom and Dad and my friends from Raleigh aren't arriving until a few hours before the ceremony tomorrow, so it's been nice having some emotional backup."

"Hey," said Liam, his tone aggrieved. "*We* love you."

Mia kissed his cheek. "I know you do. But sometimes a woman needs a break from all that testosterone."

Emma walked to where her vehicle was parked, her feet crunching on the frost-covered grass. The truth was, she had no good plan to look for Aidan...none at all. When she made it back to town, she cruised the darkened streets, trying to spot his fancy sports car. She even made a pass through the parking lot of the Silver Dollar Saloon. But no Aidan.

Driving up the mountain was her last shot. Aidan was staying at the lodge, true, but there was at least a possibility that he had left town. When she handed her keys to the valet and stepped out, she shivered. The wind had picked up, making the night seem even colder. She bundled her coat around her, hurrying up the steps of the hotel.

In the lobby, she paused. Aidan might be outside, though it was unlikely. The young man working the desk tonight was an employee she didn't recognize, so that might be to her advantage.

She approached him casually, removing her coat and straightening her dress and duster. "Hello," she said, beaming him a bright smile. "I'm trying to catch up with Mr. Kavanagh, Aidan Kavanagh," she clarified. "Did you happen to see him go up to his room earlier?"

The barely twenty-something blinked, seeming dazzled by her deliberately cozy manner. "Yes, ma'am," he said. "About an hour ago. May I ring his room for you?"

Emma reached in her purse and pressed a large bill into his hand. "No, thank you. He's expecting me."

Leaving the flustered clerk to ponder the fact that he might have been indiscreet, Emma headed for the elevator. She had no clue what she was going to say to Aidan or how she could make things better, but she had to try. The memory of his face as he left the party hurt her deeply.

Stepping out of the elevator, she paused a moment. The elegant hallway was quiet. It was possible that some guests had retired for the night, though unlikely. Even still, she didn't have the luxury of making a scene.

At Aidan's door, she knocked softly and listened for any sound inside his room. Nothing. Knocking harder, she held her breath, praying that he wouldn't ignore her.

At last, she was pretty sure she heard him on the other side of the door. She knocked a third time. "I know you're in there, Aidan. Let me come in. Please."

Thirteen

Aidan unlocked the door with a sense of fatalism and swung it open, stepping back to allow Emma to enter. She would not leave until she was satisfied that he was okay. It was his own damned fault for reacting so viscerally to her innocent observations. But somehow, the thought of Emma on a ski slope had made his heart stop and his stomach revolt.

No surprise, really, given his past with her. But she didn't need to know that. His job now was to convince her that he was fine…that he'd had a momentary crisis, but it had passed.

He saw her glance at the whiskey decanter. "I'm not drowning my sorrows," he said, leaning heavy on the sarcasm.

"I didn't say that."

"But you were thinking it."

She removed her coat and tossed it on a chair. Only hours before he had been holding her, his body taut with need. What he wouldn't give to rewind the clock and pretend this evening had never happened.

"I'm so sorry, Aidan."

He shrugged, her sympathy about as comfortable to him as a hair shirt. "It's no big deal. I was caught off guard, that's all."

And stunned at the thought that you could die...just like poor Danielle.

"It was more than that, and you know it." She cupped his face in her hands, her eyes filled with tears. "I can't imagine how horrible it must have been for you... losing someone you loved that way. No wonder Christmas is a bad time."

He couldn't bear her touch. Not now. He was raw inside. "Feel free to go," he said, pushing her hands away along with her gentle empathy. "As you can see, I'm neither drunk nor high and I have no plans to harm myself in a dramatic show of grief."

Turning his back, he paced the room, wondering how long it would take to get rid of her. The longer she stayed, the more he wanted her. And he'd done enough stupid things for one night.

Emma curled up in a chair. "Tell me about Danielle," she said softly. "What was she like?"

He continued to traverse the room, in danger of wearing a path in the carpet. Talking to Emma about Danielle was both ironic and terribly sad. "She was delightful," he said, casting back for memories. "A good person in every sense of the word. She threw herself into life with abandon—charming, funny, always kind to those who were out of step with the world."

"She sounds like a lovely woman."

"She was. I never heard her say an unkind word about anyone."

"How long had the two of you been together?"

"Four years."

Emma winced visibly. "And the accident?"

He didn't want to go there. But that moment was as vivid in his mind as if it had happened yesterday. Some days he thought he would never be able to erase the recollection. So why did it matter if he told Emma at least part of the truth?

"Liam told you, I guess, that I brought Danielle home to meet my family. It was December, and the town was decked out for the holidays. Danielle fell in love with Silver Glen."

"That doesn't surprise me. Who could resist?"

"True. At any rate, we had been here a couple of days when we got a surprise. An early snowfall, almost six inches. Conor and I were jazzed. We made plans to go skiing and took Danielle with us."

"Had she skied before?"

"She knew *how* to ski, but she wasn't very good at it, and it had been a long time. So we kept to the easy runs, not quite the bunny slopes, but close. She regained her confidence finally, and we decided to tackle something a little more challenging. Conor went first. Then Danielle. I brought up the rear. About halfway down, she lost her balance and careened off the course, headed for a clump of trees. I heard her laughing, and then she screamed, and then she crumpled in a broken heap on the ground."

He wasn't looking at Emma as he struggled through the dark tale. So he was startled when he felt her arms come around him.

She pressed her cheek to his chest. "I can't even imagine what you went through. How dreadful."

"We got her down the mountain with the help of the ski patrol, but she was unconscious. At the hospital, they determined that the blow to her head had caused a massive brain bleed. She never woke up. Two days later, she was dead."

Emma hugged him so tightly he thought his ribs would crack. He rested his chin on the top of her head. He knew Emma was crying...for him. He wished he could cry, too. But he had buried his wounds and his emotions so deeply they were fossilized.

"There's more," he said, the two words hoarse.

She took him by the hand and drew him to the sofa. He sprawled in the corner and draped an arm around her shoulders when she nestled close.

"You don't have to do this," she said. "I've heard enough."

"But not the worst part. There's something I've never told anyone."

"You can trust me with your secret." She squeezed his hand.

"I was the one who thought Danielle should come with us. I'll never forget asking her. She was curled up by the fire—wrapped in a cozy afghan, reading. I told her the plan, but she said for me to go on with my brother...that she was perfectly happy to sit with her book and enjoy a quiet morning."

Emma moved restlessly, perhaps sensing what was to come. But she didn't speak.

"I'm to blame," he said, shuddering inwardly. "I begged her to go with us. Told her how much fun it would be. And in the end, I won her over."

"Oh, Aidan."

He ignored the loaded comment.

"It was my fault she died. I have to live with that."

Emma sat in silence, her world in ashes. Aidan hadn't lied to her after all. When he told her the sex was only sex, it had been the truth. Because he was still in love with his dead fiancée.

He might not realize it. But she heard the emotional pain in his words...heard him describe Danielle with such love and affection. And because his grief was so all-encompassing and so deep, he had been unable to move on.

Clearly, coming to Silver Glen at Christmas for his brother's wedding was a decision he had made at great personal cost. Every Christmas tree and wreath and sprig of holly must be a bitter reminder of all he had lost.

His reaction, more than anything, told Emma she'd never had a chance at rekindling their old romance. There was nothing to rekindle. She was the only one who had kept the glow of a youthful relationship alive. For a man to love so faithfully and so well that he still grieved years later and continued to carry a load of guilt, meant that his heart was not his own. He had buried it with Danielle.

She cleared her throat. "Thank you for telling me. She must have been a very special woman."

Suddenly, everything seemed awkward. Should she go…leave him to his own devices? Or should she stay to give him comfort…any kind of comfort she could offer?

Aidan sat up and rested his elbows on his knees, his head in his hands. "Did I upset Dylan and Mia?"

Emma chose her words carefully. "If you're asking was the party ruined…no. But of course your family is worried about you. We could go back if you want."

"God, no." His rough laugh held no humor at all. "I did enough damage earlier. I'm sure they don't need me throwing a damper on things. I'll have an early night, and tomorrow I'll make it up to them somehow. I feel like an idiot."

She touched his arm. "You're a man who cares deeply. Nothing wrong with that." Since she still had not resolved her inner struggle, she rose to her feet. "I should go now. I'll see you at the wedding tomorrow." She put a hand on his shoulder. "I'm really sorry. About Danielle, I mean."

He stood and faced her. "Will you think it incredibly crass if I ask you to stay tonight?"

She searched his eyes, looking for any indication that he truly wanted her. Was it enough to know that she would be giving him comfort in a way no one else could at the moment? "I thought you said physical intimacy between the two of us was a bad idea."

"It's been a hell of an evening. Being rational is not high on my list at the moment. But you're free to say no. I would say no to me if I were you."

The humor was weak, but it was there. He had turned a corner. "I don't believe saying *no* to you is my strong suit."

He curled a strand of her hair around his finger. "I want to make one thing clear before we go any further..."

"Okay." She braced inwardly.

"When I went all psycho tonight, it wasn't only because I was remembering Danielle's accident. It was also a gut-deep reaction to the idea that you could get hurt. You mean something to me, Emma. Maybe it's not what it was in the past, and maybe it's not what you deserve, but I do have feelings, despite my efforts to the contrary."

Her heart warmed more than it should have. His eyes were filled with *something*. Affection? Attraction? What self-respecting female went to bed with a man who was in love with another woman? Was she a masochist?

"You mean something to me as well. But you should know that I don't expect anything beyond tonight. I want to be with you. If that brings us both pleasure, that's reason enough."

Fourteen

Aidan was so deeply enmeshed in his lies of omission that he couldn't even *reach* the moral high ground, much less stand on it. He was too busy protecting himself from Emma. And now…tonight…with deliberate intent, he was going to take what she was offering and damn the consequences.

When Emma mentioned skiing earlier, it *did* bring back the past and Danielle's accident. But what had really prompted his abrupt departure was a vicious jolt of panic at the thought that the world could lose Emma as well.

For the last ten years, in the midst of anger and grief and frustration with himself for still caring about her, at least he had known that somewhere on the planet she was alive and well.

He hadn't truly realized until this evening that if she were to die, he couldn't bear it. Emma married to another man and happy with babies? That, he could wrap his head around. But dead? Like Danielle? The notion was unfathomable.

Gripping one of her wrists, he reeled her into his embrace. "I have fantasies about your hair," he muttered.

"My hair?" A little squiggle of a frown appeared between her brows. "Surely you can do better than that."

"Oh, no," he said, drawing her toward the bedroom

before she could change her mind. "It's a guy thing. The more you pin and twist and tuck it, the more I want to muss you up."

She laughed softly. "Be my guest. This fancy updo is giving me a headache anyway."

Once they crossed the threshold into the inner room of the suite, he closed the door and leaned against it. A single small lamp cast an intimate circle of light. Emma eyed him warily, perhaps wondering if he were in his right mind. Maybe he was and maybe he wasn't. Ever since the moment he came face-to-face with her in the emergency room, he had questioned his sanity.

Ten years ago she had betrayed him and made a fool of him, and yet at the same time she had been the center of his world for three amazing months. Now, the good memories battled the bad, as if trying to convince him that the past was the past…that the future held endless possibilities.

Emma had asked again and again for the chance to explain her actions. To make amends. To request absolution. He had shut her down every time she tried.

Should he let her speak of that terrible day? Let her attempt to make sense of it? Or did it even matter from the vantage point of a decade in time? He was a man. He understood that life included disappointments. The blessings of family and friends were balanced with the inevitable struggles of living. Not that all struggles were as tragic as Danielle's death.

Shaking his head slightly, he decided such questions could wait. Emma wasn't going anywhere. Maybe he would let her open the door to the past. But not here. And not now.

"Come closer, my English rose," he muttered, unbuttoning his shirt and pulling it free of his pants. When he shrugged out of it and tossed it toward the closet, Emma's eyes widened.

She sighed, lips parted, as she obeyed his command. Placing her hands flat on his chest, she flicked his flat, copper-colored nipples with sharp fingernails. The tiny stings of pain arrowed to his groin and joined the rush of arousal that already had his sex lifting to attention.

"I won't regret this," she said softly. "I'm glad we had this chance to see each other again. Maybe we both needed closure."

He didn't like the finality in her description, even though he'd been the one to say they had no future. "You talk too much," he said, only half-joking. He didn't want to *think* tonight. All he wanted was to feel her body straining against his.

Without asking, he pulled the pins from her hair one at a time and dropped them into a crystal dish. Each small *clink* was quiet music to his ears. When he was done, he used both hands to winnow through her hair, separating the strands and smoothing the wavy tresses. "That's better," he said softly.

The prelude to sex was easier this time, more natural. Removing Emma's clothes was a reverent task not to be rushed. When he had her down to a set of ultrafeminine undies and bra, he finished his own disrobing. Lowering the zipper on his slacks was tricky. His erection bobbed thick and eager as he eased it free of confinement.

Together, they climbed into the enormous hedonistic bed. The Silver Beeches Lodge spared no expense when it came to their guests' comfort. Whether for sleep or more intimate pursuits, the bedding and mattress provided an island of physical bliss.

He leaned over Emma on one elbow, studying the dewy perfection of her skin. Maybe something about the air and water in the British Isles produced this exquisite variety of female.

"Tell me one of *your* fantasies," he said. "Something naughty you've always wanted to do but never had the chance."

Her instant, cheeky grin made him shiver. She sighed. "I've always wanted to have sex in a lift."

"A lift?" All the blood in his head had rushed south, making him slow to comprehend.

"You know...an elevator. Preferably one with glass on the top half. So people watching might have a clue as to what's happening, but wouldn't know for sure."

He gaped at her. "Emma. You wicked girl."

Her shrug was epic. "You asked."

"So I did." And now all he could think about was where such an elevator might exist. Certainly not in the town of Silver Glen. "I'm going to forget you said that," he muttered. "Although getting the image out of my head will be hard."

"You said *hard*." She snickered. "Is that a Freudian slip?"

He touched her smooth thigh, running his hand from her knee to the crevice where leg joined torso. Her underwear was tiny and sexy. Twisting a finger in the side band, he snapped it deliberately. "Freud might want to study my caveman tendencies." Tugging the small piece of fabric to uncover her secrets, he nudged her hip. "Lift your butt."

Now she was completely bare from the waist down. He took the opportunity to tease her with kisses that ranged from playful to deliberately sexual.

Emma moved restlessly, her hands gripping his head. "Aidan."

"Hmmm...?" Her taste was exquisite.

"I want to do something."

"Pretty sure we're already doing it."

"I'm serious."

He winced when she pulled his hair. "Okay, okay." Rolling to his back, he turned his head to look at her. "You have my attention."

Emma, in turn, surprised the hell out of him by moving agilely and straddling his waist. "I want to take care of you tonight," she said. "Will you let me?"

Her body was a pleasant weight at his hips. "I'm not sure what you mean."

She leaned forward, her lace-covered breasts in kissing distance, and took his wrists in her hands. "I want you to grab hold of the spindles in the headboard. We don't have anything to tie you with, so you'll have to promise not to let go."

A fresh current of arousal flooded his veins. "Please don't tell me being a dominatrix is on your bucket list. I'll never believe it." People often made jokes in tense situations. This definitely counted. "A lady never acts out of character," he said. "I think you've been reading too many erotic novels."

"I'm not always a lady, Aidan. Perhaps you don't know me as well as you think."

Well, hell's bells. That shut him up. With her small hands guiding his wrists, he found the slender pieces of wood and wrapped his fingers around two of them. The stretch in his shoulders was pleasant. So far.

"What next?" he asked, trying to gauge her mood.

Emma shifted her weight back to his hips again. Her expression defied analysis. Not uncertainty. More like assessment. He wasn't sure if that aroused him or worried him. In all honesty, a bit of both.

"Are you comfortable?" she asked, her hands flat on

her thighs. Considering that her lady parts were tantalizingly close to his rigid sex, it was a loaded question.

"Yes."

She nodded once. "Good. Now close your eyes."

"Um..." He flexed his feet, his toes cold.

"Are you afraid of me, Aidan?" Her question could have been flirtatious, but the tone suggested she was serious.

"Should I be?" he asked, dodging the truth.

"I want to make you feel good...that's all. No need for alarm. You can trust me."

He wondered if this were some kind of test. To prove to him that she had changed. "I'm in your hands. Be gentle with me."

His half-hearted teasing didn't even coax a smile from her. "I'm waiting for you to close your eyes." She said it patiently in the tone of someone dealing with a stubborn toddler.

"Are you going to ditch the bra?" he asked hopefully. The pastel lace was mostly transparent, but that didn't mean he didn't want to uncover what was underneath. He simply hadn't gotten to it when she turned the tables so unexpectedly.

Emma shrugged. "It won't matter," she said softly. "You won't be able to see."

The simple statement struck him as a threat, even though there was nothing of menace in the words. Apparently, his trust issues went deeper than he realized. Now that he thought about it, he'd never allowed any woman this kind of physical control.

He'd played naughty games with females in the past, but Aidan had always wielded the power. From this side of the metaphorical whip, he felt distinctly uneasy. But he wasn't about to reveal his reservations. Not at this particular moment.

Inhaling a deep gulp of air that lifted his chest, he let it out slowly as he closed his eyes and tightened his grip.

Fifteen

Aidan Kavanagh was an extraordinarily masculine and beautiful man. Though he had complied with her orders, Emma sat motionless for a moment, enjoying the tableau. His skin was lightly tanned, the hair on his torso and beneath his arms a shade darker than his deep brown locks with the hint of fire in them.

With his arms extended above his head, she could see the tendons and muscles that delineated his strength. Broad shoulders and a hair-dusted chest tapered to a trim waist, flat stomach and below...*Oh, lordy...*

His sex, though still somewhat turgid, lay against his thigh. Perhaps her offer to make him feel good was ambiguous enough to make it difficult for him to relax.

"I'm going to start with a massage," she said quietly.

Aidan made no response, but he muttered something inaudible.

Scooting up onto his chest, she leaned forward until she could reach his wrists. Pressing her thumbs to his pulse, she dug into his flesh and ran a path all the way to the crook of his elbows. Then, using both hands on one arm at a time, she worked her way from his elbow to his upper arm.

Perhaps because of the posture she insisted he adopt, his shoulder muscles were tight. She spent some time there, finding knots and working them out. It might have been easier if he had been on his stomach, but she wanted to watch his face.

At one point, he flinched. "Too hard?" she asked. One of her college friends had studied sports medicine, and Emma had picked up tips from her. But sometimes people couldn't take too firm a pressure.

"Your *assets* are in my face."

"Ah." She blushed, though he couldn't see her. "Almost done with this part." She moved on to his neck and behind his ears. As her hands warmed his skin, she inhaled the smell of him…the yummy *guy* aroma that made a girl's knees weak and led to all sorts of improper thoughts.

The next bit was very personal. Letting her fingertips glide gently, she feathered her way across his forehead, down his nose and cheeks, along his chin and over his firm jaw to his throat.

Aidan's Adam's apple bobbed visibly when she pressed lightly where his pulse beat in the side of his neck. Moving to his collarbone, she stroked it slowly. As she shifted back a couple of inches so she could reach his chest, she realized that his sex was no longer at rest. It was firm and erect and bumped her bottom eagerly.

From this particular angle, she could have joined their bodies easily. But there was time for that later. She concentrated on rubbing his chest, tracing his rib cage, following the line of his sternum.

She saw his tongue come out to wet his lips. It seemed as if his breathing had picked up in tempo. At one time, she'd had the freedom to touch Aidan however and whenever she wanted, knowing that every brush of skin made them both drunk with happiness and arousal.

For one painful moment, the stab of grief consumed

her. Even if Aidan eventually forgave her for the past, they would never be the same two people. What they had shared at Oxford was exhilarating. They had been young and in love and frightfully full of themselves.

Determined to forget the past, she moved quickly, avoiding Aidan's straining erection and settling in between his legs. She heard him curse, possibly because he thought she had been preparing to join their bodies by sliding down onto his shaft.

She crouched on her knees. Avoiding his groin area, she rubbed his hipbones. His thighs were next, then his bony knees, his calves, his ankles and finally his big feet. When she slid her fingers between his toes, his back arched off the bed.

"Enough," he wheezed.

"I'm trying to relax you. These are standard massage techniques."

"Screw that." He sat up, raking his hands through his hair. His eyes glittered with desire. "Either your technique sucks, or when you touch me I go insane. I'm betting on the latter."

"Oh." She'd been trying to calm him, to make him feel good after a crappy evening. "I didn't even touch your…"

"My penis?" he offered helpfully.

Frowning at him, she eased back onto her bottom and pretzeled her legs. "I don't like that word."

"It's a perfectly good word…unless you prefer di—"

She slapped a hand across his mouth. "I prefer not to talk about it at all. I'm more into *doing*."

One side of his mouth kicked up in a grin. "Happy to oblige." He mimicked her position, then took her hands and tucked them around his shaft. "Feel free to massage this poor neglected body part."

It was her turn to swallow. His sex was proportionally large, the shaft veined and strong, the head weeping for her. "I don't think they covered this in the manuals," she muttered.

When she ran her thumb beneath the flange and used her other hand to squeeze, Aidan's eyes rolled back in his head. Well, they might have. She didn't exactly know since his face was scrunched up and his lashes fanned out against his cheeks.

So far, so good. "You really are tense," she breathed.

Despite his advanced state of arousal, Aidan laughed, opening his eyes to look at her with a glazed expression. "*Tense* doesn't even begin to describe it. You have an unfair advantage with that upper crust British accent. Everything out of your mouth sounds like a sexual come-on."

"Close your eyes, naughty boy," she said, channeling her old headmistress. "I'm not done yet."

Emma might not be done, but Aidan was almost there. His skin was so sensitive to the touch that it hurt. He took her hand and removed it from the trigger. "Not like this, Emma. I want to be inside you."

Her lower lip pouted the tiniest bit. "I wanted to make you feel good," she said.

He groaned, shaking his head in bemusement. "Mission accomplished. Now turn around."

"Why?"

"Don't you trust me?"

"Not funny, Kavanagh."

"Don't be so prissy. I'm only going to undo you." When she gave him her back, he unfastened the band of her bra carefully and slid the straps down her shoulders. "There. Now was that so bad?"

She faced him again, her breasts high and firm and

beautiful. Although she had been bold when his eyes were closed, now she seemed hesitant...even shy. He cupped one breast in his hand. "You don't have to stay. I'm fine." Why he was giving her the chance to leave, he wasn't sure. But it seemed somehow important.

She took his free hand and held it to her cheek. "I don't want to leave, Aidan."

"Are you staying because you feel sorry for me?" The thought of her sympathy chafed.

But she shook her head vigorously. "I'd be lying if I said yes. I really did want to make you feel better, but the real reason is selfish."

He cocked his head. "Tell me. Please."

Pale, narrow shoulders lifted and fell. "I want to feel it again."

"It?"

"The high. At the risk of giving you a swelled ego, you're very good at satisfying a woman sexually."

Her explanation was not what he expected to hear. It seemed impersonal and cold. Though paradoxically, he and Emma were anything but at the moment. Hunger sizzled between them. It seemed, however, as if they were reading from a script, both of them afraid to speak the truth.

Refusing to acknowledge her confession, bogus or not, he took her with him under the covers. Their arms and legs tangled. "I want you, Emma. You have no idea how much."

She nestled against him. "I want you, too, Aidan."

Still, he felt dissatisfied. Perhaps this was payback for the way he had insisted that anything physical between them was *only* sex. Who had he been trying to convince?

Emma had asked him if there was still a spark. He had

denied it. But with her here in his bed, he seemed like the worst kind of liar.

He ran his hands over her back, tracing her spine, feeling the press of her breasts against his chest. If he closed his eyes, he could pretend he was twenty-one again. Eager. Painfully naive about women. Standing on the precipice of a moment that would change his life forever.

How could he have made such a wrong choice? Such a desperately wrong choice? He'd been hurt, true. But he liked to think he was wiser now. Even in the face of Emma's betrayal, he should have fought for her.

Her cheek rested trustingly against his chest. Could she feel his heart thump? To him, it felt like a runaway train. Beating out a rhythm on the tracks.

Last chance. Last chance. Last chance.

Confusion and lust were poor bedfellows. Lust won every time, even in the absence of clear thinking. He moved over her and kissed her roughly. She arched into his embrace, giving him everything. Her softness. Her kindness. Her capacity for loving.

Love. The word was so damned dangerous. As he entered her with one hard thrust, he felt the syllable reverberate in his head, in his heart, in his loins. He did not love her. He wouldn't allow it. Never again.

But as his body stroked into hers, as her arms linked around his neck, binding him to her, he felt his will crumble. How could this be wrong? How could anything this good be wrong?

They loved wildly, passionately, battling almost to see who could give the other more pleasure. He lost the ability to speak, to reason, to keep her at bay.

He wanted everything she was, everything *he* was when he was with her. Emotions he had denied for years washed over him, drowning every one of his stupid life rules. His need for release bore down on him, but he didn't want this to end. He wanted to love her all night long.

When Emma cried out his name, though, shuddering beneath him, he had no choice but to follow her. The intensity of his climax tore him apart and rebuilt him cell by cell.

Eons later, he clutched her close and slept. But it was a fitful slumber. He jerked awake, time and again, dreaming that he had lost her. In his nightmares, he stood inside a train car, watching her wave to him as some immoveable force carried him away.

After the third time when he awoke sweating and trembling, he eased from the bed and went in search of a drink of water. He stood naked in the living room area of the suite and peered out at the night between a crack in the drapes. The world was still and dark.

Today was his brother's wedding day. Dylan was gaining a wife and a daughter in one fell swoop. What must it be like to know that people depended on you? That their health and well-being directly impacted your own happiness?

In Dylan's shoes, Aidan would be scared to death. That was a hell of a thing for a grown man to admit. Even now, with Emma asleep in the other room, Aidan had to resist the urge to run. He remembered his early twenties all too well. He'd been a mess. Drinking too much. Sleeping with too many women. Teaching himself not to feel.

All because Emma Braithwaite's betrayal had crushed him. The pain had made it hard to breathe. And it had made him stupid. Unfortunately, Danielle had borne the brunt of that.

His breath fogged the glass. Rubbing his thumb across the condensation, he told himself to let go of the memories. But what was the old saying? He who forgets the past is doomed to repeat it?

Aidan couldn't live through such a cataclysm again. He wouldn't. He'd been as vulnerable as a newborn pup, no defenses at all.

This time he was smarter.

When he was chilled to the bone, he returned to the bedroom. The small lamp still burned. Emma looked like a painting, her golden hair strewn across the pillow, her ivory breasts rising and falling with each breath.

He climbed beneath the covers, his heart catching sharply in his chest when she murmured and curled into his embrace.

"You're so cold," she said. She didn't open her eyes, but her face scrunched up in dismay.

"Sorry." Her skin felt like velvet—warm, supple and soft.

Even half-asleep, she tried to protect him. She patted his thigh. "Stay close to me." The words were slurred. "I'll warm you up."

For the remainder of the early morning, he listened to her gentle breathing, his body wrapped around hers. It was too important a moment to be lost in sleep. He loved her.

I love you.

No one was there to hear when he whispered the admission, dry-eyed. He loved Emma Braithwaite. Perhaps he had never stopped. But now was all there was. Come daybreak he had to let her go.

Though he closed his eyes, he kept slumber at bay. Around seven-thirty, she stirred. He feigned sleep, giving her the chance to make a trip to the bathroom, to find her clothes and to dress.

When she was ready, he pretended to wake up, rearing up on one elbow to gaze at her sleepily. "You're leaving?"

Emma's smile was shy. "I have to go home and shower and open the shop. Mrs. Correll is coming at two so I can get ready for the wedding, but I'll be on my own until then."

She sat down on the side of the bed and touched his arm. "I wanted to ask you one more thing. If you don't mind."

He tensed inwardly. "What is it?"

Emma glanced down, her expression troubled. When she looked up at him again, he felt as if he could see into her soul. "How long ago was it that Danielle died?" she asked, the words barely audible.

Here it was. This was his chance. All he had to do was tell the truth and he'd be free of Emma forever. She would be hurt, but she deserved to suffer a little. It was only fair.

Feeling cold to his bones, even though the bed still carried the warmth of their two bodies, he looked at her grimly. "Ten years." When the words left his mouth, it was too late to change his mind.

As he watched, Emma's forehead creased. He saw her do the math. "But you left England ten years ago... the first week in December. And you were engaged by Christmas?" Her voice broke on the last word as she stumbled to her feet. "You and Danielle were together before you came to England, weren't you?" Her tone was less accusatory than grief-stricken. She had gone so white, he feared for a moment she would faint.

"I guess you weren't the only one with secrets, Emma. Perhaps no one is ever who they seem."

Sixteen

Emma didn't react outwardly. Not even a single tear. She couldn't. Not with him watching. The hurt ran too deep. It was all she could do to breathe and move one foot in front of the other. She was perfectly calm as she walked out of Aidan's suite and rode the elevator down to the lobby. In the early morning there were few people around other than employees. She was not a hotel guest. Anyone could draw a conclusion from that. But what did it matter?

Perhaps she shouldn't have gotten behind the wheel of a car. But the choking need to put distance between herself and Aidan won out. She kept her speed ten miles under the limit. The mountain road was tricky.

By the time she made it to her apartment, she hovered on the brink of an ugly crying jag. Her chest felt as if someone had ripped it open with a dull blade. Her eyes burned. Her stomach revolted.

Upstairs, she glanced at the clock. In barely an hour she had to open the store for one of the biggest shopping days of the year. What was she going to do? She lay across her bed, utterly lost. Aidan was lying. He had to be. He could never have spent time with her at Oxford, adoring her, having sex with her, making plans with her…if he had been in love with another woman. It was impossible. She refused to believe it.

But then she saw his face as it had been when she walked out of his bedroom. She remembered his dark-eyed stare. And she realized he was right. She didn't know him at all.

Raw, brokenhearted sobs wet her pillow and left her feeling hollow and sick to her stomach. Somehow she had to make it through this day. Somehow she had to survive seeing him one more time. Tonight was Dylan and Mia's wedding. Neither Emma nor Aidan had the luxury of avoiding one another.

Though the thought of it was beyond comprehension, she knew she had no choice. She gave herself twenty minutes to cry out her misery and pain. It wasn't enough. It would never be enough. The empty cavity where her heart normally resided was frightening…like a black hole waiting to swallow her until she was nothing but a spot of darkness.

She dragged herself to her feet and undressed, ashamed that she had no underwear. What had seemed sexy and fun the night before now carried the tawdry feel of regret. A blistering hot shower did nothing to warm her soul. She dried her hair, applied light makeup with trembling hands, and dressed in a wool sweater and pants.

In a very real sense, Silver Memories became her salvation during the day. The heavy flow of customers, the constant *ching* of the cash register…all of it anesthetized her so that she could function.

When Mrs. Correll arrived midafternoon, the older woman didn't appear to notice anything amiss in her boss's demeanor. They exchanged a few words, Emma handed over the keys and fled upstairs.

For the longest time she sat huddled in her chair by

the fire, remembering how Aidan had looked sleeping in this very spot. She wanted to wail and throw things and smash bits of glass, but she was very afraid if she gave in to the emotions tearing her apart, she would never regain control.

The afternoon ticked away until it was far past time to prepare. She forced herself to heat a can of soup and eat it. She had skipped lunch. Though hunger was the last thing on her mind, she knew she needed the sustenance.

At last, she went to her tiny closet and reached for the green velvet dress. It was as beautiful as when she had first opened the box and lifted it out. The style was reminiscent of the 1940s, nipped in at the waist, full-skirted and cut low at the bodice with a sweetheart neckline. Trying it on had made her feel like a movie star.

Now, looking at herself in the mirror, all she saw was the ghost of a woman with sad eyes and a barely beating heart.

The skies had been clear all day, which meant that by five, the temperatures started to plummet. Emma was to be at the church at five thirty for pictures. Although she was only in charge of the guestbook, Mia had insisted she be included.

The small chapel where Mia and Dylan had chosen to have their ceremony was one of the oldest structures in Silver Glen. In lean, hard times, the early townspeople had erected a place of worship, nondenominational, welcoming all who wanted to come.

Only two blocks from Emma's apartment, the historic building was a favorite stop for tourists in the summertime. Tonight, even though Emma walked quickly in her high heels, the wind cut through her thick wool coat as if she were naked.

Breathless when she arrived, she paused at the doors

to the church, drawing on the faith taught to her as a child for strength to face the night ahead. Then lifting her chin, she turned the polished tin knob and let herself in.

The well-worn pews were original wood, as was the floor. Etched windows had been a later addition. Instead of stained glass, they were clear, affording grand views of the mountains in the daytime.

Candles in hurricane globes flickered softly on the high windowsills. Someone, Maeve perhaps, had surrounded them with fresh evergreens and red bows. The scent took Emma back to England, when her rambling, drafty home was decked out in holiday array.

A small group of people milled at the front of the chapel. Mia had refused to give credence to silly superstitions, as she called them, so all the pictures were to be taken with bride and groom together. Dylan couldn't take his eyes off her. His pride and happiness wrapped his woman in a romantic glow. Cora was passed from arm to arm, everyone fighting for the privilege of holding her.

Emma and Aidan stayed on opposite sides of the group, never making eye contact. No one seemed to notice. The photographer was talented and socially adept. He managed to get what he wanted without making anyone feel rushed or stressed. By a quarter 'til seven, it was all done.

Mia disappeared into a small room at the back, where she would wait until it was time for the ceremony. Her parents took a seat on the front row, left-hand side. Four of Mia's friends from Raleigh sat behind them. The Kavanagh boys, resplendent in formal wear, settled beside and behind their mother on the opposite side of the church.

The guest list was relatively small. Over the next half hour, thirty or so people drifted in, all of them longtime friends of the Kavanaghs. Emma offered the book and pen as each couple appeared. Standing so near the door, she shivered, but at least she was as far away from Aidan as possible.

At seven twenty-five, a violinist began to play softly. Emma made sure the old paneled door was firmly latched before taking a seat in the back row. Moments later, the musician began playing an evocative piece that echoed Mia's Russian heritage.

The bride appeared and stood in the center of the aisle. Her eye caught Emma's for a split second. The two women exchanged a smile. Then as the music swelled and danced, Mia walked slowly toward Dylan carrying a bouquet of red roses and eucalyptus tied with gold braid.

Her traditional wedding gown suited her small frame. White satin with long transparent sleeves, the dress's simplicity was a perfect foil for the antique lace that covered the bride's head and reached the floor in back. The veil and pearl-studded headpiece had belonged to Mia's Russian great-grandmother.

The bridal couple had chosen not to have attendants. Only the robed minister stood with them at the chancel rail.

Dearly beloved...

At that moment, Emma lost her composure. Tears rolled, one after the other, down her cheeks. If she had not made such foolish mistakes when she was younger, she and Aidan might have been married a long time by now...perhaps even had children.

Extracting an embroidered handkerchief that had belonged to her grandmother from her clutch purse, she dabbed her cheeks. This was why she felt so much passion for preserving the past. Tangible objects carried the memories of loved ones. They recalled the beauty of earlier times.

Silver Glen had made a point of preserving its heritage, of telling the town's story. And on virtually every street, some evidence of Kavanagh influence could be seen. Aidan was a part of that, though he chose to live elsewhere. Would he ever want to come home for good?

All she could see of him at the moment was the back of his head. She was grateful for that. If he had stood beside his brother, Emma would have been hard-pressed to look away.

She refocused her attention on the minister, who was guiding his charges in repeating wedding vows to each other. Dylan, sensitive to his struggles with the written word, had wanted to use the traditional liturgy. *To have and to hold, in sickness and in health, 'til death do us part.*

The words resonated, beautiful and timeless.

Even in profile, holding hands, Dylan and Mia looked so happy. The tenderness on his face was almost too personal to witness.

When Aidan became part of Emma's life in Oxford, he had looked at her much the same way. She had felt his love to the marrow of her bones. Had never doubted him for a minute. Despite what he told her this morning about the timing of his engagement, she knew he had loved her once upon a time.

Maybe she was blind...or ridiculously naive, but she refused to believe that the Aidan Kavanagh she knew in England was that good an actor.

The minister gave the pronouncement. Dylan and Mia faced their guests, arm in arm, beaming. Someone handed Cora to them. Cheers broke out in the small chapel.

There was no recessional. Everyone stood in the aisle,

talking and laughing. Emma made her way to the front, hugged Dylan and Mia, and prepared to make her escape.

But she hadn't counted on Maeve Kavanagh. Emma was four rows away from the back door and a clean get-away when Aidan's mother hailed her. "Slow down, Emma, for heaven's sake. You don't want to be the first one at the reception."

It didn't seem polite to say that Emma had planned to avoid the post-ceremony soiree all together. "Did I forget something? I put the guestbook in Mia's tote bag like she asked me to..."

Maeve shook her head. "This isn't about the guest-book. I wanted to let you know that I booked a room at the hotel for you tonight."

"Why would you do that? I live here."

"We Kavanaghs know how to throw a party. And though this group tonight will be small, don't underes-timate their enthusiasm. We're going to give Dylan and Mia the send-off they deserve. Which means a late night. Grab a toothbrush and whatever else you need and don't argue with the mother of the groom."

"Seriously, Maeve. I'm touched that you want me there, but I don't know any of your guests."

"You know Aidan." Something about the other woman's sly glance told Emma that Maeve was perhaps a bit too perceptive when it came to her sons. "And here he is now."

Emma's stomach flipped hard. Maeve had crooked a finger, and her son, clearly not willing to spoil a family occasion, had come as commanded. But the cold, closed look on his face when he looked at Emma said he was not happy about the situation.

Maeve ignored any tension. "Aidan...I need you to give Emma a ride to her apartment so she can pack a

few things. Then bring her up the mountain. I've promised her a room."

"Why?"

Even Maeve faltered at the incredulity in that one syllable. "Well," she said, soldiering on despite the awkward
moment, "she will want to have some wine, at least, and
no one should drive that mountain road on a dark winter
night when she's been drinking."

Aidan shoved the heels of his hands in his eyes.
"Mother, you're meddling...and not very subtly. Emma
has a perfectly fine vehicle and impeccable driving skills.
If she wants to come to the party, she can come on her
own."

Maeve bristled. "Watch your tongue, Aidan. You
might be a grown man, but you're still my little boy.
And I raised you better than that. Apologize to Emma."

Aidan glanced at Emma, his jaw tight. "I'm sorry. I'll
be happy to give you a ride up the mountain. Let me get
my coat and keys." The bitter sarcasm in his tone was
barely veiled, yet Maeve seemed oblivious.

When Aidan strode away, Maeve touched Emma's
arm. "Be patient with him, my dear."

"I don't know what you mean." Emma shifted from
one foot to the other, uncomfortable and embarrassed.

Maeve shook her head slightly, her eyes filled with a
mix of emotions, the clearest of which was determination. "I saw you leave the hotel this morning, Emma."

Bloody hell. "Oh, but I—"

Aidan's mother stopped her with an upheld hand. "It's
none of my business. And I don't want or need explanations. But I love my son. And I want to see him happy."

Emma looked toward the front of the church, where
Aidan stood talking to James and Conor. She bit her lip.

"I think you've misunderstood. Aidan doesn't have feelings for me. At least not the good kind."

"He's angry with you right now." It wasn't a question.

"Yes, ma'am."

"And you knew each other before you came here."

Emma nodded. She wasn't a very good liar. "We did."

"That's all I need to know. If you have a past with my son, I'm asking you to not give up on whatever this is between you. He can be bullheaded and emotionally distant, but I swear to you that he feels things deeply. Like the silver mines in these hills, sometimes you have to dig through the layers to find what's worth keeping."

Aidan was on his way back down the aisle.

"I understand," Emma whispered. "But there's a lot you don't know."

Maeve patted her arm. "And I don't need to know. Just remember what I said." She touched the skirt of Emma's dress as Aidan joined them. "Doesn't Emma look gorgeous in this shade of green, Aidan?"

"Stop it, Mother."

His parent lifted both eyebrows with an innocent expression. "I don't know what you mean."

"Matchmaking. You're embarrassing Emma."

"Am I?" She looked at Emma beseechingly.

With Aidan standing there like judge and jury, Emma had no choice but to tell the truth. "Yes, ma'am. A little bit."

Maeve waved a hand, dismissing their concerns. "Very well. I'll leave you two alone. But don't be long. We don't want to start the party without you."

Seventeen

Aidan strode around the corner, retrieved his car and turned the heater on full blast as he approached the church and idled at the curb. The door of the old building opened a crack. Emma spotted him and hurried outside, bundled to the chin as she slid into the passenger seat.

"Thank you," she said quietly. "I could have walked back, but I appreciate the lift. It's colder now than it was when I came. And don't worry. I'll drive myself up the mountain."

"Oh, no," he said. "My mother has spoken. My life wouldn't be worth two cents if she found out I didn't follow her directive."

The brief drive was silent after that. Aidan parked in front of Silver Memories. "I'll wait here." He didn't want to see Emma's cozy apartment again. Nor did he want to remember the first time they had made love. Damn his mother for interfering.

He could have told Maeve to go to the devil, but given all that she had sacrificed over the years for Aidan's sorry hide, he didn't have it in him to treat her so shabbily. She was simply trying to help in the only way she knew how.

When Emma reappeared carrying a small suitcase, he hopped out of the car, took it from her and placed it carefully in the trunk. After that, neither of them spoke as they made their way up the winding mountain road. Despite the silence, however, he was stingingly aware of everything about his passenger.

Her scent. Her body language. The way her soft velvet skirt spread across the seat, nearly touching his thigh.

This morning he had been so sure about everything. But tonight, seated in a hundred-year-old church, watching his brother marry the love of his life amidst the romantic glow of candlelight, even Aidan's calcified heart had begun to quiver and crack.

When all was said and done, did it matter that Emma had betrayed him once upon a time? Could he put the past behind him?

His introspection was short-lived. Soon, the magnificent hotel, ablaze with lights, welcomed them. Though all the family benefitted materially from the hotel's success, Liam and Maeve were the forces behind the day-to-day operations.

As Aidan exited the car and handed over the keys, Emma walked on ahead of him. To any onlooker, it might have seemed as if she were trying to get in out of the cold. But Aidan knew the truth. She didn't want him to touch her…even something as innocuous as holding her elbow as they ascended the steps.

The elegant lobby was festive and crowded. The long-time concierge, Pierre, directed them to a private room at the back of the hotel. Aidan and Emma were the last to arrive. Only Cora was missing. Dylan's housekeeper had taken the baby home to put her to bed.

Aidan grabbed a beer and some food and made a beeline for an unoccupied seat near Gavin. His brother shot him a look rife with curiosity. "You not hanging with your girlfriend?"

Stabbing a canapé with a silver fork, Aidan shook his head. "Not my girlfriend."

"Mom seems to think differently."

"Mom is a busybody."

Maeve appeared out of nowhere to thump him on the back of his head. "I heard that."

Aidan gave her a measured look. "If the shoe fits…"

She bent to kiss his cheek. "My job is to see my children settled happily."

Gavin blanched. "Don't get any ideas about me. Two out of seven isn't bad, Mom."

"Don't worry," she said. "When the right woman comes along, I won't have to do a thing. I love seeing my big strong boys give in to love." She didn't pause to sit down. "Pay attention now. Mia and Dylan are about to cut the cake."

Aidan turned his gaze to the appropriate spot in the room, but he couldn't help tracking Emma. So far tonight, she had been introduced to Mia's Raleigh friends, and she had danced with at least three of Aidan's brothers, including the groom.

As far as he could tell, she was having a wonderful time.

The more Emma glowed, the more Aidan glowered. He'd told her today that he had lied to her and cheated on her. Did she not believe him? Or did his confession not matter at all?

He couldn't understand her. That infuriated him more than anything. He was accustomed to sizing up a man or a woman at first meeting. Such people skills made him successful in his work.

But Emma remained an enigma. When he was in bed with her, it was easy to pretend she was the girl he knew in England, the young woman who made his life complete.

With a bit of emotional distance, though, his cynicism returned in full force. People didn't change. If Emma had betrayed him before, it was in her DNA to do it again. No matter how good the sex—and even he would admit that it was pretty damn spectacular—he would be a fool to set himself up for disappointment and loss a second time.

It was bad enough that he loved her. But he would get over that. He had to. He also had to make it clear to her and to himself that whatever her reasons for coming to Silver Glen...he wasn't interested.

The hours passed slowly. Never once did Emma glance his way. In her deep emerald pin-up-girl dress, she laughed and chatted and danced and partied the night away. He studied her for long chunks of time, trying to decide what it was about her that called to him. Was it the classic features? The golden hair? The female chuckle that went straight to his gut and ignited a slow burn? Seeing Conor pull her out onto the floor a second time made Aidan clench his jaw. But he kept his seat.

Emma could dance with every man in Silver Glen for all he cared.

Only for Mia did Aidan make an exception. His new sister-in-law sparkled with happiness. "I've danced with everyone but you," she said, taking him by the hand and pulling him to his feet. "You're acting like Scrooge over here in your corner. Don't make me beg."

"I wouldn't dream of it," he said, smiling at her with affection. "You've made my brother a very happy man."

Mia returned the smile. "Your whole family has welcomed me so sweetly. It's a novelty to have brothers after all this time. But I think I like it." He steered her around the floor, responding to her happy chatter when appropriate. Mia was an exceptional woman in every way. But never once had he felt anything for her other than fondness and admiration.

Even if Dylan hadn't been in the picture, Aidan wouldn't have made a play for Mia. Because no matter how foolish and self-destructive it was, the only female who gave him sleepless nights and unfulfilled sexual dreams was Emma Braithwaite.

At the song's end, he delivered Mia back to her new groom. Then, trying not to be obvious about it, he scouted the room for Emma's location. She was nowhere to be seen.

He couldn't ask about her, or he'd risk setting off his mother's radar. After half an hour, when it was clear Emma hadn't merely slipped out to the restroom, Aidan gave the bridal couple and his mother one last set of hugs and said his goodbyes. If they were suspicious, they gave no sign.

In the lobby, he hesitated. Everyone on staff knew him. It wasn't as if he could make an inquiry on the sly. So he might as well sin and sin boldly.

He approached the check-in area, giving Marjorie, the desk clerk who had known him since he was a boy, his best winsome smile.

Lowering his voice, he leaned an elbow on the granite counter. "Can you please give me Emma Braithwaite's room number? She slipped out before I had a chance to tell her good-night."

Marjorie eyed him with a wry twist of her lips. "Is this going to get me in trouble, Aidan?"

He held up his hands. "Not at all. I swear."

Shaking her head, she jotted the number on a slip of paper and pushed it toward him. "Don't make me regret this."

"I'm on my best behavior."

She snorted. "When it comes to Kavanagh men, that definition has all sorts of interpretations. Good luck."

"With what?" He lifted an eyebrow.

"The pretty English lady. You could do a lot worse."

"Forget that," he chuckled, though his throat was tight. "I haven't caught wedding fever, despite all the festivities. This confirmed bachelor is completely content with his lot."

Emma unpinned her hair and brushed it out. After taking off her stockings and shoes, she curled up on the sofa. Though this room was nowhere near as large as Aidan's suite, it was nevertheless extremely luxurious. More for company than anything else, she turned on the television and muted it.

Two different channels were showing the classic holiday movie *White Christmas*. She paused on one, but it was late in the film. Rosemary Clooney and Bing Crosby had argued and were in the midst of a party, trying to ignore each other. The similarities between the fictional couple and Aidan and Emma were hard to miss.

Even Rosemary's clothing struck a chord, perhaps the reason Emma had ordered this particular style and color for Mia's wedding. She couldn't bring herself to take off the dress yet. The soft green velvet buoyed her spirits and made her feel feminine, despite her sad mood.

When the knock sounded at her door, she couldn't even say she was surprised. But her heart skipped a few beats anyway.

After glancing through the peephole, she unlocked the dead bolt and opened it. Aidan lingered in the hallway, his expression hard to read.

"May I come in?" he asked, his formal tone at odds with the turbulence in his gaze.

"Of course." She stepped back to allow him to enter.

He prowled the confines of her room, hands shoved in his pockets. "I thought you would be angry," he said.

"About what?"

"Don't play dumb. About what I told you this morning. The timing of my engagement."

She debated how to answer him. "We both made mistakes, Aidan. I'm hardly one to criticize."

"Are you even human?" he snapped. "Why aren't you calling me names? Why aren't you throwing things at me?"

"For the same reason that you're in my room right now," she said quietly, her heart breaking. "We don't know how to be together because we ruined the past, but there's something between us that we haven't managed to kill."

He ripped off his tie and ran a hand behind his neck. "I'm leaving in the morning." The dark-eyed gaze dared her to protest.

Emma shook her head vehemently. "Your mother will be crushed, Aidan. She's so looking forward to having her whole family together on Christmas Day. And the special events this week, the children's party, the caroling—please don't leave. I'll go instead. You won't have to see me again."

"Where would you go?"

"Back to England, I suppose."

"But your mother is traveling. That's why Mia and my mom have included you as part of our family this past week."

"It doesn't matter. I'm not a Kavanagh. But you *are*, Aidan. You can't forsake your family this year. If you do, they'll realize that you've never gotten over losing Danielle. And somehow, I think you don't want them to know that."

"What makes you think I've never gotten over Danielle?" Hostility crackled in the words.

"I heard it in your voice this morning. You loved her. And you lost her in a tragic accident. Being here in Silver Glen at Christmas has revived those terrible memories."

Aidan felt as if were being ripped apart. He knew exactly what kind of ass he would be to abandon his family now. But God knows, it seemed like his only choice at the moment.

Allowing Emma to leave Silver Glen would accomplish nothing. He was deliberately fostering the lie that Danielle was his long-lost love...that he had kept an emotional vigil for her all these years.

If that lie was supposed to be a punishment for Emma, then why was *he* the one who felt like hell?

"I can't stay," he said bluntly. "I don't want to."

Emma wrung her hands. "But you have to," she cried. In her bare feet, and with her hair loose around her face, she looked more like the girl he had loved in Oxford.

"Perhaps you could convince me," he said slowly. *Bastard.* His mind was made up, and yet he was willing to use Emma's concern as a bargaining chip. In his defense, if he were never going to see her again, surely it wasn't such a terrible crime to steal one more night in her arms.

She stared at him in silence. Even disheveled and upset, her dignity was unassailable. Inevitably, he felt like a peasant begging for crumbs.

"Say something," he growled. "Yes or no?"

He watched her chest rise and fall. Blue eyes, tinged

with some painful emotion, judged him and found him wanting.

"Yes."

The exultation that swept through his veins was at odds with Emma's expression. Her misery infuriated him. "You don't have to look like a condemned woman on her way to the guillotine. If you don't want me, say so. I'm done playing games."

Her quiet laugh held no amusement at all. "It's not a game, Aidan, believe me."

When she turned on her heel and left him standing alone in the sitting area, he gaped. The bathroom door opened and closed. He heard water running.

Grim-faced, he pounded on the wood. "Quit hiding from me, damn it. And don't undress. That's my job."

She swung open the barrier between them so quickly he almost pitched forward. Her eyes flashed blue fire. "Fine. Have it your way." She stalked toward the bed and stood beside it, her back to him. She had swept her hair over one shoulder, baring the nape of her neck.

A pulse, low and sweet, began to thrum in his veins. He closed the distance between them. "I'm not a big fan of angry sex," he whispered, kissing the top of her spine. "Let's forget everything tonight except for the way we make each other feel."

Glancing at him over her shoulder, she gave him a mocking smile. "You mean the way we want to strangle each other?"

Eighteen

How could she make him want to laugh at the oddest moments? He shook his head. "I don't want to strangle you, Emma. At least not most of the time." He was forced to add that last bit in the interest of honesty.

She sighed and bowed her head, her posture submissive despite her sarcasm. "We seem to make better enemies than we do friends."

The phrasing bothered him. "I don't want to be your friend." These feelings he had were too strong for friendship and too complicated for anything else.

When she turned to face him, he held her by the shoulders…suddenly afraid she would bolt.

Emma was smaller and more vulnerable in her bare feet. She tilted her face up to his and studied him intently, as if trying to see inside his soul. "We were friends once upon a time."

"No." He shook his head, the word vehement. "We were lovers. I never had time to be your friend, because the first day I met you I fell head over heels in lust with you."

"Lust? Not love?"

He had no doubt he was hurting her now. "Lust, Emma," he said flatly, "a young man's physical passion for a beautiful woman. Love lasts. Lust fades. That's how you know the difference. If we ever had a shot at love, it ended before it began."

"And yet you still want me."

Only then did he see the trap he had set for himself. *Damn.* He backtracked quickly. "But only because we've been thrown together in this Christmas-wedding, romantic atmosphere. It's not real. *We're* not real. I wasn't kidding when I said I'm leaving in the morning. And no matter what I intimated, you can't change my mind."

Her small smile was wistful. "Final answer?"

He steeled himself against her charm. "Final answer. Now, do you want me under those conditions, or not?"

Two soft hands cupped his face. Feminine fingers slid cool against his overheated skin. Her eyes searched his. "I love you, Aidan. I know you'd rather not hear it. Perhaps you don't believe it. Or maybe our history discredits what I say. But before you leave, I want you to understand how I feel. I don't know what Danielle has to do with all of this, but she's gone and I'm here. I can't change what happened in England. I'm sorry for that. But please, Aidan. Don't live in the past."

Every word she spoke was a shard of glass, piercing his skin and finding its way to his heart. *Emma loved him.* He wanted to crow with masculine triumph. Beat his chest. Shout it from the rooftops.

Yet in the midst of all that rose a terrible pain. He'd believed her once upon a time. Had handed over his heart with the carelessness of youth, not realizing what he risked.

Three times he'd been betrayed by love. His father had not loved his sons enough to put them before his obsession with finding a lost silver mine. Danielle had died, leaving Aidan with the guilt of knowing he hadn't loved her enough. And Emma…Emma had made him *believe* in love. That was the cruelest blow of all.

His heart encased in ice, he removed her hands from his face and forced her arms behind her back, manacling her wrists with one hand. Her bones, delicate in his grasp, struck him as feminine and helpless. "I don't want you to love me," he said. He crushed his mouth over hers taking the kiss he wanted, feeling the way her lips quivered against his. "All I want is you."

Emma felt the sting of hot tears and blinked them back. She had gambled her all on one roll of the dice and lost. Gasping, she struggled to free her arms. "I want you, too," she whispered. "But I don't like angry sex, either. Come to bed with me, Aidan."

He let her go instantly and stood stone faced as she reached behind her to lower the zipper. When she faltered, he finished the task, holding her hand as she stepped out of a sea of velvet. Carefully, he draped the dress over a nearby chair.

She saw Aidan's eyes burn as he took in the matching bra, undies and garter belt she wore. Her nipples tightened in helpless pleasure. His hot gaze raked her from head to toe, leaving no doubt about his desire for her. A less pragmatic woman might have told herself that love was there buried somewhere under that brusque facade.

But she had come too far to fool herself now. Aidan wanted her body—not her soul, not her heart, not her whispered confession of devotion. And because she loved him enough for two, she would give him everything. If that left her with nothing, she would not cry.

Taking his hand, she climbed into the bed. He was on her instantly, his face flushed, the bulge in his trousers impossible to miss. They kissed wildly. He tasted of coffee and wedding cake.

"God, you drive me insane," he muttered, sucking one nipple through a covering of ecru lace. "Tell me you want me."

She unbuttoned his shirt with fumbling fingers. "I do, Aidan. I do."

The juxtaposition of those five words so close to tonight's wedding ceremony made him wince. Emma saw his involuntary response. Though she hadn't meant to make the connection—obviously, he had.

He rolled away from her long enough to toe off his shoes and unfasten his trousers. When he freed his sex, it was dark red and rigid. "Can't wait," he groaned. "Not this time."

The fact that he didn't bother to finish undressing either of them was as arousing as the touch of his big warm hands on her body. "Then don't," she said, tugging him closer.

He took two seconds to move aside the narrow fabric between her legs. Then he positioned himself and shoved to the hilt in one forceful thrust that smacked the headboard against the wall.

A ragged laugh shook his chest. "Please tell me I didn't bust a hole in the wall. I'd never live it down."

"Do you really care?" She linked her ankles at the small of his back. Neither of them was naked. Yet this was the most intimate time she had shared with him since he'd arrived in Silver Glen.

For a flash—a split second—he looked down at her with the face of the young man who had stolen her heart. Carefree. Happy. Determined to make her his. "No. I suppose not," he muttered.

Keeping his gaze locked on her face, he moved inside her. One steady push after another. His skin heated. So did hers. The pace was lazy, but the look in his eyes was anything but.

"Tell me what you're thinking," she said, the words tumbling out impulsively.

It was a mistake. Instantly, his expression shuttered. His jaw rigid, he closed his eyes and closed her out.

Beneath her fingertips, his hair was soft and springy. Her thighs ached from the effort of clinging to him. He overwhelmed her suddenly, so much a man that she could almost forget the boy.

But even as he stroked her intimately, she felt echoes of sweetness from the past. Almost everything had changed. The world. Their lives. Their bodies. Yet when she closed her eyes and gave herself over to the intense pleasure of the moment, she could pretend she was back in England. Back with a young Aidan. Back under the influence of a love that was innocent and perfect.

Without warning, he shifted suddenly, putting pressure where her body craved his touch. She shivered, so close to her climax that she felt little flutters of anticipation in her sex.

Aidan nipped her earlobe with sharp teeth. "I'll stay 'til morning." The promise was hoarse.

"Yes." It was all she could manage. He took her with him then to a place that held a poignant mixture of regret and physical bliss.

"Emma…"

She couldn't answer him in words. Her throat was too tight. Instead, she rained kisses across his face and canted her hips to take him deeper. He groaned as if he were in pain when he came. And she followed him. But the pleasure was hollow and the end incomplete.

Because what he gave her was not enough. And it never would be.

Nineteen

Aidan huddled into his wool overcoat, turning up the collar in a vain attempt to escape the howling wind from the arctic front that had blasted through New York that morning. Snow fell, but it was dry and icy...nothing to hamper shoppers on the next-to-last shopping day before Christmas.

He'd been walking the streets of Manhattan for hours, his hands and his feet numb. The physical discomfort was some kind of punishment, though he didn't know exactly what for or why. All he knew was that he'd been compelled to leave his apartment in search of relief from his pain.

Booze hadn't done it. Nor back-to-back movies at the closest theater. Not even an impulsive volunteer shift at a local soup kitchen...though that last stint had at least reminded him that holiday misery took on a far more serious face in many corners and back alleys of the city.

Everywhere he went he faced incessant, relentless good cheer. Even the poor and downtrodden found something to smile about in the presence of an artificial tree and modest gifts from local charities.

Aidan was so lost he couldn't even begin to find the path. The life he'd been so pleased with before he decided to spend Christmas at Silver Glen was gone, eradicated by the memories of Emma.

He saw her in every window display, in every shiny package carried by smiling passersby. Everything good and joyful and meaningful about Christmas conspired to remind him that true love meant forgiveness. It was that simple. And that impossible.

He could forgive Emma for just about anything, if the truth were told. But what if he had her and lost her again?

Imagining such a thing made him shudder with a biting chill that was far worse than any winter weather he could conjure. He wanted his old life back...the one where he didn't *have* to feel anything. A satisfying job. A pleasant social life. And plenty of his own company.

Where was *that* Aidan Kavanagh?

At last, when his face was in danger of frostbite, he headed for home. Leftover pizza in the fridge would be his companion tonight. Hopefully, none of his family would ring him up again. He'd already fielded one tearful phone call from his mother that left him feeling like the worst kind of vermin on the planet.

Hell, Dylan had even texted Aidan from his honeymoon and called him a handful of choice names that were spot on. Without even trying, Aidan had become something worse than a Scrooge...if there was such a thing.

When he reached his building, he gave the doorman a fifty-dollar tip and a muttered "Merry Christmas." But he never made it to his apartment. When he stepped off the elevator, Mr. Shapiro, his across-the-hall neighbor, appeared, wild-eyed.

"Help me, Aidan," he cried. "Mrs. S. fell in the kitchen and she's out cold."

Aidan dashed into the apartment with him. "Have you called 911?"

The old man wrung his hands. "Yes. But how long will it take?"

As Aidan knelt beside the white-haired lady, he thought he heard sirens in the distance. "Hang on, Mr. Shapiro. She's breathing." That was a relief. Surely things couldn't be too bad. Had she passed out and fallen, or had she fallen and passed out after she hit her head? "Grab me a pillow and something to cover her with. We don't want her to get cold here on the floor."

Aidan was not a trained medic, but even he could see that the poor guy needed something to do.

Fortunately, the EMTs made it upstairs in the next ten minutes. They loaded the elderly woman onto a gurney and rolled her out into the hall. Mr. Shapiro looked pale enough to pass out himself.

A uniformed kid who looked all of twenty smiled encouragingly. "We're taking her to Lenox Hospital. Don't worry. She seems to be stable."

Suddenly, the professionals were gone. Mr. Shapiro seemed at a loss. He had to be ninety if he were a day. And the poor guy was shaking all over. "Let me get you something to drink," Aidan said. "I think you need to sit down."

Suddenly the man's spine snapped straight. "I'm fine. Take me to see her. Please?"

The naked entreaty in his wrinkled face was impossible to resist, even if Aidan had possessed a heart of stone. "Of course." Aidan pulled out his phone and summoned a cab. When he turned around, Mr. Shapiro was standing in front of a menorah, his lips moving in a quiet prayer.

"Are you ready?" Aidan asked quietly.

The man nodded, plucking his jacket from an antique coat tree. "What should I take for her?" he asked suddenly, the agitation returning to his face.

"If she needs anything later, I'll bring you back here," Aidan promised.

Aidan's apartment was only three blocks from the hospital, but the old man was in no condition to walk, especially not on a night that was as wickedly cold as this one.

The cab ride took no time at all. Aidan paid the fare and jumped out to help Mr. Shapiro. They didn't need a broken bone to add to the evening's trauma.

Inside the hospital, the emergency room admitting nurse was kind but firm. "No one can go back yet. Give them time to assess her condition and make sure she's stable. I'll keep you posted."

Aidan found a couple of chairs, and the two of them sat down. Moments later, Mr. Shapiro's chin rested on his chest. He was either sleeping or praying again.

When he lifted his head and spoke suddenly, it startled Aidan. His gaze was clear and sharp in a face that was worn with time. "We've been married seventy-one years. Came over during the Second World War as newlyweds. Our families pooled money for our passage. We lost them all in the holocaust. Esther is all I have in the world."

"No children?" Aidan asked quietly.

"We couldn't have any."

The silence lengthened after that. Aidan felt the story in his bones. Love and loss. The fabric of life.

At last, when the summons came, Mr. Shapiro jumped to his feet like a young lad.

Aidan touched his arm. "Do you want me to go back with you?"

"I'd like that. You're a good boy."

It had been many years since Aidan had considered himself a boy, but from Mr. Shapiro's perspective, the reference made sense.

They made their way back to a tiny exam room. "I'll

stay in the hall for now," Aidan said. "You tell me if you need me."

The door was open and stayed open, so Aidan hovered just out of sight. When he took a quick peek, he saw Mrs. Shapiro's arms go up to embrace her husband. The look on the old woman's face made something hurt in Aidan's chest. The moment was intensely personal, yet he couldn't look away. For a split second he could see the couple as twenty-somethings, walking the streets of New York arm in arm.

Forcing himself to back up, he leaned against the wall in the corridor and shut his eyes. Five minutes passed, maybe ten, before Mr. Shapiro touched his arm. Though stooped and shuffling, the devoted husband smiled with relief. "It was a mild heart attack," he said. "But she's going to be okay. They're keeping her overnight. She wants me to go home and get some rest."

Aidan nodded. "Sounds good."

In Mr. Shapiro's apartment, Aidan prepared to say his goodbyes. But his neighbor sank into a chair, his gnarled hands gripping the arms white-knuckled. "I'll sit here tonight," he said.

"Why on earth would you do that?"

Mr. Shapiro grimaced. "My hearing's gone. I don't want to miss the phone if the hospital calls. She might need me."

"What if I sleep on your sofa?" Aidan said. "You need to keep up your strength so you can take care of your wife. If the hospital contacts you, I'll make sure to wake you up."

The old man sniffed and wiped his nose with the back of his hand. His rheumy eyes held a wealth of gratitude. "God bless you, Mr. Kavanagh."

"Call me Aidan...please."

"And I'm Howard."

The two men stared at each other, opposites in every way. One young, one old. Two different faiths. One with more family than he knew what to do with. The other alone in the world.

Aidan knew in that moment that something had changed. No longer would he be able to hide behind the anonymity of the city. From the first moment he set eyes on Emma again and realized he still wanted her, the painful process of metamorphosis had begun. The man he had been was gone. But who would surface in his place?

Twenty

Emma locked the door to Silver Memories at four o'clock and pulled the shade over the glass. Fastened to the other side was a notice that said: Closed until January 3rd. It had been a good holiday season for her fledgling business. Though financially it wouldn't have mattered one way or another, she took quiet pride in knowing she had pulled it off.

It was Christmas Eve. Maeve had offered numerous invitations to join the Kavanagh clan for the evening and the next day, but Emma declined them all. Holidays were a family time. If that weren't reason enough, Emma bore the guilt of feeling responsible for Aidan's absence.

Maeve hadn't said much on that subject, but Emma knew the Kavanagh matriarch was deeply disappointed not to have her whole clan together. Dylan and Mia had chosen to take a brief honeymoon with a longer trip planned for later. They had returned midday today and were looking forward to spending Christmas Eve with their daughter and the rest of the family.

Mia hadn't called Emma this afternoon. But she was undoubtedly busy. Perhaps she, too, blamed Emma for Aidan's return to New York. Unless Aidan had made any explanations—and that didn't sound like him at all—none of the Kavanaghs could know for sure what was going on. If, however, Maeve had shared what she knew about seeing Emma at the hotel in the early morning hours, then speculation might have filled in the details.

When the shop was set to rights and the till counted, Emma grabbed her coat and the day's deposit in hopes of making a dash to the bank before it closed. The weather was far balmier today than it had been a week ago. She didn't even need gloves or a hat.

People on the street bustled happily. Some of the die-hard shoppers made last-minute purchases, though like Emma, most business owners were closing up for the long weekend.

With her errand done, Emma found herself walking aimlessly, enjoying the waning sunshine and the scent of wood smoke and evergreen in the air. Even though she felt very much alone, she drew comfort from the cheerful "busy"-ness of small-town life.

She recognized many faces now that she had been around for a few months. Silver Glen was a close-knit community and would be a wonderful spot to put down permanent roots. Emma's mother was already talking about coming over for a visit in the New Year.

And as for Aidan...well, that situation would resolve itself. He didn't come home to visit very often, and when he did, Emma planned to make herself scarce.

Without conscious thought, she found herself in front of the chapel where Dylan and Mia had exchanged vows. The town council had decided long ago to leave the little church unlocked at all times, not only for tourists' benefit, but so that the people of Silver Glen could also stop by and say a prayer or light a candle.

Emma opened the door and closed it behind her. It was cold inside the small sanctuary. With the sun going down, shadows spread long and dark across the wooden pews.

In one corner, a simply decorated tree stood ready for the late night service. Candles burned on the altar already. The evergreen boughs from the wedding still adorned the windows.

She sat down on the second row and ran her hand over the velvet cushion. Several generations of Silver Glen's families had worshipped here. Emma felt an unseen connection to the little abbey back home in the Cotswolds.

Breathing slowly, she took stock of her disappointment and grief. Aidan was not hers. He didn't want anything *from* her. She had been so sure she could convince him they deserved a second chance. But in the end, she was forced to recognize the futility of her hopes and dreams.

Whatever Aidan had felt for her once upon a time didn't matter. All that was important now was for Emma to move on.

Even with all that grown-up reasoning, surely a girl deserved a moment to indulge in self-pity. Resting her arms on the pew in front of her, she buried her face and let the tears fall.

But her catharsis was short.

"Emma…"

When a voice sounded behind her, she jerked upright and wiped her cheeks with trembling fingers before turning around. The shadows were deeper now. Even so, she recognized the figure standing tall and still in the center aisle.

"Aidan?"

"Yep."

He sounded resigned. Or mildly amused. Or maybe both.

"What are you doing here?"

"Here, where? In Silver Glen? Or in this church?"

"Either. Both." She felt dizzy—hot one minute and cold the next.

"It's Christmas Eve."

He said it calmly as if it were perfectly normal for him to be in the one place that held so many dark memories.

When he took two steps in her direction, she held up both hands. "Stop. Don't come any closer."

He obeyed, but he cocked his head. "Are you scared of me, Emma?" Now, he was near enough for the candles on the altar to illuminate his face. In his dear, familiar features she saw fatigue...but something else as well. Light. Steadiness. Contentment. As if someone had wiped away his customary air of cynicism.

"Please don't say whatever you're going to say," she cried. "I can't bear it. I've made my peace with this whole mess. I need you to go away." Ruthlessly, she stomped on the hope that tried to gain a tiny foothold in the hushed atmosphere.

"I can't, Emma. I owe you an apology and an explanation."

"I don't want it. It's too late. Your family is waiting for you up on the mountain. Go."

He took two more steps, his posture confident and relaxed. "I've made you miserable, Emma. I'm so sorry."

Literally backed into a corner because of the closed-in pew, she inhaled sharply. "I need you to respect my wishes." Unfortunately, the words came out quavering and tearful instead of firm and demanding.

Aidan must have made his own interpretation. He crowded her, his scent and the warmth of his body making her pulse jump. "I love you, Emma."

She put her hands over her ears. "No. Don't say things you think I want to hear. You're in a sacred place. Lightning will strike."

He ran his hands down her arms and tugged her by the wrists until she landed firmly against his chest. One of his thighs lodged between hers. His gray sweater was soft against her cheek. If she listened hard enough, she could hear his heart beating in time with hers.

"Neither of us can dance around the facts beneath this roof, can we? It has to be the truth and nothing but the truth." He stroked her hair. "Sit down with me, Emma."

He didn't give her much choice. Tucking her in the crook of the arm, he cuddled her close.

But she couldn't bear it. Jerking away and standing abruptly, she kept him at bay. "Let me out."

"No."

Emma started to shake. "We've come to the end of the road, Aidan. Don't make things worse."

"I was a free agent when I came to England," he said. "Danielle and I had been dating for a long time. But we weren't sure if what we had was merely comfortable. The decision was mutual. We agreed to see other people while I was gone."

"And at Christmas, you went home and realized that you had loved her all along." It seemed petty and wrong to be jealous of a dead woman, but however unpleasant, the reality was clear.

Their intense conversation was interrupted momentarily when the minister came in and turned on the lights. He halted abruptly when he saw them. "Sorry to interrupt. Just getting ready for tonight. Merry Christmas." He departed as quickly as he had come.

The fixtures were original to the building and could only handle low-wattage bulbs, so even now the room was softly lit. Emma wasn't sure if it were better or worse that she could see Aidan's face more clearly. He remained seated, but she sensed his determination.

"When I left England," he said, "I was a mess. But I was a guy, so I wasn't about to let anyone know how I felt."

"I called you and sent emails for weeks, but you didn't answer."

"In case you haven't noticed, I'm a stubborn man. Even worse, back then I was too young to know that few situations in life are entirely black or white. You had betrayed me. That was all I knew. I got back to campus and saw Danielle. She represented everything uncomplicated and easy. Without thinking about the consequences, I proposed."

"And she accepted."

"Yes. It was something we had thought about for a long time, so the proposal was almost anticlimactic. We made plans to go to Silver Glen and spend Christmas with my family. But by the time we made it to North Carolina, I realized I had made a mistake."

"What kind of mistake?"

"I *loved* her, but I wasn't *in* love with her. I knew I couldn't drag things out, so as soon as the holidays were over, I planned to tell her the truth and to apologize."

"But she died."

After all this time, his face reflected a pain that was still deep. "I failed her on so many levels."

"But you made her happy, too."

"God, I hope so." He raked his hands through his hair, leaning forward with his elbows on his knees. "As soon as I broke things off with Danielle, I planned to go back to England and confront you...to fight for what we had."

"But you didn't..."

"I couldn't." He sat back against the pew, his expression bleak as he stared at her. "How was it fair for me to reach for happiness when her life was over?"

Hearing that Aidan had wanted to come back to England healed some of the raw places in Emma's heart. "I'm so sorry."

He shrugged. "It all happened a long time ago."

"Is it my turn now?" she asked quietly. "Will you let me tell you my story?"

He stood up and took her in his arms a second time, smoothing the hair from her face. "It doesn't matter, Emma. Whatever mistakes you made back then were no better or worse than mine. It's over." She saw the love in his eyes, but she couldn't let him believe that she had betrayed him.

It was her turn to pull him down onto the pew. She half turned to face him, taking his hands in hers. "Richard lied to you."

Aidan frowned. "He introduced himself to me as your fiancé. And when I looked at you to ask if it was true, you hesitated. I saw in your face that you knew who he was and you weren't surprised."

"I wasn't surprised, because my father had been telling Richard for two years that if he only waited for me to finish college, my father was sure that I would consent to an engagement."

"And would you have? Had it not been for me?"

"No," she said firmly. "I'd made that clear to my father, but Richard's estate adjoined ours, and my father had visions of joining two great families, even though Richard was a decade older than I was. Poor Richard was not a malicious man, but he let himself be manipulated by my father. When Daddy got wind of my romance with you, he sent Richard to London to stake a claim."

Aidan closed his eyes momentarily as a pained look crossed his face. "So none of it was true…"

"No. But I handled things poorly. When you asked me

if Richard was my fiancé, I should have denied it immediately. I'd been brought up to keep the peace whenever possible, though. I didn't want to hurt Richard's feelings, because he hadn't really done anything wrong except for letting my father fill his head with nonsense. But in my naïveté, I hurt the one person I loved more than anything else in the world."

"Was that incident what caused the rift with your father?"

"Yes. I was furious and distraught and completely at a loss as to what to do. He ruined my life."

"Or maybe you and I ruined our lives together."

She grimaced, nodding. "A decade lost."

Aidan cupped her face in his hands. "That decade taught me some important lessons, my love. I've come to understand that forgiveness has to be unconditional. And it's finally been pounded into my hard skull that the people who love me don't deserve to be shut out…that our connection and commitment to one another make life rich." He paused, his throat working. "I won't ever let you go again."

Emma trembled, afraid to assume too much. "Meaning what, Aidan?"

He kissed her softly on the lips, a reverent, sweet caress. When he pulled back, his eyes gleamed. "It means that you're going to marry me. The sooner, the better. My work, your antique business—we can handle those details as we go along."

Joy welled in her chest. "Don't I get a say in the matter?"

"Not at all. This is nonnegotiable. But I think we'd better get out of here quickly."

"Why?"

"Because the thoughts I'm having about you right now are definitely not appropriate in this setting."

Outside, he took her in his arms again, and kissing her deeply, backed her up against the door of the church and sealed his vow. He had come so close to losing her a second time, it terrified him. "I love you, Em. Body and soul. I never stopped. I've lied to myself for years, living on the surface of life, never willing to admit that there was more."

Her smile was radiant, warming him even as the chill of night swirled around him. "You're the best Christmas present I've ever received. I love you, too, Aidan. My apartment is close. What if we go there and I show you exactly how much?"

He shuddered, already imagining the feel of her body pressed against his. "Hold that thought, my little tease. There's one thing we have to do first."

Her eyes widened in comprehension. "Of course…"

The Silver Beeches Lodge was booked to capacity. Aidan held Emma's hand as they walked up the steps. As the doorman welcomed then into the lobby, Emma hung back.

"I'm nervous," she whispered.

"Why, my love? You've already met everyone."

"But it's Christmas. And I'm the reason you almost missed it."

"You're also the reason I came back."

Emma's brow furrowed as they headed back toward the small dining room that had been set aside for the Kavanagh celebration. "I forgot to ask. Did you have some kind of epiphany about us?"

He stood in the doorway, his arm around her waist

and surveyed his loud, wonderful family before they had a chance to notice him. The remnants of dinner littered the large table. In the far corner, a mountain of brightly wrapped gifts waited to be opened.

Pressing a kiss to the top of Emma's head, Aidan paused to savor the incredible feeling of happiness and joy that swept over him. "Let's just say that I did the math, and I realized if we start right now, we can still make it to our fiftieth wedding anniversary."

Emma leaned into him, the woman he'd always loved and needed. "Merry Christmas, Aidan," she said.

"Merry Christmas, my English rose…"

* * * * *

"That comes naturally to you, doesn't it?"

"Rescuing damsels in distress?"

"No, that slow, sexy, let's-get-naked grin."

"Is that the message it sends?"

"Yes."

"Is it working?"

She pursed her lips. "No."

"Ah, *drágám*," he said, laughter springing into his eyes, "every time you do that, I want to do this."

She'd thought it would end there. One touch. One pass of his mouth over hers. It *should* have ended there. Traffic was coursing along the busy street, for pity's sake. A streetcar clanged by. Yet Natalie didn't move as his arm went around her waist, drawing her closer, while her pulse pounded in her veins.

She was breathing hard when Dominic lifted his head. So was he, she saw with intense relief. She couldn't remember if she'd ever kissed a man on a public sidewalk in the middle of the afternoon before. She didn't think so. Somehow it didn't seem like something she would do. If she had, though, she hoped it hit him with the same impact it had her.

* * *

Her Unforgettable Royal Lover
is part of The Duchess Diaries series: Two royal
granddaughters on their way to happily-ever-after!

HER
UNFORGETTABLE
ROYAL LOVER

BY
MERLINE LOVELACE

MILLS & BOON

Published in Great Britain 2014
by Mills & Boon, an imprint of Harlequin (UK) Limited,
Eton House, 18-24 Paradise Road, Richmond, Surrey, TW9 1SR

© 2014 Merline Lovelace

ISBN: 978-0-263-91487-0

51-1214

Harlequin (UK) Limited's policy is to use papers that are natural, renewable and recyclable products and made from wood grown in sustainable forests. The logging and manufacturing processes conform to the legal environmental regulations of the country of origin.

Printed and bound in Spain
by CPI, Barcelona

A career Air Force officer, **Merline Lovelace** served at bases all over the world. When she hung up her uniform for the last time she decided to combine her love of adventure with a flair for storytelling, basing many of her tales on her own experiences in uniform. Since then she's produced more than ninety action-packed sizzlers, many of which have made the *USA TODAY* and Waldenbooks bestseller lists. Over eleven million copies of her books are available in some thirty countries.

When she's not tied to her keyboard, Merline enjoys reading, chasing little white balls around the fairways of Oklahoma and traveling to new and exotic locales with her handsome husband, Al. Check her website at www.merlinelovelace.com or friend her on Facebook for news and information about her latest releases.

To Neta and Dave, friends, traveling buds and the source of all kinds of fodder for my books. Thanks for the info on research grants and nasty bugs, Neta!

Prologue

Who would have imagined my days would become this rich and full, and at such a late point in my life! My darling granddaughter Sarah and her husband, Dev, have skillfully blended marriage with their various enterprises, their charitable work and their travels to all parts of the world. Yet Sarah still finds time to involve me in the book she's writing on lost treasures of the art world. My input has been limited, to be sure, but I've very much enjoyed being part of such an ambitious undertaking.

And Eugenia, my carefree, high-spirited Eugenia, has surprised herself by becoming the most amazing wife and mother. Her twins are very much like she was at that age. Bright-eyed and lively, with very distinct personalities. And best of all, her husband, Jack, is being considered for appointment as US Ambassador to the United Nations. If he's confirmed, he and Gina and the babies would live only a few blocks away.

Until that happens, I have the company of my longtime friend and companion, Maria. And Anastazia, my lovely, so serious Anastazia. Zia's in her second year of a residency in pediatric medicine and I played shamelessly on our somewhat tenuous kinship to convince her to live with me for the three-year program. She wears herself to the bone, poor dear, but Maria and I see that she eats well and gets at least some rest.

It's her brother, Dominic, I fret about. Dom insists he's not ready to settle down, and why should he with all the women who throw themselves at him? His job worries me, however. It's too dangerous, too high-risk. I do wish he would quit working undercover, and may have found just the enticement to encourage him to do so. How surprised he'll be when I tell him about the document Sarah's clever research assistant has discovered!

From the diary of Charlotte,
Grand Duchess of Karlenburgh

One

August was slamming New York City when Dominic St. Sebastian climbed out of a cab outside the castle-like Dakota. Heat waves danced like demented demons above the sidewalks. Across the street, moisture-starved leaves drifted like yellowed confetti from the trees in Central Park. Even the usual snarl of cabs and limos and sightseeing buses cruising the Upper West Side seemed lethargic and sluggish.

The same couldn't be said for the Dakota's doorman. As dignified as ever in his lightweight summer uniform, Jerome abandoned his desk to hold the door for the new arrival.

"Thanks," Dom said with the faint accent that marked him as European despite the fact that English came as naturally to him as his native Hungarian. Shifting his carry-all to his right hand, he clapped the older man's shoulder with his left. "How's the duchess?"

"As strong-willed as ever. She wouldn't listen to the rest of us, but Zia finally convinced her to forego her daily constitutional during this blistering heat."

Dom wasn't surprised his sister had succeeded where others failed. Anastazia Amalia Julianna St. Sebastian combined the slashing cheekbones, exotic eyes and stunning beauty of a supermodel with the tenacity of a bulldog.

And now his beautiful, tenacious sister was living with

Grand Duchess Charlotte. Zia and Dom had met their long-lost relative for the first time only last year and formed an instant bond. So close a bond that Charlotte had invited Zia to live at the Dakota during her pediatric residency at Mt. Sinai.

"Has my sister started her new rotation?" Dom asked while he and Jerome waited for the elevator.

He didn't doubt the doorman would know. He had the inside track on most of the Dakota's residents but kept a close eye on his list of favorites. Topping that list were Charlotte St. Sebastian and her two granddaughters, Sarah and Gina. Zia had recently been added to the select roster.

"She started last week," Jerome advised. "She doesn't say so, but I can see oncology is hard on her. Would be on anyone, diagnosing and treating all those sick children. And the hospital works the residents to the bone, which doesn't help." He shook his head, but brightened a moment later. "Zia wrangled this afternoon off, though, when she heard you were flying in. Oh, and Lady Eugenia is here, too. She arrived last night with the twins."

"I haven't seen Gina and the twins since the duchess's birthday celebration. The girls must be, what? Six or seven months old now?"

"Eight." Jerome's seamed face folded into a grin. Like everyone else, he'd fallen hard for an identical pair of rose-bud mouths, lake-blue eyes and heads topped with their mother's spun-sugar, silvery-blond curls.

"Lady Eugenia says they're crawling now," he warned. "Better watch where you step and what you step in."

"I will," Dom promised with a grin.

As the elevator whisked him to the fifth floor, he remembered the twins as he'd last seen them. Cooing and blowing bubbles and waving dimpled fists, they'd already developed into world-class heartbreakers.

They'd since developed two powerful sets of lungs,

Dom discovered when a flushed and flustered stranger yanked open the door.

"It's about time! We've been…"

She stopped, blinking owlishly behind her glasses, while a chorus of wails rolled down the marble-tiled foyer.

"You're not from Osterman's," she said accusingly.

"The deli? No, I'm not."

"Then who…? Oh! You're Zia's brother." Her nostrils quivered, as if she'd suddenly caught a whiff of something unpleasant. "The one who goes through women like a hot knife through butter."

Dom hooked a brow but couldn't dispute the charge. He enjoyed the company of women. Particularly the generously curved, pouty-lipped, out-for-a-good-time variety.

The one facing him now certainly didn't fall into the first two of those categories. Not that he could see more than a suggestion of a figure inside her shapeless linen dress and boxy jacket. Her lips were anything but pouty, however. Pretty much straight-lined, as a matter of fact, with barely disguised disapproval.

"Igen," Dom agreed lazily in his native Hungarian. "I'm Dominic. And you are?"

"Natalie," she bit out, wincing as the howls behind her rose to high-pitched shrieks. "Natalie Clark. Come in, come in."

Dom had spent almost seven years now as an Interpol agent. During that time, he'd helped take down his share of drug traffickers, black marketeers and the scum who sold young girls and boys to the highest bidders. Just last year he'd helped foil a kidnapping and murder plot against Gina's husband right here in New York City. But the scene that greeted him as he paused at the entrance to the duchess's elegant sitting room almost made him turn tail and run.

A frazzled Gina was struggling to hang on to a red-faced, furiously squirming infant in a frilly dress and a lacy headband with a big pink bow. Zia had her arms full with the second, equally enraged and similarly attired baby. The duchess sat straight-backed and scowling in regal disapproval, while the comfortably endowed Honduran who served as her housekeeper and companion stood at the entrance to the kitchen, her face screwed into a grimace as the twins howled their displeasure.

Thankfully, the duchess reached her limit before Dom was forced to beat a hasty retreat. Her eyes snapping, she gripped the ivory handle of her cane in a blue-veined, white-knuckled fist.

"Charlotte!" The cane thumped the floor. Once. Twice. "Amalia! You will kindly cease that noise at once."

Dom didn't know whether it was the loud banging or the imperious command that did the trick, but the howls cut off like a faucet and surprise leaped into four tear-drenched eyes. Blessed silence reigned except for the babies' gulping hiccups.

"Thank you," the duchess said coolly. "Gina, why don't you and Zia take the girls to the nursery? Maria will bring their bottles as soon as Osterman's delivers the milk."

"It should be here any moment, *Duquesa*." Using her ample hips, the housekeeper backed through the swinging door to the kitchen. "I'll get the bottles ready."

Gina was headed for the hall leading to the bedrooms when she spotted her cousin four or five times removed. "Dom!" She blew him an air kiss. "I'll talk to you when I get the girls down."

"I, as well," his sister said with a smile in her dark eyes.

He set down his carryall and crossed the elegant sitting room to kiss the duchess's cheeks. Her paper-thin skin carried the faint scent of gardenias, and her eyes were cloudy with age but missed little. Including the wince he couldn't quite hide when he straightened.

"Zia told me you'd been knifed. Again."

"Just nicked a rib."

"Yes, well, we need to talk about these nicked ribs and bullet wounds you collect with distressing frequency. But first, pour us a…" She broke off at the buzz of the doorbell. "That must be the delivery. Natalie, dear, would you sign for it and take the milk to Maria?"

"Of course."

Dom watched the stranger head back to the foyer and turned to the duchess. "Who is she?"

"A research assistant Sarah hired to help with her book. Her name's Natalie Clark and she's part of what I want to talk to you about."

Dominic knew Sarah, the duchess's older granddaughter, had quit her job as an editor at a glossy fashion magazine when she married self-made billionaire Devon Hunter. He also knew Sarah had expanded on her degree in art history from the Sorbonne by hitting every museum within taxi distance when she accompanied Dev on his business trips around the world. That—and the fact that hundreds of years of art had been stripped off walls and pedestals when the Soviets overran the Duchy of Karlenburgh decades ago—had spurred Sarah to begin documenting what she learned about the lost treasures of the art world. It also prompted a major New York publisher to offer a fat, six-figure advance if she turned her notes into a book.

What Dom *didn't* know was what Sarah's book had to do with him, much less the female now making her way to the kitchen with an Osterman's delivery sack in hand. Sarah's research assistant couldn't be more than twenty-five or twenty-six but she dressed like a defrocked nun. Mousy-brown hair clipped at her neck. No makeup. Square glasses with thick lenses. Sensible flats and that shapeless linen dress.

When the kitchen door swung behind her, Dom had to

ask. "How is this Natalie Clark involved in what you want to talk to me about?"

The duchess waived an airy hand. "Pour us a *pálinka*, and I'll tell you."

"Should you have brandy? Zia said in her last email that..."

"Pah! Your sister fusses more than Sarah and Gina combined."

"With good reason, yes? She's a doctor. She has a better understanding of your health issues."

"Dominic." The duchess leveled a steely stare. "I've told my granddaughters, I've told your sister, and I'll tell you. The day I can't handle an aperitif before dinner is the day you may bundle me off to a nursing home."

"The day you can't drink us all under the table, you mean." Grinning, Dom went to the sideboard and lined up two cut-crystal snifters.

Ah, but he was a handsome devil, Charlotte thought with a sigh. Those dark, dangerous eyes. The slashing brows and glossy black hair. The lean, rangy body inherited from the wiry horsemen who'd swept down from the Steppes on their sturdy ponies and ravaged Europe. Magyar blood ran in his veins, as it did in hers, combined with but not erased by centuries of intermarriage among the royals of the once-great Austro-Hungarian Empire.

The Duchy of Karlenburgh had been part of that empire. A tiny part, to be sure, but one with a history that had stretched back for seven hundred years. It now existed only in dusty history books, and one of those books was about to change Dominic's life. Hopefully for the better, although Charlotte doubted he would think so. Not at first. But with time...

She glanced up as the instigator of that change returned to the sitting room. "Ah, here you are, Natalie. We're just about to have an aperitif. Will you join us?"

"No, thank you."

Dom paused with his hand on the stopper of the Bohemian crystal decanter he and Zia had brought the duchess as a gift for their first meeting. Thinking to soften the researcher's stiff edges, he gave her a slow smile.

"Are you sure? This apricot brandy is a specialty of my country."

"I'm sure."

Dom blinked. *Mi a fene!* Did her nose just quiver again? As though she'd picked up another bad odor? What the hell kind of tales had Zia and/or Gina fed the woman?

Shrugging, he splashed brandy into two snifters and carried one to the duchess. But if anyone could use a shot of *pálinka*, he thought as he folded his long frame into the chair beside his great-aunt's, the research assistant could. The double-distilled, explosively potent brandy would set more than her nostrils to quivering.

"How long will you be in New York?" the duchess asked after downing a healthy swallow.

"Only tonight. I have a meeting in Washington tomorrow."

"Hmm. I should wait until Zia and Gina return to discuss this with you, but they already know about it."

"About what?"

"The Edict of 1867." She set her brandy aside, excitement kindling in her faded blue eyes. "As you may remember from your history books, war with Prussia forced Emperor Franz Joseph to cede certain concessions to his often rambunctious Hungarian subjects. The Edict of 1867 gave Hungary full internal autonomy as long as it remained part of the empire for purposes of war and foreign affairs."

"Yes, I know this."

"Did you also know Karlenburgh added its own codicil to the agreement?"

"No, I didn't, but then I would have no reason to," Dom

said gently. "Karlenburgh is more your heritage than mine, Duchess. My grandfather—your husband's cousin—left Karlenburgh Castle long before I was born."

And the duchy had ceased to exist soon after that. World War I had carved up the once-mighty Austro-Hungarian Empire. World War II, the brutal repression of the Cold War era, the abrupt dissolution of the Soviet Union and vicious attempts at "ethnic cleansing" had all added their share of upheavals to the violently changing political landscape of Eastern Europe.

"Your grandfather took his name and his bloodline with him when he left Karlenburgh, Dominic." Charlotte leaned closer and gripped his arm with fingers that dug in like talons. "You inherited that bloodline and that name. You're a St. Sebastian. And the present Grand Duke of Karlenburgh."

"What?"

"Natalie found it during her research. The codicil. Emperor Franz Joseph reconfirmed that the St. Sebastians would carry the titles of Grand Duke and Duchess forever and in perpetuity in exchange for holding the borders of the empire. The empire doesn't exist anymore, but despite all the wars and upheavals, that small stretch of border between Austria and Hungary remains intact. So, therefore, does the title."

"On paper, perhaps. But the lands and outlying manors and hunting lodges and farmlands that once comprised the duchy have long since been dispersed and redeeded. It would take a fortune and decades in court to reclaim any of them."

"The lands and manor houses are gone, yes. Not the title. Sarah will become Grand Duchess when I die. Or Gina if, God forbid, something should happen to her sister. But they married commoners. According to the laws of primogeniture, their husbands can't assume the title of

Grand Duke. Until either Sarah or Gina has a son, or their daughters grow up and marry royalty, the only one who can claim it is you, Dom."

Right, he wanted to drawl. That and ten dollars would get him a half-decent espresso at one of New York's over-priced coffee bars.

He swallowed the sarcasm but lobbed a quick glare at the woman wearing an expression of polite interest, as if she hadn't initiated this ridiculous conversation with her research. He'd have a thing or two to say to Ms. Clark later about getting the duchess all stirred up over an issue that was understandably close to her heart but held little relevance to the real world. Particularly the world of an undercover operative.

He allowed none of those thoughts to show in his face as he folded Charlotte's hand between his. "I appreciate the honor you want to bestow on me, Duchess. I do. But in my line of work, I can hardly hang a title around my neck."

"Yes, I want to speak to you about that, too. You've been living on the edge for too many years now. How long can you continue before someone nicks more than a rib?"

"Exactly what I've been asking him," Zia commented as she swept into the sitting room with her long-legged stride.

She'd taken advantage of her few hours away from the hospital to pull on her favorite jeans and a summer tank top in blistering red. The rich color formed a striking contrast to her dark eyes and shoulder-length hair as black and glossy as her brother's. When he stood and opened his arms, she walked into them and hugged him with the same fierce affection he did her.

She was only four years younger than Dom, twenty-seven to his thirty-one, but he'd assumed full responsibility for his teenage sibling when their parents died. He'd been there, too, standing round-the-clock watch beside her hospital bed when she'd almost bled to death after a uterine cyst ruptured her first year at university. The complications that resulted from the rupture had changed her life in so many ways.

What hadn't changed was Dom's bone-deep protectiveness. No matter where his job took him or what dangerous enterprise he was engaged in, Zia had only to send a coded text and he would contact her within hours, if not minutes. Although he always shrugged off the grimmer aspects of his work, she'd wormed enough detail out of him over the years to add her urging to that of the duchess.

"You don't have to stay undercover. Your boss at Interpol told me he has a section chief job waiting for you whenever you want it."

"You can see me behind a desk, Zia-mia?"

"Yes!"

"What a poor liar you are." He made a fist and delivered a mock punch to her chin. "You wouldn't last five minutes under interrogation."

Gina had returned during their brief exchange. Shoving back her careless tumble of curls, she entered the fray. "Jack says you would make an excellent liaison to the State Department. In fact, he wants to talk to you about that tomorrow, when you're in Washington."

"With all due respect to your husband, Lady Eugenia, I'm not ready to join the ranks of bureaucrats."

His use of her honorific brought out one of Gina's merry, irreverent grins. "Since we're tossing around titles here, has Grandmother told you about the codicil?"

"She has."

"Well then…" Fanning out the skirts of her leafy-green sundress, she sank to the floor in an elegant, if theatrical, curtsy.

Dom muttered something distinctly unroyal under his breath. Fortunately, the Clark woman covered it when she pushed to her feet.

"Excuse me. This is a family matter. I'll leave you to discuss it and go back to my research. You'll call me when it's convenient for us to continue our interview, Duchess?"

"I will. You're in New York until Thursday, is that correct?"

"Yes, ma'am. Then I fly to Paris to compare notes with Sarah."

"We'll get together again before then."

"Thank you." She bent to gather the bulging briefcase that had been resting against the leg of her chair. Straightening, she nudged up her glasses back into place. "It was good to meet you, Dr. St. Sebastian, and to see you again, Lady Eugenia."

Her tone didn't change. Neither did her polite expression. But Dom didn't miss what looked very much like a flicker of disdain in her brown eyes when she dipped her head in his direction.

"Your Grace."

He didn't alter his expression, either, but both his sister and his cousin recognized the sudden, silky note in his voice.

"I'll see you to the door."

"Thank you, but I'll let myself… Oh. Uh, all right."

Natalie blinked owlishly behind her glasses. The smile didn't leave Dominic St. Sebastian's ridiculously handsome face and the hand banding her upper arm certainly wouldn't leave any bruises. That didn't make her feel any less like a suspect being escorted from the scene of a crime, however. Especially when he paused with a hand on the door latch and skewered her with a narrow glance from those dark eyes.

"Where are you staying?"

"I beg your pardon?"

"Where are you staying?"

Good Lord! Was he hitting on her? No, he couldn't

be! She was most definitely not his type. According to Zia's laughing reports, her bachelor brother went for leggy blondes or voluptuous brunettes. A long string of them, judging by the duchess's somewhat more acerbic references to his sowing altogether too many wild oats.

That more than anything had predisposed Natalie to dislike Dominic St. Sebastian sight unseen. She'd fallen for a too-handsome, too-smooth operator like him once and would pay for that stupidity for the rest of her life. Still, she tried, she really tried, to keep disdain from seeping into her voice as she tugged her arm free.

"I don't believe where I'm staying is any of your business."

"You've made it my business with this nonsense about a codicil."

Whoa! He could lock a hand around her arm. He could perp-walk her to the door. He could *not* disparage her research.

Thoroughly indignant, Natalie returned fire. "It's not nonsense, as you would know if you'd displayed any interest in your family's history. I suggest you show a little more respect for your heritage, *Your Grace*, and for the duchess."

He muttered something in Hungarian she suspected was not particularly complimentary and bent an elbow against the doorjamb, leaning close. Too close! She could see herself in his pupils, catch the tang of apricot brandy on his breath.

"My respect for Charlotte is why you and I are going to have a private chat, yes? I ask again, where are you staying?"

His Magyar roots were showing, Natalie noted with a skitter of nerves. The slight thickening of his accent should have warned her. Should have sent her scurrying back into the protective shell she'd lived inside for so long it was now as much a part of her life as her drab hair and clothes. But some spark of her old self tilted her chin.

"You're supposed to be a big, bad secret agent," she said coolly. "Dig out the information yourself."

He would, Dom vowed as the door closed behind her with a small thud. He most definitely would.

Two

All it took was one call to arm Dom with the essential information. Natalie Elizabeth Clark. Born Farmington, Illinois. Age twenty-nine, height five feet six inches, brown hair, brown eyes. Single. Graduated University of Michigan with a degree in library science, specializing in archives and presentation. Employed as an archivist with Centerville Community College for three years, the State of Illinois Civil Service Board for four. Currently residing in L.A. where she was employed by Sarah St. Sebastian as a personal assistant.

An archivist. Christ!

Dom shook his head as his cab picked its way downtown later that evening. He envisioned a small cubicle, her head bent toward a monitor screen, her eyes staring through those thick lenses at an endless stream of documents to be verified, coded and electronically filed. And she'd done it for seven years! Dom would have committed ritual hara-kiri after a week. No wonder she'd jumped when Sarah put out feelers for an assistant to help research her book.

Ms. Clark was still running endless computer searches. Still digging through archives, some electronic, some paper. But at least now she was traveling the globe to get at the most elusive of those documents. And, Dom guessed as his cab pulled up at the W New York, doing that traveling on a very generous expense account.

He didn't bother to stop at the front desk. His phone call had confirmed that Ms. Clark had checked into room 1304 two days ago. And a tracking program developed for the military and now in use by a number of intelligence agencies confirmed her cell phone was currently emitting signals from this location.

Two minutes later Dom rapped on her door. The darkening of the peephole told him she was as careful in her personal life as she no doubt was in her work. He smiled his approval, then waited for the door to open.

When neither of those events happened, he rapped again. Still no response.

"It's Dominic St. Sebastian, Ms. Clark. I know you're in there. You may as well open the door."

She complied but wasn't happy about it. "It's generally considered polite to call ahead for an appointment instead of just showing up at someone's hotel room."

The August humidity had turned her shapeless linen dress into a roadmap of wrinkles, and her sensible pumps had been traded for hotel flip-flops. She'd freed her hair from the clip, though, and it framed her face in surprisingly thick, soft waves as she tipped Dom a cool look through her glasses.

"May I ask why you felt compelled to come all the way downtown to speak with me?"

Dom had been asking himself the same thing. He'd confirmed this woman was who she said she was and verified her credentials. The truth was he probably wouldn't have given Natalie Clark a second thought if not for those little nose quivers.

He'd told himself the disdain she'd wiped off her face so quickly had triggered his cop's instinct. Most of the scum he'd dealt with over the years expressed varying degrees of contempt for the police, right up until they were cuffed and led away. His sister, however, would probably insist those small hints of derision had pricked his male ego. It was true that Dom could never resist a challenge. But despite Zia's frequent assertions to the contrary, he didn't try to finesse *every* female who snagged his attention into bed.

Still, he was here and here he intended to remain until he satisfied his curiosity about this particular female. "I'd like more information on this codicil you've uncovered, Ms. Clark."

"I'm sure you would. I'll be happy to email you the documentation I've…"

"I prefer to see what you have now. May I come in, or do we continue our discussion in the hall?"

Her mouth pursing, she stood aside. Her obvious reluctance intrigued Dom. And, all right, stirred his hunting instincts. Too bad he had that meeting at the National Central Bureau—the US branch of Interpol—in Washington tomorrow. It might have been interesting to see what it would take to get those prim, disapproving lips to unpurse and sigh his name.

He skimmed a glance around the room. Two queen beds, one with her open briefcase and neat stacks of files on it. An easy chair angled to get the full benefit of the high-definition flat-screen. A desk with a black ergonomic chair, another stack of files and a seventeen-inch laptop open to a webpage displaying a close-up of an elaborately jeweled egg.

"One of the Fabergé eggs?" he asked, moving closer to admire the sketch of a gem-encrusted egg nested in a two-wheeled gold cart.

"Yes."

"The Cherub with a Chariot," Dom read, "a gift from Tsar Alexander III to his wife, Maria Fyodorovna for Easter, 1888. One of eight Fabergé eggs currently lost."

He glanced at the researcher hovering protectively close to her work, as if to protect it from prying eyes.

"And you're on the hunt for it?"

"I'm documenting its history."

Her hand crept toward the laptop's lid, as if itching to slam it down.

"What have you found so far?"

The lips went tight again, but Dom was too skilled at interrogations to let her off the hook. He merely waited until she gave a grudging nod.

"Documents show it was at Gatchina Palace in 1891, and was one of forty or so eggs sent to the armory at the Kremlin after the 1917 Revolution. Some experts believe it was purchased in the 1930s by Victor and Armand Hammer. But…"

He could see when her fascination with her work overcame her reluctance to discuss it. Excitement snuck into her voice and added a spark to her brown eyes. Her very velvety, very enticing brown eyes, he thought as she tugged off her glasses and twirled them by one stem.

"I found a reference to a similar egg sold at an antiques shop in Paris in 1930. A shop started by a Russian émigré. No one knows how the piece came into his possession, but I've found a source I want to check when I'm in Paris next week. It may…"

She caught herself and brought the commentary to an abrupt halt. The twirling ceased. The glasses whipped up, and wariness replaced the excitement in the doe-brown eyes.

"I'm not trying to pump you for information," Dom assured her. "Interpol has a whole division devoted to lost, stolen or looted cultural treasures, you know."

"Yes, I do."

"Since you're heading over to Paris, I can set up a meeting for you with the division chief, if you like."

The casual offer seemed to throw her off balance. "I… Uh… I have access to their database but…" Her glance went to the screen, then came back to Dom. "I would appreciate that," she said stiffly. "Thank you."

A grin sketched across his face. "There now. That didn't taste so bad going down, did it?"

Instant alarms went off in Natalie's head. She could almost hear their raucous clanging as she fought to keep her chin high and her expression politely remote. She would *not* let a lazy grin and a pair of glinting, bedroom eyes seduce her. Not again. Never again.

"I'll give you my business card," she said stiffly. "Your associate can reach me anytime at my mobile number or by email."

"So cool, so polite." He didn't look at the embossed card she retrieved from her briefcase, merely slipped it into the pocket of his slacks. "What is it about me you don't like?"

How about everything!

"I don't know you well enough to dislike you." She should have left it there. Would have, if he hadn't been standing so close. "Nor," she added with a shrug, "do I wish to."

She recognized her error at once. Men like Dominic St. Sebastian would take that as a challenge. Hiding a grimace, Natalie attempted some quick damage control.

"You said you wanted more information on the codicil. I have a scanned copy on my computer. I'll pull it up and print out a copy for you."

She pulled out the desk chair. He was forced to step back so she could sit, but any relief she might have gained from the small separation dissipated when he leaned a hand on the desk and bent to peer over her shoulder. His breath stirred the loose tendrils at her temple, moved lower, washed warm and hot against her ear. She managed to keep from hunching her shoulder but it took an iron effort of will.

"So that's it," he said as the scanned image appeared, "the document the duchess thinks makes me a duke?"

"Grand Duke," Natalie corrected. "Excuse me, I need to check the paper feed in the printer."

There was nothing wrong with the paper feed. Her little portable printer had been cheerfully spitting out copies before St. Sebastian so rudely interrupted her work. But it was the best excuse she could devise to get him to stop breathing down her neck!

He took the copy and made himself comfortable in the armchair while he tried to decipher the spidery script. Natalie was tempted to let him suffer through the embellished High German, but relented and printed out a translation.

"I stumbled across the codicil while researching the Canaletto that once hung in the castle at Karlenburgh," she told him. "I'd found an obscure reference to the painting in the Austrian State Archives in Vienna."

She couldn't resist an aside. So many uninformed thought her profession dry and dull. They couldn't imagine the thrill that came with following one fragile thread to another, then another, and another.

"The archives are so vast, it's taken years to digitize them all. But the results are amazing. Really amazing. The oldest document dates back to 816."

He nodded, not appearing particularly interested in this bit of trivia that Natalie found so fascinating. Deflated, she got back to the main point.

"The codicil was included in a massive collection of letters, charters, treaties and proclamations relating to the Austro-Prussian War. Basically, it states what the duchess told you earlier. Emperor Franz Joseph granted the St. Sebastians the honor of Karlenburgh in perpetuity in exchange for defending the borders for the empire. The duchy may not exist anymore and so many national lines have been redrawn. That section of the border between

Austria and Hungary has held steady, however, through all the wars and invasions. So, therefore, has the title."

He made a noise that sounded close to a snort. "You and I both know this document isn't worth the paper you've just printed it on."

Offended on behalf of archivists everywhere, she cocked her chin. "The duchess disagrees."

"Right, and that's what you and I need to talk about."

He stuffed the printout in his pocket and pinned her with a narrow stare. No lazy grin now. No laughter in those dark eyes.

"Charlotte St. Sebastian barely escaped Karlenburgh with her life. She carried her baby in her arms while she marched on foot for some twenty or thirty miles through winter snows. I know the story is that she managed to bring away a fortune in jewels, as well. I'm not confirming the story..."

He didn't have to. Natalie had already pieced it together from her own research and from the comments Sarah had let drop about the personal items the duchess had disposed of over the years to raise her granddaughters in the style she considered commensurate with their rank.

"...but I am warning you not to take advantage of the duchess's very natural desire to see her heritage continue."

"Take advantage?"

It took a moment for that to sink in. When it did, she could barely speak through the anger that spurted hot and sour into her throat.

"Do you think...? Do you think this codicil is part of some convoluted scheme on my part to extract money from the St. Sebastians?"

Furious, she shoved to her feet. He rose as well, as effortlessly as an athlete, and countered her anger with a shrug.

"Not at this point. If I discover differently, however, you and I will most certainly have another chat."

"Get out!"

Maybe after she cooled down Natalie would admit flinging out an arm and stabbing a finger toward the door was overly melodramatic. At the moment, though, she wanted to slam that door so hard it knocked this pompous ass on his butt. Especially when he lifted a sardonic brow.

"Shouldn't that be 'Get out, *Your Grace*'?"

Her back teeth ground together. "Get. Out."

As a cab hauled him back uptown for a last visit with the duchess and his sister, Dom couldn't say his session with Ms. Clark had satisfied his doubts. There was still something he couldn't pin down about the researcher. She dressed like a bag lady in training and seemed content to efface herself in company. Yet when she'd flared up at him, when fury had brought color surging to her cheeks and fire to her eyes, the woman was anything but ignorable.

She reminded him of the mounts his ancestors had ridden when they'd swept down from the Steppes into the Lower Danube region. Their drab, brown-and-dun-colored ponies lacked the size and muscle power of destriers that carried European knights into battle. Yet the Magyars had wreaked havoc for more than half a century throughout Italy, France, Germany and Spain before finally being defeated by the Holy Roman Emperor Otto I.

And like one of those tough little ponies, Dom thought with a slow curl in his belly, Ms. Clark needed taming. She might hide behind those glasses and shapeless dresses, but she had a temper on her when roused. Too bad he didn't have time to gentle her to his hand. The exercise would be a hell of a lot more interesting than the meetings he had lined up in Washington tomorrow. Still, he entertained himself for the rest of the cab ride with various techniques he might employ should he cross paths with Natalie Elizabeth Clark anytime in the near future.

He'd pretty much decided he would make that happen when Zia let him into the duchess's apartment.

"Back so soon?" she said, her eyes dancing. "Ms. Clark didn't succumb to your manly charms and topple into bed with you?"

The quip was so close to Dom's recent thoughts that he answered more brusquely than he'd intended. *"I didn't go to her hotel to seduce her."*

"No? That must be a first."

"Jézus, Mária és József! The mouth on you, Anastazia Amalia. I should have washed it with soap when I had the chance."

"Ha! You would never have been able to hold me down long enough. But come in, come in! Sarah's on FaceTime with her grandmother. I think you'll be interested in their conversation."

FaceTime? The duchess? Marveling at the willingness of a woman who'd been born in the decades between two great world wars to embrace the latest in technology, Dom followed his sister into the sitting room. One glance at the tableau corrected his impression of Charlotte's geekiness.

She sat upright and unbending in her customary chair, her cane close at hand. An iPad was perched on her knees, but she was obviously not comfortable with the device. Gina sat cross-legged on the floor beside her, holding the screen to the proper angle

Sarah's voice floated through the speaker and her elegant features filled most of the screen. Her husband's filled the rest.

"I'm so sorry, Grandmama. It just slipped out."

"What slipped out?" Dom murmured to Zia.

"You," his sister returned with that mischievous glint in her eyes.

"Me?"

"Shh! Just listen."

Frowning, Dom tuned back into the conversation.

"Alexis called with an offer to hype my book in *Beguile*," Sarah was saying. "She wanted to play up both angles." Her nose wrinkled. "My former job at the magazine and my title. You know how she is."

"Yes," the duchess drawled. "I do."

"I told Alexis the book wasn't ready for hype yet. Unfortunately, I also told her we're getting there much quicker since I'd hired such a clever research assistant. I bragged about the letter Natalie unearthed in the House of Parma archives, the one from Marie Antoinette to her sister describing the miniature of her painted by Le Brun that went missing when the mob sacked Versailles. And..." She heaved a sigh. "I made the fatal mistake of mentioning the codicil Nat had stumbled across while researching the Canaletto."

Although the fact that Dom's cousin had mentioned that damned codicil set his internal antennae to vibrating, it didn't appear to upset the duchess. Mention of the Canaletto had brought a faraway look to her eyes.

"Your grandfather bought me that painting of the Grand Canal," she murmured to Sarah. "Right after I became pregnant with your mother."

She lapsed into a private reverie that neither of her granddaughters dared break. When she emerged a few moments later, she included them both in a sly smile.

"That's where it happened. In Venice. We were supposed to attend a *cárnival* ball at Ari Onassis's palazzo. I'd bought the most gorgeous mask studded with pearls and lace. But...how does that rather obnoxious TV commercial go? You never know when the mood will hit you? All I can say is something certainly hit your grandfather that evening."

Gina hooted in delight. "Way to go, Grandmama!"

Sarah laughed, and her husband issued a joking curse. "Damn! My wife suggested we hit the carnival in Venice this spring but I talked her into an African photo safari instead."

"You'll know to listen to her next time," the duchess sniffed, although Dom would bet she knew the moment could strike as hot and heavy in the African savannah as it had in Venice.

"I don't understand," Gina put in from her perch on the floor. "What's the big deal about telling Alexis about the codicil?"

"Well…" Red crept into Sarah's cheeks. "I'm afraid I mentioned Dominic, too."

The subject of the conversation muttered a curse, and Gina let out another whoop. "Ooh, boy! Your barracuda of an editor is gonna latch on to that with both jaws. I foresee another top-ten edition, this one listing the sexiest single royals of the male persuasion."

"I know," her sister said miserably. "It'll be as bad as what Dev went through after he came out on *Beguile*'s top-ten list. When you see Dominic tell him I'm so, so sorry."

"He's right here." Hooking a hand, Gina motioned him over. "Tell him yourself."

When Dominic positioned himself in front of the iPad's camera, Sarah sent him a look of heartfelt apology. "I'm so sorry, Dom. I made Alexis promise she wouldn't go crazy with this, but…"

"But you'd better brace yourself, buddy," her husband put in from behind her shoulder. "Your life's about to get really, really complicated."

"I can handle it," Dom replied with more confidence than he was feeling at the moment.

"You think so, huh?" Dev returned with a snort. "Wait

till women start trying to stuff their phone number in your pants pocket and reporters shove mics and cameras in your face."

The first prospect hadn't sounded all that repulsive to Dom. The second he deemed highly unlikely...right up until he stepped out of a cab for his scheduled meeting at Washington's Interpol office the following afternoon and was blindsided by the pack of reporters, salivating at the scent of fresh blood.

"Your Highness! Over here!"

"Grand Duke!"

"Hey! Your lordship!"

Shaking his head at Americans' fixation on any and all things royal, he shielded his face with his hands like some damned criminal and pushed through the ravenous newshounds.

Three

Two weeks later Dominic was in a vicious mood. He had been since a dozen different American and European tabloids had splashed his face across their front pages, trumpeting the emergence of a long-lost Grand Duke.

When the stories hit, he'd expected the summons to Interpol Headquarters. He'd even anticipated his boss's suggestion that he take some of the unused vacation time he'd piled up over the years and lie low until the hoopla died down. He'd anticipated it, yes, but did *not* like being yanked off undercover duty and sent home to Budapest to twiddle his thumbs. And every time he thought the noise was finally dying down, his face popped up in another rag.

The firestorm of publicity had impacted his personal life, as well. Although Sarah's husband had tried to warn him, Dom had underestimated the reaction to his supposed royalty among the females of his acquaintance. The phone number he gave out to non-Interpol contacts had suddenly become very busy. Some of the callers were friends, some were former lovers. But many were strangers who'd wrangled the number out of *their* friends and weren't shy about wanting to get to know the new duke on a very personal level.

He'd turned most of them off with a laugh, a few of the more obnoxious with a curt suggestion they get a life. But one had sounded so funny and sexy over the phone that he'd arranged to meet her at a coffee bar. She turned out to be a tall, luscious brunette, as bright and engaging in person as she was over the phone. Dom was more than ready to agree with her suggestion they get a second cup to go and down it at her apartment or his loft. Before he could put in the order, though, she asked the waiter to take their picture with her cell phone. Damned if she hadn't zinged it off by email right there at the table. Just to a few friends, she explained with a smile. One, he discovered when yet another story hit the newsstands, just happened to be a reporter for a local tabloid.

In addition to the attention from strangers, the barrage of unwanted publicity seemed to make even his friends and associates view him through a different prism. To most of them he wasn't Dominic St. Sebastian anymore. He was Dominic, Grand Duke of a duchy that had ceased to exist a half century ago, for God's sake.

So he wasn't real happy when someone hammered on the door of his loft apartment on a cool September evening. Especially when the hammering spurred a chorus of ferocious barking from the hound who'd followed Dom home a year ago and decided to take up residence.

"Quiet!"

A useless command, since the dog considered announcing his presence to any and all visitors a sacred duty. Bred originally to chase down swiftly moving prey like deer and wolves, the Magyar Agár was as lean and fast as a greyhound. Dom had negotiated an agreement with his downstairs neighbors to dog-sit while he was on assignment, but man and beast had rebonded during this enforced vacation. Or at least the hound had. Dom had yet to reconcile himself to sharing his Gold Fassl with the pilsner-guzzling pooch.

"This better not be some damned reporter," he muttered as he kneed the still-barking hound aside and checked the spy hole. The special lens he'd had installed gave a

180-degree view of the landing outside his loft. The small area was occupied by two uniformed police officers and a bedraggled female Dom didn't recognize until he opened the door.

"Mi a fene!" he swore in Hungarian, then switched quickly to English. "Natalie! What happened to you?"

She didn't answer, being too preoccupied at the moment with the dog trying to shove his nose into her crotch. Dom swore again, got a grip on its collar and dislodged the nose, but he still didn't get a reply. She merely stared at him with a frown creasing her forehead and her hair straggling in limp tangles around her face.

"Are you Dominic St. Sebastian?" one of the police officers asked.

"Yes."

"Aka the Grand Duke?"

He made an impatient noise and kept his grip on the dog's collar. "Yes."

The second officer, whose nametag identified him as Gradjnic, glanced down at a newspaper folded to a grainy picture of Dom and the brunette at the coffee shop. "Looks like him," he volunteered.

His partner gestured to Natalie. "And you know this woman?"

"I do." Dom's glance raked the researcher, from her tangled hair to her torn jacket to what looked like a pair of men's sneakers several sizes too large for her. "What the devil happened to you?"

"Maybe we'd better come in," Gradjnic suggested.

"Yes, yes, of course."

The officers escorted Natalie inside, and Dom shut the dog in the bathroom before joining them. The Agár whined and scratched at the door but soon nosed out the giant chew-bones Dom stored in the hamper for emergencies like this.

Aside from the small bathroom, the loft consisted of a single, barn-like attic area that had once stored artifacts belonging to the Ethnological Museum. When the museum moved to new digs, their old building was converted to condos. Zia had just nailed a full scholarship to medical school, so Dom had decided to sink his savings into this loft apartment in the pricy Castle Hill district on the Buda side of the river. He'd then proceeded to sand and varnish the oak-plank floors to a high gloss. He'd also knocked out a section of the sloping roof and opened up a view of the Danube that usually had guests gasping.

Tonight's visitors were no exception. All three gawked at the floodlit spires, towering dome, flying buttresses and stained-glass windows of the Parliament Building across the river. Equally elaborate structures flanked the massive building, while the usual complement of river barges and brightly lit tour boats cruised by almost at its steps.

Ruthlessly, Dom cut into their viewing time. "Please sit down, all of you, then someone needs to tell me what this is all about."

"It's about this woman," Gradjnic said in heavily accented English when everyone had found a place to perch. He tugged a small black notebook from his shirt pocket. "What did you say her name was?"

Dom's glance shot to Natalie. "You didn't tell them your name?"

"I…I don't remember it."

"What?"

Her frown deepened. "I don't remember anything."

"Except the Grand Duke," Officer Gradjnic put in drily.

"Wait," Dom ordered. "Back up and start at the beginning."

Nodding, the policeman flipped through his notebook. "The beginning for us was 10:32 a.m. today, when dispatch called to report bystanders had fished a woman out of the

Danube. We responded, found this young lady sitting on the bank with her rescuers. She had no shoes, no purse, no cell phone, no ID of any kind and no memory of how she ended up in the river. When we asked her name or the name of a friend or relative here in Budapest, all she could tell us was 'the Grand Duke.'"

"Jesus!"

"She has a lump the size of a goose egg at the base of her skull, under her hair."

When Dom's gaze shot to Natalie again, she raised a tentative hand to the back of her neck. "More like a pigeon's egg," she corrected with a frown.

"Yes, well, the lump suggests she may have fallen off a bridge or a tour boat and hit her head on the way down, although none of the tour companies have reported a missing passenger. We had the EMTs take her to the hospital. The doctors found no sign of serious injury or concussion."

"No blurred vision?" Dom asked sharply. He'd taken—and delivered—enough blows to the head to know the warning signs. "No nausea or vomiting or balance problems?"

"Only the memory loss. The doctor said it's not all that unusual with that kind of trauma. Since we had no other place to take her, it was either leave her at the hospital or bring her to the only person she seems to know in Budapest—the Grand Duke."

Hit by a wicked sense of irony, Dom remembered those quivering nostrils and flickers of disdain. He suspected Ms. Clark would rather have been left at a dog pound than delivered to him.

"I'll take care of her," he promised, "but she must have a hotel room somewhere in the city."

"If she does, we'll let you know." Gradjnic flipped to an empty page and poised his pen. "Now what did you say her name was?"

"Natalie. Natalie Clark."

"American, we guessed from her accent."

"That's right."

"And she works for your cousin?"

"Yes, as research assistant." Angling around, Dom tried a tentative probe. "Natalie, you were supposed to meet with Sarah sometime this week. In Paris, right?"

"Sarah?"

"My cousin. Sarah St. Sebastian Hunter."

Her first response was a blank stare. Her second startled all three men.

"My head hurts." Scowling, she pushed out of her chair. "I'm tired. And these clothes stink."

With that terse announcement, she headed for the unmade bed at the far end of the loft. She kicked off the sneakers as she went. Dom lurched to his feet as she peeled out of the torn jacket.

"Hold on a minute!"

"I'm tired," she repeated. "I need sleep."

Shaking off his restraining hand, she flopped facedown across the bed. The three men watched with varying expressions of surprise and resignation as she buried her face in the pillow.

Gradjnic broke the small silence that followed. "Well, I guess that does it for us here. Now that we have her name, we'll trace Ms. Clark's entry into the country and her movements in Hungary as best we can. We'll also find out if she's registered at a hotel. And you'll call us when and if she remembers why she took that dive into the Danube, right?"

"Right."

The sound of their departure diverted the Agár's attention from the chew-bone he'd dug out of the hamper. To quiet his whining, Dom let him out of the bathroom but kept a close watch while he sniffed out the stranger sprawled sideways across the bed. Apparently deciding she posed no threat, the dog padded back to the living area and stretched out in front of the window to watch the brightly lit boats cruising up and down the river.

Dom had his phone in hand before the hound's speckled pink belly hit the planks. Five rings later, his sleepy-sounding cousin answered.

"Hullowhozzis?"

"It's Dom, Sarah."

"Dom?"

"Where are you?"

"We're in…uh…Dalian. China," she added, sounding more awake…and suddenly alarmed by a call in what had to be the middle of the night on the other side of the globe. "Is everyone okay? Grandmama? Gina? Zia? Oh, God! Is it one of the twins?"

"They're all fine, Sarah. But I can't say the same for your research assistant."

He heard a swift rustle of sheets. A headboard creaking.

"Dev! Wake up! Dom says something's happened to Natalie!"

"I'm awake."

"Tell me," Sarah demanded.

"The best guess is she fell off a bridge or a cruise boat. They fished her out of the river early this morning."

"Is she…? Is she dead?"

"No, but she's got a good-size lump at the base of her skull and she doesn't remember anything. Not even her name."

"Good Lord!" The sheets rustled again. "Natalie's been hurt, Dev. Would you contact your crew and have them prep the Gulfstream? I need to fly back to Paris right away."

"She's not in Paris," Dom interjected. "She's with me, in Budapest."

"In Budapest? But…how? Why?"

"I was hoping you could tell me."

"She didn't say anything about Hungary when we got together in Paris last week. Only that she might drive down to Vienna again, to do more research on the Canaletto." A note of accusation slipped through Sarah's concern. "She was also going to dig a little more on the codicil. Something you said about it seemed to have bothered her."

He'd said a lot about it, none of which he intended to go into at the moment. "So you don't know why she's here in Hungary?"

"I have no clue. Is she there with you now? Let me speak to her."

He flicked a glance at the woman sprawled across his bed. "She's zoned out, Sarah. Said she was tired and just flopped into bed."

"This memory thing? Will she be all right?"

"Like you, I have no clue. But you'd better contact her family just in case."

"She doesn't have any family."

"She's got to have someone. Grandparents? An uncle or aunt stashed away somewhere?"

"She doesn't," Sarah insisted. "Dev ran a detailed background check before I hired her. Natalie doesn't know who her parents are or why she was abandoned as an infant. She lived with a series of foster families until she checked herself out of the system at age eighteen and entered the University of Michigan on full scholarship."

That certainly put a different spin on the basic age-height-DOB info he'd gathered.

"I'll fly to Budapest immediately," Sarah was saying, "and take Natalie home with me until she recovers her memory."

Dom speared another glance at the researcher. His gut

told him he'd live to regret the suggestion he was about to make.

"Why don't you hang loose for now? Could be she'll be fine when she wakes up tomorrow. I'll call you then."

"I don't know…"

"I'll call you, Sarah. As soon as she wakes up."

When she reluctantly agreed, he cut the connection and stood with the phone in hand for several moments. He'd worked undercover too long to take anything at face value…especially a woman fished out of the Danube who had no reason to be in Budapest that anyone knew. Thumbing the phone, he tapped in a number. His contact at Interpol answered on the second ring.

"Oui?"

"It's Dom," he replied in swift, idiomatic French. "Remember the query you ran for me two weeks ago on Natalie Clark?"

"Oui."

"I need you to dig deeper."

"Oui."

The call completed, he contemplated his unexpected houseguest for a few moments. Her rumpled skirt had twisted around her calves and her buttoned-to-the-neck blouse looked as though it was choking her. After a brief inner debate, Dom rolled her over. He had the blouse unfastened and was easing it off when she opened her eyes to a groggy squint and mumbled at him.

"Whatryoudoin?"

"Making you comfortable."

"Mmm."

She was asleep again before he got her out of her blouse and skirt. Her panties were plain, unadorned white cotton but, Dom discovered, covered slender hips and a nice, trim butt. Nobly, he resisted the urge to remove her underwear and merely tucked the sheets around her. That done, he popped the cap on a bottle of a pilsner for himself, opened another for the hound and settled in for an all-night vigil.

He rolled her over again just after midnight and pried up a lid. She gave a bad-tempered grunt and batted his hand away, but not before he saw her pupil dilate and refract with reassuring swiftness.

He woke her again two hours later. "Natalie. Can you hear me?"

"Go away."

He did a final check just before dawn. Then he stretched out on the leather sofa and watched the dark night shade to gold and pink.

Something wet and cold prodded her elbow. Her shoulder. Her chin. She didn't come awake, though, until a strap of rough leather rasped across her cheek. She blinked fuzzily, registered the hazy thought that she was in bed, and opened her eyes.

"Yikes!"

A glistening pink mouth loomed only inches from her eyes. Its black gums were pulled back and a long tongue dangled through a set of nasty-looking incisors. As if in answer to her startled yip, the gaping mouth emitted a blast of powerful breath and an ear-ringing bark.

She scurried back like a poked crab, heart thumping and sheets tangling. A few feet of separation gave her a better perspective. Enough to see the merry eyes above an elongated muzzle, a broad forehead topped with one brown ear and one white, and a long, lean body with a wildly whipping tail.

Evidently the dog mistook her retreat for the notion that she was making space for him in the bed. With another loud woof, he landed on the mattress. The tongue went to work again, slathering her cheeks and chin before she could hold him off.

"Whoa! Stop!" His joy was contagious and as impossible to contain as his ecstatically wriggling body. Laughing now, she finally got him by the shoulders. "Okay, okay, I like you, too! But enough with the tongue."

He got in another slurp before he let her roll him onto his back, where he promptly stuck all four legs into the air and begged for a tickle. She complied and raised quivers of ecstasy on his short-haired ribs and speckled pink-and-brown belly.

"You're a handsome fellow," she murmured, admiring his sleek lines as her busy fingers set his legs to pumping. "Wonder what your name is?"

"He doesn't have one."

The response came from behind her. Twisting on the bed, she swept her startled gaze across a huge, sparsely furnished area. A series of overhead beams topped with A-frame wooden trusses suggested it was an attic. A stunningly renovated attic, with gleaming oak floors and modern lighting.

There were no interior walls, only a curved, waist-high counter made of glass blocks that partitioned off a kitchen area. The male behind the counter looked at home there. Dark-haired and dark-eyed, he wore a soccer shirt of brilliant red-and-black stripes with some team logo she didn't recognize emblazoned on one breast. The stretchy fabric molded his broad, muscular shoulders. The wavy glass blocks gave an indistinct view of equally muscular thighs encased in running shorts.

She watched him, her hand now stilled on the dog's belly, while he flicked the switch on a stainless-steel espresso machine. Almost instantly the machine hissed out thick, black liquid. Her eyes never left him as he filled two cups and rounded the glass-block counter.

When he crossed the huge room, the dog scrambled to sit up at his approach. So did she, tugging the sheet up with her. For some reason she couldn't quite grasp, she'd slept in her underwear.

He issued an order in a language she didn't understand. When he repeated it in a firmer voice, the dog jumped off the bed with obvious reluctance.

"How do you feel?"

"I...uh... Okay."

"Head hurt?"

She tried a tentative neck roll. "I don't... Ooh!" Wincing, she fingered the lump at the base of her skull. "What happened?"

"Best guess is you fell off a bridge or tour boat and hit your head. Want some aspirin?"

"God, yes!"

He handed her one of the cups and crossed to what she guessed was a bathroom tucked under one of the eaves. She used his brief absence to let her gaze sweep the cavernous room again, looking for something, *anything* familiar.

Panic crawled like tiny ants down her spine when she finally accepted that she was sitting cross-legged on an unmade bed. In a strange apartment. With a hound lolling a few feet away, grinning from ear to ear and looking all too ready to jump back in with her.

Her hands shaking, she lifted the china cup. The rim rattled against her teeth and the froth coated her upper lip as she took a tentative sip.

"Ugh!"

Her first impulse was to spit the incredibly strong espresso back into the cup. Politeness—and the cool, watchful eyes of the bearer of aspirin—forced her to swallow.

"Better take these with water."

Gratefully, she traded the cup for a glass. She was

reaching for the two small white pills in his palm when she suddenly froze. Her heart slamming against her chest, she stared down at the pills.

Oh, God! Had she been drugged? Did he intend to knock her out again?

A faint thread of common sense tried to push through her balled-up nerves. If he wanted to drug her, he could just as easily have put something in her coffee. Still, she pulled her hand back.

"I...I better not. I, uh, may be allergic."

"You're not wearing a medical alert bracelet."

"I'm not wearing much of anything."

"True."

He set the pills and her cup on a low bookshelf that doubled as a nightstand. She clutched the water glass, looked at him, at the grinning dog, at the rumpled sheets, back at him. Ants started down her spine again.

"Okay," she said on a low, shaky breath, "who *are* you?

Four

"I'm Dominic. Dominic St. Sebastian. Dom to my friends and family."

He kept his eyes on her, watching for the tiniest flicker of recognition. If she was faking that blank stare, she was damned good at it.

"I'm Sarah's cousin," he added.

Nothing. Not a blink. Not a frown.

"Sarah St. Sebastian Hunter?" He waited a beat, then decided to go for the big guns. "She's the granddaughter of Charlotte, Grand Duchess of Karlenburgh."

"Karlenburgh?"

"You were researching a document pertaining to Karlenburgh. One with a special codicil."

He thought for a moment he'd struck a chord. Her brows drew together, and her lips bunched in an all-too-familiar moue. Then she blew out a breath and scooted to the edge of the bed, pulling the sheet with her.

"I don't know you, or your cousin, or her grandmother. Now, if you don't mind, I'd like to get dressed and be on my way."

"On your way to where?"

That brought her up short.

"I...I don't know." She blinked, obviously coming up empty. "Where...? Where am I?"

"Maybe this will help."

Dom went to the window and drew the drapes. Morning light flooded the loft. With it came the eagle's-eye view of the Danube and the Parliament's iconic red dome and forest of spires.

"Ooooh!" Wrapping the sheet around her like a sari, she stepped to the glass wall. "How glorious!"

"Do you recognize the building?"

"Sort of. Maybe."

She sounded anything but sure. And, Dom noted, she didn't squint or strain as she studied the elaborate structure across the river. Apparently she only needed her glasses for reading or close work. Yet…she'd worn them during both their previous meetings. Almost like a shield.

"I give up." She turned to him, those delicate nostrils quivering and panic clouding her eyes. "Where *am* I?"

"Budapest"

"Hungary?"

He started to ask if there was a city with that same name in another country but the panic had started to spill over into tears. Although she tried valiantly to gulp them back, she looked so frightened and fragile that Dom had to take her in his arms.

The sobs came then. Big, noisy gulps that brought the Agár leaping to all fours. His ears went flat and his long, narrow tail whipped out, as though he sensed an enemy but wasn't sure where to point.

"It's all right," Dom said, as much to the dog as the woman in his arms. She smelled of the river, he thought as he stroked her hair. The river and diesel spill and soft, trembling female still warm from his bed. So different from the stiff, disdainful woman who'd ordered him out of her New York hotel room that his voice dropped to a husky murmur.

"It's all right."

"No, it's not!"

The tears gushed now, soaking through his soccer shirt and making the dog whine nervously. His claws clicked on the oak planking as he circled Dom and the woman clinging to his shirt with one hand and the sheet with her other.

"I don't understand any of this! Why can't I remember where I am? Why can't I remember *you*?" She jerked back against his arm and stared up at him. "Are we...? Are we married?"

"No."

Her glance shot to the bed. "Lovers?"

He let that hang for a few seconds before treating her to a slow smile.

"Not yet."

Guilt pricked at him then. Her eyes were so huge and frightened, her nose red and sniffling. Gentling his voice, he brushed a thumb across her cheek to wipe the tears.

"Do you remember the police bringing you here last night?"

"I...I think so."

"They took you to a hospital first. Remember?"

Her forehead wrinkled. "Now I do."

"A doctor examined you. He told the police that short-term memory loss isn't unusual with a head injury."

She jumped on that. "How short?"

"I don't know, *drágám*."

"Is that my name? *Drágám*?"

"No, that's a nickname. An endearment, like 'sweetheart' or 'darling.' Very casual here in Hungary," he added when her eyes got worried again. "Your name is Natalie. Natalie Elizabeth Clark."

"Natalie." She rolled it around in her head, on her tongue. "Not a name I would pick for myself," she said with a sniffle, "but I guess it'll do."

The brown-and-white hound poked at her knee then, as if demanding reassurance that all was well. Natalie eased out of Dom's arms and knuckled the dog's broad, intelligent forehead.

"And who's this guy?"

"I call him *kutya*. It means 'dog' in Hungarian."

Her eyes lifted to his, still watery but accusing. "You just call him 'dog'?"

"He followed me home one night and decided to take up residence. I thought it would be a temporary arrangement, so we never got around to a baptismal ceremony."

"So he's a stray," she murmured, her voice thickening. "Like me."

Dom knew he'd better act fast to head off another storm of tears. "Stray or not," he said briskly, "he needs to go out. Why don't you shower and finish your coffee while I take him for his morning run? I'll pick up some apple pancakes for breakfast while I'm out, yes? Then we'll talk about what to do next."

When she hesitated, her mouth trembling, he curled a knuckle under her chin and tipped her face to his. "We'll work this out, Natalie. Let's just take it one step at a time."

She bit her lip and managed a small nod.

"Your clothes are in the bathroom," Dom told her. "I rinsed them out last night, but they're probably still damp." He nodded to the double-doored wardrobe positioned close to the bath. "Help yourself to whatever you can find to fit you."

She nodded again and hitched the sheet higher to keep from tripping over it as she padded to the bathroom. Dom waited until he heard the shower kick on before dropping into a chair to pull on socks and his well-worn running shoes.

He hoped to hell he wasn't making a mistake leaving her alone. Short of locking her in, though, he didn't see how he could confine her here against her will. Besides which, they needed to eat and Dog needed to go out. A point the hound drove home by retrieving his leash from its hook by the door and waiting with an expression of acute impatience.

Natalie. Natalie Elizabeth Clark.

Why didn't it feel right? Sound right?

She wrapped her freshly shampooed hair in a towel and stared at the steamed-up bathroom mirror. The image it reflected was as foggy as her mind.

She'd stood under the shower's hot, driving needles and tried to figure out what in the world she was doing in Budapest. It couldn't be her home. She didn't know a word of Hungarian. Correction. She knew two. *Kutya* and... What had he called her? *Dragon* or something.

Dominic. His name was Dominic. It fit him, she thought with a grimace, much better than Natalie did her. Those muscled shoulders, the strong arms, the chest she'd sobbed against, all hinted at power and virility and, yes, dominance.

Especially in bed. The thought slipped in, got caught in her mind. He'd said they weren't lovers. Implied she'd slept alone. Yet heat danced in her belly at the thought of lying beneath him and feeling his hands on her breasts, his mouth on her...

Oh, God! The panic came screaming back. She breathed in. Out. In. Then set her jaw and glared at the face in the mirror.

"No more crying! It didn't help before! It won't help now."

She snatched up a dry washcloth and had started to scrub the fogged glass when she caught the echo of her words. Her fist closed around the cloth, and her chest squeezed.

"Crying didn't help before *what*?"

Like the steam still drifting from the shower stall,

the mists in her mind seemed to curl. Shift. Become less opaque. Something was there, just behind the thin gray curtain. She could almost see it. Almost smell it. She spun around and hacked out a sound halfway between a sob and a laugh.

She could smell it, all right. The musty odor emanated from the wrinkled items hanging from hooks on the door. The steam from the hot shower must have released the river stink.

Her nose wrinkling, she fingered the shapeless jacket, the unadorned blouse, the mess that must once have been a skirt. Good grief! Were these really her clothes? They looked like they'd come from a Goodwill grab bag. The bra and panties she'd discarded before getting in the shower were even worse.

He—Dominic—said he'd rinsed her things out. He should have tossed them in a garbage sack and hauled them to a dumpster.

"Well," she said with a shrug, "he told me to help myself."

The helping included using his comb to work the tangles from her wet hair and squirting a length of his toothpaste onto her forefinger to scrub her teeth. It also included poking her head through the bathroom door to make sure he was still gone before she raided his closet.

It was a European-style wardrobe, with mirror double doors and beautiful carving. The modern evolution of the special room in a castle where nobles stored their robes in carved wooden chests. Called an armoire in French, a shrunk in German, this particular wardrobe wasn't as elaborate as some she'd seen but...

Wait! How did she know about castles and nobles and shrunks? What other, more elaborate armoires had she seen? She stared at the hunting scene above the doors, feeling as though she was straining every brain cell she possessed through a sieve, and came up empty.

"Dammit!"

Angry and more than a little scared, she yanked open the left door. Suits and dress shirts hung haphazardly from the rod, while an assortment of jeans, T-shirts and sporting gear spilled from the shelves below. She plucked out a soccer shirt, this one with royal-blue and white stripes but with the same green-and-gold emblem on the right sleeve. The cool, slick material slithered over her hips. The hem hung almost to her knees.

Curiosity prompted her to open the right door. This side was all drawers. The top drawer contained unmatched socks, tangled belts, loose change and a flashlight.

The middle drawer was locked. Securely locked, with a gleaming steel mechanism that didn't give a hair when she tested it.

She slid the third drawer out and eyed the jumble of jock straps, Speedos and boxers. She thought about appropriating a Speedo but couldn't quite bring herself to climb into his underwear.

"Not the neatest guy in the world, are you?" she commented to the absent Dominic.

She started to close the drawer, intending to go back to the bathroom and give her panties a good scrubbing, when she caught a glimpse of delicate black lace amid boxers.

Oh, Lord! Was he into kink? Cross-dressing? Transgender sex play? Did that locked drawer contain whips and handcuffs and ball gags?

She gulped, remembering her earlier thought about strength and power and dominance, and used the tip of a finger to extract a pair of lace-trimmed silk hipsters. A new and very expensive pair of hipsters judging by the embossed tag still dangling from the band. Natalie's eyes widened when she saw the hand-lettered price.

Good grief! Three hundred pounds? Could that be right?

When she recovered from sticker shock, she found it interesting that the price was displayed in British pounds and not in Hungarian...Hungarian whatever. Also interesting, the light-as-air scrap of silk had evidently been crafted by an "atelier" who described her collection as feminine and ethereal, each piece a limited edition made to measure for the client. The matching garter belt and triangle bra, the tag advised, would put the cost for the complete ensemble at just over a thousand pounds.

Well, she thought with a low whistle, if he was into kink, he certainly did it up right. She was about to stuff the panties back in the drawer when she noticed handwriting on the back of the tag.

I stuck these in your suitcase so you'll know what I won't be wearing next time you're in London.
Kiss, kiss, Arabella.

Oh, yuck! Her lip curling, she started to stuff the hipsters back in the drawer. Common sense and a bare butt made her hesitate several seconds too long. She still had the panties in hand when the front door opened and the hound burst in. Sweat darkened the honey-brown patches on the dog's coat. Similar damp splotches stained Dominic's soccer shirt.

"Find everything you need?" he asked as he dropped a leash and a white paper sack on the kitchen counter.

"Almost everything." She lifted her hand. The scrap of silk and lace dangled from her forefinger. "Do you think Arabella will mind if I borrow her knickers?"

"Who?"

"Arabella. London. Kiss, kiss."

"Oh. Right. That Arabella." He eyed the gossamer silk

with a waggle of his brow. "Very nice. Where'd you find them?"

"In with your socks," she drawled. "There's a note on the back of the tag."

He flipped the tag over and skimmed the handwriting. She could smell the sharp tang of his sweat, see the bristles darkening his cheeks and chin. See, too, the smile that played at the corners of his mouth. He managed to keep it from sliding into a full grin as he handed back the panties.

"I'm sure Arabella wouldn't mind you borrowing them," he said solemnly.

But *he* would. The realization hit Dom even before she whirled and the hem of his soccer shirt flared just high enough to give him a glimpse of her nicely curved butt.

"That might have been a mistake," he told the hound when the bathroom door shut. "Now I'm going to be imagining her in black silk all day."

The Agár cocked his head. The brown ear came up, the white ear folded over, and he looked as though he was giving the matter serious consideration.

"She's fragile," Dom reminded the dog sternly. "Confused and frightened and probably still hurting from her dive into the Danube. So you refrain from slobbering all over her front and I'll keep my mind off her rear."

Easier said than done he discovered when she re-emerged. She wore a cool expression, the blue crew shirt and, as Dom could all-too-easily visualize, a band of black silk around her slender hips.

And here he'd thought her nondescript back in New York. She certainly looked different with her face flushed and rosy from the shower and her damp hair showing streaks of rich, dark chestnut. The oversize glasses had dominated her face in New York, distracting from those cinnamon-brown eyes and the short, straight nose. And, he remembered, her full lips had been set in such thin, disapproving lines for most of their brief acquaintance. They were close to that now but still looked very kissable.

Not that he should be thinking about her eyes or her lips or the length of bare leg visible below the hem of his shirt. She's vulnerable, he had to remember. Confused.

"I bought some apple pancakes from my favorite street seller," he told her, indicating the white sack on the counter. "They're good cold, if you're hungry now, but better when crisped a bit in the oven. Help yourself while I take my turn in the shower."

"I'll warm them up."

Rounding the glass counter, she stooped to study the knobs on the stovetop. The soccer shirt rode up again. Barely an inch. Two at the most. All it showed were the backs of her thighs, but Dom had to swallow a groan as he grabbed a pair of jeans and a clean shirt and hit the bathroom.

He didn't take long. A hot, stinging shower and a quick shampoo. He scraped a palm over his three or four days' worth of bristles, but a shave lost out to the seductive scent of warm apples.

She was perched on one of the counter stools, laughing at the shivering bundle of ecstasy hunkered between her bare legs. "No, you idiot! Don't give me that silly grin. I'm not feeding you another bite."

She glanced up, her face still alight, and spotted Dom. The laughter faded instantly. He felt the loss like a hard right jab to the solar plexus.

Jézus, Mária és József! Did she dislike all men, or just him? He couldn't tell but sure as hell intended to find out.

The woman represented so many mysteries. There was the disdain she'd treated him to in New York. That ridiculous codicil. The memory loss. The yet-to-be-explained reason she was here in his loft, swathed in his soccer shirt. Dom couldn't remember when a woman had challenged him in so many ways. He was about to tell her so when the cell phone he'd left on the counter buzzed.

"It's Sarah," he said after a quick glance at the face that came up on the screen. "My cousin and your boss. Do you want to talk to her?"

"I…uh… All right."

He accepted the FaceTime call and gave his anxious cousin the promised update. "Natalie's still here with me. Physically she seems okay but no progress yet on recovering her memory. Here, I'll put her on."

He positioned the phone so the screen captured Natalie still seated on the high stool. Both he and Sarah could see the desperate hope and crushing disappointment that chased across the researcher's features as she stared at the face on the screen.

"Oh, Nat," Sarah said with a tremulous smile, "I'm so, so sorry to hear you've been hurt."

Her hand crept to her nape. "Thank you."

"Dev and I will fly to Budapest today and take you home."

Uncertainty flooded her eyes. "Dev?"

Sarah swallowed. "Devon Hunter. My husband."

The name didn't appear to register, which caused Natalie such obvious dismay that Dom intervened. Leaning close, he spoke into the camera.

"Why don't you and Dev hold off for a while, Sarah? We haven't spoken to the police yet this morning. They were going to trace Natalie's movements in Hungary and might have some information for us. Also, they might have found her purse or briefcase. If not, we'll need to go to the American Embassy and get a replacement passport before she can leave the country. That could take a few days."

"But…"

Sarah struggled to mask her concern. Dom guessed she felt personally responsible for her assistant being hurt and stranded in a foreign country.

"Are you good with remaining in Hungary a little while yet, Nat?"

"I..." She looked from the screen to Dom to the hound, who now sat with his head plopped on her knee. "Yes."

"Would you feel better staying at a hotel? I can make a reservation in your name today."

Once again Dom felt compelled to intercede. Natalie was in no condition to be left on her own. Assuming, of course, her memory loss was real. He had no reason to believe otherwise but the cop in him went too deep to take anyone or anything at face value.

"Let's leave that for now, too," he told Sarah. "As I said, we need to talk to the police and start the paperwork for a replacement passport if necessary. While we're working things at this end, you could make some inquiries back in the States. Talk to the duchess and Zia and Gina. Maybe the editor you're working with on your book. Find out if anyone's called inquiring about Natalie or her research. It might help jog her memory if we can discover what brought her to Budapest from Vienna."

"Of course. I'll do that today." She hesitated, clearly distressed for her assistant. "You'll need money, Natalie. I'll arrange a draft... No, we'd better make it cash since you don't have any ID. I'll have it delivered to Dom's address this afternoon. Just an advance on your salary," she added quickly when Natalie looked as though she'd been offered charity.

Dom considered telling his cousin that the money could wait, too. He was more than capable of covering his unexpected guest's expenses. More to the point, it might be better to keep her dependent on him until they sorted out her situation. On reflection, though, he decided the leash was short enough.

The brief conversation left Natalie silent for several long moments. She scratched the hound's head, obviously dismayed over not recognizing the woman she worked for and with. Dom moved quickly to head off another possible panic attack.

"Okay, here's today's agenda," he said with brisk cheerfulness. "First, we finish breakfast. Second, we hit the shops to buy you some shoes and whatever else you need. Third, we visit police headquarters to find out what, if anything, they've learned. We also get a copy of their incident report and contact the embassy to begin the paperwork for a replacement passport. Finally, and most important, we arrange a follow-up with the doctor you saw yesterday. Or better yet, with a specialist who has some expertise dealing with amnesia cases."

"Sounds good to me," she said, relief at having a concrete plan of action edging aside the dismay. "But do you really think we can swing an appointment with a specialist anytime soon? Or even find one with expertise in amnesia?"

"I've got a friend I can call."

He didn't tell her that his "friend" was the internationally renowned forensic pathologist who'd autopsied the victims of a particularly savage drug cartel last year. Dom had witnessed each autopsy, groaning at the doc's morbid sense of humor as he collected the evidence Interpol needed to take down key members of the cartel.

He made the call while Natalie conducted another raid on his wardrobe. By the time she'd dug out a pair of Dom's flip-flops and running shorts with a drawstring waist, one of Budapest's foremost neurologists had agreed to squeeze her in at 11:20 a.m.

Five

The short-notice appointment with the neurologist necessitated a quick change in the day's agenda. Almost before Natalie had downed her last bite of apple pancake, Dom hustled her to the door of the loft and down five flights of stairs to the underground garage.

It'd been dark when she'd arrived the previous evening, so she'd caught only glimpses of the castle dominating the hill on the Buda of the river. The bright light of morning showed the royal palace in its full glory.

"Oh, look!" Her glance snagged on the bronze warrior atop a muscled warhorse that guarded the entrance to the castle complex. "That's Prince Eugene of Savoy, isn't it?"

Dominic slanted her a quick look. "You know about *Priz Eugen*?"

"Of course." She twisted in her seat to keep the statue in view as they negotiated the narrow, curving streets that would take them down to the Danube. "He was one of the greatest military leaders of the seventeenth century. As I recall, he served three different Holy Roman Emperors and won a decisive victory against the Ottoman Turks in 1697 at…"

She broke off, her eyes rounding. "Why do I know that?"

She sank back against her seat and stared through the windshield at the tree-dappled street ahead. Dom said nothing while she struggled to jam together the pieces of the puzzle.

"Why do I know the Hapsburgs built this palace on the site of the Gothic castle originally constructed by an earlier Holy Roman Emperor? Why do I know it was reconstructed after being razed to the ground during World War II?" Her fists bunched, drummed her thighs. "Why can I pull those details out of my head and not know who I am or how I ended up in the river?"

"Recalling those details has to be a good sign. Maybe it means you'll start to remember other things, as well."

"God, I hope so!"

Her fists stayed tight through the remainder of the descent from Castle Hill and across the majestic Chain Bridge linking Buda and Pest.

Their first stop was a small boutique, where Natalie traded Dom's drawstring shorts, soccer shirt and flip-flops for sandals, slim designer jeans, a cap-sleeved tank in soft peach and a straw tote. A second stop garnered a few basic toiletries. Promising to shop for other necessities later, Dom hustled her back to the car for her appointment with Dr. Andras Kovacs.

The neurologist's suite of offices occupied the second floor of a gracious nineteenth-century town house in the shadow of St. Stephen's Basilica. The gray-haired receptionist in the outer office confirmed Natalie's short-notice appointment, but showed more interest in her escort than the patient herself.

"I read about you in the paper," she exclaimed to Dom in Hungarian. "Aren't you the Grand Duke of...of...something?"

Swallowing a groan, he nodded. "Of Karlenburgh, but the title is an empty one. The duchy doesn't exist any longer."

"Still, it must be very exciting to suddenly find yourself a duke."

"Yes, very. Is Dr. Kovacs running on time for his appointments?"

"He is." She beamed. "Please have a seat, Your Highness, and I'll let his assistant know you and Ms. Clark are here."

When he led Natalie to a set of tall wingback chairs, she sent him a quick frown. "What was all that about?"

"She was telling me about a story she'd read in the paper."

"I heard her say 'Karlenburgh.'"

He eyed her closely. "Do you recognize that name?"

"You mentioned it this morning. I thought for a moment I knew it." Still frowning, she scrubbed her forehead with the heel of her hand. "It's all here, somewhere in my head. That name. That place. You."

Her eyes lifted to his. She looked so accusing, he had to smile.

"I can think of worse places to be than in your head, *drágám.*"

He wasn't sure whether it was the lazy smile or the casual endearment or the husky note to his voice that brought out the Natalie Clark he'd met in New York. Whatever the reason, she responded with a hint of her old, disapproving self.

"You shouldn't call me that. I'm not your sweetheart."

He couldn't help himself. Lifting a hand, he brushed a knuckle over the curve of her cheek. "Ah, but we can change that, yes?"

She pulled away, and Dom was cursing himself for the mix of wariness and confusion that came back to her face when a slim, thirtysomething woman in a white smock coat emerged from the inner sanctum.

"Ms. Clark? I'm Dr. Kovacs's assistant," she said in Hungarian. "Would you and your husband please follow me?"

"Ms. Clark is American," Dom told her. "She doesn't speak our language. And we're not married."

"Oh, my apologies."

Switching to English, she repeated the invitation and advised Natalie it was her choice whether she wished to have her friend join her for the consult. Dom half expected her to refuse but she surprised him.

"I'd better have someone with me who knows who I am."

The PA showed them to a consultation room lined with mahogany bookshelves displaying leather-bound volumes and marble busts. No desk, just high-backed wing chairs in Moroccan leather arranged around a marble-topped pedestal table. The physician fit his surroundings. Tall and lean, he boasted an aristocratic beak of a nose and kind eyes behind rimless glasses.

"I reviewed the computer results of your examination at the hospital yesterday," he told Natalie in flawless English. "I would have preferred a complete physical exam with diagnostic imaging and cognitive testing before consulting with you, of course. Despite the limited medical data available at this point, however, I doubt your memory loss resulted from an organic issue such as a stroke or brain tumor or dementia. That's the good news."

Natalie's breath hissed softly on the air. The sound made Dom reach for her hand.

"What's the bad?" she asked, her fingers closing around his.

"Despite what you see in movies and on television, Ms. Clark, it's very rare for persons suffering from amnestic syndrome to lose their self-identity. A head injury such as the one you sustained generally leads to confusion and problems remembering *new* information, not old."

"I'm starting to remember things." Her fingers curled tighter, the nails digging into Dom's palm. "Historical dates and facts and such."

"Good, that's good. But for you to have blocked your sense of self…"

Kovacs slid his rimless glasses to the tip of his nose. Dom found himself wondering again about Natalie's glasses, but pushed the thought to the back of his mind as the doctor continued.

"There's another syndrome. It's called psychogenic, or dissociative, amnesia. It can result from emotional shock or trauma, such as being a victim of rape or some other violent crime."

"I don't think…" Her nails gouged deeper, sharper. "I don't remember any…"

"The hospital didn't run a rape kit," Dom said when she stumbled to a halt. "There was no reason to. Natalie—Ms. Clark—doesn't have any defensive wounds or bruises other than the swelling at the base of her skull."

"I'm aware of that. And I'm not suggesting the trauma is necessarily recent. It could have happened weeks or months or years ago." He turned back to Natalie. "The blow to your head may have triggered a memory of some previous painful experience. Perhaps caused you to throw up a defensive shield and block all personal memories."

"Will…" She swiped her tongue over her lower lip. "Will these personal memories come back?"

"They do in most instances. Each case is so different, however, it's impossible to predict a pattern."

Her jaw set. "So how do I pry open Pandora's box? Are there drugs I should take? Mental exercises I can do?"

"For now, I suggest you just give it a little time. You're a visitor to Budapest, yes? Soak in the baths. Enjoy the opera. Stroll in our beautiful parks. Let your mind heal along with the injury to your head."

The neurologist's parting advice didn't sit well with Natalie.

"Hit the opera," she huffed as they exited the town house. "Soak in the baths. Easy for him to say!"

"And easy for us to do."

The drawled comment brought her up short. Coming to a dead stop in the middle of the wide, tree-shaded sidewalk, she cocked her head.

"How can you dawdle around Budapest with me? Don't you have a job? An office or a brickyard or a butcher shop wondering where you are?"

"I wish I worked in a butcher shop," he replied, laughing. "I could keep the hound in bones for the rest of his life."

"Don't dodge the question. Where do you work?"

"Nowhere at the moment, thanks to you."

"Me?" A dozen wild possibilities raced through her head but none of them made any sense. "I don't understand."

"No, I don't suppose you do." He hooked a hand under her elbow and steered her toward a café a short distance away. "Come, let's have a coffee and I'll explain."

If Budapest's many thermal springs and public baths had made it a favorite European spa destination since Roman times, the city owed its centuries-old café culture to the Turks. Suleyman the Magnificent first introduced coffee to Europe when he invaded Hungary in the 1500s.

Taste for the drink grew during the Austro-Hungarian Empire. Meeting friends for coffee or just claiming a table to linger over a book or newspaper became a time-honored tradition. Although Vienna and other European cities developed their own thriving café cultures, Budapest remained its epicenter and at one time boasted more than six hundred *kávébáz.*

Hungarians still loved to gather at cafés. Most were small places with a dozen or so marble-topped tables, serving the inevitable glass of water along with a pitcher of milk and a cup of coffee on a small silver tray. But a few of the more elegant nineteenth-century cafés still remained. The one Dom escorted Natalie to featured chandeliers dripping with Bohemian crystal and a monstrous brass coffeemaker that took up almost one whole wall.

They claimed an outside table shaded by a green-and-white-striped awning. Dom placed the order, and Natalie waited only until they'd both stirred milk and sugar into their cups to pounce.

"All right. Please explain why I'm responsible for you being currently unemployed."

"You uncovered a document in some dusty archives in Vienna. A codicil to the Edict of 1867, which granted certain rights to Hungarian nobles. The codicil specifically confirmed the title of Grand Duke of Karlenburgh to the house of St. Sebastian forever and in perpetuity. Does any of this strike a chord?"

"That name. Karlenburgh. I know I know it."

"It was a small duchy, not much larger than Monaco, that straddled the present-day border between Austria and Hungary. The Alps cut right through it. Even today it's a place of snow-capped peaks, fertile valleys and high mountain passes guarded by crumbling fortresses."

"You've been there?"

"Several times. My grandfather was born at Karlenburgh Castle. It's just a pile of rubble now, but Poppa took my parents, then my sister and me back to see it."

"Your grandfather was the Grand Duke?"

"No, that was Sarah's grandfather. Mine was his cousin." Dom hesitated, thinking about the blood ties that had so recently and dramatically turned his life upside down. "I suppose my grandfather could have tried to claim the title when the last Grand Duke was executed."

He stirred his coffee again and tried to imagine those long ago days of terror and chaos.

"From what he told me, that was a brutal time. The Soviet invasion leveled everyone—or elevated them, depending on how you looked at it—to the status of comrade. Wealth and titles became dangerous liabilities and made their holders targets. People tried to flee to the West. Neighbors spied on neighbors. Then, after the 1956 Uprising, the KGB rounded up thousands of nationalists. Charlotte, Sarah's grandmother, was forced to witness her husband's execution, and barely escaped Hungary with her life."

The history resonated somewhere in Natalie's mind. She'd heard this story before. She knew she had. She just didn't know how it connected her and the broad-shouldered man sitting across from her.

"So this dusty document you say I uncovered? It links you to the title?"

"Charlotte thinks it does. So, unfortunately, do the tabloids." His mouth twisted. "They've been hounding me since news of that damned document surfaced."

"Well, excuse me for making you aware of your heritage!"

His brows soared. He stared at her with such an arrested expression that she had to ask.

"What?"

"You said almost the same thing in New York. While you were tearing off a strip of my hide."

The revelation that she'd taken him down a peg or two did wonders for her self-confidence. "I'm sure you deserved it," she said primly.

This time he just laughed.

"What?" she demanded again.

"That's you, *drágám*. So proper. So prissy. That's the Natalie who made me ache to tumble her to the bed or a sofa and kiss the disapproval from those luscious lips. I hurt for an hour after I left you in New York."

Her jaw dropped. She couldn't speak. Could barely breathe. Some distant corner of her mind warned that she would lose, and lose badly, if she engaged Dominic St. Sebastian in an exchange of sexual repartee.

Yet she couldn't seem to stop herself. Forcing a provocative smile, she leaned her elbows on the table and dropped her voice to the same husky murmur Dom had employed in Dr. Kovacs's reception area.

"Ah, but we can fix that, yes?"

His blank astonishment shot her ego up another notch. For the first time since she'd come awake and found herself eye to eye with a grinning canine, Natalie was able to shelve her worry and confusion.

The arrival of a waiter with their lunch allowed her to revel in the sensation awhile longer. Only after she'd forked down several bites of leafy greens and crunchy cucumber did she return to their original topic.

"You still haven't explained how inheriting the title associated with a long-defunct duchy put you on the rolls of the unemployed."

He swept the café with a casual glance. So casual she didn't realize he was making sure no one was close enough to overhear until he delivered another jaw-dropper.

"I'm an undercover agent, Natalie. Or I was until all this Grand Duke business hit."

"Like...?" She tried to get her head around it. "Like James Bond or something?"

"Closer to something. After my face got splashed across the tabloids, my boss encouraged me to take a nice, long vacation."

"So that explains the drawer!"

He leaned back in his chair. Slowly. Too slowly. Although the September sun warmed the cozy space under the awning and the exhaust from the cabs clogging the boulevard shimmered on the afternoon air, Natalie had the eerie sensation that the temperature around their table had dropped at least ten degrees.

"What drawer?"

"The locked one in your wardrobe. You store all your 007-type gadgets in there, don't you? Poison pens and jet-propelled socks and laser-guided minimissiles?"

He didn't answer for several moments. When he did, her brief euphoria at being in control evaporated.

"This isn't about me, Nat. You're the one with the empty spaces that need filling. Let's finish our coffee, yes? Then we'll swing by police headquarters. With any luck, they will have found the answers to at least some of your questions."

Dom called before they left the café to make sure Officer Gradjnic, his partner or their supervisor would be available to speak with them. Natalie didn't say a word during the short drive. Budapest traffic was nerve-racking enough to tie anyone in knots. The possibility that the police might lift a corner of the curtain blanketing her mind only added to her twist of nerves.

The National Police Department occupied a multistory, glass-and-steel high-rise on the Pest side of the Danube. Command and control of nationwide operations filled the upper stories. The Budapest PD claimed the first two floors. Officer Gradjnic's precinct was crammed into a corner of the second floor.

Natalie remembered Gradjnic from yesterday. More or less. Enough to smile when he asked how she was feeling, anyway, and thank him for their help yesterday.

"So, Ms. Clark. Do you remember how you ended up in the Danube?"

"No."

"But you might, yes?"

"The doctor we consulted this morning said that was possible." She swiped her tongue over suddenly dry lips. "What have you discovered?"

"A little."

Computers sat on every desk in the office but Officer Gradjnic tugged out his leather notepad, licked his finger and flipped through the pages.

"We've verified that you flew from Paris to Vienna last week," he reported. "We've also learned that you rented a vehicle from the Europcar agency in Vienna three days ago. We had the car rental company retrieve the GPS data from the vehicle and discovered you crossed into Hungary at Pradzéc."

"Where's Pradzéc?"

"It's a small village at the foot of the Alps, straddling the border between Austria and Hungary."

Her glance shot to Dom. They'd been talking about the border area less than an hour ago. He didn't so much as flick an eyelid but she knew he'd made the connection, just as she had.

"According to the GPS records, you spent several hours in that area, then returned to Vienna. The next day you crossed into Hungary again and stopped in Győr. The vehicle is still there, Ms. Clark, parked at a tour dock on the Danube. We called the tour office and verified that a woman matching your description purchased a ticket for a day cruise to Budapest. Do you recall buying that ticket, Ms. Clark?"

"No."

"Do you remember boarding the tour boat? Watching the scenery as you cruised down the Danube, perhaps?"

"No."

He shrugged and closed his notebook. "Well, that's all I have for you, I'm afraid. You'll have to make arrangements to return the rental car."

Dom nodded. "We'll take care of it. In the meantime, we'd like a copy of your report."

"Of course."

When they walked out into the afternoon sunshine, Natalie couldn't wait to ask. "Was Győr part of the duchy of Karlenburgh?"

"At one time."

"Is Karlenburgh Castle anywhere in that vicinity?"

"It's farther west, guarding a mountain pass. Or was. It's just a pile of ruins now."

"I need to retrace my steps, Dominic. Maybe if I see the ruins or the towns or the countryside I drove through, I'll remember why I was there."

"We'll go tomorrow."

A part of her cringed a bit at being so dependent on this man, who was still almost a stranger to her. Yet she couldn't help feeling relieved he would accompany her.

"We can have someone from Europcar meet us in Győr with a set of master keys," he advised. "That way you can retrieve any luggage you might have left locked in the trunk."

"Assuming it's still there. Rental cars are always such targets."

"True. Now we'd better see about getting you a replacement passport."

He pulled up the necessary information from the US Embassy's consular services on his iPhone. "As I thought. You'll need proof of US citizenship. A birth certificate, driver's license or previous passport."

"None of which I have."

"I can help there. I'll have one my contacts obtain a copy of your driver's license."

"You can do that?"

When he just smiled, she slapped the heel of her hand against her forehead. "Of course you can. You're 007."

They walked to the car and he opened the passenger door for her. Before she slid into the seat, Natalie turned. "You're a man of many different personas, Dominic St. Sebastian. Grand Duke. Secret agent. Rescuer of damsels in distress."

His mouth curved. "Of the three, I enjoy the last most."

"Hmm." He was so close, almost caging her in, that she had to tip her chin to look up at him. "That comes naturally to you, doesn't it?"

"Rescuing damsels in distress?"

"No, that slow, sexy, let's-get-naked grin."

"Is that the message it sends?"

"Yes."

"Is it working?"

She pursed her lips. "No."

"Ah, *drágám*," he said, laughter springing into his eyes, "every time you do that, I want to do this."

She sensed what was coming. Knew she should duck under his arm, drop into her seat and slam the door. Instead she stood there like an idiot while he stooped, placed his mouth over hers and kissed the disapproval off her lips.

Six

It was just a kiss. Nothing to get all jittery about. And certainly no reason for a purr to start deep in Natalie's throat and heat to ball in her belly. She could feel both, though, right along with the sensual movement of Dominic's lips over hers.

She'd thought it would end there. One touch. One pass of his mouth over hers. It *should* have ended there. Traffic was coursing along the busy street, for pity's sake. A streetcar clanged by. Yet Natalie didn't move as his arm went around her waist, drawing her closer, while her pulse pounded in her veins.

She was breathing hard when Dominic raised his head. He was, too, but recovered much quicker than she did.

"There," he teased. "That's better. You don't want to walk around with your mouth all pruned up."

She couldn't think of an appropriate response, so she merely sniffed and ducked into the car.

She struggled to regain her equilibrium as the car negotiated the narrow, winding streets of Castle Hill. Yet with every turn of the wheels she could feel Dominic's mouth on hers, still taste him.

She snuck a sideways glance, wondering if he was experiencing any aftershocks. No, of course not. He was supercool Mr. Secret Agent. Sexy Mr. Grand Duke, who had women slipping outrageously expensive panties into his carryall. The thought of him cuddling with Kissy Face Arabella struck a sour note in Natalie's mind. Not that it was any of her business *who* he cuddled with, she reminded herself sternly. She certainly had no claim on the man, other than being dropped on his doorstep like an abandoned baby.

That thought, in turn, triggered alternating ripples of worry and fear. She had to battle both emotions as Dom pulled into his parking space in the underground garage and they climbed the five flights of stairs. The enclosed stairwell blocked any glimpse of the river but it did afford a backside view of the uniformed delivery man trudging up ahead of them.

When they caught up with him at the landing outside the loft, Dom gestured to the large envelope in his hand. "Is that for me?"

"It is if you're Dominic St. Sebastian."

He signed for the delivery, noting the address of the sender. "It's from Sarah."

He pulled the tab on the outer envelope and handed Natalie the one inside. She fingered the bulging package before slipping it into her new straw tote. She didn't know the currency or the denomination of the notes her employer had sent but it felt like a fat wad. More than enough, she was sure, to repay Dom for her new clothes and the consult with Dr. Kovacs.

The money provided an unexpected anchor in her drifting world. When Dom unlocked the door to the loft and stood aside for her to enter, the hound provided another. Delirious with joy at their return, he woofed and waggled and whirled in ecstatic circles.

"Okay, Dog, okay." Laughing, Natalie dropped to her knees and fondled his ears. "I missed you, too."

He got in a few quick licks on her cheeks and chin

before she could dodge them. The silly grin on his face tugged at her heart.

"You can't keep calling him 'Dog,'" she scolded Dom. "He needs a proper name."

"What do you suggest?"

She studied the animal's madly whipping tail and white coat with its saddle-brown markings. "He looks a lot like a greyhound, but he's not, is he?"

"There may be some greyhound in him but he's mostly Magyar Agár."

"Magyar Agár." She rolled the words around in her head but drew a blank. "I'm not familiar with that breed."

"They're long-distance-racing and hunting hounds. In the old days, they would run alongside horsemen, often for twenty miles or more, to take down fast game like deer or hare. Anyone could own one, but big fellows like this one normally belonged to royalty."

"Royalty, huh. That settles it." She gave the cropped ears another tug. "You have to call him Duke."

"No."

"It's perfect," she insisted with a wicked glint in her eyes.

"No, Natalie."

"Think of the fun you can have if some pesky reporter wants to interview the duke."

Even better, think of the fun *she* could have whistling and ordering him to heel. "What do you say?" she asked the hound. "Think you could live with a royal title?"

Her answer was an ear-rattling woof.

"There, that settles the matter." She rose and dusted her hands. "What happens to Duke here when you're off doing your James Bond thing?"

"There's a girl in the apartment downstairs who looks after him for me."

Of course there was. Probably another Arabella-From-

London type. Natalie could just imagine what kind of payment she demanded for her dog-sitting services.

The thought was small and nasty and not one she was proud of. She chalked it up to these bizarre circumstances and the fact that she could still feel the imprint of Dom's mouth on her.

"I'd better take his highness out," he said. "Do you want to walk with us?"

She did, but she couldn't get the memory of their kiss out of her head. It didn't help that Dom was leaning against the counter, looking at her with those bedroom eyes.

"You go ahead," she said, needing some time and space. As an excuse she held up the straw tote with its cache of newly purchased toiletries. "Do you mind if I put some of these things in your bathroom?"

"Be my guest, *drágám.*"

"I asked you not to call me that."

Nerves and a spark of temper made her sound waspish even to her own ears. He noted the tone but shrugged it off.

"So you did. I'll call you Natushka, then. Little Natalie."

That didn't sound any more dignified but she decided not to argue.

When he left with the dog, she emptied the tote. The toothbrush came out of its protective plastic sleeve first. A good brushing made up for her earlier finger-work, but she grimaced when she tried to find a spot in the bathroom for the rest of her purchases.

The sink area was littered with shaving gear, a hairbrush with a few short hairs that might or might not belong to the dog, dental floss and a dusty bottle of aftershave with the cap crusted on. The rest of the bathroom wasn't much better. Her wrinkled clothes occupied the towel rack. A shampoo bottle lay tipped on its side in the shower. The damp towels from their morning showers were draped over the shower door.

When she swept her skirt, blouse and jacket from the rack, her nose wrinkled at the faint but still-present river smell. They were too far gone to salvage. Not that Natalie wanted to. She couldn't believe she'd traipsed around the capitals of Europe in such a shapeless, ugly suit. Wadding it into a ball, she took it to the kitchen and searched for a wastebasket.

She found one in the cupboard under the sink, right next to some basic cleaning supplies. The suit and blouse went in. A sponge, a bottle of glass cleaner and a spray can of foaming disinfectant came out. Since Dominic was letting her crash at his loft, the least she could do was clean up a little.

The bathroom was small enough that it didn't take her long to get it gleaming and smelling like an Alpine forest. On a roll, she attacked the kitchen next. The coffee mugs and breakfast plates hit the dishwasher. The paper napkins and white bag with its grease stains from the apple pancakes joined her clothes in the trash. The stovetop and oven door got a scrubbing, as did the dog dish in a corner next to a cupboard containing a giant-size bag of dried food. She opened the refrigerator, intending to wipe down the shelves, and jumped back.

"Omig…!"

Gulping, she identified the gory objects in the gallon-size plastic bag as bones. Big bones. Belonging, she guessed, to a cow or boar. The kind of bones a Hungarian hunting dog would gnaw to sharpen his teeth.

The only other objects in the fridge were a to-go carton from an Asian restaurant and a dozen or so bottles of beer with labels touting unfamiliar brands. Curiosity had her opening the cupboards above the sink and stove. She found a few staples, some spices and a half loaf of bread keeping company with a dusty bottle of something called

Tokaji. Dominic St. Sebastian, she decided, was not into cooking at home.

Abandoning the cupboards, she turned her attention to the stainless-steel sink. The scrubbing gave Natalie a sense of fierce satisfaction. She might not be a James Bond type but she knew how to take out sink and shower grunge!

The kitchen done, she attacked the sitting area. Books got straightened, old newspapers stacked. The sleek little laptop nested next to a pair of running shoes on the floor was moved to the drop-down shelf that doubled as a desk. Natalie ran her fingers over the keyboard, gripped by a sudden urge to power up the computer.

She was a research assistant, according to Dom. An archivist. She probably spent most of her waking hours on the computer. What would she find if she went online and researched one Natalie Clark? Or had Dom already done that? She'd have to ask him.

She was dusting the black-and-glass stand of the wide-screen TV when he and the hound returned. The dog burst in first, of course, his claws tattooing on the oak floor. Dominic followed and placed a brown paper sack on the counter. Lifting a brow, he glanced at the now spotless kitchen.

"You've been busy."

"Just straightened up a bit. I hope you don't mind."

"Why would I mind?" Amusement glinted in his eyes. "Although I can think of better ways for both of us to work off excess energy than cleaning and dog walking."

She didn't doubt it for a moment. She was wearing proof of one of his workouts in the form of black silk hipsters. No doubt Kiss Kiss Arabella would supply an enthusiastic endorsement of his abilities in that area.

Not that Natalie required a second opinion. He'd already given her a hint of just how disturbing he could be to her equanimity if she let him. Which she wouldn't. She couldn't! Her life was in enough turmoil without adding the complication of a wild tumble between the sheets with Dominic St. Sebastian. The mere thought made her so nervous that she flapped the dust cloth like a shield.

"What's in the bag?"

"I stopped by the butcher shop and picked up our supper."

"I hope you've got more than bones in there," she said with a little grimace.

"You found those, did you?"

"They were hard to miss."

"Not to worry. Dog will take care of those, although I'm sure he would much rather share our goulash."

Natalie eyed the tall, round carton he extracted dubiously. "The butcher shop sells goulash?"

"No, but Frau Kemper, the butcher's wife, always makes extra for me when she cooks up a pot."

"Oh?" She caught the prune before it formed but couldn't quite keep the disdain from her tone. "It must be a burden having so many women showering you with gifts."

"It is," he said sadly. "A terrible burden. Especially Frau Kemper. If she keeps forcing stews and cakes on me, I'll soon match her weight of a hundred and fifty kilos or more."

"A hundred and fifty kilos?" Natalie did the math. "Ha! I'd like to see you at three hundred plus pounds."

"No, you would not." He cocked his head. "But you did that calculation very quickly."

"I did, didn't I?" Surprise gave way to panic. "How can I remember metric conversions and not my name? My past? Anything about my family?"

Dom hesitated a fraction of a second too long. He knew something. Something he didn't want to reveal.

"Tell me!" she said fiercely.

"Sarah says you have no family."

"What?" Her fist bunched, crumpling the cloth she'd forgotten she still held. "Everyone has family."

"Let me put the goulash on to simmer, and I'll tell you what I know. But first…" He reached into the bag again and produced a gold-labeled bottle. "I'll open this and we'll drink a glass while we talk, yes?"

A vague memory stirred. Something or someone splashing pale gold liquid into crystal snifter. A man? This man? Desperately, she fought to drag the details to the front of her mind.

"What's in the bottle?"

"A chardonnay from the Badacsony vineyards."

The fragments shifted, realigned, wouldn't fit together.

"Not…? Not apple brandy?"

"*Pálinka*? No," he said casually. Too casually. "That's what the duchess and I drank the last time I visited her in New York. You chose not to join us. This is much less potent."

He retrieved two wineglasses and rummaged in a drawer for an opener. She held up a hand before he poured. "None for me, thanks."

"Are you sure? It's light and crisp, one of Hungary's best whites."

"I'm not a drinker." As soon as the words were out, she sensed they were true. "You go ahead. I'm good with water."

"Then I'll have water, also."

With swift efficiency, he poured the goulash into a pot that had seen much better days. Once it was covered and set on low heat, he retrieved a bone for the hound and left him happily gnawing on the mat strategically placed under one of the eaves. Then he added ice to the two wineglasses and filled them with water.

"Let's take them to the balcony."

"Balcony," Natalie discovered when he held aside the

drapes on one side of the windows and opened an access door, was a grandiose term for the narrow platform that jutted out from the steep, sloping roof. Banded by a wrought-iron safety rail, it contained two bar chairs and a bistro-style table. Dominic edged past the table and settled in the farther chair.

Natalie had to drag in a deep breath before feeling her way cautiously to the closer chairs. She hitched up and peered nervously at the sheer drop on the other side of the railing.

"You're sure this is safe?"

"I'm sure. I built it myself."

Another persona. How many was that now? She had to do a mental recap. Grand Duke. Secret agent. Sex object of kissy-faced Englishwomen and full-bodied butcher's wives. General handyman and balcony-builder. All those facets to his personality, and hers was as flat and lifeless as a marble slab. More lifeless than she'd realized.

"You said I don't have any family," she prompted.

His glance strayed to the magnificence across the river. The slowly setting sun was gilding the turrets and spires and towering dome. The sight held him for several seconds. When it came back to her, Natalie braced herself.

"Sarah ran a background check on you before she hired you. According to her sources, there's no record of who your parents were or why they abandoned you as an infant. You were raised in a series of foster homes."

She must have known. On some subconscious level, she must have known. She'd been tossed out like trash. Unwanted. Unwelcome.

"You said a 'series' of foster homes. How many? Three? Five?"

"I don't have a number. I'll get one if you want."

"Never mind." Bitterness layered over the aching emptiness. "The total doesn't really matter, does it? What does is that in a country with couples desperate to adopt, apparently no one wanted me."

"You don't know that. I'm not familiar with adoption laws in the United States. There may have been some legal impediment."

He played with his glass, his long fingers turning the stem. There was more coming, and she guessed it wouldn't be good. It wasn't.

"We also have to take into account the fact that no one appears to have raised an alarm over your whereabouts. The Budapest police, my contacts at Interpol, Sarah and Dev…none of them have received queries or concerns that you may have gone missing."

"So in addition to no family, I have no friends or acquaintances close enough to worry about me."

She stared unseeing at the stunning vista of shining river and glittering spires. "What a pathetic life I must lead," she murmured.

"Perhaps."

She hadn't been fishing for a shoulder to cry on, but the less-than-sympathetic response rankled…until it occurred to her that he was holding something back.

The thought brought her head up with a snap. She scowled at him, sitting so calm and relaxed on his tiny handkerchief of a balcony. The slanting rays of the late-afternoon sun highlighted the short, glossy black hair, the golden oak of his skin, the strong cheekbones and chin. The speculative look in his dark eyes…

"What do you know that you're not telling me?" she snapped.

"There," he said, tipping his glass toward her in mock salute. "That's what I know."

"Huh?"

"That spark of temper. That flash of spirit. You try so

hard to hide them behind the prim, proper facade you present to the world but every so often they slip out."

"What are you talking about? What facade?"

He parried her questions with one of his own. "Do you see the ironmonger's cast there, right in front of you, stamped into the balcony railing?"

"What?"

"The cast mark. Do you see it?"

Frowning, she surveyed the ornate initial entwined with ivy. The mark was worn almost smooth but still legible. "You mean that *N*?"

He gestured with his glass again, this time at the panorama view across the river. "What about the Liberation Monument, high on that hill?

"Dominic..."

"Do you see it?"

She speared an impatient glance at the bronze statue of a woman holding a palm leaf high aloft. It dominated the hill in the far distance and could obviously be seen from anywhere in the city.

"Yes, I see it." The temper he'd commented on earlier sparked again. "But I'm in no mood for games or quizzes, Mr. Grand Duke. What do you know that I don't?"

"I know you wore glasses in New York," he replied evenly. "Large, square glasses with thick lenses that you apparently don't require for near or distance vision. I know you scraped your hair back most unattractively instead of letting it fall loose to your shoulders, as it does now. I know you chose loose clothes in an attempt to disguise your slender hips and—" his glance drifted south, and an appreciative gleam lit his eyes "—very delightful breasts."

Her mouth had started sagging at the mention of glasses. It dropped farther when he got to her hair, and snapped shut at the mention of her breasts. Fighting the urge to cross her arms over her chest, she tried to make sense of his observations.

She couldn't refute the part about the clothes. She'd questioned her fashion sense herself before she'd tossed the garments in the trash this morning. But the glasses? The hair?

She scrubbed her palms over her thighs, now encased in the formfitting designer jeans she'd purchased at the boutique. The jeans, the sandals, the short-sleeve T-shirt didn't feel strange or uncomfortable. From what Dom had said, though, they weren't her.

"Maybe what you saw in New York is the real me," she said a little desperately. "Maybe I just don't like drawing attention to myself."

"Maybe," he agreed, his gaze steady on her face. "And maybe there's a reason why you don't."

She could think of several reasons, none of them particularly palatable. Some were so far out she dismissed them instantly. She just couldn't see herself as a terrorist in training or a bank robber on the run. There was another explanation she couldn't shrug off as easily. One Dom brought up slowly, carefully.

"Perhaps your desire to hide the real you relates to a personal trauma, as Dr. Kovacs suggested this morning."

She couldn't deny the possibility. Yet...

She didn't *feel* traumatized. And she'd evidently been doing just fine before her dive into the Danube. She had a job that must have paid very well, judging by the advance on her salary Sarah had sent. She'd traveled to Paris, to Vienna, to Hungary. She must have an apartment back in the States. Books, maybe. Framed prints on the wall or a pen-and-ink sketch or a...

Her thoughts jerked to a stop. Rewound. Focused on a framed print. No, not a print. A painting. A canal scene with strong, hazy colors and a light so natural it looked as though the sun was shimmering on the water.

She could see it! Every sleek black gondola, every window arch framed by mellow stone, every ripple of the green waters of the lagoon.

"Didn't Sarah tell you I went to Vienna to research a painting?" she asked Dom eagerly.

"She did."

"A Venetian canal scene." She clung to the mental image with a fierce effort of will. "By...by..."

"Canaletto."

"Yes!" She edged off the tall chair and kept a few careful inches away from the iron railing. "Let's go inside. I need to use your laptop."

Seven

The spicy scent of paprika and simmering beef filled the loft when they went inside. Natalie sniffed appreciatively but cut a straight line for the laptop.

"Do I need a password to power up?"

"Just hit the on switch."

"Really?" She dropped into the leather armchair and positioned the laptop on her knees. "I would have thought 007 would employ tighter security."

Dom didn't bother to explain that all electronic and digital communications he received from or sent to Interpol were embedded with so many layers of encryption that no one outside the agency could decipher them. He doubted she would have heard him in any case. She was hunched forward, her fingers hovering over the keys.

"I hope you have Wi-Fi," she muttered as the screen brightened to display a close-up of the hound. All nose and bright eyes and floppy ears, the image won a smile from Natalie. The real thing plopped down on his haunches before Dom and let his tongue loll in eager anticipation of a libation.

Idly, Dom tipped some lager into his dish and watched as Natalie skimmed through site after site relating to the eighteenth-century Italian painter. The cop in him kept returning to their conversation outside on the balcony. He wasn't buying her quick dismissal of the suggestion she'd tried to downplay her natural beauty.

She most definitely had, and the ploy hadn't worked. Not with Dom, anyway. Despite her disdainful sniffs, daunting glasses and maiden-aunt clothes, she'd stirred his interest from the moment she'd opened the door of the duchess's apartment. And she'd damned near tied him in knots when she'd paraded out of the shower this morning with that crew shirt skimming her thighs.

Now...

His fist tightened on the dew-streaked pilsner bottle. She should see herself through his eyes. The shoulder-length, honey-streaked brown hair. The fierce concentration drawing her brows into a straight line. The lips pooched into a tight rosebud.

Jézus, Mária és József! Those lips!

Swallowing a groan, Dom took another pull of the lager and gave the rest to the ecstatic hound.

"You shouldn't let him have beer."

He glanced over to find her looking all prudish and disapproving again. Maybe it wasn't a disguise, he thought wryly. Maybe there was room in that sexy body for a nun, a shower scrubber and a wanton.

God, he hoped so!

It didn't take her long to find what she was looking for. Dom was still visualizing a steamy shower encounter when she whooped.

"This is it! This is the painting I was researching. I don't know how I know it, but I do."

He crossed the room and peered over her shoulder. Her scent drifted up to him, mingling with that of the goulash to tease his senses. Hair warmed by the sun. Skin dusted from their day in the city. The faint tang of cleaning solutions. Excitement radiated from her as she read him the details she'd pulled up on the laptop.

"It's one of Canaletto's early works. Commissioned by a Venetian doge and seized by Napoleon as part of the spoils of war after he invaded Venice in 1797. It reportedly hung in his study at the Tuileries Palace, then disappeared sometime before or during a fire in 1871."

She scrolled down the page. She was in full research mode now, inhaling every detail with the same eagerness the hound did pilsner.

"The painting disappeared for almost a half a century, until it turned up again in the early '30s in the private collection of a Swiss industrialist. He died in 1953 and his squabbling heirs auctioned off his entire collection. At that point... Look!"

She stabbed a finger at the screen. Dom bent closer.

"At that point," she recited eagerly, "it was purchased by an agent acting for the Grand Duke of Karlenburgh."

She swiveled around, almost tilting the laptop off her knees in her eagerness. Her face was alive, her eyes bright with the thrill of discovery.

"The Grand Duke of Karlenburgh," she repeated. "That was you, several times removed."

"*Many* times removed."

Despite his seeming insouciance, the connection couldn't be denied. It wove around him like a fine, silken thread. Trapping him. Cocooning him.

"The painting was a gift from the duke to his duchess," he related, remembering the mischievous look in Charlotte's eyes. "To commemorate a particularly pleasant visit to Venice."

Natalie's face went blank for a moment, then lit with excitement. "I remember hearing that story! Venice is where she got pregnant, right? With her only child?"

"Right."

They were so close, her mouth just a breath away from

his, that Dom couldn't help himself. He had to drop a kiss on those tantalizing lips.

He kept it light, playful. But when he raised his head confusion and a hint of wariness had replaced the excitement. Kicking himself, he tried to coax it back.

"Charlotte said the painting hung in the Red Salon at Karlenburgh Castle. Is there reference to that?"

"I, uh... Let me look."

She ducked her head and hit the keys again. Her hair feathered against her cheek like a sparrow's wing, shielding her face. He knew he'd lost serious ground when she shook her head and refused to look at him.

"No mention here. All it says is that the painting was lost again in the chaos following the Soviet suppression of the 1956 Hungarian Uprising."

"The same uprising that cost the Grand Duke his life and forced his wife to flee her homeland."

"How sad." With a small sigh, Natalie slumped against the chair back. "Charlotte's husband purchased the painting to celebrate one of the most joyous moments of their lives. And just a little more than a year later, both he and the painting were lost."

Her voice had gone small and quiet. She was drawing parallels, Dom guessed. Empathizing with the duchess's tragic losses. Feeling the emptiness of her own life.

The thought of her being a forgotten, helpless cog in a vast social welfare bureaucracy pulled at something deep inside him. He'd known her for such a short time. Had spoken to her twice in New York. Spent less than twenty-four hours with her here in Budapest. Yet he found himself wanting to erase the empty spaces in her heart. To pull her into his arms and fill the gaps in her mind with new, happy and extremely erotic memories. The urge was so powerful it yanked him up like a puppet on a twisted string.

Christ! He was a cop. Like all cops, he knew that trust

could—and too often did—shift like the sand on a wave-swept shore. Identities had to be validated, backgrounds scrubbed with a wire brush. Until he heard back from his contact at Interpol, he'd damned well better keep his hands to himself.

"The duke was executed," he said briskly, "but Charlotte survived. She made a new life for herself and her baby in New York. Now she has her granddaughters, her great-grandchildren. And you, Ms. Clark, have the finest goulash in all of Budapest to sample."

The abrupt change in direction accomplished precisely what he'd intended. Natalie raised her head. The curtain of soft, shiny hair fell back, and a tentative smile etched across her face.

"I'm ready."

More than ready, she realized. They hadn't eaten since their hurried breakfast and it was now almost seven. The aroma filling the loft had her taste buds dancing in eagerness.

"Ha!" Dom said with a grin. "You may think you're prepared, but Frau Kemper's stew is in a class by itself. Prepare for a culinary tsunami."

While he sniffed and stirred the goulash, Natalie set the counter with the mismatched crockery and cutlery she'd found during her earlier explorations of the kitchen cupboards.

Doing the homey little task made her feel strange. Strange and confused and nervous. Especially when her hip bumped Dominic's in the narrow kitchen area. And when he reached for a paper towel the same time she did. And…

Oh, for pity's sake! Who was she kidding? It wasn't the act of laying out bowls and spoons that had her mind and nerves jumping. It was Dominic. She couldn't look at him without remembering the feel of his mouth on hers.

Couldn't listen to him warning the dog—Duke!—to take himself out of the kitchen without thinking about how he'd called her sweetheart in Hungarian. And not just in Hungarian. In a husky, teasing voice that seemed so intimate, so seductive.

She didn't really know him. Hell, she didn't even know herself! Yet when he went to refill her glass with water she stopped him.

"I'd like to try that wine you brought home."

He looked up from the spigot in surprise. "Are you sure?"

"Yes."

She was. She really was. Natalie had no idea what lay at the root of her aversion to alcohol. A secretive, guilt-ridden tasting as a kid? An ugly drunk as a teen? A degrading experience in college? Whatever had caused it remained shrouded in her past. Right here, though, right now, she felt safe enough enjoy a glass of wine.

Safe?

The word echoed in her mind as Dom worked the cork on the chilled bottle and raised his glass to eye level. *"Egészségére!"*

"I'll drink to that, whatever it means."

"It means 'to your health.' Unless you mispronounce it," he added with a waggle of his brows. "Then it means 'to your arse.'"

She didn't bother to ask which pronunciation he'd used, just took a sip and waited for some unseen ax to fall. When the cool, refreshing white went down smoothly, she started to relax.

The goulash sped that process considerably. The first spoonful had her gasping and reaching desperately for the wineglass. The second, more cautious spoonful went down with less of an assault by the paprika and garlic. By the third, she'd recovered enough to appreciate the subtle flavors of caraway seed, marjoram and sautéed onions. By the fourth, she was spearing the beef, pork and potatoes with avid enthusiasm and sopping up gravy with chunks of dark bread torn from the loaf Frau Kemper had thoughtfully included with her stew.

She limited her wine intake to a single glass but readily agreed to a second helping of goulash. The Agár sat on his haunches beside her stool as she spooned it down. When she didn't share, his liquid brown eyes filled with such reproach that she was forced to sneak him several dripping morsels. Dom pretended not to notice, although he did mention drily that he'd have to take the hound for an extralong run before bed to flush the spicy stew out of his system.

As casual as it was, the comment started Natalie's nerves jumping again. The loft boasted only one bed. She'd occupied it last night. She felt guilty claiming it again.

"Speaking of bed…"

Dom's spoon paused in midair. "Yes?"

Her cheeks heating, she stirred the last of her stew. He had to be wondering why she hadn't taken Sarah up on her offer of a hotel room. At the moment, she couldn't help wondering the same thing.

"I don't like ousting you out of yours."

"Oh?" His spoon lowered. "Are you suggesting we share?"

She was becoming familiar with that slow, provocative grin.

"I'm suggesting," she said with a disdainful sniff, "I sleep on the sofa tonight and you take the bed."

She hadn't intended her retort as a challenge, but she should have known Dom would view it that way. Laughter leaped into his face, along with something that started Natalie's breath humming in her throat.

"Ah, sweetheart," he murmured, his eyes on her mouth.

"You make it very difficult for me to ignore the instincts bred into me by my wild, marauding ancestors."

Even Duke seemed to sense the sudden tension that arced through her. The dog wedged closer to Natalie and propped his head on her knee. She knuckled his forehead and tried desperately to blank any and all thought of Dom tossing her over his shoulder. Carrying her to his bed. Pillaging her mouth. Ravishing her body. Demanding a surrender she was all too willing to...

"Don't look so worried."

The wry command jolted her back to the here and now. Blinking, she watched Dom push off his stool.

"My blood may run as hot as my ancestors', but I draw the line at seducing a woman who can't remember her name. Come, Dog."

Still racked by the erotic images, Natalie bent her head to avoid looking at Dom as he snapped the Agár's lead to his collar. She couldn't avoid the knuckle he curved under her chin, however, or the real regret in his eyes when he tipped her face to his.

"I'm sorry, Natushka. I shouldn't tease you. I know this is a frightening time for you."

Oh, sure. Like she was going to tell him that fright was *not* what she was feeling right now? Easing her chin from his hold, she slid off her stool and gathered the used utensils.

"I'll wash the dishes while you're gone."

"No need. Just stick them in the dishwasher."

"Go!" She needed to do something with her hands and her overactive, overheated mind. "I'll take care of the kitchen."

She did the dishes. Spritzed the sink and countertop. Drew the drapes. Fussed with paperbacks she'd stacked earlier that afternoon. Curled up in the chair and reached for the laptop. And grew more annoyed with each passing moment.

Her glance kept darting from the wide sofa with its worn leather cushions to the bed tucked under the eaves at the far end of the loft. She didn't understand why she was so irritated by Dom's assurance that he wouldn't seduce her. Those brief moments of fantasy involving marauding Magyars aside, she didn't really *want* him to. Did she?

Lips compressed, she tried to balance her contradictory emotions. On the one hand, Dominic St. Sebastian constituted the only island in the empty sea of her mind. It was natural that she would cling to him. Not want to antagonize him or turn him away.

Yet what she was feeling now wasn't mental. It was physical, and growing more urgent by the moment. She wanted his hands on her, dammit! His mouth. She wanted that hard, muscled body pinning hers to the wall, the sheets, even the floor.

The intensity of the hunger pumping through her veins surprised her. It also generated an enormous relief. All that talk about a possible past trauma had raised some ugly questions in her mind. In Dom's, too, apparently, judging by his comment about her deliberately trying to downplay her looks. The realization that she could want a man as much as she appeared to want this one was as reassuring as it was frustrating.

Which brought her right back to square one. She threw another thoroughly annoyed look at the bed. She should have taken Sarah up on her offer to arrange a hotel room, she thought sourly. If she had, she wouldn't be sitting here wondering whether she should—or could!—convince Dom to forget about being all noble and considerate.

Shoving out of the chair, she stalked to the wardrobe and reclaimed the shirt she'd slept in last night. She took it into the bathroom to change, and her prickly irritation ratcheted up another notch when she found the hand towel she'd left folded neatly over the rack tossed in a damp pile atop the counter. Worse, the toiletries she'd carefully arranged to make room for her few purchases were once again scattered haphazardly around the sink.

Muttering, she stripped off her new jeans and top. She didn't think she was obsessive-compulsive. And even if she was, what was so wrong with keeping things neat and orderly?

The sight of her borrowed undies didn't exactly improve her mood. Dom obviously hadn't suffered from an excess of scruples with Kissy Face Arabella. Natalie would have dumped the black silk hipsters in the trash if she'd had another pair to step into. She'd have to do more shopping tomorrow.

Yanking the crew shirt over her head, she scrubbed her face and teeth. Then she carefully refolded *her* towel and scooped up her jeans and top. Just as she exited the bathroom, the front door opened and Duke bounded in. His ecstatic greeting soon had her laughing. Hard to stay in a snit with a cold nose poking her bare thighs and a pink tongue determined to slather her with kisses.

"Okay, enough, stop." She fended off a determined lunge and pointed a stern finger at the floor. "Duke! Sit!"

He looked a little confused by the English command but the gesture got through to him. Ears flopping, he dropped onto his haunches.

"Good boy." She couldn't resist sending his master a smug look. "See, he recognizes his name."

"I think he recognized your tone."

"Whatever." She chewed on her lower lip for a moment. "We didn't resolve the issue of the bed earlier. I don't feel right consigning you to the sofa. I'll sleep there tonight."

"No, you won't."

"Look, I'm very grateful for all you've done for me. I

don't want to inconvenience you any more than I already have."

Dom managed not to snort. If she had any idea of just how badly she was "inconveniencing" him at this moment, she'd shimmy back into her jeans and run like hell. Instead she just stood there while his gaze gobbled up the long, slender legs showing below the hem of his shirt. The mere thought of those legs tangled with his started an ache in his groin.

He damned well better not fantasize about what was *under* the shirt. If he did, neither one of them would make it to the bed. They might not even make it to the sofa.

"I've fallen asleep more nights than I can count in front of the TV," he bit out. "You've got the bed."

He could tell from the way her mouth set that he'd come across more brusque than he'd intended. Tough. After just a little more than twenty-four hours in her company, Ms. Clark had him swinging like a pendulum. One moment his cop's instincts were reminding him that things weren't always what they seemed. The next, he ached to take her in his arms and kiss away the fear she was doing her best to disguise.

Now he just plain ached, and he wasn't happy about the fact that he couldn't—wouldn't!—do anything to ease the hurt. And why was she tormenting him like this, anyway?

"You're not going to bed now, are you?" he asked her.

"It's almost ten."

He managed to keep his jaw from sagging, but it took a heroic effort. He could understand her crashing facedown on the bed last night. She'd been hurt. She'd spent who knew how long in the Danube, and had a lump the size of a softball at the base of the skull.

She'd seemed to recover today, though. Enough for him to make an incautious comment. "At ten o'clock most Hungarians are trying to decide where to go for coffee and dessert."

Her chin tilted. "If you want to go out for coffee and dessert, please don't let me stop you."

Whoa! He'd missed something here. When he left to take out the dog twenty minutes ago, Natalie had been all soft and shy and confused. Now she was as stiff and prickly as a horsehair blanket.

Dom wanted to ask what happened in that short time span but he'd learned the hard way to keep his mouth shut. He'd guided his sister through her hormone-driven teen years. He'd also enjoyed the company of his fair share of women. Enough, anyway, to know that any male who attempted to plumb the workings of the female mind had better be wearing a Kevlar vest. Since he wasn't, he quickly backpcdaled.

"Probably just as well we make it an early night. We have a full day tomorrow."

She acknowledged his craven retreat with a regal dip of her head. "Yes, we do. Good night."

"Good night."

Dom and the hound both watched as she made her way to the far end of the loft and arranged her jeans and tank top into neat folds before placing them on the table beside the bed. Dom didn't move while she turned back the comforter and slid between the sheets.

The dog didn't exercise the same restraint. His claws scrabbling on the oak floorboards, he scrambled across the open space and made a flying leap. He landed on the bed with paws outstretched and announced his arrival with a happy woof. Natalie laughed and eased to one side to make room for him.

With a muttered curse, Dom turned away from the sight of the Agár sprawled belly-up beside her.

Eight

The next day dawned achingly bright and gloriously cool. The first nip of fall had swept away the exhaust-polluted city air and left Budapest sparkling in the morning light.

Dom woke early after a restless night. Natalie was still hunched under the featherbed when he took the hound for his morning run. Halfway through their usual five miles he received a text message with a copy of her driver's license. He saved the attachment to print out at the loft and thumbed his phone to access the US Embassy website. Once he'd downloaded the application to replace a lost passport, he made a note to himself to call the consular office and set up an appointment.

He was tempted to make another call to his contact at Interpol. When he'd asked Andre to dig deeper, he hadn't expected the excavation to take more than a day. Two at the most. But he knew Andre would get back to him if he uncovered anything of interest.

Dom also knew he belonged in the field! He'd taken down vicious killers, drug traffickers, the remorseless sleaze who sold children to the highest bidders. He didn't claim to be the best at what he did, but he'd done his part. This extended vacation was pure crap.

Or had been, until Natalie had dropped into his life. If Dom hadn't been at such loose ends he might not have been so quick to assume complete responsibility for her.

Now that he had, he felt obligated to keep her close until her memory returned.

It was already trickling back. Bits and pieces had started to pierce the haze. And when the fog dissipated completely, he thought with a sudden tightening of his belly, he intended to do his damnedest to follow up on that one, searing kiss. He'd spent too many uncomfortable hours on the sofa last night, imagining just that eventuality.

A jerk on the leash checked his easy stride. He glanced down to see the hound dragging his rear legs and glaring at him reproachfully.

"Don't look at me like that. You're already in bed with her."

Still the dog wouldn't move.

"Oh, all right. Have at it."

Dom jogged in place while the Agár sniffed the interesting pile just off the track, then majestically lifted a leg to spray it.

As soon as Dom and the hound entered, they were hit with the aroma of sizzling bacon and freshly baked cinnamon bread. The scents were almost as tantalizing as the sight of Natalie at the stove, a spatula in hand and a towel tucked apronlike around her slim hips. Dom tried to remember the last woman who'd made herself at home in his kitchen. None of those who'd come for a drink and stayed for the night, as best he could recall. And certainly not his sister. Even as a child, Anastazia had always been too busy splinting the broken wings of sparrows or feeding baby squirrels with eyedroppers to think about nourishing herself or her brother.

"I went down to the grocery shop on the corner," Natalie said by way of greeting. "I thought we should have breakfast before we took off for Karlenburgh Castle."

"That sounds good. How long before it's ready?"

"Five minutes."

"Make it ten," he begged.

He snagged a cup of coffee and had to hide a grimace. She'd made it American style. Closer to colored water than the real thing. The weak brew provided barely enough punch to get him through a quick shower and shave.

He emerged eager for a taste of the bacon laid out in crisp strips on a paper towel. The fluffy eggs scrambled with mushrooms and topped with fresh-grated Gruyère cheese had his tongue hanging out almost as far as the hound's. But the warm cinnamon rolls tucked in a napkin made him go weak at the knees. Groaning, he sank onto a stool at the counter.

"Do you cook breakfast for yourself every morning?"

She paused with the spatula hovering above the platter of eggs. "I don't know."

"No matter," Dom said fervently. "You're doing fine."

Actually, she was doing great. Her movements concise and confident, she set out his mismatched plates and folded paper napkins into neat, dainty triangles. Amused, he saw that she'd purchased a small bouquet of flowers during her quick trip to the grocers. The purple lupines and pink roses now sprouted from his prized beer stein. He had to admit they added a nice touch of color to the otherwise drab kitchen area.

So did she. She wore the jeans she'd purchased yesterday and had borrowed another of his soccer shirts. The hem of the hunter-green shirt fell well below her hips, unfortunately, but when she leaned across the counter to refill his coffee mug, the deep-V neckline gave him a tantalizing glimpse of creamy slopes.

Promising the hopeful hound he would be fed later, she perched on the stool beside Dom and served them both. The eggs tasted as good as they looked. He was halfway through his when he gave her an update.

"While I was out jogging, I got a text with a copy of your driver's license attached. I also downloaded the application form for a replacement passport. I'll print both after breakfast, then we'll make an appointment with the consular office."

Natalie nodded. The bits and pieces of her life seemed to be falling into place. She just wished they would fall faster. Maybe this excursion to Karlenburgh Castle would help. Suddenly impatient, she hopped off her stool and rinsed her dish in the sink.

"Are you finished?" she asked.

He relinquished his plate but snagged the last cinnamon bun before she could whisk the basket away. She did a quick kitchen cleanup and changed back into her red tank top. Her straw tote hooked over her shoulder, she waited impatiently while Dom extracted a lightweight jacket from his wardrobe.

"You'll need this. It can get cool up in the mountains."

She was disappointed when he decreed the hound wouldn't join them on the expedition…and surprised when he introduced her to the girl in the apartment downstairs who looked after the animal during his frequent absences.

The dog-sitter wasn't the sultry, predatory single Natalie had imagined. Instead she looked to be about nine or ten, with a splash of freckles across her nose and a backpack that indicated she'd been just about to depart for school.

When she dropped to her knees to return the hound's eager kisses, her papa came to the door. Dom introduced Natalie and explained that they might return late. "I would appreciate it if Katya would walk him after school, as per our usual agreement."

The father smiled fondly at his daughter and replied in heavily accented English. "But of course, Dominic. They will both enjoy the exercise. We still have the bones and bag of food you left last time. If you are late, we'll feed him, yes?"

"We should not call him Dominic anymore, Papa." The girl sent Dom an impish grin. "We should address you as Your Grace, shouldn't we?"

"You do," he retorted, tugging on her ear, "and I won't let you download any more songs from my iTunes account."

Giggling, she pulled away and reminded him of a promise he looked as though he would prefer to forget. "You're coming to my school, aren't you? I want to show off my important neighbor."

"Yes, yes. I will."

"When?"

"Soon."

"When?"

"Katya," her father said in gentle reproof.

"But Dom's on vacation now. He told us so." Her arm looped around the dog's neck, she turned accusing eyes on her upstairs neighbor. "So when will you come?"

Natalie had to bite the inside of her lip to keep from laughing. The kid had him nailed and knew it.

"Next week," he promised reluctantly.

"When next week?"

"Katya, enough!"

"But, Papa, I need to tell my teacher when to expect the Grand Duke of Karlenburgh."

Groaning, Dom committed to Tuesday afternoon if her teacher concurred. Then he grasped Natalie's elbow and steered her toward the garage stairs.

"Let's get out of here before she makes me promise to wear a crown and a purple robe."

"Yes, Your Grace."

"Watch yourself, woman."

"Yes, Your Grace."

She knew him well enough now to laugh off his bad-tempered growl. As they started down the winding streets of Castle Hill, though, she added another facet to his growing list of alter egos. Undercover Agent. Grand Duke. Rescuer of damsels in distress. Loving older brother. Adopter of stray hounds. And now friend to an obviously adoring preteen.

Then there was that other side to him. The hot, sexy marauder whose ancestors had swept down from the Steppes. Sitting right next to her, so close that all she had to do was slide a glance at his profile to remember his taste and his scent and the feel of all those hard muscles pressed against her.

Natalie bit her lip in dismay when she realized she couldn't decide which of Dom's multiple personalities appealed to her most. They were all equally seductive, and she had the scary feeling that she was falling a little bit in love with each one of them.

Lost in those disturbing thoughts, she didn't see they'd emerged onto a broad boulevard running parallel to the Danube until Dom pointed out an impressive complex with an elaborate facade boasting turrets and fanciful wrought-iron balconies.

"That's Gellért Hotel. Their baths are among the best in Budapest. We'll have to follow Dr. Kovacs's advice and go for a soak tomorrow, yes?"

Natalie couldn't remember if she'd been to a communal bath before. Somehow it didn't seem like her kind of thing. "Do the spa-goers wear bathing suits?"

"In the public pools." He tipped her a quick grin. "But we can book a private session, where suits are optional."

Like that was going to happen! Natalie could barely breathe sitting here next to him fully clothed. She refused to think about the two of them slithering into a pool naked.

Hastily, she shoved her thoughts in a different direction. "How far did you say it was to where I left the rental car?"

"Győr's only a little over a hundred kilometers."

"And Pradzéc, where I crossed over from Austria?"

"Another sixty or seventy kilometers. But the going will be slower as we get closer to the border. The road winds as it climbs into the Alps."

"Where it reaches Karlenburgh Castle," she murmured.

She'd been there. She *knew* she'd been there. Dom claimed the castle was nothing but a pile of tumbled rock now but something had pulled Natalie to those ruins. Even now, she could feel the tug. The sensation was so strong, so compelling, that it took her some time to let go of it and pay more attention to the countryside they passed through.

They zipped along the M1 motorway as it cut through the region that Dom told her was called Northern Transdanubia. Despite its bloody history as the traditional battleground between Hungary and the forces invading from the west, the region was one of gentle hills, green valleys and lush forests. The international brown signs designating a significant historic landmark flashed by with astonishing frequency. Each town or village they passed seemed to boast an ancient abbey or spa or fortified stronghold.

The city of Győr was no exception. When Dom pointed out that it was located exactly halfway between Vienna and Budapest, she wondered how many armies had tramped through its ancient, cobbled streets. Natalie caught only a glimpse of Old Town's battlements, however, before they turned north. Short moments later they reached the point where two smaller rivers flowed into the mighty Danube.

A double-decker tour boat was just departing the wharf. Natalie strained every brain cell in an effort to identify with the day-trippers crowding the rails on the upper decks. Nothing clicked. Not even when Dom turned into the parking lot and parked next to the motorized matchbox she'd supposedly rented in Vienna almost two days ago.

Dom had arranged for a rental agency rep to meet them. When the agent popped the trunk with a spare set of keys a tingle began to feather along her nerves. The tingle surged to a hot, excited rush the moment she spotted a bulging leather briefcase.

"That's mine!"

Snatching the case out of the trunk, she cradled it against her breasts like a long-lost baby. She allowed it out of her arms only long enough for Dom to note the initials embossed in gold near the handle...and the fact that it wasn't locked. Her heart pounding, she popped the latch and whooped at the sight of a slim laptop jammed between stacks of fat files.

"This must be yours, too," the rental agency rep said as he lifted out a weekender on wheels.

She didn't experience the same hot rush when the ID tag on the case verified the case was, in fact, hers. Maybe because when she opened it to inspect the contents they looked as though they belonged to an octogenarian. Everything was drab, colorless and eminently sensible. She tried to pump herself up with the realization that she now had several sets of clean undies in her possession. Unfortunately, they were all plain, unadorned undies that Kiss Kiss Arabella wouldn't be caught dead in!

A check of the vehicle's interior produced no purse, passport, ID or credit cards. Nor was there any sign of the glasses Dominic insisted she hadn't really needed. They must have gone into the river with her. Hugging the briefcase, she watched as Dom transferred the weekender to his own car and provided a copy of the police report to the rep from the rental agency. In view of her accident and injury and the fact that there was no apparent damage to the vehicle, the rep agreed to waive the late return charges.

Natalie almost shivered with impatience to delve into the files in the briefcase but Dom wanted to talk to the people at the tour office first on the off-chance they might remember her. They didn't, nor could they provide any more information than the police had already gleaned by tracking her credit card charges.

Natalie stood with Dom next to the ticket booth and stared at the sleek boat now little more than a speck in the distance. "This is so frustrating! Why did I take a river cruise? I don't even like boats."

"How do you know?"

She blinked. "I'm not sure. I just don't."

"Maybe we'll find a clue in your briefcase."

She glanced around the wharf area, itching to get into those fat files, but knew they couldn't spread their contents out on a picnic table where the breeze off the river might snatch them away. Dom sensed her frustration and offered a suggestion.

"We're less than an hour from Karlenburgh Castle. There's an inn in the village below the castle ruins. We can have lunch and ask Frau Dortmann for the use of her parlor to lay everything out."

"Let's go!"

She couldn't resist extracting a few of the files and skimming through them on the way. Each folder was devoted to a lost treasure. A neat table of contents listed everything inside—printed articles from various computer sources, copies of handwritten documents, color photos, black-and-whites, historical chronologies tracing last known ownership, notes Natalie had made to herself on additional sources to check.

"Ooh," she murmured when she flipped to a sketch of jewel-studded egg nested in a gold chariot pulled by a winged cherub. "How beautiful."

Dom glanced at the photo. "Isn't that the Fabergé egg Tsar Alexander gave his wife?"

"I…uh…" She checked her notes and looked up in surprise. "It is. How do you know that?"

"You were researching it in the States. You told me about it when we got together in your hotel room in New York."

"We got together in New York? In my hotel room?"

Dom was tempted, really tempted, but he stuck with the truth. "I thought you might be scheming to rip off the duchess with all that business about the codicil so I came to warn you off. You," he added with a quick grin, "kicked me out on my ass."

The Natalie he knew and was beginning to seriously lust after emerged. "I'm sure you deserved it."

"Ah, Natushka. Don't go all prim and proper on me. We might not make it to the inn."

He said it with a smile but they both knew he was only half kidding. Cheeks flushed, Natalie dug into the file again.

She saw the castle ruins first. She could hardly miss them. The tumbled walls and skeletal remains of a single square tower were set high on a rocky crag and visible from miles away. As they got closer, Natalie could see how the road cut through the narrow pass below——the only pass connecting Austria and Hungary for fifty miles in either direction, Dom informed her.

"No wonder the Habsburgs were so anxious to have your ancestors hold it for the Empire."

Only after they'd topped a steep rise did she see the village at the base of the cliffs. The dozen or so structures were typically Alpine, half-timbered and steep-roofed to slough off snow. A wooden roadside shrine housing a statue of the Virgin Mary greeted them as they approached the village. In keeping with the mingled heritage of the residents, the few street signs and notices were in both German and Hungarian.

The gasthaus sat at the edge of the village. Its mossy shingles and weathered timbers suggested it had welcomed wayfarers for centuries. Geraniums bloomed in every window box and an ivy-covered beer garden beckoned at one side of the main structure.

When Natalie and Dom went up the steps and entered the knotty-pine lobby, the woman who hustled out to greet them didn't match her rustic surroundings. Dom's casual reference to Frau Dortmann had evoked hazy images of an apron-clad, rosy-cheeked matron.

The fortysomething blonde in leggings and a tiger-striped tunic was as far from matronly as a woman could get. And if there was a Herr Dortmann hanging around anywhere, Natalie was certain he wouldn't appreciate the way his wife flung herself into Dom's arms. Wrapping herself around him like a half-starved boa constrictor, she kissed him. Not on both cheeks like any other polite European, but long and hard and full on the lips.

He was half laughing, half embarrassed when he finally managed to extricate himself. With a rueful glance at Natalie, he interrupted the blonde's spate of rapid Hungarian liberally interspersed with German.

"Lisel, this is Natalie Clark. A friend of mine from America."

"America!" Wide, amethyst eyes turned to Natalie. Eager hands reached out to take both of hers. *"Wilkommen!* You must come in. You'll have a lager, *ja*? And then you will tell me how you come to be in the company of a rogue such as Dominic St. Sebastian." Her laughing glance cut back to Dom. "Or do I address you as 'Your Grace'? *Ja, ja,* I must. The whole village talks of nothing else but the stories about you in the papers."

"You can thank Natalie for that," he drawled.

The blonde's brows soared. "How so?"

"She's an archivist. A researcher who digs around in musty old ledgers. She uncovered a document in Vienna that appears to grant the titles of Grand Duke and Duchess of Karlenburgh to the St. Sebastians until the Alps crumble. As we all know, however, it's an empty honor."

"Ha! Not here. As soon as word gets around that the Grand Duke has returned to his ancestral home, the taproom will be jammed and the beer will flow like a river. Just wait. You will see."

They didn't have to wait long. Dom had barely finished explaining to Frau Dortman that he'd only come to show Natalie the ruins and aid her in her research when the door opened. A bent, craggy-faced gentleman in worn leather pants hobbled in and greeted Dom with the immense dignity of a man who'd lived through good times and bad. This, Natalie soon grasped, was a good time. A very good time, the older man indicated with a wide smile.

He was followed in short order by a big, buff farmer who carried the sharp tang of the barn in with him, two teenagers with curious eyes and earbuds dangling around their necks and a young woman cradling a baby on her hip. Natalie kept waiting for Herr Dortmann to make an appearance. When he didn't show, a casual query revealed Lisel had divorced the lazy good-for-nothing and sent him packing years ago.

Dom tried his best to include Natalie in the conversations that buzzed around them. As more and more people arrived, though, she edged out of the inner circle and enjoyed the show. St. Sebastian might downplay this whole royalty thing, she mused as she settled on a bar stool and placed her briefcase on a counter worn smooth by centuries of use, but he was a natural. It wasn't so much that he stood two or three inches above the rest of the crowd. Or that he exuded such an easy self-confidence. Or, she thought wryly, that he had already informed Lisel that he would pay for the beer that flowed as freely as the inn-keeper had predicted.

He also, Natalie guessed, paid for the platters piled with sausages and spaetzle and fried potatoes and pickled beets that emerged in successive waves from the kitchen. The feasting and toasts and storytelling lasted through the afternoon and into the evening. By then, Dom had downed too much beer to get behind the wheel again.

Lisel had anticipated just such an eventuality. "You will stay here tonight," she announced and drew an old-fashioned iron key from the pocket of her tiger-striped tunic. "The front bedroom has a fine view of the castle," she confided to Natalie. "You and Dominic can see it as you lie in bed."

"It sounds wonderful." She plucked the room key out of the innkeeper's hand. "But Dominic will need other sleeping arrangements."

After Lisel Dortmann's enthusiastic welcome, Natalie preferred not to speculate on what those arrangements might be. All she knew was that she wasn't going to share a bed with the man—as much as she wanted to.

Nine

She took the narrow wooden stairs to the second floor and found the front bedroom easily enough. It contained a good-size bath and an alcove tucked under the slanting eaves that housed a small desk and overstuffed easy chair. The beautifully carved wooden headboard and washstand with its porcelain pitcher and bowl provided antique touches, while the flat-screen TV and small placard announcing the inn offered free Wi-Fi were welcome modern conveniences.

As Lisel had promised, the lace-draped windows offered an unimpeded view of the ruins set high atop the rocky promontory. The early evening shadows lent them a dark and brooding aspect. Then the clouds shifted, parted, and the last of the sun's rays cut like a laser. For a few magical moments what remained of Karlenburgh Castle was bathed in bright gold.

She'd seen these ruins before! Natalie knew it! Not all shimmery and ethereal and golden like this but...

A rap on the door interrupted her tumultuous thoughts. Dom stood in the hall with the weekender he'd brought in from the car.

"I thought you might need your case."

"Thanks." She grabbed his arm and hauled him toward the window. "You've got to see this."

He glanced through the windows at the sight she pointed

to but almost immediately his gaze switched back to Natalie. Her eyes were huge, her face alive with excitement. She could hardly contain it as she turned to him.

"Those ruins... That setting... I went up there, Dom."

Her forehead scrunched with such an intense effort to dredge up stubborn memories that it hurt him to watch. Aching for her, he raised his hand and traced his thumb down the deep crease in her brow. He followed the slope of her nose, the line of her tightly folded lips.

"Ah, Natushka." The husky murmur distracted her, as he'd intended. "You're doing it again."

"Doing wh...? Oh."

He couldn't help himself. He had to coax those lips back to lush, ripe fullness. Then, of course, he had to take his fill of them. To his delight, she tilted her head to give him better access.

He wasn't sure when he knew a mere taste wouldn't be enough. Maybe when she gave a little sigh and leaned into him. Or when her hands slid up and over his shoulders. Or when the ache he'd felt when he'd watched her struggling to remember dropped south. Hard and heavy and suddenly hurting, he tried to disentangle.

"No!"

The command was breathy and urgent. She tightened her arms around his neck, dragging him in for another kiss. This time she gave, and Dom took what she offered. The eager mouth, the quick dance of her tongue against his, the kick to his pulse when her breasts flattened against his chest.

He dropped his hands, cupped her bottom and pulled her closer. A serious mistake, he realized the instant her hip gouged into his groin. Biting down a groan, he eased back an inch or two.

"I want you, Natalie. You can see it. Feel it. But..."

"I want you, too."

"But," he continued gruffly, "I'm not going to take advantage of your confusion and uncertainty."

She leaned back in his arms and considered that for several moments while Dom shifted a little to one side to ease the pressure of her hip.

"I think it's the other way around," she said at last. "I'm the one taking advantage. You didn't have to let me stay at the loft. Or go with me to Dr. Kovacs, or get a copy of my driver's license, or come with me today."

"So I was just supposed to set you adrift far from your home with no money and no identity?"

"The point is, you didn't set me adrift." Her voice softened, and her eyes misted. "You're my anchor, Dominic. My lifeline." She leaned in again and brushed his mouth with hers. "Thank you."

The soft whisper sliced into him like a double-bladed ax. Wrapping his hands around her upper arms, he pushed her away. Surprise left her slack-jawed and gaping up at him.

"Is that what this is about, Natalie? You're so grateful you feel you have to respond when I kiss you? Perhaps sleep with me in payment for services rendered?"

"No!" Indignation sent a tide of red to her cheeks. "Of all the arrogant, idiotic..."

She stopped, dragged in a breath and tilted her chin to a dangerous angle.

"I guess you didn't notice, St. Sebastian, but I happen to like kissing you. I suspect I would also like going to bed with you. But I'll be damned if I'll do it with you thinking I'm so pathetic that I should be grateful for any crumbs that you and the hound and Kissy Face Arabella and..." She waved an irate hand. "And all your other friends toss my way."

The huffy speech left Dom swinging from anger to amusement. He didn't trust himself to address her comment about Arabella. Just the thought of Natalie wearing the Londoner's black silk put another kink in his gut. The hound was a different matter.

"This is a first," he admitted. "I've never been lumped in the same category as a dog before."

"You're not in the same category," she retorted. "Duke at least recognizes honest emotions like friendship and loyalty and affection."

"Affection?" His ego dropped another notch. "That's what you feel for me?"

"Oh, for….!" Exasperated, she twisted out of his arms and planted both fists on her hips. "What do you want, *Your Highness*? A written confession that I lay awake last night wishing it was you snuffling beside me instead of Duke? An engraved invitation to take his place?"

He searched her face, her eyes, and read only indignation and frustration. No subliminal fear stemming from a traumatic past event. No prim, old-maidish reluctance to get sweaty and naked. No confusion about what she wanted.

His scruples died an instant death as hunger rushed hot and greedy through his veins. "No engraved invitation required. I'll take this." He reached for her again and found her mouth. "And this," he murmured, nipping at her throat. "And this," he growled as his hand found her breast.

When he scooped her into his arms several long, mind-drugging moments later, his conscience fought through the red haze for a last, desperate battle. She was still lost, dammit! Still vulnerable. Despite her irate speech, he shouldn't carry her to the bed.

Shouldn't, but did. Some contrary corner of his mind said it was her very vulnerability that made him want to strengthen the lifeline she mentioned. Anchor her even more securely.

The last thought shook him. Not enough to stop him,

though. Especially with the moonlight spilling through the windows, bathing her face and now well-kissed lips in a soft glow.

His hunger erupted in a greedy, gnawing need. He stood her on her feet beside the bed and peeled away her clothes with more haste than finesse. Impatience made him clumsy but fired a similar urgency in Natalie. She tugged his shirt over his head and dropped hungry kisses on his chest as she fumbled with the snap of his jeans.

When he dragged back the thick, down-filled feather-bed and tumbled her to the sheets, her body was smooth and warm, a landscape of golden lights and dark shadows. And when she hooked a calf around one of his, he had to fight the primal need to drive into her. He had to get something straight between them first. Thrusting his hands into her hair, he delivered a quick kiss and a wry confession.

"Just so you don't think this is your idea, you should know I was plotting various ways to get you into bed when I came to your hotel room in New York."

Natalie's heart kicked. In a sudden flash, she could see the small hotel room. Two double beds. An open laptop. Herself going nose to nose with Dom about... About...

"You thought I was some kind of schemer, out to fleece the duchess."

He went still. "You remember that?"

"Yes!" She clung to the image, sorting through the emotions that came with it. One proved especially satisfying. "I also remember slamming the door in your face," she said gleefully.

"You do, huh?" He got even for that with a long, hard kiss that left her gasping. "Remember anything else?"

"Not at the moment," she gulped.

He released her hair and slid his hands down her neck, over her shoulders, down her body. "Then I guess we'd better generate a few new memories."

Natalie gasped again as he set to work exploring her body. Nipping her earlobe. Kneading her breasts. Teasing her nipples. Tracing a path down her belly to the apex of her thighs. She was quivering with delight when he used a knee to part her legs.

His hair-roughened thigh rasped against hers. His breathing went fast and harsh. And his hand—his busy, diabolical hand—found her center. She was hot and wet and eager when he slid a finger in. Two. All the while his thumb played over the tight bud at her center and his teeth brought her nipples to taut, aching peaks. As the sensations piled one on top of the other, she arched under him.

"Dom! Dom, I… Ooooooh!"

The cry ripped from deep in her throat. She tried to hold back but the sensations spiraling up from her belly built to a wild, whirling vortex. Shuddering, she rode them to the last, gasping breath.

Minutes, maybe hours later, she pried up eyelids that felt as heavy as lead. Dom had propped his weight on one elbow and was watching her intently. He must be thinking of Dr. Kovacs's hypothesis, she realized. Worrying that some repressed trauma in her past might make her wig out.

"That," she assured him on a ragged sigh, "was wonderful."

His face relaxed into a smile. "Good to hear, but we're not done yet."

Still boneless with pleasure, she stretched like a cat as he rolled to the side of the bed and groped among the clothes they'd left in a pile on the floor. Somehow she wasn't surprised when he turned back with several foil-wrapped condoms. By the time he'd placed them close at hand on the table beside the bed, she was ready for round two.

"My turn," she murmured, pushing up on an elbow to

explore his body with the same attention to detail he'd explored hers.

God, he was beautiful! That wasn't an adjective usually applied to males but Natalie couldn't think of any other to categorize the long, lean torso, the roped muscle at shoulder and thigh, the flat belly and nest of thick, dark hair at his groin. His sex was flaccid but came to instant, eager attention when she stroked a finger along its length.

But it was the scar that caught and held her attention. Healed but still angry in the dim glow of the moon, it cut diagonally along his ribs. Frowning, she traced the tip of her finger along the vicious path.

"What's this?"

"A reminder not to trust a rookie to adequately pat down a seasoned veteran of the Cosa Nostra."

She spotted another scar higher on his chest, this one a tight, round pucker of flesh.

"And this?"

"A parting gift from an Albanian boat captain after Interpol intercepted the cargo of girls he was transporting to Algeria."

He said it with a careless shrug, as if knife wounds and kidnappings were routine occurrences in the career of a secret agent. Which they probably were, Natalie thought with a swallow. Suddenly the whole James Bond thing didn't seem quite so romantic.

"Your employer's brother-in-law took part in that op," Dom was saying. "Gina's husband, Jack Harris."

"He's undercover, too?"

"No, he's a career diplomat. He was part of a UN investigation into child prostitution at the time."

"Have I met him?"

"I don't know."

"Hmm."

It was hard to work up an interest in her employer's

brother-in-law while she was stretched out hip-to-naked-hip with Dominic St. Sebastian. Aching for the insults done to his body, she kissed the puckered scar on his shoulder.

One kiss led to another, then another, as she traced a path down his chest. When she laved her tongue along the scar bisecting his stomach, his belly hollowed and his sex sprang to attention again. Natalie drew a nail lightly along its length and would have explored the smooth satin further but Dom inhaled sharply and jerked away from her touch.

"Sorry! I want you too much."

She started to tell him there was no need for apologies, but he was already reaching for one of the condoms he'd left so conveniently close at hand. Heat coiled low in her belly and then, when he turned back to her, raced through her in quick, electric jolts. On fire for him, she took his weight and welcomed him eagerly into her body.

There was no slow climb to pleasure this time. No delicious heightening of the senses. He drove into her, and all too soon Natalie felt another climax rushing at her. She tried desperately to contain it, then sobbed with relief and sheer, undiluted pleasure when he pushed both her and himself over the edge.

She sprawled in naked abandon while the world slowly stopped spinning. Dom lay next to her, his eyes closed and one arm bent under his head. As she stared at his profile in the dim light of the moon, a dozen different emotions bounced between her heart and her head.

She acknowledged the satisfaction, the worry, the delight and just the tiniest frisson of fear. She hardly knew this man, yet she felt so close to him. *Too* close. How could she tell how much of that was real or the by-product of being too emotionally dependent on him?

As if to underscore her doubts, she glanced over his shoulder at the open window. Silhouetted against a midnight-blue sky were the ruins that had brought her to Hungary and to Dom.

Somehow.

The need to find the missing pieces of the puzzle put a serious dent in the sensual satisfaction of just lazing next to him. She bit her lip and shifted her attention to the desk tucked in the alcove under the eaves. Her briefcase lay atop the desk, right where she'd placed it. Anticipation tap-danced along her nerves at the thought of attacking those fat files and getting into her laptop.

Dom picked up on her quiver of impatience and opened his eyes. "Are you cold?"

"A little," she admitted but stopped him before he could drag up the down-filled featherbed tangled at their feet. "It's early yet. I'd like to go through my briefcase before we call it a night."

Amusement colored his voice. "Do you think we're done for the night?"

"Aren't we?"

"Ah, Natushka, we've barely begun. But we'll take a break while you look through your files." He rolled out of bed with the controlled grace of a panther and pulled on his clothes. "I'll go down and get us some coffee, yes?"

"Coffee would be good."

While he was gone she made a quick trip to the bathroom, then dug into her suitcase. She scrambled into clean panties but didn't bother with a bra. Or with either of the starched blouses folded atop a beige linen jumper that had all the grace and style of a burlap sack. Frowning, she checked the tag and saw the jumper was two sizes larger than the clothes she'd bought in Budapest.

Was Dom right? Had she deliberately tried to disguise her real self in these awful clothes? Was there something in her past that made her wary of showing her true colors? If so, she might find a clue to whatever it was in the briefcase. Impatient to get to it, she stuffed the jumper back in the case and slipped on the soccer shirt she'd appropriated from Dom to use as a sleep shirt. It hung below her hips but felt soft and smooth against her thighs.

She lifted the files out of her briefcase and arranged them in neat stacks. She was flipping through one page by page when Dom returned with two mugs of foaming latte.

"Finding anything interesting?" he asked as he set a mug at her elbow.

"Tons of stuff! So far it all relates to missing works of art, like that Fabergé egg and a small Bernini bronze stolen from the Uffizi Gallery in Florence. I haven't found information on the Canaletto painting yet. It's got to be in one of these files, though."

He nodded to the still-closed laptop. "You probably cross-indexed the paper files on your computer. Why don't you check it?"

"I tried." She blew out a frustrated breath. "The laptop's password-protected."

"And you can't remember the password."

"I tried a dozen different combinations, but none worked."

"Do you want me to get into it?"

"How can you…? Oh. Another useful skill you picked up at Interpol, right?"

He merely smiled. "Do you have a USB cord in your briefcase? Good. Let me have it."

He deposited the latte on the table beside the easy chair and settled in with the computer on his lap. It booted up to a smiley face and eight blinking question marks in the password box. Dom plugged one end of the USB cord into the laptop, the other into his cell phone. He tapped a series of numbers on the phone's keypad and waited to connect via a secure remote link to a special program developed by Interpol's Computer Crimes Division for use by agents in the field. The handy-dandy program whizzed through hundreds of thousands of letter/number/character combinations at the speed of light.

Scant minutes later, the password popped up letter by letter. Dom made a note of it and hit Return. The smiley face on Natalie's laptop dissolved and the home screen came up. The icons were arranged with military precision, he saw with an inner smile. God forbid his fussy archivist should keep a messy electronic filing cabinet. He was about to tell Natalie that he was in when a message painted across the screen.

D—I see you're online. Don't know whose computer you're using. Contact me. I have some info for you. A.

About time! Dom erased the message and de-linked before passing the laptop to Natalie. "You're good to go."

She took it eagerly and wedged it onto the desk between the stacks of paper files. Fingers flying, she conducted a quick search.

"Here's the Canaletto folder!"

A click of the mouse opened the main file. When dozens of subfolders rippled down the screen, Natalie groaned.

"It'll take all night to go through these."

"You don't have all night," Dom warned, dropping a kiss on her nape. "Just till I get back."

"Where are you going?"

"I need to let Katya and her father know we won't be home tonight. I'll get a stronger signal outside."

It wasn't a complete lie. He did need to call his downstairs neighbors. That bit about the stronger signal shaded the truth, but the habit of communicating privately with his contacts at headquarters went too deep to compromise.

He slipped on a jacket and went downstairs. The bar was still open. Lisel waved, inviting him in for another coffee or a beer, but he shook his head and held up his phone to signal his reason for going outside.

He'd forgotten how sharp and clean and cold the nights could be here in the foothills of the Alps. And how bright the stars were without a haze of smog and city lights to blur them. Hiking up the collar of his jacket, he contacted Andre.

"What have you got for me?"

"Some interesting information about your Natalie Elizabeth Clark."

Dom's stomach tightened. "Interesting" to Andre could mean anything from an unpaid speeding ticket to enrollment in a witness protection program.

"It took a while, but the facial recognition program finally matched to a mug shot."

Hell! His gut had told him Natalie was hiding her real self. He almost didn't want to hear the reason behind the disguise now but forced himself to ask.

"What were the charges?"

"Fraud and related activities in connection with computers."

"When?" he bit out.

"Three years ago. But it looks like the charges were dropped and the arrest record expunged. Someone missed the mug shot, though, when they wiped the slate."

Dom wanted to be fair. The fact that the charges had been dropped could mean the arrest was a mistake, that Natalie hadn't done whatever the authorities thought she had. Unfortunately, he'd seen too many sleazy, high-priced lawyers spring their clients on technicalities.

"Do you want me to contact the feds in the US?" Andre asked. "See what they've got on this?"

Dom hesitated, his gaze going to the brightly illuminated window on the second floor of the gasthaus. Had he just made love to a hacker? Had she tracked him down, devised a ploy to show up at his loft dripping wet and help-less? Was this whole amnesia scene part of some elabo-rate sting?

Every one of his instincts screamed no. She couldn't have faked the panic and confusion he'd glimpsed in her eyes. Or woven a web of lies and deceit, then flamed in his arms the way she had. The question now was whether he could trust his instincts.

"Dom? What do you want me to do?"

He went with his gut. "Hang loose, Andre. If I need more, I'll get back to you."

He disconnected, hoping to hell he wasn't thinking with the wrong head, and made a quick call to his downstairs neighbors.

Ten

Natalie was still hard at it when Dom went back upstairs. Her operation had spread from the desk to the armchair and the bed, which was now neatly remade. With pillows fluffed and the corners of the counterpane squared, he noted wryly. He also couldn't help noticing how her fingers flew over the laptop's keyboard.

"How's it coming?" he asked.

"So-so. The good news is I'm now remembering many of these details. The bad news is that I went through the Canaletto folder page by page. I also searched its corresponding computer file. I didn't find an entry that would explain why I drove down from Vienna, nor any reference to Győr or Budapest. Nothing to tell me why I hopped on a riverboat and ended up in the Danube." Sighing, she flapped a hand at the stacks now spread throughout the room. "I hope I find something in one of those."

Dom eyed the neat array of files. "How have you separated them?"

"The ones on the chair contain paper copies of documents and reports of lost art from roughly the same period as the Canaletto. The ones on the bed detail the last known locations of various missing pieces from other periods."

"Sorted alphabetically by continent and country, I see."

She looked slightly offended. "Of course. I thought I might have stumbled across something in reports from a gallery or museum or private collection that gained a new acquisition at approximately the same time the Canaletto disappeared from Karlenburgh Castle."

"What about information unrelated to missing art treasures? Any personal data in the files or on the computer that triggered memories?"

"Plenty," she said with a small sigh. "Apparently I'm as anal about my personal life as I am about professional matters. I've got everything on spreadsheets. The service record for my car. The books I've read and want to read. Checking and savings accounts. A household inventory with purchase dates, cost, serial numbers where appropriate. Restaurants I've tried, sorted by type of food and my rating. In short," she finished glumly, "my entire existence. Precise, well-organized and soulless."

She looked so frustrated, so dejected and lost, that Dom had to fight the urge to take her in his arms. He'd get into the computer later, when she was asleep, and check out the household inventory and bank accounts. Right now he was more interested in her responses to his careful probing.

"How about your email? Find anything there?"

"Other than some innocuous correspondence from people I've tagged in my address book as 'acquaintances,' everything relates to work." Her shoulders slumped. "Is my life pathetic, or what?"

If she was acting, she was the best he'd ever seen. To hell with fighting the urge. She needed comforting. Clearing the armchair, he caught her hand and tugged her into his lap.

"There's more to you than spreadsheets and color-coded files, Ms. Clark."

With another sigh, she laid her head on his shoulder. "You'd think so."

"There are all your little quirks," he said with a smile,

stroking her hair. "The lip thing, the fussiness, the questionable fashion sense."

"Gee, thanks."

"Then there's your rapport with the Agár."

"Ha! I suspect he bonds instantly with everyone."

"And there's tonight," he reminded her. "You, me, this gasthaus."

She tipped her head back to search his face. He supported her head, careful of the still-tender spot at the base of her skull.

"About tonight... You, me, this place..."

"Don't look so worried. We don't have to analyze or dissect what happened here."

"I'm thinking more along the lines of what happens after we leave. Next week. Next month."

"We let them take care of themselves."

As soon as he said it, he knew it was a lie. Despite the mystery surrounding this woman—or maybe because of it—he had no intention of letting her drop out of his life the same way she'd dropped into it. She was under his skin now.

That last thought made him stop. Rewind. Take a breath. Think about the other women he'd been with. The hard, inescapable fact was that none of them had ever stirred this particular mix of lust, tenderness, worry, suspicion and fierce protectiveness.

He might have to change his tactics if and when Natalie's memory fully returned, Dom acknowledged. At the moment she considered him an anchor in a sea of uncertainty. He couldn't add to that uncertainty by demanding more than she was ready to give.

"For now," he said with a lazy smile, "this is good, isn't it?"

"Oh, yes."

She leaned in, brought her mouth to his, gave him a

promise of things to come. He was ready to take her up on that promise when she made a brisk announcement.

"Okay, I'm done wallowing in self-pity. Time to get back to work."

"What do you want me to do?"

She glanced at the files on the bed and caught her lower lip between her teeth. Dom waited, remembering how antsy she'd been about letting him see her research when he'd shown up unannounced at her New York hotel room. He'd chalked that up to a proprietary desire to protect her work. With Andre's call still fresh in his mind, he couldn't help wondering if there was something else in those fat folders she wanted to protect.

"I guess you could start on those," she said with obvious reluctance. "There's an index and a chronology inside each file. The sections are tabbed, the documents in each section numbered. That's how I cross-reference the contents on the computer. So keep everything in order, okay?"

Dom's little bubble of suspicion popped. The woman wasn't nervous about him digging into her private files, just worried that he'd mess them up. Grinning, he pushed out of the chair with her still in his arms and deposited her back at the desk.

"I'll treat every page with care and reverence," he promised solemnly.

She flushed at little at the teasing but stood her ground. "You'd better. We archivists don't take kindly to anyone who desecrates our files."

It didn't take Dom long to realize Natalie could land a job with any investigative agency in the world, including Interpol. She hadn't just researched facts about lost cultural treasures. She'd tracked every rumor, followed every thread. Some threads were so thin they appeared to have no relation to the object of her research. Yet in at least two of the files he dug through, those seemingly unrelated, unconnected tidbits of information led to a major find.

"Jesus," Dom muttered after following a particularly convoluted trail. "Do you remember this?"

She swiveled around and frowned at a scanned photo depicting a two-inch-long cylinder inscribed with hieroglyphics. "Looks familiar. It's Babylonian, isn't it? About two thousand years old, I'd guess."

"You'd guess right."

"What's the story on it?"

"It went missing in Iraq in 2003, shortly after Saddam Hussein was toppled."

"Oh, I remember now. I found a reference to a similar object in a list of items being offered for sale by a little-known dealer. Best I recall, he claimed he specialized in Babylonian artifacts."

She rubbed her forehead, trying to dredge up more detail. Dom helped her out.

"You sent him a request for a more detailed description of that particular item. When it came in, you matched it to a list the US Army compiled of Iraqi antiquities that were unaccounted for."

"I can't remember…did the army recover the artifact?"

He flipped through several pages of notes and correspondence. "They did. They also arrested the contractor employee who'd lifted it during recovery efforts at the Baghdad Archeological Museum."

"Well! Maybe I'm not so pathetic after all."

She turned back to the laptop with a smug little smile that crushed the last of Dom's doubts. Those two inches of inscribed Babylonian clay were damned near priceless. If Natalie was into shady deals, she wouldn't have alerted the army to her find. The fact that she had convinced Dom. Whatever screwup had led to her arrest, she was no hacker or huckster.

He dug into the next folder and soon found himself absorbed in the search for a thirteenth-century gold chalice studded with emeralds that once graced the altar of an Irish abbey. He was only halfway through the thick file when he glanced up and saw Natalie's shoulders drooping again, this time with fatigue. So much for his anticipation of another lively session under the featherbed. He closed the folder, careful not to dislodge any of its contents, and stretched.

"That's it for me tonight."

She frowned at the remaining files. "We've still got a half dozen to go through."

"Tomorrow. Right now, I need bed, sleep and you. Not necessarily in that order, although you look as whipped as I feel."

"I might be able to summon a few reserves of energy."

"You do that," he said as he headed for the bathroom.

His five-o'clock shadow had morphed into a ten-o'clock bristle. He'd scraped Natalie's tender cheeks enough the first time around. He better shave and go a little more gentle on her this time. But when he reentered the bedroom a scant ten minutes later, she was curled in a tight ball under the featherbed and sawing soft, breathy Z's.

Taking advantage of the opportunity, he settled at the desk. His conscience didn't even ping as he powered up her laptop. Forty minutes later he'd seen everything he needed to. His skills weren't as honed as those of the wizards in Interpol's Computer Crimes Division, but they were good enough for him to feel confident she wasn't hacking into unauthorized databases or shifting money into hidden accounts. Everything he saw indicated she'd lived well within her salary as an archivist for the State of Illinois and was now socking most of the generous salary Sarah paid her into a savings account.

Satisfied and more than a little relieved to have his instincts validated, Dom shed his clothes and slid in beside her lax, warm body. He was tempted to nudge her awake and treat himself to a celebration of his nonfindings. He restrained himself but it required a heroic effort.

Natalie woke to bright morning sunshine, the distant clang of cowbells and a feeling of energy and purpose. She ascribed the last to a solid night's sleep—until she tried to roll over and realized she probably owed it more to the solid wall of male behind her.

God, he felt good! What's more, he made *her* feel good. Just lying nested against his warmth and strength generated all kinds of wild possibilities. Like maybe waking up in the same nest for the next few weeks or months. Or even, her sneaky little subconscious suggested, years.

The thought struck her that Dominic St. Sebastian might be all she needed to feel complete. All she would ever need. Apparently, she had no family. Judging by the dearth of personal emails on her laptop, she didn't have a wide circle of friends. Yet lying here with Dom, she didn't feel the lack of either.

Maybe that's why the details of her personal life were so slow returning. Her life was so empty, so blah, she didn't *want* to remember it. That made her grimace, which must have translated into some small movement because a lazy voice sounded just behind her ear.

"I've been waiting for you to wake up."

Sheets rustling, she angled a look over her shoulder and sighed. "It's not fair."

"What isn't?"

"My eyes feel goopy from sleep, my hair's probably sticking out in all directions and I know my teeth need brushing. You, on the other hand, look fresh and wide-awake and good enough to eat."

Good enough to gobble whole, actually. Those black

eyes and hair, the golden-oak hue of his skin, the square chin and chiseled cheekbones…the whole package added up to something really spectacular to start the day with. Only the nicks and scars of his profession marred the perfection.

"In fact," she announced, "I think I'll have you for breakfast."

She rolled onto her side, trying not to treat him to a blast of morning breath, and wiggled down a few inches. She started with the underside of his jaw and slowly worked her way south. Teasing, tasting, nibbling the cords in his neck, dropping kisses on alternate ribs, circling his belly button with her tongue. By the time she dragged the sheets down to his hips, he was stiff and rampant.

Her own belly tight and quivering now, she circled him with her palm. The skin was hot and satin smooth, the blood throbbing in his veins. She slid her hand up, down, up again, delighted when he grunted and jerked involuntarily.

"Okay," she told him, her voice throaty with desire, "I need a little of that action."

All thought of ratty hair and goopy eyes forgotten, she swung a leg over his thighs and raised her hips. Dom was straining and eager but held her off long enough to tear into another foil package.

"Let me," she said, brushing his hands aside.

She rolled on the condom, then positioned her hips again. Together they rode to an explosive release that had him thrusting upward and her collapsing onto his chest in mindless, mewling pleasure.

Natalie recovered first. Probably because she had to pee really, really bad. She scooped up her jeans and the green-and-white-striped rugby shirt she now claimed as her own on the way to the bathroom. When she emerged, she found Dom dressed and waiting for his turn.

"Give me five minutes and I'll be ready to go."

Since she wasn't sure whether they would return to the gasthaus, she stuffed the files and laptop back into her briefcase and threw her few miscellaneous items into her weekender. The sight of those plain, sensible, neatly folded blouses made her wrinkle her nose. Whatever happened when—*if*—she regained her memory, she was investing in an entire new wardrobe.

Dom agreed that it was probably better to check out of the gasthaus and head back to Budapest after going up to the castle. "But first, we'll eat. I guarantee you've never tasted anything like Lisel's *bauernfrühstück*."

"Which is?"

"Her version of a German-Austrian-Hungarian farmer's breakfast."

Their hostess gave them a cheerful smile when they appeared in the dining room and waved them to a table. She was serving two other diners, locals by the looks of them, and called across the room.

"Frühstück, ja?"

"Ja," Dom called back as he and Natalie helped themselves to the coffee and fresh juice set out on an elaborately carved hutch.

A short time later Lisel delivered her special. Natalie gaped at the platter-size omelette bursting with fried potatoes, onions, leeks, ham and pungent Munster cheese. The Hungarian input came from the pulpy, stewed tomatoes flavored with red peppers and the inevitable paprika.

When their hostess returned with a basket of freshly baked rolls and a crock of homemade elderberry jam, she lingered long enough to knuckle Dom's shoulder affectionately.

"So you leave us today?"

His mouth full, Dom nodded.

"You must come again soon." The blonde's amethyst eyes twinkled as she included his companion in the invitation. "You, as well. You and Dominic found the bed in my front room comfortable, yes?"

Natalie could feel heat rushing into her cheeks but had to laugh. "Very comfortable."

With a respectable portion of her gargantuan breakfast disposed of and the innkeeper's warm farewells to speed them on their way, Natalie's spirits rose with every twist and turn of the road that snaked up to the mountain pass. Something had drawn her to the ruins dominating the skyline ahead. She felt it in her bones, in the excitement bubbling through her veins. Impatience had her straining against her seat belt as Dom turned off the main road onto the single lane that led to what was left of Karlenburgh Castle.

The lane had once been paved but over the years frost heaves had buckled the asphalt and weeds now sprouted in the cracks. The weedy approach took nothing away from the dramatic aspect of the ruins, however. They rose from a base of solid granite, looking as though they'd been carved from the mountain itself. To the west was a breath-stealing vista of the snow-covered Austrian Alps. To the east, a series of stair-stepping terraces that must once have contained gardens, vineyards and orchards. The terraces ended abruptly in a sheer drop to the valley below.

Natalie's heart was pounding by the time Dom pulled up a few yards from the outer wall. The wind slapped her in the face when she got out of the car and knifed through the rugby shirt.

"Here, put this on."

Dom held up the jacket he'd retrieved from the backseat. She slid her arms into the sleeves and wrapped its warmth around her gratefully.

"Watch your step," he warned as they approached a gap in the outer ring of rubble. "A massive portcullis used to guard this gate, but the Soviets claimed the iron for scrap—along with everything else of any value. Then," he said, his voice grim, "they set charges and destroyed the castle itself as a warning to other Hungarians foolish enough to join the uprising."

Someone had cleared a path through the rubble of the outer bailey. "My grandfather," Dom explained, "with help from some locals."

Grasping her elbow to guide her over the rough spots, he pointed out the charred timbers and crumpled walls of the dairy, what had been the kitchens in earlier centuries, and the stables-turned-carriage house and garage.

Another gate led to what would have been the inner courtyard. The rubble was too dense here to penetrate but she could see the outline of the original structure in the tumbled walls. The only remaining turret jutted up like a broken tooth, its roof blown and stone staircase exposed to the sky. Natalie hooked her arm through Dom's and let her gaze roam the desolation while he described the castle he himself had seen only in drawings and family photographs.

"Karlenburgh wasn't as large as some border fortresses of the same era. Only thirty-six rooms originally, including the armory, the great hall and the duke and duchess's chambers. Successive generations of St. Sebastians installed modern conveniences like indoor plumbing and electric lights, but for comfort and luxury the family usually wintered in their palazzos on the Italian Riviera or the Dalmatian Coast." A smile lightened his somber expression. "My grandfather had a photo of him and his cousin dunking each other in the Mediterranean. They were very close as children, he and the last Grand Duke."

"Except," Natalie said, squeezing his arm with hers, "he wasn't the last Grand Duke."

For once Dominic didn't grimace or shrug or otherwise downplay his heritage. He couldn't, with its very dramatic remains staring him in the face.

"I've told the duchess she should come back for a visit," he murmured almost to himself. "But seeing it like this…"

They stood with shoulders hunched against the wind, Dom thinking of the duchess and Natalie searching the ruins for something to jog her memory. What had drawn her here? What had she found among the rubble that propelled her from here to Győr and onto that damned boat?

It was there, just behind the veil. She knew it was there! But she was damned if she could pull it out. Disappointment ate into her, doubly sharp and bitter after her earlier excitement.

Dom glanced down and must have read the frustration in her face. "Nothing?" he asked gently.

"Just a sort of vague, prickly sensation," she admitted, "which may or may not be goose bumps raised by the cold."

"Whichever it is, we'd best get you out of the wind."

Dejected and deflated and feeling dangerously close to tears, she picked her way back through the rubble. She'd been so sure Karlenburgh Castle was the key. So certain she'd break through once she stood among the ruins.

Lost in her glum thoughts, her eyes on the treacherous path, it took a moment for a distant, tinny clanging to penetrate her preoccupation. When it did, her head jerked up. That sound! That metallic tinkling! She'd heard it before, and not long ago.

Her heart started pumping. Her mouth went dry. Feeling as though she was teetering on the edge of a precipice, she followed the clanging to a string of goats meandering along the overgrown lane in their direction. A gnarled gnome of a man trailed the flock. His face was shadowed by the wide brim of his hat and he leaned heavily on a burled wood staff.

"That's old Friedrich," Dom exclaimed. "He helped tend the castle's goats as a small boy and now raises his own. Those are *cou noirs*—black necks—especially noted for their sweet milk. My grandfather always stopped by Friedrich's hut to buy cheese when he brought Zia and me back for a visit."

Natalie stood frozen as Dom forged a path through the goats to greet their herder. She didn't move, couldn't! Even when the lead animals milled inquisitively around her knees. True to their name, their front quarters were black, the rest of their coat a grayish-white. The does were gentle creatures but some instinct told Natalie to keep a wary eye on the buck accompanying them.

A bit of trivia slipped willy-nilly into her mind. She'd read somewhere that Alpine goats were among the earliest domesticated animals. Also that their adaptability made them good candidates for long sea voyages. Early settlers in the Americas had brought this breed with them to supply milk and cheese. And sea captains would often leave a pair on deserted islands along their trade routes to provide fresh milk and meat on return voyages.

Suddenly, the curtains in her mind parted. Not all the way. Just far enough for her to know she hadn't picked up that bit of trivia "somewhere." She'd specifically researched Alpine goats on Google after... After...

Her gaze shot to the herder hobbling alongside Dom, a smile on his wrinkled walnut of a face. Excitement rushed back, so swift and thrilling she was shaking with it when Friedrich smiled and greeted her in a mix of German and heavily accented English.

"*Guten tag, fraülein. Es gut* to see you again."

Eleven

Natalie had spent all those hours soul- and mind- and computer-searching. She'd tried desperately to latch on to something, *anything*, that would trigger her memory. Never in her wildest dreams would she have imagined that trigger would consist of a herd of smelly goats and a wizened little man in a floppy felt hat. Yet the moment Friedrich greeted her in his fractured English, the dam broke.

Images flooded the empty spaces in her mind. Her, standing almost on this same spot. The goatherd, inquiring kindly if she was lost. These same gray-white does butting her knees. The buck giving her the evil eye. A casual chat that sent her off on a wild chase.

"*Guten tag*, Herr Müller." Her voice shook with excitement. "*Es gut* to see you again, too."

Dom had already picked up on the goatherd's greeting to Natalie. Her reply snapped his brows together. "When did you and Friedrich meet?"

"A week ago! Right here, at the castle! I remember him, Dom. I remember the goats and the bells and Herr Müller asking if I was lost. Then...then..."

She was so close to hyperventilating she had to stop and drag in a long, hiccuping breath. Müller looked confused by the rapid-fire exchange, so Natalie forced herself to slow down, space the words, contain the hysterical joy that bubbled to the surface.

"Then we sat there, on that wall, and you told me about the castle before the Soviets came. About the balls and the hunting parties and the tree-lighting ceremony in the great hall. Everyone from the surrounding villages was invited, you said. On Christmas Eve. Uh...*Heiliger Abend*."

"Ja, ja, Heiliger Abend."

"When I mentioned that I'd met the duchess in New York, you told me that you remember when she came to Karlenburgh Castle as a bride. So young and beautiful and gracious to everyone, even the knock-kneed boy who helped tend the goats."

She had to stop and catch her breath again. She could see the scene from last week so clearly now, every detail as though etched in glass. The weeds poking from the cracks in the road. The goats wandering through the rubble. This hunched-shouldered man in his gray felt hat, his gnarled hands folded atop the head of his walking stick, describing Karlenburgh Castle in its glory days.

"Then," she said, the excitement piling up again, "I told you I was searching for a painting that had once hung in the Red Salon. You gave me a very hard look and asked why I, too, should want to know about that particular room after all these years."

Everything was coming at her so fast and furiously and seemingly in reverse, like a DVD rewound at superhigh speed. The encounter with Herr Müller. The drive down from Vienna. A burning curiosity to see the castle ruins. The search for the Canaletto. Sarah and Dev. The duchess and Gina and the twins and Anastazia and meeting Dom for the first time in New York.

The rewind came to a screeching halt, stuck at that meeting with Dom. She could see his laughing eyes. His lazy grin. Hear his casual dismissal of the codicil and the title it conferred on him.

That was one of the reasons she'd returned to Vienna!

Why she'd decided to make a day trip to view the ruins of Karlenburgh Castle, and why she'd been so blasted determined to track the missing Canaletto. She'd wanted to wipe that cynical smile off Dominic St. Sebastian's face. Prove the validity of her research. Rub his nose in it, in fact. And, oh, by the way, possibly determine what happened to a priceless work of art.

And why, when the police tried to determine who she was and what she was doing in Budapest, the only response she could dredge from her confused mind was the Grand Duke of Karlenburgh!

With a fierce effort of will, she sidelined those tumultuous memories and focused on the goatherd. "I asked you who else had enquired about the Red Salon. Remember? You told me someone had come some months ago. And told you his name."

"Ja." His wrinkled face twisting in disgust, Müller aimed a thick wad of spittle at the ground. "Janos Lagy."

Dom had been listening intently without interruption to this point, but the name the goatherd spit out provoked a startled response. "Janos Lagy?"

Natalie threw him a surprised glance but he whipped up a palm and stilled the question he saw quivering on her lips.

"Ja," Müller continued in his thick, accented English. "Janos Lagy, a banker, he tells me, from Budapest. He tells me, too, he is the grandson of a Hungarian who goes to the military academy in Moscow and becomes a *mladshij lejtenant* in the Soviet Army. And I tell him I remember this lieutenant," the goatherd related, his voice shaking with emotion. "He commands the squad sent to destroy Karlenburgh Castle after the Grand Duke is arrested."

Dom mumbled something in Hungarian under his breath. Something short and terse and sounding very unnice to Natalie. She ached to ask him what he knew about

Lagy but Herr Müller was just getting to the crux of the story he'd shared with her less than a week ago.

"When I tell this to the grandson, he shrugs. He shrugs, the grandson of this traitorous lieutenant, as if it's of no matter, and asks me if I am ever in the Red Salon!"

The old man quivered with remembered rage. Raising his walking stick, he shook it in the air.

"I threatened to knock his head. He leaves very quickly then."

"Jézus," Dom muttered. "Janos Lagy."

Natalie couldn't contain herself. "You know him?"

"I know him."

"How!"

"I'll explain in the car, and you can tell me what you did with the information Friedrich gave you. But first…"

He probed for more information but when it was clear the goatherd had shared all he knew, he started to take a gracious leave. To his surprise and acute embarrassment, the old man grabbed his hand and kissed it.

"The Grand Duke and Duchess, they are still missed here," he said with tears swimming in his eyes. "It's good, what I read in the papers, that you are now duke. You'll come back again? Soon?"

"I will," he promised. "And perhaps I can convince the duchess to come, too."

"Ahhhh, I pray that I live to see her again!"

They left him clinging to that hope and picked their way through the weeds back to the car. Natalie was a quivering bundle of nerves but the deep crease between Dom's eyes kept her silent while he keyed the ignition, maneuvered a tight turn and regained the road that snaked up and over the pass. Neither of them spoke until he pulled into a scenic turnout that gave an eagle's-eye view of the valley below.

When Dom swung toward her, his face was still tight. "Start at the beginning. Tell what you remember."

She rewound the DVD again. She focused her growing absorption with both the codicil and Canaletto but glossed over the ignoble desire to rub a certain someone's nose in her research.

"I was there in Vienna, only a little over an hour away. I wanted to see the castle the duchess had told me about during our interviews, perhaps talk to some locals who might remember her."

"Like Friedrich Müller."

"Like Friedrich Müller," she confirmed. "I'd done a review of census records and knew he was one of only a handful of people old enough to have lived through the 1956 Uprising. I intended to go to the address listed as his current residence, but met him by chance there at the ruins instead."

"What a string of coincidences," Dom muttered, shaking his head. "Incredible."

"Not really," she countered, defensive on behalf of her research. "Pretty much everything one needs to know is documented somewhere. You just have to look for it."

He conceded the point. "So you met Friedrich, and he told you about Lagy. What did you do then?"

"I researched him on Google as soon as I got back to my hotel in Vienna. Took me a while to find the right Lagy. It's a fairly common name in Hungary. But I finally tracked him to his office at his bank. His secretary wouldn't put me through until I identified myself as Sarah St. Sebastian Hunter's research assistant and said I was helping with her book dealing with lost works of art. Evidently Janos is something of a collector. He came on the line a few minutes later."

"Did you tell him you were trying to track the Canaletto?"

"Yes, and he asked why I'd contacted him about it. I didn't want to go into detail over the phone, just said I thought I'd found a possible link through his grandfather that I'd like to pursue with him. He asked if I'd discussed this link with anyone else and I told him no, that I wanted to verify it first. I offered to drive to Budapest but he generously offered to meet me halfway."

"In Györ."

"On the tour boat," she confirmed. "He said cruising the Danube was one of his favorite ways to relax, that if I hadn't taken a day trip on the river before I would most certainly enjoy it. I knew I wouldn't. I hate boats, loathe being on the water. But I was so eager to talk to him I agreed. I drove down to Györ the next day."

"And you met Lagy aboard?"

"No. He called after the damned boat had left the dock and said he'd been unavoidably detained. He apologized profusely and said he would meet me when it docked in Budapest instead."

She made a moue of distaste, remembering the long, queasy hours trying not to fixate on the slap of the current against the hull or the constant engine vibration under her feet.

"We didn't approach Budapest until late afternoon. By then I was huddled at the rail near the back of the boat, praying I wouldn't be sick. I remember getting another call. Remember reaching too fast for my phone and feeling really dizzy. I leaned over the rail, thinking I was going to puke." Frowning, she slid her hand under her hair and fingered the still tender spot at the base of her skull. "I must have banged my head on one of the support poles because there was pain. Nasty, nasty pain. And the next thing I know someone's leaning on my chest, pumping water out of my lungs!"

"You never saw Janos Lagy? Never connected with him?"

"Not unless he was one of the guys who fished me out of the river. Who *is* he, Dom? How do you know him?"

"We went to school together."

"You're friends with him?" she asked incredulously.

"Acquaintances. My grandfather was not one to forgive or forget old wrongs. He knew Jan's grandfather had served in the Soviet Army and didn't want me to have anything to do with the Lagy family. He didn't know the bastard had commanded the squad that leveled Karlenburgh Castle, though. I didn't either, until today."

Natalie had been certain that once she regained her memory, every blank space would fill and every question would have an answer. Instead, all new questions were piling up.

"This is so frustrating." She shook her head. "Like a circle that doesn't quite close. You, me, the duchess, the castle, the painting, this guy Lagy. They're all connected, but I can't see how they come together."

"Nor do I," he said, digging his cell phone out of his jeans pocket, "but I intend to find out."

She watched wide-eyed as he pressed a single key and was instantly connected. She understood just enough of his fluid French to grasp that he was asking someone named Andre to run a check on Janos Lagy.

Their return sent the hound into a paroxysm of delight. When Natalie laughed and bent to accept his joyous adulation, he got several quick, slurpy kisses past her guard before she could dodge them.

As a thank-you to the dog-sitters, Dom gave Katya the green light to purchase the latest Justin Bieber CD on his iTunes account and download it to her iPod—with her father's permission, he added. The indulgent papa received the ten-pound Westphalia ham that Dom had picked up at the butcher's on the way home. The hound got a bag of bones, which tantalized him all the way up to the loft.

When Dom unlocked the front door and stood aside for Natalie to precede him, she was hit with a sudden attack of nerves. Now that she'd remembered her past, would it overshadow the present? Would the weight of all those months and years in her "real" life smother the brief days she'd spent here, with Dom?

Her heart thumping, she stepped inside and felt instant relief. And instantly at home...despite the dust motes dancing on a stray sunbeam and the rumpled bedcovers she'd straightened so meticulously before the hound had pounced on them. She knew she was just a guest, yet the most ridiculous sense of belonging enveloped her. The big fat question mark now was how long she'd stay camped out here. At least until she and Dom explored this business with Lagy, surely.

Or not. Doubt raised its ugly head when she glanced over her shoulder and saw him standing just inside the still-open door.

"Aren't you coming in?"

He gave himself a little shake, as if dragging his thoughts together, and dredged up a crooked smile.

"We left your case in the car. I'll go get it."

She used his absence to open the drapes and windows to let in the crisp fall air. Conscious of how Dom had teased her about her neat streak, she tried to ignore the rumpled bed but the damned thing pulled her like a magnet. She was guiltily smoothing the cover when he returned.

Propping her roller case next to the wardrobe, he made for the fridge. "I'm going to have a beer. Would you like one? Or wine, or tea?"

"Tea sounds good. Why don't I brew a fresh pitcher while you check with your friend to see what he's turned up on Lagy?"

Dom took the dew-streaked pilsner and cell phone out to the balcony. Not because he wanted privacy to make the call to Andre. He'd decided last night to trust Natalie in spite of that unexplained arrest and nothing had happened since to change his mind. Unless whatever he learned about Lagy was classified "eyes only," he intended to share it with her. No, he just needed a few moments to sort through everything that had happened in the past twenty-four hours.

Oh hell, who was he kidding?

What he needed was, first, a deep gulp of air. Second, a long swallow of Gold Fassl. And third, a little more time to recover from the mule kick that'd slammed into his midsection when he'd opened the door to the loft and Natalie waltzed in with the Agár frisking around her legs.

He liked having her here. Oddly, she didn't crowd him or shrink his loft to minuscule proportions the way Zia did whenever she blew into Budapest on one of her whirlwind visits, leaving a trail of clothes and scarves and medical books and electronic gadgets in her wake. In fact, Natalie might lean a bit too far in the opposite direction. She would alphabetize and color-code his life if he didn't keep a close eye on her.

He would have to loosen her up. Ratchet her passion for order and neatness down to human levels. He suspected that might take some work but he could manage it. All he had to do was take her to bed often enough—and keep her there long enough—to burn up any surplus energy.

As he gazed at the ornate facades on the Pest side of the river, he could easily envision fall rolling into winter while he lazed under the blankets with Natalie and viewed these same buildings dusted with snow. Or the two of them exercising the hound when the park below was tender and green with spring.

The problem was that he wasn't sure how Natalie felt

about resuming her real life now that she'd remembered it. He suspected she wasn't sure, either. Not yet, anyway. His conscience said he should stick to the suggestion he'd made last night to take things between them slowly, step-by-step. But his conscience couldn't stand up to the homey sounds of Natalie moving around inside the loft, brewing her tea, laughing at the hound's antics.

He wanted her here, with him. Wanted to show her more of the city he loved. Wanted to explore that precise, fascinating mind, hear her breathy gasps and groans when they made love.

And, he thought, his eyes going cold and flat, he wanted to flatten whoever'd hurt her. He didn't believe for a moment she'd hit her head on a support pole and tumbled into the Danube. Janos Lagy had lured her onto that tour boat and Dom was damned well going to find out why.

For once Andre didn't have the inside scoop. Instead, he referred Dom back to the Hungarian agency that conducted internal investigations. The individual Dom spoke to there was cautious and closemouthed and unwilling to share sensitive information with someone she didn't know. She did, however, agree to meet with him and Natalie in the morning.

That made two appointments for tomorrow—one at the US Embassy to obtain a replacement passport and one at the National Tax and Customs Administration.

"Tax and Customs?" Natalie echoed when he told her about the appointments. "Is that like the Internal Revenue Service in the US?"

"More like your IRS and Department of the Treasury combined. The NTCA is our focus for all financial matters, including criminal activities like money laundering and financing terrorist activities."

Her eyes rounded. "And they have something on Lagy?"

"They wouldn't say, but they're interested in talking to you."

"I can't tell them any more than I told you."

"No, but they can tell us what, if anything, Lagy's involved in."

"Well, this has been an amazing day. Two days, actually." Her eyes met his in a smile. "And a pretty amazing night."

The smile clinched it. No way was he letting this woman waltz out of his life the same way she'd waltzed in. Dom thought seriously about plucking the glass out of her hand and carrying her to the bed. Which he would, he promised himself. Later. Right now, he'd initiate a blitz-style campaign to make her develop a passion for all things Hungarian—himself included.

"Did you bring a bathing suit?"

She blinked at the abrupt change of topic. "A bathing suit?"

"Do you have one in your suitcase?"

"I packed for business, not splashing around in hotel pools."

"No matter. We can rent one."

"Rent a bathing suit?" Her fastidious little nose wrinkled. "I don't think so."

"They're sanitized and steam-cleaned. Trust me on this. Stuff a couple of towels in your tote while I feed the hound and we'll go."

"Dom, I don't think public bathing is really my thing."

"You can't leave Budapest without experiencing what gives this city its most distinctive character. Why do you think the Romans called their settlement here Aquincum?"

"Meaning water something?"

"Meaning abundant waters. All they had to do was poke a stick in the ground and a hot spring bubbled up. Get the towels."

* * *

Natalie was even less sure about the whole communal spa thing when they arrived at the elegant Gellért Hotel. The massive complex sat at the base of Gellért Hill, named, Dom informed her, for the unfortunate bishop who came from Venice at the request of King Istivan in 1000 A.D.

"My rebellious Magyar ancestors took exception to the king's conversion to Christianity," Dom related as he escorted her to the columned and colonnaded entrance. "They put the bishop in a barrel, drove long spikes in it and rolled him down the hill."

"Lovely."

"Here we go."

He ushered her into a grand entry hall two or three stories high. A long row of ticket windows lining one side of the hall offered a bewildering smorgasbord of options. Dom translated a menu that included swimming pools, thermal baths with temperatures ranging from a comfortable 86 degrees to a scorching 108 degrees, whirlpools, wave pools, saunas and steam rooms. And massages! Every sort of massage. Natalie gave up trying to pick out options and left the choice to him.

"Don't you need to know what bathing suit size I need?" she asked as they approached a ticket booth.

He cut her an amused glance. "I was with you when you bought those jeans, remember? You're a size forty-two."

Ugh! She hated European sizing. She stood beside him while he purchased their entry and noted that a good number of people passed through the turnstiles with just a flash of a blue card.

"They don't have to pay?"

"They have a medical pass," he explained as he fastened a band around her wrist. "The government operates all spas in Hungary. They're actually part of our health care system. Doctors regularly send patients here for massage or hot soaks or swimming laps."

Impressed but still a little doubtful, Natalie accompanied him into a gloriously ornate lobby, then to a seemingly mile-long hall with windows offering an unimpeded view of a sparkling swimming pool. Swimmers of all ages, shapes and sizes floated, dog-paddled or cut through the water with serious strokes.

"Here's where we temporarily part ways," Dom told her, extracting one of the towels from her tote. "The men's changing area is on the right, the women's on the left. Just show the attendant your wristband and she'll fix you up with a suit. Then hold the band up to the electronic pad and it'll assign you a changing cabin and locker. Once you've changed, flash the band again to enter the thermal baths. I'll meet you there."

That sounded simple enough—until Natalie walked through the entrance to the women's area. It was huge, with marble everywhere, stairs leading up and down, and seemingly endless rows of massage rooms, saunas, showers and changing rooms. A friendly local helped her locate the alcove containing the suit rental desk.

She still harbored distinct doubts about shimmying into a used bathing suit. But when she slid the chit Dom had given her across the desk, the attendant returned with a sealed package containing what looked like a brand-new one-piece. She held her wristband up to the electronic pad as Dom had instructed and got the number of a changing room. Faced with long, daunting rows of cubicles, she had to ask another local for help locating hers. Once they'd found it, the smiling woman took Natalie's wrist and aimed the band at the electronic lock.

"Here, here. Like this."

The door popped open, and her helpful guide added further instructions.

"It locks behind you, yes? You leave your clothes and towels in the cabin, then go through to the thermal pool."

"Thank you."

"Szívesen."

The room was larger than Natalie had expected, with a bench running along one wall and a locker for her clothes and tote. She was still leery of the rented bathing suit but a close inspection showed it to be clean and fresh-smelling.

And at least one size too small!

Cut high on the thighs and low in the front, the sleek black Spandex revealed far more skin than Natalie wanted to display. She tried yanking up the neck but that only pulled the Spandex into an all-too-suggestive V at her crotch. She tugged it down again, determined not to give Dom a peep show.

Not that he would object. The man was nothing if not appreciative of the opposite sex. Kiss Kiss Arabella and lushly endowed Lisel were proof of that. And, Natalie now remembered, his sister Zia and Sarah's sister Gina had both joked about how women fell all over him. And why not? With that sexy grin and too-handsome face, Dominic St. Sebastian could have his pick of...

She froze, her fingers still tugging at the bottom of the suit, as another handsome face flashed into her mind.

Oh, God!

She dropped onto the bench. Blood drained from her heart and gathered like a cold, dead pool in her belly.

Oh God, oh God, oh God!

Wrapping her arms around her middle, she rocked back and forth on the bench. She remembered now the "traumatic" event she'd tried to desperately to suppress. The ugly incident that had caused her to lose her sense of self.

How could she have forgotten for a day—an hour!— the vicious truth she'd kept buried for more than three years? Tears stung her eyes, raked her throat. Furiously, she fought them back. She'd cried all the tears she had in her three years ago. She was damned if she'd shed any more for the bastard who destroyed her life then. And would now destroy it again, she acknowledged on a wave of despair.

How could she have let herself believe last night could lead to something more between her and Dominic St. Sebastian? When she told him about her past, he'd be so disappointed, so disgusted. She sat there, aching for what might have been, until the urge to howl like a wounded animal released its death grip on her throat. Then she got off the bench and pushed through the door at the other end of the changing room.

The temperature in the marble hall shot up as she approached the first of the thermal pools. Dom was there, waiting for her as promised. Yesterday, even this morning, she would have drooled at the sight of his tall, muscled torso sporting a scant few inches of electric-blue Speedo. Now all she could do was gulp when he got a look at her face and stiffened.

"What's wrong?"

"I…I…"

"Natalie, what is it? What's happened?"

"I have to tell you something." She threw a wild look around the busy spa. "But not here. I'll…I'll meet you at the car."

Whirling, she fled back to her changing room.

Twelve

Her mind drowning in a cesspool of memories, Natalie scrambled into her clothes and had to ask for directions several times before she emerged from the maze of saunas and massage rooms.

Dom waited at the entrance to the women's changing rooms instead of at the car. His face was tight with concern and unspoken questions when she emerged. He swept a sharp glance around the hall, as though checking to see if anyone lingered nearby or appeared to be waiting or watching for Natalie, then cut his gaze back to her.

"What happened in the changing area to turn your face so pale?"

"I remembered something."

"About Janos Lagy?"

"No." She gnawed on her lower lip. "An incident in my past. I need to tell you about it."

Something flickered in his eyes. Surprise? Caution? Wariness? It came and went so quickly she couldn't have pinned a label on it even if her thoughts weren't skittering all over the place.

"There's a café across the street. We can talk there."

"A café? I don't think… I don't know…"

"We haven't eaten since breakfast. Whatever you have to tell me will go down easier with a bowl of goulash."

Natalie knew nothing could make it go down easier,

but she accompanied him out of the hotel and into the fall dusk. Lights had begun to glow on the Pest side of the Danube. She barely registered the glorious panorama of gold and indigo as Dom took her arm and steered her to the brightly lit café.

Soon—too soon for her mounting dread—they were enclosed in a high-backed booth that afforded both privacy and an unimpeded view of the illuminated majesty across the river. Dom ordered and signaled for her to wait until the server had brought them both coffee and a basket of thick black bread. He cut Natalie's coffee with a generous helping of milk to suit her American taste buds, then nudged the cup across the table.

"Take a drink, take a breath and tell me what has you so upset."

She complied with the first two instructions but couldn't find a way to broach the third. She stirred more milk into her coffee, fiddled with her spoon, gnawed on her lower lip again.

"Natalie. Tell me."

Her eyes lifted to his. "The scum you hunt down? The thieves and con artists and other criminals?" Misery choked her voice. "I'm one of them."

She'd dreaded his reaction. Anticipated his disgust or icy withdrawal. The fact that he didn't even blink at the anguished confession threw her off for a moment. But only a moment.

"Oh, my God! You know?" Shame coursed through her, followed almost immediately by a scorching realization. "Of course you do! You've known all along, haven't you?"

"Not all along, and not the details." His calm, even tone countered the near hysteria in hers. "Only that you were arrested, the charges were later dropped and the record wiped clean."

Her laugh was short and bitter. "Not clean enough, apparently."

The server arrived then with their goulash. The brief interruption didn't give her nearly enough time to swallow the fact that Dom had been privy to her deepest, darkest, most mortifying secret. The server departed, but the steaming soup sat untouched while Natalie related the rest of her sorry tale.

"I'm not sure how much you know about me, but before Sarah hired me I worked for the State of Illinois. Specifically, for the state's Civil Service Board. I was part of an ongoing project to digitize more than a hundred years' worth of paper files and merge them with current electronic records. I enjoyed the work. It was such a challenge putting all those old records into a sortable database."

She really *had* loved her job, she remembered as she plucked a slice of coarse black bread from the basket and played with it. Not just the digitizing and merging and sorting, but the picture those old personnel records painted of previous generations. Their work ethic, their frugal saving habits, their large numbers of dependents and generous contributions to church and charity. For someone like Natalie with no parents or grandparents or any known family, these glimpses into the quintessential American working family were fascinating.

"Then," she said with a long, slow, thoroughly disgusted sigh, "I fell in love."

She tore a thick piece off the bread, squeezed it into a wad, rolled it around and around between her fingers.

"He was so good-looking," she said miserably. "Tall, athletic, blue-eyed, always smiling."

"Always smiling? Sounds like a jerk."

Her lips twisted. "I was the jerk. I bought his line about wanting to settle down and start a family. Actually started weaving fantasies about a nursery, a minivan with car seats, the whole baby scene. I should've known I wasn't the type to interest someone as smooth and sophisticated as Jason DeWitt for longer than it took for him to hack into my computer."

Dom reached out and put his palm over the fingers still nervously rolling the bread. His grip was strong and warm, his eyes glinting with undisguised anger.

"We'll discuss what type you are later. Right now, I can pretty well guess what came next. Mr. Smooth used your computer to access state records and mine thousands of addresses, dates of birth and social security numbers."

"Try hundreds of thousands."

"Then he sold them, right? I'm guessing to the Russians, although the marketplace is pretty well wide-open these days. And when the crap hit the fan, the feds tracked the breach to you."

"He hadn't sold them yet. They caught him with his hand still in my cookie jar."

Shame and misery engulfed her again. Tears burned as the images from that horrible day played through her head.

"Oh, Dom, it was so awful! The police came to my office! Said they'd been after Jason—the man I *knew* as Jason DeWitt—for over a year. They'd decoded his electronic signature and knew he'd hacked into several major databases. They'd finally penetrated his shields and not only pinpointed his exact location, they kicked in the door to my apartment and nailed him in the act. Then they charged me with being an accomplice to unauthorized access to public records with intent to commit fraud. They arrested me right there in front of all my coworkers and… and…"

She had to stop and gulp back the stinging tears. "Then they hauled me downtown in handcuffs."

"At which point they discovered you weren't a party to the hacking and released you."

Dom's unquestioned acceptance of her innocence should have soothed her raw nerves. Instead, it made it even tougher to finish the sordid tale.

"Not quite."

Writhing inside, she tried to pull her hand away but he kept it caged.

"Jason tried to convince the police it was all my idea. He said I'd teased and taunted him with sex. That would have been laughable," she said, heat surging into her cheeks, "if the police hadn't found a closet full of crotch-high leather skirts, low-cut blouses and peek-a-boo lingerie. Jason kept pestering me to wear that kind of…of slut stuff when we went out. It was enough to make the investigators wring me inside out before they finally released me."

Dom played his thumb over the back of her hand and fought to keep his fury in check. It wasn't enough that the hacker had played on Natalie's lonely childhood and craving for a family. The bastard had also cajoled her into decking herself out like a whore. No wonder she'd swung to the opposite extreme and started dressing like a refugee from a war zone.

Even worse, she'd had no one to turn to for help during what had to be one of the most humiliating moments of her life. No parents to rush downtown and bail her out. No sister to descend like an avenging angel, as Zia would have done. No brother to pulverize the man who'd set her up.

She wasn't alone now, though. Nor would she be alone in the future. Not as long as Dominic had a say in the matter. The absolute certainty of that settled around his heart like a glove as he quietly prompted her to continue.

"What did you do then?"

"I hired a lawyer and got the arrest expunged. Or so I thought," she amended with a frown. "Then I had the lawyer negotiate a deal with my boss. Since the state records hadn't actually been compromised, I said I would quietly disappear if he agreed that my employment record would contain no reference to the whole sorry mess. After some weeks of wrangling with the state attorney general's office, I packed up and left town. I worked at odd jobs for a while until…"

"Until you went to work for Sarah," he finished when she didn't.

Guilt flooded her face. "I didn't lie to her, Dom. I filled out my employment history truthfully. I knew she would check my references, knew my chances were iffy at best. But my former boss stuck to his end of the deal, and my performance reports before…before that big mess were so glowing and complimentary that Sarah hired me after only one interview."

She turned away, shamefaced.

"I know you think I should have told her. I wanted to. I really did. And I intended to. I just thought…maybe if I tracked down the Canaletto first…helped return it to its rightful owner…Sarah and Dev and the duchess would know I wasn't a thief."

"You're not a thief. Natalie, look at me. You're not a thief or a con artist or a criminal. Trust me, I've been around the breed enough to know. Now I have two questions for you before we eat the soup that's been sitting here for so long."

"Only two?"

Her voice was wobbly, her eyes still tear-bright and drenched with a humiliation that made Dom vow to pulverize the scum who'd put it there.

"Where is this Jason character now?"

"Serving five to ten at the Danville Correctional Facility."

"Well, that takes him off my hit list. For now."

An almost smile worked through her embarrassment. "What's question two?"

"How long are you going to keep mashing that piece of bread?"

She blinked and looked down in surprise at the pulpy glob squishing through her fingers.

"Here." He passed her a napkin. "Eat your soup, *drágám*. Then we'll go home and get back to work on finding your painting."

Home. The word reverberated in Natalie's mind when Dom opened the door to the loft and Duke treated them to an ecstatic welcome. She clung to the sound of it, the thought of it, like a lifeline while man and dog took a quick trip downstairs and she went to unpack the roller suitcase still propped next to the wardrobe.

Her toiletries went into the bathroom, her underwear onto the corner of a shelf in the wardrobe. When she lifted the neatly folded blouses, her mouth twisted.

Natalie knew she'd never been a Princess Kate. She wasn't tall or glamorous or as poised as a supermodel. But she'd possessed her own sense of style. She'd preferred a layered look, she now remembered. Mostly slim slacks or jeans with belted tunics or cardigans over tanks...until Jason.

He'd wanted sexier, flashier. She cringed, remembering how she'd suppressed her inner qualms and let him talk her into those thigh-hugging skirts and lace-up bustiers. She'd burned them. The leather skirts, the bustiers, the stilettos and boob tubes and garter belts and push-up bras. Carted the whole lot down to the incinerator in her building, along with every other item in her apartment that carried even a whiff of Jason's scent or a faint trace of his imprint.

Then she'd gone out and purchased an entire new wardrobe of maiden aunt blouses and shapeless linen dresses. She'd also stopped using makeup and began scraping her hair back in a bun. She'd even resorted to wearing glasses she didn't need. Paying penance, she now realized, for her sins.

She was still staring at the folded blouses when Dom and the hound returned. When he saw what she was holding, he dropped the dog's lead on the kitchen counter and crossed the room.

"You don't need these anymore." He took the blouses and dumped them back in the case. "You don't need any of this."

When he zipped the case and propped it next to the wardrobe again, Natalie experienced a heady sense of freedom. As though she'd just shed an outer skin that'd felt as unnatural and uncomfortable as the one she'd tried to squeeze into for Jason.

Buoyed by the feeling, she flashed Dom a smile. "If you don't want me to continue raiding your closet, you'll have to take me shopping again."

"You're welcome to wear anything of mine you wish. Although," he confessed with a quick grin, "I must admit I prefer when you wear nothing at all."

The need that splintered through her was swift and clean and joyous. The shame she'd tried to bury for three long years was still there, just below the surface. She suspected traces of it would linger there for a long while. But for now, for this moment, she could give herself completely to Dom and her aching hunger for his touch.

She looped her arms around his neck and let the smile in his eyes begin healing the scars. "I must admit I prefer you that way, too."

"Then I suggest we both shed some clothes."

They made it to the bed. Barely. A stern command prevented Duke from jumping in with them, but Natalie had to force herself not to look at the hound's reproachful face until Dom's mouth and teeth and busy, busy hands made her forget everything but him.

She was boneless with pleasure and half-asleep when he tucked her into the curve of his body and murmured something in Hungarian.

"What does that mean?"

"Sleep well, my darling."

Her heart tripped, but she didn't ask him to expand on that interesting translation. She settled for snuggling closer to his warmth and drifting into a deep, dreamless sleep.

Natalie woke the next morning to the sound of hammering. She pried one eye open and listened for several moments before realizing that was rain pounding against the roof. Burrowing deeper under the featherbed, she resurfaced again only when an amused voice sounded just over her shoulder.

"The dog and I are going for our run. Coffee's on the stove when you're ready for it."

She half rolled over. "You're going out in the rain?"

"That's one of the penalties of being adopted by a racing hound. He needs regular exercise whatever the weather. We both do, actually."

Natalie grunted, profoundly thankful that she wasn't invited to participate in this morning ritual.

"I'll bring back apple pancakes for breakfast," Dom advised as he and the joyously prancing Agár headed for the door. "Then we'll need to leave for the appointments at the embassy and the Tax and Customs Administration."

"And shopping," Natalie called to his back. "I need to shop!"

The prospect of replenishing her wardrobe with bright colors and soft textures erased any further desire to burrow. By the time Dom and Duke returned she'd showered and dressed in her one pair of jeans and tank top. She'd also made the bed, fussed with the folds in the drapes and dust-mopped the loft's wood-plank floors.

Her welcome smile slipped a little when the runners tracked wet foot- and paw-prints across the gleaming floors. She had to laugh, though, and hold up her hands against a flying spray when the hound planted all four paws and shook from his nose to his tail.

She and Dom feasted on the pancakes that he'd somehow protected from the rain. Then he, too, got ready for the morning's appointments. He emerged from the bathroom showered and shaved and looking too scrumptious for words in jeans and a cable-knit fisherman's sweater.

"You'd better bring the Canaletto file," he advised.

"I have it," she said, patting her briefcase. "I made copies of the key documents, just in case."

"Good." He held up the jacket she'd pretty much claimed as her own. "Now put this on and we'll go."

Natalie was glad of its warmth when they went down to the car. The rain had lessened to a misty drizzle but the damp chill carried a bite. Not even the gray weather could obscure the castle ramparts, though, as Dom negotiated the curving streets of Castle Hill and joined the stream of traffic flowing across Chain Bridge.

The US Embassy was housed in what had once been an elegant turn-of-the century palazzo facing a lush park. High metal fencing and concrete blocks had turned it into a modern-day fortress and long lines waited to go through the security checkpoint. As Dom steered Natalie to a side entrance with a much shorter line, she noted a bronze plaque with a raised relief religious figure.

"Who's that?"

"Cardinal József Mindszenty, one of the heroes of modern Hungary. The communists tortured and imprisoned him for speaking out against their brutal regime. He got a temporary reprieve during the 1956 Revolution, but when the Soviets crushed the uprising, the US Embassy granted him political asylum. He remained here for more than fifteen years.

"Fifteen *years*?"

"Cardinal Mindszenty is one of the reasons Hungary and the United States enjoy such close ties today."

Dom's Interpol credentials got them into the consular offices through the side entrance. After passing through security and X-ray screening, they arrived at their appointment right on time

Replacing Natalie's lost passport took less than a half hour. She produced the copy of her driver's license Dom's contact had procured and the forms she'd already completed. After signing the form in front of a consular officer and having it witnessed by another official, the computer spit out a copy of her passport's data page.

She winced at the photo, taken when she'd renewed her passport just over a year ago, but she thanked the official and slipped the passport into her tote with an odd, unsettled feeling. She should have been relieved to have both her memory and her identity back. She could leave Hungary now. Go home to the States, or anywhere else her research took her. How stupid was she for wishing this passport business had taken weeks instead of minutes?

Their second appointment didn't go as quickly or as well. Dom's Interpol credentials seemed to have a negative effect on the two uniformed officers they met with at the NTCA. One was a spare, thirtysomething woman who introduced herself as Patrícia Czernek, the other a graying older man who greeted Natalie with a polite nod before engaging Dom in a spirited dialogue. It didn't take a genius or a working knowledge of Hungarian to figure out they were having a bit of a turf war. Natalie kept out of the line of fire until the female half of the team picked up the phone and made a call that appeared to settle the matter.

With a speaking glance at her partner, Officer Czernek turned to Natalie. "So Ms. Clark, we understand from Special Agent St. Sebastian that you may have knowledge of a missing painting by a Venetian master. One taken from Karlenburgh Castle during the 1956 Uprising. Will you tell us, please, how you came by this knowledge?"

"Certainly."

Extracting the Canaletto file, she passed each of the officers a copy of the chronology she'd run earlier. "This summarizes my research, step-by-step. As you can see, it began three months ago with a computer search."

The NTCA officers flipped through the four-sheet printout and exchanged looks. Dom merely smiled.

"If you'll turn to page three, line thirty-seven," Natalie continued briskly, "you'll see that I did a search of recently declassified documents from the Soviet era relating to art treasures owned by the state and found an inventory of items removed from Karlenburgh Castle. The inventory listed more than two dozen near priceless works of art, but not the Canaletto. Yet I knew from previous discussions with Grand Duchess Charlotte that the painting *was* hanging in the Red Salon the day the Soviets came to destroy the castle."

She walked them through her search step-by-step. Her decision to drive down from Vienna to interview local residents. Her stop at the ruins and meeting with Friedrich Müller. His reference to an individual who'd inquired previously at the Red Salon.

"Janos Lagy," the older of the two officers murmured. He skimmed down several lines and looked up quickly. "You spoke with him? You spoke with Lagy about this painting?"

"I did."

"And arranged to meet with him on a riverboat?"

"That was his idea, not mine. Unfortunately, he didn't show."

"Do you have a recording of this conversation?" Officer Czernek asked hopefully. "On your cell phone, perhaps?"

"I lost my purse and phone when I went overboard."

"Yes, Special Agent St. Sebastian told us about your accident." A frown etched between her brows. "We also reviewed a copy of the incident report from the metropolitan police. It's very strange that no one saw you fall from the boat or raised an alarm."

"I was at the back of the ship and not feeling very well. Also, this happened in the middle of the week. There weren't many other passengers aboard."

"Still…"

She and her partner engaged in a brief exchange.

"We, too, have a file," she said, turning back to Natalie. "Would you be so kind as to look at some pictures and tell me if you recognize any of the people in them?"

She produced a thin folder and slid out three eight-by-tens. One showed a lone figure in a business suit and tie. The second picture was of the same individual in a tux and smiling down at the svelte beauty on his arm. In the third, he strolled along a city street wearing an overcoat and smart fedora.

"Do you recognize that man?" Czernek asked, her gaze intent on Natalie.

She scrutinized the lean features again. The confident smile, the dark eyes and fringe of brown hair around a head going bald on top. She'd never seen him before. She was sure of it.

"No, I don't recognize him. Is it Lagy?"

The police officer nodded and blew out an obviously disappointed breath. When she reached over to gather the pictures, Natalie had to battle her own crushing disappointment. Lagy's link to the Canaletto had been tenuous at best but she'd followed thinner threads. Suddenly, she frowned and took another look at the street shot.

"Him!" She stabbed a finger at a figure trailing a little way behind Lagy. "I recognize this man. He was on the boat."

"Are you sure?"

"Very sure. When I got sick, he asked if he could help but I waved him away. I didn't want to puke all over his shoes." She looked up eagerly. "Do you know who he is?"

"He's Janos Lagy's bodyguard."

The air in the small office suddenly simmered with rigidly suppressed excitement. Natalie looked from Czernek to her partner to Dom and back again. All of them, apparently, knew something she didn't.

"Clue me in," she demanded. "What have you got on Janos Lagy?"

The officer hesitated. A cop's natural instinct to hold her cards close to her chest, Natalie guessed. Tough! She wasn't leaving the NTCA until she got some answers.

"Look," she said mutinously, "I've chased all over Europe tracking the Canaletto. I've spent weeks digging through musty records. I whacked my head and took an unplanned swim in the Danube. I didn't know who I was for almost a week. So I think I deserve an answer. What's the story on Lagy?"

After another brief pause, Czernek relented. "We've had him under surveillance for some time now. We suspect he's been trafficking in stolen art and have unsubstantiated reports of a private collection kept in a secret vault in his home."

"You're kidding!"

"No, I am not. Unfortunately, we haven't been able to gather enough evidence to convince a judge to issue a search warrant." Patrícia Czernek's lips parted in a knife blade of a smile. "Based on what you've told us, we may be able to get that warrant."

Thirteen

After all she'd done, all she'd been through, Natalie considered it a complete and total bummer that she was forced to sit on the sidelines during the final phase of the hunt that had consumed her for so many weeks.

The task force gathered early the morning after Natalie had ID'd the bodyguard. As tenuous as that connection was to Lagy and the missing Canaletto, when combined with other evidence NCTA had compiled on the banker, it proved sufficient for a judge to grant a search warrant. Dom left the loft before dawn to join the team that would hit the banker's villa on the outskirts of Budapest. Natalie was left behind with nothing to do but walk the hound, make another excursion to the butcher shop, scrub the shower stall, dust-mop the floors again and pace.

"This is the pits," she complained to the hound as the morning dragged by.

The Agár cocked his head but didn't look particularly sympathetic.

"Okay, okay! It's true I don't have any official standing that could have allowed them to include me in the task force. And I guess I don't really want to see anyone hauled off in handcuffs. That would cut a little too close to the bone," she admitted with a grimace. "Still," she grumbled, shooting another glance at the kitchen clock, "you'd think certain people would find a way to let me know what's happening."

Dominic couldn't contact her directly. She knew that. Natalie's phone was at the bottom of the Danube and the loft didn't have a landline. He could've called his downstairs neighbors, though, and asked Katya or her father to relay a message.

Or not. There was probably some rule or protocol that prohibited disseminating information about an ongoing investigation to civilians.

"That better not include me."

The bad-tempered comment produced a nervous whine from the hound. Natalie stooped to scratch behind his ear.

"Sorry, Duke'ums. I'm just a little annoyed with your alter ego."

Annoyed and increasingly worried as morning crawled toward noon, then into the afternoon, she was seriously contemplating going downstairs to ask Katya if she could use her phone when she heard the heavy tread of footsteps on the outside stairs.

"Finally!"

She rushed to the door, startling the dog into a round of excited barking. One look at Dom's mile-wide grin sent all her nasty recriminations back down her throat. She could only laugh when he caught her by the waist and swung her in wide circles. The hound, of course, went nuts. Natalie had to call a halt before they all tripped over each other and tumbled down five flights of stairs.

"Dom, stop! You're making me dizzy."

He complied with a smooth move that shifted her from mostly vertical to horizontal. Still wearing a cheek-splitting grin, he carried her over the threshold and kicked the door shut as soon as the three of them were inside.

"I assume you got your man," she said.

"You assume right. Hold on."

He opened the fridge and dipped her almost vertical again. Squealing, she locked her arms around his neck while he retrieved two frosty bottles from the bottom shelf, then carried her to the sofa. He sank onto the cushions with Natalie in his lap and thumped his boots up on the coffee table.

She managed to keep from pelting him with questions while he offered her one of the dew-streaked bottles of pilsner. When she shook her head, he popped the cap and tilted his head. She watched, fascinated, as he downed half the contents in long, thirsty swallows. He hadn't had time to shave before he'd left. The beginnings of a beard shadowed his cheeks and chin. And his knuckles, she noted with a small gasp, had acquired a nasty set of scrapes and bruises.

"What happened to your knuckles?"

"Lagy's bodyguard ran into them." Something dark and dangerous glinted in his eyes. "Several times."

"What? Why?"

"We had a private discussion about your swim in the Danube. He disavowed any responsibility for it, of course, but I didn't like the way his lip curled when he did."

She gaped at him, her jaw sagging. She'd been alone so long. And so sickened by the way Jason had tried to pin the blame for his illegal activities on her. The idea that Dom had set himself up as her protector and avenger cut deep into her heart. Before she could articulate the chaotic emotions those bruised knuckles roused, however, the hound almost climbed into her lap.

She held him off, but it took some effort. "You'd better give him some of your beer before he grabs the bottle out of your hand, and tell me the rest of the story!"

He tipped the bottle toward the Agár's eager jaws. Natalie barely registered an inward cringe as pale gold lager slopped in all directions. Duke dropped the empty bottle on the floor and was scooting it across the oak planks to extract the last drops when Dom launched into a detailed account.

"We hit the villa before Lagy had left for the bank. When Czernek showed him the search warrant, he wouldn't let us proceed until his high-priced lawyer arrived on the scene."

"Did Lagy recognize you?"

"Oh, yeah. He made some crack about the newspaper stories, but I could tell the fact that a St. Sebastian had showed up at his door with an armed squad made him nervous. Especially when I flashed my Interpol credentials."

"Then what happened?"

"We cooled our heels until his lawyer showed up. Bastard had the nerve to play lord of the manor and offer us all coffee."

"Which you accepted," she guessed, all too mindful of the Hungarian passion for the brew.

"Which we accepted," he confirmed. "By the time his lawyer arrived, though, we'd all had our fill of acting polite. His attorney tried to posture and bluff, but folded like an accordion when Czernek waved the search warrant under his nose. Apparently he'd gotten crosswise of this particular judge before and knew he couldn't fast-talk his client out of this one. Then," Dom said with savage satisfaction, "we tore the villa apart. Imagine our surprise when infrared imaging detected a vault hidden behind a false wall in Lagy's study."

When he paused to pop the cap on the second bottle, Natalie groaned in sheer frustration.

"Don't you dare drink that before you tell me what was in the vault!"

"See for yourself." Shifting her on his lap, he jammed a hand in the pocket of his jeans and extracted a folded printout. "That's just a preliminary inventory. Each piece has to be examined and authenticated by a team of experts."

Her hands shaking with excitement, Natalie unfolded the printout and skimmed the fourteen entries.

"Omigod!"

The list read like a who's who of the art world. Edgar Degas. Josef Grassi. Thomas Gainsborough. And there, close to the bottom, Giovanni Canaletto.

"Did you see the Canaletto?" she asked breathlessly. "Is it the one from Karlenburgh Castle?"

"Looked like it to me."

"I can't believe it!"

"Lagy couldn't, either, when Czernek called for a team to crate up his precious paintings and take them in evidence."

She skimmed the list again, stunned by its variety and richness. "How incredible that he managed to amass such an extensive collection. It must be worth hundreds of millions."

"He may have acquired some of it through legitimate channels. As for the rest…" Dom's jaw hardened. "I'm guessing he inherited many of those paintings from his grandfather. Karlenburgh Castle wasn't the only residence destroyed in retribution for their owners' participation in the '56 Uprising. *Mladshij Lejtenant* Lagy's company of sappers would have been only too eager help take them down. God knows how many treasures the bastards managed to appropriate for themselves in the process."

Natalie slumped against his chest and devoured the brief descriptions of the paintings removed from Lagy's villa. Several she recognized immediately from Interpol's database of lost or stolen art. Others she would need more detail on before she could be sure.

"This," she said, excitement still singing through her veins, "is going make a fantastic final chapter in Sarah's book. Her editors will eat up the personal angle. A painting purchased for a young duchess, then lost for decades. The hunt by the duchess's granddaughter for the missing masterpiece. The raid that recovered it, which just happened to include the current Grand Duke."

"Let's not forget the part you played in the drama."

"I'm just the research assistant. You St. Sebastians are the star players."

"You're not 'just' anything, Natushka."

To emphasize the point, he tugged on her hair and tilted her head back for a long, hard kiss. Neither of them held back, taking and giving in both a welcome release of tension and celebration.

Natalie was riding high when Dom raised his head. "I can't wait to tell Sarah about this. And the duchess! When do you think her painting will be returned to her?"

"I have no idea. They'll have to authenticate it first, then trace the provenance. If Lagy can prove he purchased it or any of these paintings in good faith from a gallery or another collector, the process could take weeks or months."

"Or longer," she said, scrunching her nose. "Can't you exert some royal influence and hurry the process along?"

"Impatient little thing, aren't you?"

"And then some!" She scooted off his lap and onto the cushion next to him. "Let's contact Sarah via FaceTime. I want to see her reaction when we tell her."

They caught Sarah in midair aboard Dev's private jet. The moment Dom made the connection, her employer fired an anxious query.

"How's Natalie? Has her memory returned?"

"It has."

"Thank God! Where is she now?"

"She's here, with me. Hang on."

He angled the phone to capture Natalie's eager face. "Hello, Sarah."

"Oh, Natalie, we've been so worried. Are you really okay?"

"Better than okay. We've located the Canaletto!"

"What?" Sarah whipped her head to one side. "Dev, you're not going to believe this! Natalie's tracked down Grandmama's Canaletto."

"I didn't do it alone," Natalie protested, aiming a quick smile at Dom. "It was a team effort."

When she glanced back at the screen, Sarah's brows had inched up. "Well," she said after a small pause, "if I was going to team with anyone other than my husband, Dominic would certainly top my list."

A telltale heat rushed into Natalie's cheeks but she didn't respond to the curiosity simmering just below the surface of her employer's reply. Mostly because she wasn't really sure how to define her "teaming" with Dom, much less predict how long it would last. But she couldn't hold back a cheek-to-cheek grin as she related the events of the past few days. Sarah's eyes grew wider with the telling, and at the end of the recital she echoed Natalie's earlier sentiments.

"This is all so incredible. I can't wait to tell Grandmama the Canaletto's been recovered."

Dom leaned over Natalie's shoulder to issue the same warning he had earlier. "They'll have to assemble a team of experts to authenticate each painting and validate its provenance. That could take several months or more."

Dev's face crowded next to his wife's on the small screen. "We'll see what we can do to expedite the process, at least as far as the Canaletto is concerned."

"And I'll ask Gina to get Jack involved," Sarah volunteered. "He can apply some subtle pressure through diplomatic channels."

"I also suggested to the Grand Duke here that he should exercise a little royal muscle," Natalie put in.

"Good for you. With all three of our guys weighing in, I'm sure we can shake Grandmama's painting loose without too long a delay."

The reference to "our" guys deepened the heat in Natalie's cheeks. She floundered for a moment, but before she could think of an appropriate response to the possessive pronoun, Sarah had already jumped ahead.

"We need to update the chapter on the Canaletto, Nat. And if we put our noses to the grindstone, we ought to be able to finish the final draft of the book in two or three weeks. When can you fly back to L.A.?"

"I, uh…"

"Scratch that. Instead of going straight home, let's rendezvous in New York. I'd like you to personally brief my editor. I know she'll want to take advantage of the publicity all this is going to generate. We can fly to L.A. from there."

She could hardly say no. Sarah St. Sebastian Hunter had offered her the job of a lifetime. Not only did Natalie love the work, she appreciated the generous salary and fringe benefits that came with it. She owed her boss loyalty and total dedication until her book hit the shelves.

"No problem. I can meet you in New York whenever it works for you."

"I'll call my editor as soon as we hang up. I'll try to arrange something on Thursday or Friday. Did you get a replacement passport? Great. You should probably fly home tomorrow, then. I'll have a ticket waiting for you at the airport."

She disconnected with a promise to call back as soon as she'd nailed down the time and place of the meeting. Dominic tossed his phone on the coffee table and turned to Natalie.

She couldn't quite meet his eyes. She felt as though

she'd just dropped down an elevator shaft. Mere moments ago she'd been riding a dizzying high. In a few short seconds, she'd plunged back into cold, hard reality. She had a job, responsibilities, a life back in the States, such as it was. And neither she nor Dom had discussed any alternative. Still, the prospect of leaving Hungary drilled a hole in her heart.

"Sarah's been so good to me," she said, breaking the small silence. "I need to help put the final touches on her book."

"Of course you do. I, too, must go back to work. I've been away from it too long."

She plucked at the hem of her borrowed shirt. She should probably ask Dom to take her on a quick shopping run. She could hardly show up for a meeting with Sarah's editor in jeans and a tank top, much less a man's soccer shirt. Yet she hated to spend her last hours in Budapest cruising boutiques.

She tried to hide her misery at the thought of leaving, but Dom had to see it when he curled a knuckle under her chin and tipped her face to his.

"Perhaps this is for the best, *drágám*. You've had so much thrown at you in such a short time. The dive into the Danube. The memory loss. Me," he said with a crooked grin. "You need to step back and take a breath."

"You're probably right," she mumbled.

"I know I am. And when you've helped Sarah put her book to bed, you and I will decide where we go from there, yes?"

She wanted to believe him. Ached all over with the need to throw herself into his arms and make him *swear* this wasn't the end. Unfortunately, all she could think of was Kiss Kiss Arabella's outrageously expensive panties and Lovely Lisel's effusive greeting and Gina's laughing comments about her studly cousin and...

Dominic cut into those lowering thoughts by tugging her up and off the sofa with him. "So! Since this is your last night in Budapest for a while at least, we should make it one to remember."

For a while at least. Natalie clung to the promise of that small phrase as Dom scooped up his phone and stuffed it in his jeans pocket. Taking time only to pull on the red-and-black soccer shirt with its distinctive logo on the sleeve, he insisted she throw on the jacket she'd pretty much claimed as her own before hustling her to the door.

"Where are we going?"

"My very favorite place in all the city."

Since the city boasted spectacular architecture, a world-class opera house, soaring cathedrals, palatial spas and a moonlit, romantic castle perched high on its own hill, Natalie couldn't begin to guess which was Dom's favorite spot. She certainly wouldn't have picked the café/bar he ushered her into on the Pest side of the river. It was tiny, just one odd-shaped room, and noisy and crammed with men decked out in red-and-black-striped shirts. Most were around Dom's age, although Natalie saw a sprinkling of both freckles and gray hair among the men. Many stood with arms looped over the shoulders or around the waists of laughing, chatting women.

They were greeted with hearty welcomes and backslaps and more than one joking "His Grace" or "Grand Duke." Dom made so many introductions Natalie didn't even try to keep names and faces matched. As the beer flowed and his friends graciously switched to English to include her in the lively conversation, she learned she would have a ringside seat—via satellite and high-definition TV—at the World Cup European playoffs. Hungary's team had been eliminated in the quarterfinals, much to the disgust of everyone in the bar, but they'd grudgingly shifted their allegiance to former rival Slovakia.

With such a large crowd and such limited seating, Natalie watched the game, nestled on Dom's lap. Hoots and boos and foot-stomping thundered after every contested call. Cheers and ear-splitting whistles exploded when Slovakia scored halfway through the first quarter. Or was it the first half? Third? Natalie had no clue.

She was deafened by the noise, jammed knee to knee with strangers, breathing in the tang of beer and healthy male sweat, and she loved every minute of it! The noise, the excitement, the color, the casually possessive arm Dom hooked around her waist. She filed away every sensory impression, every scent and sound and vivid visual image, so she could retrieve them later. When she was back in New York or L.A. or wherever she landed after Sarah's book hit the shelves.

She refused to dwell on the uncertain future during the down-to-the-wire game. Nor while she and Dom took the hound for a romp through the park at the base of the castle. Not even when they returned to the loft and he hooked his arms around her waist as she stood in front of the wall of windows, drinking in her last sight of the Parliament's floodlit dome and spires across the river.

"It's so beautiful," she murmured.

"Like you," he said, nuzzling her ear.

"Ha! Not hardly."

"You don't see what I see."

He turned her, keeping her in the circle of his arms, and cradled her hips against his. His touch was featherlight as he stroked her cheek.

"Your skin is so soft, so smooth. And your eyes reflect your inner self. So intelligent, so brave even when you were so frightened that you would never regain your memory."

"Terrified" was closer to the mark, but she wasn't about to interrupt this interesting inventory.

Smiling, he threaded his fingers through her hair.

"I love how this goes golden-brown in the sunlight. Like thick, rich honey. It's true, your chin hints at a bit of a stubborn streak but your lips… Ah, Natushka, your lips. Have you any idea what that little pout of yours does to me?"

"Children pout," she protested. "Sultry beauties with collagen lips pout. I merely express…"

"Disapproval," he interjected, nipping at her lower lip. "Disdain. Disgust. All of which I saw in your face the first time we met. I wondered then whether I could make these same lips quiver with delight and whisper my name."

The nipping kisses achieved the first of his stated goals. Pleasure rippled across the surface of Natalie's skin even as Dom's husky murmur sent up a warning flag. She'd represented a challenge. She'd sensed that from the beginning. She remembered, too, how his sister and cousins had teased him about his many conquests. But now? Was the slow heat he stirred in her belly, the aching need in her chest, merely the by-product of a skilled seduction? Had she tumbled into love with the wrong man again?

She knew the answer before the question even half formed. Dominic St. Sebastian was most definitely the right man. The *only* man she wanted in her heart. In her life. She couldn't tell him, though. Her one and only previous foray into this love business had left her with too much baggage. Too many doubts and insecurities. And she was leaving in the morning. That more than anything else blocked the words she ached to say.

It didn't keep her from cradling his face in her palms while she kissed him long and hard. Or undressing him slowly, savoring every taut muscle, every hollow and hard plane of his body. Or groaning his name when he drove them both to a shattering climax.

Fourteen

Natalie couldn't classify the next five weeks as totally miserable.

Her first priority when she landed in New York was refurbishing her wardrobe before the meeting with Sarah and her editors. After she'd checked into her hotel she made a quick foray to Macy's. Sarah had smiled her approval at her assistant's conservative but nicely tailored navy suit and buttercup-yellow blouse.

Her smile had morphed to a wide grin when she and Natalie emerged from the meeting at Random House. Her editors were enthusiastic about how close the manuscript was to completion and anxious to get their hands on the final draft.

After a second meeting to discuss advance promo with Sarah's former boss at *Beguile* magazine, the two women flew back to California and hit the ground running. They spent most of their waking hours in Sarah's spacious, glass-walled office on the second floor of the Pacific Palisades mansion she shared with Dev. The glorious ocean view provided no distraction as they revised and edited and polished and proofed.

The final draft contained twenty-two chapters, each dedicated to a specific lost treasure. The Fabergé egg rated one chapter, the Bernini bronze another. The final chapter was devoted to the Canaletto, with space left for a photograph of the painting being restored to its rightful owner. *If* it was ever restored!

The authentication and provenance process was taking longer than any of the St. Sebastians had hoped. Several big-time insurance companies were now involved, anxious to recoup the hundreds of thousands of dollars they'd paid out over the years.

The Canaletto didn't fall into that category. It *had* been insured, as had many of the valuable objects in Karlenburgh Castle, but the policy contained exclusions for loss due to war and/or acts of God. By categorizing the 1956 Uprising as war, the insurer had wiggled out of compensating the duchess for St. Sebastian heirlooms that had either disappeared or made their way into private collections. Still, with so many conflicting claims to sort out, the team charged with verifying authenticity and rightful ownership had its hands full.

Dominic, Dev Hunter and Jack Harris had done what they could to speed the process. Dev offered to fund part of the effort. Jack helped facilitate coordination between international agencies asserting conflicting claims. Much to his disgust, Dom didn't return to undercover work. Instead, his boss at Interpol detailed him to act as their liaison to the recovery team. He grumbled about that but provided the expertise to link Lagy to several black marketeers and less reputable galleries suspected of dealing in stolen art.

He kept Sarah and Natalie apprised of the team's progress by email and texts. The personal calls came in the evenings, after Natalie had dragged back to her rented one-room condo. They'd spoken every couple of nights when she'd first returned, less frequently as both she and Dom got caught up in their separate tasks. But just the sound of his voice could make her hurt with a combination of hunger and loneliness.

The doubts crept in after she'd been home for several weeks. Dom seemed distracted when he called. After almost a month, it felt to Natalie as though he was struggling to keep any conversation going that didn't deal directly with the authentication effort.

Sarah seemed to sense her assistant's growing unease. She didn't pry, but she had a good idea what had happened between her cousin and Natalie during their time together in Budapest. She got a far clearer picture when she dropped what she thought was a casual question one rainy afternoon.

"Did Dom give you any glimmer of hope when the team might vet the Canaletto the last time he called?"

Natalie didn't look up from the dual-page layout on her computer screen. "No."

"Damn. We're supposed to fly to New York for another meeting with Random House next week. I hate to keep putting them off. Maybe you can push Dom a little next time you talk to him."

"I'm…I'm not sure when that will be."

From the corner of her eye Natalie saw Sarah's head come up. Swiveling her desk chair, she met her employer's carefully neutral look.

"Dom's been busy… The time difference… It's tough catching each other at home and…"

The facade crumbled without a hint of warning. One minute she was faking a bright smile. Two seconds later she was gulping and swearing silently that she would *not* cry.

"Oh, Natalie." Sympathy flooded Sarah's warm brown eyes. "I'm sure it's just as you say. Dom's busy, you're busy, you're continents apart…"

"And the tabloids have glommed on to him again," Natalie said with a wobbly smile.

"I know," Sarah said with a grimace. "One of these days I'll learn not to trust Alexis."

Her former boss had sworn up and down she didn't leak the story. Once it hit the press, though, *Beguile* followed almost immediately with a four-page color spread featuring Europe's sexiest single royal and his role in the recovery of stolen art worth hundreds of millions. Although the story stopped short of revealing that Dom worked for Interpol, it hinted at a dark and dangerous side to the duke. It even mentioned the Agár and obliquely suggested the hound had been trained by an elite counterterrorist strike force to sniff out potential targets. Natalie might have chuckled at that if the accompanying photo of Dom and Duke running in the park below the castle hadn't knifed right into her heart.

As a consequence, she was feeling anything but celebratory when she joined Sarah and Dev and Dev's extraordinarily efficient chief of operations, Pat Donovan, at a dinner to celebrate the book's completion. She mustered the requisite smiles and lifted her champagne flute for each toast. But she descended into a sputtering blob of incoherence when Sarah broached the possibility of a follow-on book specifically focused on Karlenburgh's colorful, seven-hundred-year history.

"Please, Natalie! Say you'll work with me on the research."

"I, uh…"

"Would you consider a one-year contract, with an option for two more? I'll double what I'm paying you now for the first year, and we can negotiate your salary for the following two."

She almost swallowed her tongue. "You're already pay-ing me twice what the average researcher's services are worth!"

Dev leaned across the table and folded his big hand around Natalie's. "You're not just a researcher, kid. We consider you one of the family."

"Th-Thank you."

She refused to dwell on her nebulous, half-formed thoughts of actually becoming a member of their clan. Those silly hopes had faded in the past month…to the point where she wasn't sure she could remain on the fringe of Sarah's family orbit.

Her outrageously expensive dinner curdled at the thought of bumping into Dom at the launch of Sarah's book six or eight months from now. Or crossing paths with him if she returned to Hungary to research the history of the St. Sebastians. Or seeing the inevitable gossip put out by the tabloids whenever the sexy royal appeared at some gala with a glamorous female looking suspiciously like Natalie's mental image of Kissy Face Arabella.

"I'm overwhelmed by the offer," she told Sarah with a grateful smile. "Can I take a little time to think it over?"

"Of course! But think fast, okay? I'd like to brief my ed-itors on the concept when we meet with them next week."

Before Natalie could even consider accepting Sarah's offer, she had to come clean. The next morning she burned with embarrassment as she related the whole sorry story of her arrest and abrupt departure from her position as an archivist for the State of Illinois. Sarah listened with wide eyes but flatly refused to withdraw her offer.

"Oh, Nat, I'm so sorry you got taken in by such a con-niving bastard. All I can say is that he's lucky he's behind bars. He'd damned well better keep looking over his shoulder when he gets out, though. Dev and Dominic both have long memories."

Relieved by Sarah's unqualified support but racked with doubts about Dom, Natalie was still agonizing over her decision the following Tuesday, when a taxi delivered her and Sarah to the tower of steel and glass housing her publisher. Spanning half a block in downtown Manhattan, the mega-conglomerate's lobby was walled with floor-to-ceiling bookcases displaying the hundreds of books put out each month by Random House's many imprints.

It was Natalie's third time accompanying Sarah to this publishing cathedral but the display of volumes hot off the press still awed her book-lover soul. While Sarah signed them both in and waited for an escort to whisk them up to the thirty-second floor, Natalie devoured the jacket and back-cover copy of a new release detailing the events leading to World War I and its catastrophic impact on Europe. Germany and the Austro-Hungarian Empire were major players in those cataclysmic events.

Karlenburgh sat smack in the juxtaposition of those cultures and epic struggles. Natalie itched to get her hands on the book. She was scrambling for her iPhone to snap a shot of the book jacket when a shrill bark cut through the low-level hum of the busy lobby. She spun around, her jaw dropping as a brown-and-white bullet hurtled straight toward her.

"Duke!" She took two front paws hard in the stomach, staggered back, dropped to her knees. "What…? How…? Whoa! Stop, fella! Stop!"

Laughing, she twisted her head to dodge the Agár's ecstatic kisses. The sight of Dom standing at the lobby entrance, his grin as goofy as the hound's, squeezed the air from her lungs. The arms fending the dog off collapsed, Duke lunged, and they both went down.

She heard a scramble of footsteps. A frantic voice shouting for someone to call 911 or animal control or whoever. A strangled yelp as a would-be rescuer grabbed Duke's collar and yanked him off her. Sarah protesting the rough handling. Dom charging across the lobby to take control of the situation.

By the time the chaos finally subsided, he'd hauled Natalie to her feet and into his arms. "Ah, Natushka," he said, his eyes alight with laughter, "the hound and I hoped to surprise you, not cause a riot."

"Forget the riot! What are you doing in here?"

"I called Sarah's office to speak with you and was told you'd both flown to New York."

"But…but…" She couldn't get her head and her heart to work in sync. "How did you know we'd be here, at the publisher? Oh! You did your James Bond thing, didn't you?"

"I did."

"I still don't understand. You? Duke? Here?"

"We missed you."

The simple declaration shimmered like a rainbow, breathing color into the hopes and dreams that had shaded to gray.

"I planned to wait until I could bring the Canaletto," he told her, tipping his forehead to hers. "I wanted you with me when we restored the painting and all the memories it holds for the duchess. But every day, every night away from you ate at my patience. I got so restless and bad-tempered even the hound would snarl or slink away from me. The team's infuriatingly slow pace didn't help. You probably didn't notice when I called but…"

"I noticed," she drawled.

"But it all boiled down to frustration," he finished with a rueful smile. "Pure, unadulterated frustration."

She started to tell him he wasn't the only one who'd twisted and turned and tied themself up in knots but he preempted any reply by cradling her face in his palms.

"I wanted to wait before I told you that I love you, *drágám*. I wanted to give you time, let you find your feet again. I was worried, too, about the weeks and months my job would take me away. Your job, as well, if you accept the offer Dev told me about when I called to speak with you. I know your work is important to you, as mine is to me. We can work it out, yes?"

She pretty much stopped listening after the "I love you" part but caught the question in the last few words.

"Yes," she breathed with absolutely no idea what she was agreeing to. "Yes, yes, yes!"

"Then you'll take this?"

She glanced down, a laugh gurgling in her throat as Dom pinned an enameled copy of his soccer club's insignia to the lapel of her suit jacket.

"It will have to do," he told her with a look in those dark eyes that promised the love and home and family she'd always craved, "until we find an engagement ring to suit the fiancée of the Grand Duke of Karlenburgh, yes?"

"Yes!"

As if that weren't enough to keep Natalie dancing on a cloud and completely delight his sister, Sarah and the duchess, Gina and her husband arrived with the twins the next afternoon.

They were house hunting, they informed the assembled family. Jack's appointment as US Ambassador to the UN still needed to be confirmed by the Senate but the chairman of the Foreign Affairs Committee had assured him the vote was purely pro forma.

"How wonderful!" Her eyes bright with tears of joy, the duchess thumped her cane and decreed this called for a toast. "Dominic, will you and Jack pour *pálinka* for us all?"

Charlotte's heart swelled with pride as she watched her tall, gold-haired grandson-in-law and darkly handsome young relative move to the sideboard and line up an array of Bohemian cut-crystal snifters. Her gaze roamed the sitting room, lingering on her beautiful granddaughters and the just-crawling twins tended by a radiant Natalie and a laughing, if somewhat tired-looking, Zia. When Maria joined them with a tray of cheese and olives, the only one missing was Dev.

"I've been thinking," Jack said quietly as he and Dom stood shoulder to shoulder, filling delicate crystal aperitif glasses with the potent apricot brandy. "Now that your face has been splashed across half the front pages of Europe, your days as an undercover operative must be numbered."

Dom's mouth twisted. "My boss agrees. He's been trying to convince me to take over management of the organized-crimes division at Interpol Headquarters."

"A desk job in Lyon couldn't be all that bad, but why not put all this hoopla about your title and involvement in the recovery of millions of dollars in stolen art to good use?" Jack's blue eyes held his. "*My* soon-to-be boss at the UN thinks the Grand Duke of Karlenburgh would make a helluva cultural attaché. He and his lovely wife would be accepted everywhere, have access to top-level social circles—and information."

Dom's pulse kicked. He'd already decided to take the promotion and settle in Lyon. He couldn't subject Natalie to the uncertainties and dangers associated with his current occupation. But deep inside he'd been dreading the monotony of a nine-to-five job.

"Cultural attaché?" he murmured. "What exactly would that involve?"

"Whatever you wanted it to. And you'd be based here in New York, surrounded by family. Which may not always be such a good thing," Jack added drily when one of his daughters grabbed a fistful of her sister's hair and gleefully yanked.

"No," Dom countered, watching Natalie scoop the howling twin into her arms to nuzzle and kiss and coo her back to smiles. "Family is a very good thing. Especially for someone who's never had one. Tell your soon-to-be boss that the Grand Duke of Karlenburgh would be honored to accept the position of cultural attaché."

Yesterday was one of the most memorable days in my long and incredibly rich life. They were all here, my ever-increasing family. Sarah and Dev. Gina and Jack and the twins. Dominic and Natalie. Zia, Maria, even Jerome, our vigilant doorman who insisted on escorting the Brink's couriers up to my apartment. I'm not ashamed to admit I cried when they uncrated the painting.

The Canaletto my husband gave me so long ago now hangs on my bedroom wall. It's the last thing I see before I fall asleep, the first thing I see when I wake. And, oh, the memories that drift in on gossamer wings between darkness and dawn! Dominic wants to take me back to Hungary for a visit. As Natalie and Sarah delve deeper into our family's history, they add their voice to his. I've said I'll return if Dom will agree to let me formally invest him with the title of Grand Duke at the black-tie affair Gina is so eager to arrange.

Then we'll settle in until Zia finishes her residency. She works herself to the bone, poor darling. If Maria and I didn't force her to eat and snatch at least a few hours' rest, she'd drop where she stands. Something more than determination to complete the residency drives her. Something she won't speak about, even to me. I tell myself to be patient. To wait until she's ready to share the secret she hides behind her seductive smile and stunning beauty. Whatever it is, she knows I'll stand with her. We are, after all, St. Sebastians.

From the diary of Charlotte
Grand Duchess of Karlenburgh

* * * * *

Don't miss Lady Sarah's story,

A BUSINESS ENGAGEMENT

and

Lady Eugenia's story,

THE DIPLOMAT'S PREGNANT BRIDE

Available now from
USA TODAY *bestselling author Merline Lovelace*

MILLS & BOON®

Why not subscribe?

Never miss a title and save money too!

Here's what's available to you if you join the exclusive **Mills & Boon Book Club** today:

✦ *Titles up to a month ahead of the shops*
✦ *Amazing discounts*
✦ *Free P&P*
✦ *Earn Bonus Book points that can be redeemed against other titles and gifts*
✦ *Choose from monthly or pre-paid plans*

Still want more?

Well, if you join today we'll even give you
50% OFF your first parcel!

So visit **www.millsandboon.co.uk/subs**
or call Customer Relations on **020 8288 2888**
to be a part of this exclusive Book Club!

_ST_7